TO LOVE A LORD

TO LOVE A LORD

Christi Caldwell

ISBN: 1519140606

ISBN-13: 9781519140609

DEDICATION

To Doug

On this journey we call life, I am so thankful that you are
my partner. These stories wouldn't be, if you didn't allow
me the time to disappear into my writing cave to tell them.
You are the world's best husband, father, chef, housekeeper,
and teacher I know. You wear many hats. But the perfect
one for you is—hero. I love you with all of my heart.

ONE

Spring 1817
London, England

"**N**o."

That terse one word utterance filled the otherwise quiet of Gabriel Edgerton, the Marquess of Waverly's office.

His sister was handling this a good deal better than he imagined she would. Gabriel sat back in his seat. "Chloe," he began, but wisely closed his mouth at the furious stare trained on him. He shifted with the slightest trace of guilt.

Chloe settled her palms on the edge of his desk. "I said nothing when you turned over the responsibility of chaperoning me to Alex."

"He is your favorite brother," he reminded her.

Her eyes narrowed. "That is neither here nor there."

His lips twitched with involuntary amusement. He hardly blamed Chloe for favoring their brother, the once roguish, now wedded Lord Alex Edgerton. He'd long been the entertaining, charming brother. Not at all like Gabriel's stodgy self, committed to his responsibilities. He pinched the bridge of his nose. "You need a companion."

"No, I need a chaperone." She gave him a pointed look until he shifted at the recrimination there.

"I have chaperoned you."

She leaned forward. "You chaperoned Philippa." His other, thankfully wedded, less difficult sibling. Or rather the *only* undifficult of all three of the Edgerton siblings. "Me, you eventually foisted off on Alex."

"Of which you appreciated," he felt inclined to point out.

1

Fire flashed in her eyes. "Not. One. Of. Mrs. Belden's. Dragons."

And this was what he had been anticipating. Gabriel scrubbed a hand over his eyes. He was glad Philippa was expecting her second child, he really was. Only after complications with her first pregnancy, Philippa wanted their mother at her side, which now left Gabriel to deal with his still unwed sister, Chloe. He made one last desperate bid at reasoning with her. "The woman will not be a chaperone. She will serve as a companion." Who would *also* serve as a chaperone. The knowing glint in his sister's eyes indicated she knew as much, too. He laid his hands down. "It is but for two months."

"Two months?" Her brow shot up. "And then, pray tell, what happens at the end of the two months?"

Well, for one the Season would be over. But not nearly soon enough. He waved a hand about. "You'll wed."

"I'll wed?"

Ah, so now the repeating back what he said business. This usually preceded the cool effrontery. He interlocked his fingers. "I expect you'll be wed by the end of the Season."

She narrowed her eyes. "You expect I'll be wed by the end of the Season?" Her tone remained remarkably even.

Gabriel tugged at his cravat and eyed the sideboard littered with crystal decanters. His mouth went dry with a sudden need for a drink, craving the liquid fortitude. He'd long known the reservations carried by all his siblings about the bonds of matrimony. Knew because he shared them, too. Having grown up the secretly abused children of the powerful former Marquess of Waverly, they'd all learned the perils of trusting oneself to another. He squared his jaw. As the eldest of the Edgerton siblings, he'd had an obligation to protect, and yet had failed—abysmally. Himself included. That failure drove all his efforts to see his siblings happy.

Clearing his throat, he then shoved back his chair and stood. "I pledge to help guide you as I did Philippa," he said walking over to the Chippendale sideboard. "You are now on your fourth Season and, as you are getting on in years, time is of the essence." He reached for a decanter and snifter. "But rest assured, the gentleman I select will be a kind, caring, and honorable man." Gabriel splashed several fingerfuls into the glass then downed a healthy swallow. He stared into the amber brew while swirling it in a slow circle.

Then, the absolute silence registered.

He turned around and nearly collided with his sister. A curse escaped him as he backed into the sideboard. "Bloody hell, you startled me." The remaining contents of his glass spilled over the rim. God, she'd always possessed a remarkable talent of sneaking up on a person. Then, years of hiding from their brute of a father had ingrained certain unwanted, but certainly warranted, lessons into each of them.

His sister stood not even a foot away with her hands planted akimbo, her eyebrows knitted into a single, dangerous line. "Getting on in years?" she repeated back, drawing out each of those four words in a "you-are-in-deuced-trouble-tone" that would have made her the envy of any stern mama.

"Yes, but you're rather focusing on the least important aspect of what I—"

"You think to wed me off to a—"

"Kind and honorable gentleman," he cut in. And *that* was the essential part. He set what remained of his brandy down hard on the sideboard. Droplets splashed his coat.

"No."

This again. And this is why he required someone of the female persuasion, because where Chloe was concerned, she'd never done anything if it had come at his bequest.

Once more he lamented she was not just a little bit like Philippa. Not all of her, for that would fundamentally alter who she was. Just the difficult parts. About wedding that was.

So when presented with the prospect of either debating the merits and necessity of her wedding, one of those honorable, caring, gentle sorts or avoiding conflict altogether, he chose the latter. "Very well." He'd allow Mrs. Belden's esteemed instructors to handle the matter of this topic.

Alas, his sister was of an altogether different mind frame. "I've no intentions of wedding."

His gut tightened. By the life they'd lived, the horrors she'd been subjected to, was it a wonder that she'd avow the marital state? "Surely you recognize you have to eventually wed."

"No." She shook her head. "No, I don't. I'll be quite content as the spinsterish aunt who bounces my nieces and nephews upon my knee." Chloe folded her arms across her chest. "Perhaps we'd both be better served by focusing our attentions on finding you a match."

He blinked. "Me?"

She gave a vigorous nod. "You."

Within the confines of his gloves, his palms grew moist and he dusted them along the sides of his breeches. "I don't care to discuss my marital state," he muttered and grabbed his snifter, particularly because there was no marital state for him, nor would there ever be. He took another swallow of the remaining contents and then set down the empty glass.

An inelegant snort escaped his sister. "Of course you don't." She paused. "Any more than I do. But," she held a finger up and wagged it under his nose. "You are in far greater need of a spouse than I am."

"Am I?" he drawled, feigning nonchalance.

Alas, by the triumphant glint in her gaze, his astute sister had already gathered his disquiet and pressed her advantage. God, she was ruthless. All of Boney's forces would have been hopeless under her dogged tenacity. She waved her gloved fingertip once more. "Oh, yes. There is the matter of you producing an heir."

He pressed the heels of his palms into his eyes. "I will not discuss the matter of an heir with you." Or anyone. Wisely his sister fell silent.

Alas, Chloe had never been one to stay quiet for long.

"I am merely pointing out that it is far more important that you wed." A twinkle lit her eyes. "Particularly with *your* advancing years."

For a long time he'd warred within himself about that obligation expected of him. To wed and produce an heir, he'd preserve a line once held by a monster. What an ultimate victory over that bastard who'd sired them, who'd loved the line more than anything and everything—to let it die and go to some distant, removed cousin. "There is Alex," Gabriel pointed out. For with his brother wed, the line wouldn't die with him.

4

She opened her mouth to continue her debate, but with glass in hand, he strode past her. "My marital state is neither here nor there," he said in clipped tones, as he reclaimed his familiar seat behind his desk. He cradled his glass in his hands. "I am worried over your being alone since Imogen and Alex married." Chloe had always been a rather lonely girl until she'd met Lady Imogen. Now since the wedding between her best friend and brother, Chloe had become that same solitary person. "Mother has written and is concerned about you and your Season." Perhaps he had more of his bastard father in him than he'd ever suspected for he pounced on his sister's weakness. "She will leave Philippa's side if it means you require her presence." It was a bold, blatant lie.

"No." The denial sprung from his sister. Some of the fight drained from her shoulders. She stomped over to the desk and then sat in the leather winged back chair. A golden curl fell over her brow. "I would not dare take her from Philippa's side."

Guilt needled his conscience. He'd known that her unflinching sisterly devotion would quell all arguments on her behalf. He took solace in knowing he merely sought to do what he'd failed to do as a youth—protect her. "I expect one of Mrs. Belden's instructors to arrive within a fortnight."

Chloe groaned and sprawled in the chair. "Does it have to be one of Mrs. Belden's instructors?" She flung an exaggerated hand over her brow. "I understand Imogen and Alex are otherwise pulled away from Society events," she pointed her eyes to the ceiling to indicate just what she thought of her favorite brother and best friend's subsequent abandonment. "But surely there is someone, *anyone*, other than one of those dour, frowning, miserable beings?"

Despite himself, his lips twitched with amusement. "I'm afraid not." Seated thusly, she resembled more the dramatic girl who'd slipped from the nursery and sought sanctuary in hidden corners of this very home to craft magical kingdoms in which to escape. His smile withered. At what point had she ceased to believe in hope and magic? After all, a person dwelling in hell always knew that one particular moment to so shatter your illusions of hope and happiness.

A curl tumbled over her eye and she blew it back on a huff of annoyance. "All those dratted instructors speak on are matters of marriage and proper husbands and proper decorum and…" She waved her hand. "Everything proper."

In short, the woman who'd be assigned to his sister for the next two months was bloody perfect and, God willing, would be able to rationalize with his sister when he'd never been able to. "It is temporary," he assured her.

"I've agreed to your foisting me off on a companion so you can be free of me, I do not, however, want a Belden dragon."

Guilt tugged once more. "Is that what you believe?" His siblings all possessed such a low opinion of him. Then how could they not when he'd so failed to care for them as he had?

She arched an eyebrow. "Isn't it true?"

He glanced over her shoulder at the wood door panel. Yes, he certainly saw how, on the surface, it appeared that way. After all, hadn't his own father gleefully pointed out that Gabriel possessed the same vices as his sire? He'd proudly noted Gabriel's ability to put his own comforts before all others. "It isn't," he said quietly. Instead, he'd spent his life fighting those addictive personalities he'd learned at his father's knee and secretly striving to put his siblings first. "I very much enjoy your company, Chloe." His lips pulled in a grimace.

A burst of laughter escaped his sister. "That is hardly convincing," she said between gasping breaths. "You don't enjoy anyone's company, Gabriel."

He'd built a fortress about his heart when his father had taken him under his wing, a boy of ten. It had been a mechanism to protect himself from hurt. To show emotion had wrought more pain at his father's hands. Yet, in so many years he'd spent proving he didn't feel, he'd done a damned convincing job of making his siblings believe that lie. In truth, he wanted her safely wed and at which point all those he loved would be properly cared for. Their security and happiness represented an absolution of sorts. Perhaps then, with Chloe wed, there would be a sense of having proved his father wrong. "That isn't true,"

2

he said defensively. "There is you and Alex and…" He slashed the air with his hand. "I'll not continue this discussion."

Chloe hopped to her feet. "Of course you won't." She leaned over the desk and patted his hand. "Because I daresay, but for your equally stodgy Lord Waterson, there isn't a single soul you'd add." Lord Waterson—a man who'd known Gabriel since he'd been a sniveling, afraid-of-everything coward at Eton. Any person who could set himself up as a devoted supporter of the miserable, cowering, weak fool he'd been was deserving of an eternal friendship.

Not wanting to traverse the path of his rotted youth, he cleared his throat. "If you'll excuse me, I've matters of business to attend."

His sister pointed her gaze to the ceiling. "My, how you do enjoy my company." A chuckle escaped her as she started for the door. She paused at the threshold. "Oh, and Gabriel?"

He inclined his head.

"If you've brought one of Mrs. Belden's Beasts to transform me into a marriage-minded miss, I warn you, their efforts proved futile at finishing school and they will be just so here." With a jaunty wave, she slipped from the room, and then pulled the door closed behind her.

Silence remained in her wake, punctuated by the tick-tocking of the long-case clock. His sister's charges from their exchange rattled around his mind. He studied the lingering droplets that still clung to the edge of his glass.

Gabriel enjoyed people's company. He just enjoyed his own more. Solitariness represented safety. The less people one was responsible for, the less a person could hurt. He'd little interest in expanding the number of individuals dependent on him—by doing something as foolhardy as adding a wife, as his sister suggested. With a wife came that heir and a spare she'd spoken of, which merely compounded the people reliant upon him. A family merely represented more opportunity for failure and disappointment. He'd had enough of such sentiments to last the course of his life and into the hereafter.

Once Chloe was wedded, nay *happily* wedded, then his obligations would be fulfilled.

Yes, the line would pass to Alex and his heirs, and Gabriel?

An ugly laugh rumbled up from his chest and split the quiet. His lips twisted in a bitterly triumphant smile. And he would have the ultimate revenge against his dead father who, even now, burned in hell.

TWO

Southampton, England
Spring 1817

S ince she'd been a child, Jane Munroe had been told her quick
tongue would land her in all manner of trouble. In fact, her
nursemaid had said as much with such a staggering frequency it had
become the same as a morning greeting. The nursemaid was ignorant,
unkind, and horribly stern. Jane had never placed much stock in anything the rail-thin, lanky woman, Mrs. Crouch, who'd been tasked with
caring for her, told her.

Which is why, seated now before her employer, Mrs. Belden, she
found great irony in learning Mrs. Crouch had been correct—about
something.

Why did it have to be that particular point?

Mrs. Belden removed her wire spectacles, folded them with an
annoying slowness and set them down on the immaculate desk before
her. And then, she uttered those words Jane knew were coming.

"I am afraid you are not working out in your current post, Mrs.
Munroe." She steepled her fingers together. "Lady Clarisse has brought
it to my attention that you have been filling the heads of her and the
other young ladies with thoughts of independence and," she wrinkled
her nose, "remaining unwed."

Lady Clarisse. The Duke of Ravenscourt's legitimate daughter.
Golden blonde and icy as a January freeze, she epitomized all a duke's
daughter should be. And unfortunately for Jane, the young woman was
astute to have heard the whispers and knew her instructor was really

9

none other than her half-sister. "I did not advise them to maintain an unmarried state." Wise though they'd be. "But rather encouraged them to exercise their own opinions and beliefs and—"

The headmistress thumped a fist on the desk hard enough she rattled the lone page upon the otherwise immaculate surface. "Enough, Mrs. Munroe." The page fluttered to the edge of the desk and then hovered there, one heavy breath from tumbling to the floor.

And even knowing the words had been coming did little to stem the tide of panic threatening to overtake her. Jane placed her trembling palms on her lap. "Mrs. Belden," she began. Having been summoned a quarter of an hour ago, she really should have placed her efforts on finding the appropriate and necessary words to save her post. "I won't make the same mistake." As soon as the words left her mouth, she bit the inside of her cheek. Blasted lie, and an obvious one at that.

To both of them.

"Ah, yes, you've said as much," Mrs. Belden said while peering down the length of her disapproving nose. "Four times."

"Surely it was not four," she murmured. She'd have wagered this very post she depended upon that it had been at the very least six times.

"Regardless, Mrs. Munroe, I simply cannot have you here any longer."

The panic climbed higher and higher, tightening her belly, and settling in her throat, threatening to choke her. She gripped the edge of her seat and held firm. "I do not have anywhere else to go." This proved to be the second worst possible response.

The stern headmistress of the esteemed finishing school sat back in her chair. "That is, unfortunately, not my problem, Mrs. Munroe. I'd had," she raked her cool gaze over Jane. "I had reservations about you but was *persuaded*," likely paid a substantial sum to take her on, "to allow you a post. In your time here, you've filled my girls' heads with dangerous talk of treason, challenging the very tenets of Society."

"I'd hardly say encouraging the ladies to strengthen their minds and not offer blind allegiance to a gentleman constitutes treason."

She couldn't keep the dryness from threading her words. The other woman snapped her eyebrows into a single line.

Blasted quick tongue. She cleared her throat. "That is, what I'd intended to say is I've striven to instruct the young ladies on the importance of using their minds to formulate productive thoughts." That extended beyond the match they'd make and instead to rely on their own strengths and capabilities. "And—"

"And lecture them on the words of your Mrs. Mary Wollstonecraft."

She was hardly Jane's Mrs. Wollstonecraft. That esteemed woman was the inspiration who had given Jane hope she could be more than mere chattel. But she was everyone's Mrs. Wollstonecraft. "Yes," she said calmly. "I have spoken to them about Mrs. Wollstonecraft's philosophies so they might formulate their own opinions."

Mrs. Belden propelled forward in her seat. She thumped her fist on the desktop once more, sending the lone page fluttering to the floor forgotten. "Mrs. Munroe, women do not have opinions. They are obedient, decorous creatures to be cared for by a husband and your Mrs. Wollstonecraft with her bastard children is not fit discourse for anyone." Crimson blotches blazed upon the woman's cheeks, and she stared at Jane with pointed condescension, her words a smidgeon shy of the insult she'd level at her.

For every employer from the previous households she'd found employment in to this dour creature, all knew the truth—the Duke of Ravenscourt's requests of employment for Jane were more of an order than anything else and stemmed from some obligatory response to his by-blow daughter.

She tipped her chin up at a mutinous angle, daring the woman with her eyes to speak the whole truth. The woman wisely remained silent, likely fearing retribution if she were to issue that insult. Little did the nasty headmistress realize that Jane would no sooner humble herself before the man who'd sired her by asking for his aid than beg the pinch-mouthed crone.

"I agreed to His Grace's request but was forthright in saying that if you did anything to jeopardize my charges, I'd be forced to release you from your responsibilities. After all, I'd heard rumors of you."

Rumors. So the grounds of her dismissal from her previous employer had found their way to the far flung corners of Kent. Not even the duke could silence those scandalous whispers. Fury tightened Jane's belly at the condescending sneer on the woman's lips. A woman who instructed young ladies on blind obedience and their rightful position in Society would never believe the word of a duke's by-blow daughter over that of a powerful earl's *respected* son and heir. So she said nothing.

"I cannot provide you a reference..." Nausea turned in Jane's belly. A knock sounded at the door and she looked blankly from the arbiter of her fate and to the wood panel. Mrs. Belden frowned and glanced briefly over at the door, and then returned her attention to Jane once again. "As I said, I cannot provide you a reference. It would not be the honorable thing for me to do as your employer."

Honor. What did this woman or the Earls of Montclairs and Dukes of Ravenscourts of the world know of honor? Fear turned her mouth dry. Where would she go? For the briefest, infinitesimal moment, she entertained sending a missive to her father. She slid her eyes closed. God help her, she'd not be so weak to rely on the assistance of a man whom her mother had thrown away all hope of respectability and honor for. She could not, nay would not, appeal to her father. She'd not ever done so on her own behalf. Her foolish mother, who'd given away all happiness for that man's love, had done so. The employers who cast her out, time and time again, had done so as a deferential respect for the revered Duke of Ravenscourt. "I ask that you allow me a fortnight, Mrs. Belden," she said at last.

"You—" Another rap interrupted the woman's words. On a huff of annoyance, she stood with slow, precise movements. "Yes?"

The door opened and one of the uniformed instructors, Mrs. Smythe, stood at the entrance. She momentarily glanced at Jane. Pity filled the woman's eyes. Ah, so all knew. Nothing was private where she was concerned. "Mrs. Belden, there is a quarrel between Lady Clarisse and Lady Nora."

Lady Clarisse. The very legitimate daughter of the Duke of Ravenscourt—the one not dependent upon the mercy of cruel employers and prey to lecherous gentlemen. Bitterness turned in her belly.

"A quarrel?"

The young woman had despised Jane from the moment she'd arrived at her new post, likely a product of a daughter who knew precisely the young woman her father had coordinated employment for.

"Yes, they are arguing about," she cleared her throat. "Mrs. Wollstonecraft and," she slid her gaze away from Jane's as though unable to meet her stare. "Mrs. Munroe."

The headmistress favored Jane with a black glower. "I will return in a moment to continue this." *This*, as in the ensuing argument between Lady Nora who'd quite taken to the enlightened ideas of free thought and freedoms of choice and Lady Clarisse, who'd quite detested anything and everything Jane had lectured on or spoken of, including mundane mentions of the weather.

Together, the two women hurried from the office, leaving Jane alone. A thunderous quiet filled the room. Her shoulders sagged as the hum of silence in her ears blended with the frantic beating of her heart, nearly deafening. Filled with a restiveness, she shoved to her feet and began to pace before Mrs. Belden's immaculate, mahogany desk.

"Twenty-five," she whispered. Never more had she wished for that magical, almost mystical, elusive age which represented her freedom.

The funds settled on her by her benevolent father would pass to her hands. Life had seen her humbled, dependent upon the duke's powerful connections once her mother had passed. The man, whom she'd met but two times in her life and then only when she'd been a small child, had purged her from his life. Beyond seeing her properly employed, he'd no dealings with her. She tightened her mouth. The funds promised her, that she would take with a sense of entitlement and no regrets. For that impressive to her, insignificant to him, amount her mother had spoken of, represented Jane's freedom.

Freedom to not find herself on her back, legs spread for some bored nobleman as her mama had been. Freedom to not be subjected to lecherous lords and their vile sons' grasping hands, merely for the station of her employment in their households. Freedom to set up a small finishing school, not at all like Mrs. Belden's, where young ladies would be encouraged to read and discuss matters of import. Only two months until freedom was at last granted her.

Jane stopped suddenly and stared blankly down at the desk. Except, two months may as well have proved endless for a woman without references, employment, and stubbornness to not ask the blasted duke for anything more.

The budding panic cloyed at her chest and she closed her eyes a moment. The options for an unwed woman of ignoble origins were not many. Rather, they were nonexistent. She dropped her gaze to the floor and her panicked musings cut short. Absently, she stooped to retrieve the forgotten page dropped by Mrs. Belden moments ago. She'd no intention of reading the contents of another person's note. She'd never been one of those nosy, eavesdropping bodies unable to mind her own affairs. No, she'd no intention of reading about the nasty headmistress' affairs. But then, her eyes snagged upon one particular word on that brief note, written in a powerful hand.

...Employment...in need of a companion...

Jane chewed her lower lip and looked to the doorway, and then guiltily returned her attention to the sheet. She quickly scanned the contents.

Mrs. Belden,
I require the services of one of your esteemed instructors for my sister,
Lady Chloe Edgerton.

She continued skimming.
...A term of two months...

Her heart started and she picked her head up, staring at the floor-length crystal windowpane. *A sign.* As a mere girl, her mother had spoken to Jane of signs and encouraged her to find hope in those signs. For all her cynicism of her lot and station in life as a bastard daughter of a powerful duke, she'd looked for and celebrated those symbols. It was the sliver of optimism she clung to; a hope in a better world—for herself, for others. Two months. Surely this was one of those carefully laid signs she was to follow.

14

Giving her head a shake, she cast one more glance at the door and then returned her attention to the remainder of the note.

...Signed,
The Marquess of Waverly.

Waverly. She ran through the name in her mind, trying to recall a student who was sister to the marquess. Jane had only been at Mrs. Belden's for a year. A giddy sensation lightened the pressure in her chest. The young woman, a Lady Chloe Edgerton, was a stranger to her. Surely another sign. Fate's way of intervening. Footsteps sounded in the hall and she quickly folded the note and, shoving aside the tendrils of guilt, stuffed the missive in the front apron of her uniform.

Mrs. Belden stepped through the entrance and did not break stride. She continued on to the seat she'd vacated a short while ago and then thumped her fist once upon the desk.

The stolen note within Jane's pocket burned and, for a numbing moment, she thought she'd been discovered. That this disobedience and theft would result in her being turned out immediately. She thrust aside the guilt. Her life had been subject to the whims and fancies of an indolent peerage early on. This moment, she would put her security and her future before all those lords and ladies.

"As I was saying, Mrs. Munroe, I can no longer continue to hold you on my staff. You've a fortnight, at which point, I expect you to leave."

A fortnight. Time enough for a missive to be sent to Jane's father and time enough for the duke to secure another post for his daughter. She tightened her jaw. The woman made the erroneous assumption that she would seek out his aid. She'd not done so before and she'd not do so now. Nor did she suspect the stern headmistress would be herself eager to write that respective note informing the duke his illegitimate daughter had been turned out on her ear. "Thank you," she said with a stoic calm, belied by the frantic pounding of her heart.

The woman inclined her head and with a flick of her hand, indicated the meeting was at an end.

With the pilfered contents in her apron, Jane marched, head held high, from the room. She made her way down the narrow, white-washed corridors. When she'd placed distance between herself and Mrs. Belden, she came to a stop beside the silver-plated knight oddly out of place in the finishing school. Positioning herself behind the massive armor from long ago, she withdrew the missive and perused the page once more.

The Marquess of Waverly's sister required a companion. At one and twenty, the young lady, a powerful marquess' sister, was likely no different than all the unkind, self-absorbed women Jane had confronted since she'd been the sneered at, giggled about bastard child, living in a country cottage kept by the duke. Jane could brave the discomforts of such an assignment. She caught her lower lip between her teeth, troubling the flesh. Could she, however, in good conscience slip into a post assigned to another?

Then, no one had truly been assigned the post. And any one of Mrs. Belden's other instructors already were in possession of a post. They were not dependent upon another position the way Jane was.

Yet, it was still not her missive. Jane tightened her grip upon the page, wrinkling the sheet. It was a level of underhandedness she disdained and she hated herself in this moment for being so very desperate that she'd abandon all honor. She lightened her grip. It wouldn't do to ruin the page. With the tip of her ragged fingernail, she ran it over the inked word *"two"*.

Two months.

She'd sacrifice her honor and pride for just two months. Jane thrust aside all guilt and hardened her mouth into a determined line. After the abuses and injustices she'd known at the hands of the peerage, she had no compunction in entering into another one of their households so she might steal her freedom. After all, noblemen and their snobbish kin were the same. She'd not feel any remorse in lying to them.

Jane drew in a shuddery sigh. "Liar," she said under her breath.

Except, when faced with the option of survival or her own sense of guilt for her deception, Jane chose survival.

THREE

In the muddied London streets, with rain stinging her cheeks, Jane at last had reservations in absconding with a note intended for Mrs. Belden and leaving in the dead of night without a word to anyone.

She jumped as the driver of the hired hack tossed down her lone valise. It landed with a hard thump in a rather impressive puddle. Water splashed the hem of her skirts and soaked her boots. She glowered up at the gap-toothed man who stuck his hand out. "Yer coin."

"Your coin," she muttered and fished around her reticule. She handed over the coins, eager for the foul-stenched, leering driver to be on his way. It wouldn't do to be discovered, arriving in a rented hack. He stuffed the half pence into his pocket and then climbed aboard his carriage—leaving her alone.

In the biting London rain. At the front steps of the Marquess of Waverly's residence. The seeds of misgivings, which had rooted around her brain the moment she'd arrived in London and blue skies had been replaced with black storm clouds and ominous rumblings of thunder, grew in her chest. She stole a skyward glance and blinked as raindrops trailed down the lenses of her spectacles, blurring the world before her. With a silent curse, she removed the pair and dried them with the fabric of her dampened cloak. To no avail. Jane placed the glasses on once again seeing the world through a rainy blur.

She sighed. It was a sign.

"Don't be silly," she muttered to herself. "The sign was a favorable one." She'd paid attention to the blasted sign. Two months. What was the likelihood of that precipitous amount of time coinciding with the timing of her attaining control of her trust?

Lightning cracked across the sky and she jumped, propelled into forward motion. She swiped her waterlogged valise from the ground and, with an unladylike speed that would have gotten her sacked by Mrs. Belden if there hadn't been the whole treasonous Mrs. Wollstonecraft talk on Jane's part, she made her way up the handful of steps.

The new signs all seemed to point to the folly in her plan. Even so, she still didn't care to be smote by lightning on a stranger's doorstep. She dropped her valise and knocked. Thunder rumbled overhead, burying the staccato rhythm of her rapping.

Another blasted sign.

"I've quite tired of signs," she said, glaring at the door. A glint of gold snagged her notice and she raised her attention up from the black panel. She wiped the rain from her eyes and stared transfixed at the erect dragon, with his vicious grip upon the knocker, daring her to knock.

The day she'd been assigned a post at Mrs. Belden's Finishing School, she'd met the other instructors—dour-faced, always frowning, as though they'd feared a grin would result in their immediate expulsion from their esteemed post. Dragons, every last one of them.... and she'd become one by default.

A dragon. Jane raised her fingertips and traced the ice cold fabled creature. A slow smile turned her lips up. She raised the knocker and pounded hard. She'd little other choice. She knocked once more. Nay, she had no alternative. Another knock. Either lie her way into a post for two months' time or face an uncertain life on the streets. She flattened her lips into a firm line. Or, she could swallow her injurious pride and appeal to the man who'd sired her until—"Bloody unlikely," she said between gritted teeth and pounded all the harder.

The door opened and the alacrity of that movement wrenched her forward. She released her grip upon the dragon so quickly she sprawled forward and came down hard, half-inside and half-outside the home of the illustrious Marquess of Waverly. Despite the chill of the rain, humiliated shame set her body ablaze with fiery heat. Mustering a smile, she raised her gaze upward to the gray-haired butler towering over her. The wrinkles lining his weathered cheeks marked him at some ancient age. She frowned. Was the marquess one of those monstrous sorts who abused his servants and didn't provide a deserved pension at the end of their years of service? Jane scoffed. Then, didn't all noblemen place their interests and desires before—?

"Ahem," the older man cleared his throat.

She started and belatedly recalled she lay prone at his feet, her backside presented to any members of polite Society who happened by. She stared up at his outstretched fingers and the burn on her cheeks threatened to set her face afire. "Er, yes. Thank you."

With the older man's assistance, Jane climbed to her feet. Her hem dripped a sizeable puddle onto the otherwise immaculate, marble foyer. Oh, dear. This was hardly an entrance that would earn her the marquess' favor. She braced for the sneering condescension in his servant's cool, blue stare and froze. A twinkle lit the servant's rheumy eyes.

He was one of the kind ones. Having been born a bastard, she'd had a good deal of experience in sorting out the kindly ones from the sneering, disapproving others. Unfortunately, there had been a shortage of the kindly ones.

She cleared her throat. "I am Mrs. Munroe."

The man stared at her in confusion.

"I am here to see the Marquess of Waverly." Jane fished around for her reticule and opened the sopping piece. She withdrew the well-read note. She held it up for the other man's inspection. "I've come from Mrs. Belden's Finishing School at the marquess' request to serve as companion." He accepted the note from her trembling fingers. Her breath caught in dreaded anticipation of the gods sending a bolt of lightning through the sweeping foyer to smite her for her lies.

The butler eyed the page in his hands and she braced for him to jab his finger at her and thunder "Liar" into the towering space. He folded the note and handed it over. There was nothing in his kindly eyes to indicate he'd seen her for the charlatan she was. Instead, he inclined his head with a smile. "Allow me to show you to the marquess." He motioned to her cloak.

Jane followed his discreet gesture and then glanced back at him. She gave her head a small shake. What was he on about?

A ghost of a smile played on his lips. "Er, your cloak, Mrs. Munroe."

"Oh, yes!" She widened her eyes. "Of course, my cloak." With jerky movements, she fiddled with the clasp of her modest, brown muslin cloak and then turned the wet garment over to his care.

A footman rushed over to claim the cloak and then disappeared. A protest sprung to her lips as he carried off the only one she had in her possession.

"If you will please follow me, Mrs. Munroe?"

Jane jumped at the servant's quietly spoken request. She wet her lips. Fear always chose the worst time to present itself. She stood rooted to the floor. Unease turned in her belly. Her future hung upon the following exchange; upon the benevolence of a nobleman who'd hired a companion for his sister and had instead received a sacked, former instructor and, well, a liar. Guilt needled at her insides. *I am a liar.*

Desperate, but a liar all the same and desperation did not pardon the sins of a liar. Alas, survival superseded honor in the cold, uncertain world in which she dwelled.

The butler coughed, breaking her from her panicked reverie. He stood at the edge of the corridor looking at her expectantly. "I—" She flitted her gaze about the foyer and then her stare collided with her bag. "I cannot—"

The old servant clapped once and a different footman instantly materialized. A startled shriek escaped her at the liveried servant's sudden appearance. Jane slipped on the dampened marble and slid forward. Her heart thudded hard, but she tossed her arms wide and managed to prevent a fall. Another fall, that is. How many blasted footmen did a person require? She managed a sheepish grin for the butler.

"If you'll follow me," he repeated. This time, he did not wait to see if she followed but continued along the halls.

Jane forced her legs to move and, with wooden steps, walked at a slower, more reluctant pace behind him. As they walked through the lavish townhouse, the trepidation that had gripped Jane all morning threatened to overwhelm her with numbing panic.

What if she was discovered as an interloper? An imposter? She glanced down at her dark, modest uniform of Mrs. Belden's. Surely the gentleman's letter returned to him with Jane and her Dragon skirts would rouse no suspicions. Because the alternative, to be turned out and ultimately forced to starve or humble herself before the father she'd met but twice as a child, and only when he'd paid visits to her mother, was unfathomable. His lover. Familiar rage rolled through her, reminding her of why she hated the nobility who saw those deemed inferior, such as a bastard Jane and her actress mother, as beneath their notice. Those gentlemen who could, with a single look or one word utterance, decide a person's fate.

She tightened her grip upon her reticule. Or who, with their roving hands, could cause a woman being turned out, labeled a whore, and—

Jane collided with the butler's back as he stopped beside a closed door. Her spectacles fell forward. "Forgive me," she said hurriedly. She adjusted the frames, pushing them back on the brim of her nose. Goodness the man moved with far greater speed than she'd expect of one of his advanced years. "I—" *Am distracted by my panic.* "Forgive me," she finished lamely.

He gave her another one of those kindly smiles and, blast, if they weren't the first smiles she'd received in…She wracked her mind, well, blast, she couldn't recall a time she'd received one of those types of smiles. The butler knocked. There had been plenty of smiles. Silence met his rapping. There had been plenty of leering grins. He knocked once more. There were also the knowing grins.

"Enter," a booming voice called from within.

She braced her shoulders as the servant pressed the handle. Jane hovered at the entrance, thinking of all the smiles she'd received in the course of her life. There had also been cruel ones and mocking ones.

"My lord, a Mrs. Munroe has arrived from Mrs. Belden's school."

But never the kindly ones. A sheen filled her eyes. Blasted rain. She removed her spectacles and dashed a hand over her eyes. How else was there to account for the sheen there other than that moisture?

21

Silence met the servant's pronouncement. She placed her wire rims on once more and looked across the room to the seated figure of the marquess. With the hard, chiseled planes of his face and the firm, noble brow and jaw, he was a regal specimen of noble perfection. She dimly registered the kindly servant backing out of the room. An irrational urge to call the kindly man back bubbled to her throat. The door closed with a quiet click that made her jump. Unnerved by the intensity of the marquess' hard, impenetrable stare, Jane dropped a curtsy. "My lord."

Belatedly, he climbed to his feet, unfurling to his full height. "Mrs. Munroe." She swallowed hard. More than a foot taller than her own five foot-three inch figure, his broad shoulders and arms strained the fabric of his midnight black coat. But for his tousled dark hair, there was nothing soft or gentle or kind about this man. The mere strength of one such as he would rouse terror in the most seasoned soldiers. Then a single loose curl fell across his brow, momentarily softening him. With long, powerful fingers he brushed it back, as though annoyed by that weakening.

Lucifer.

She'd once read that Lucifer came to Earth disguised in the form of a gloriously handsome gentleman and set a person to sinning. Jane thrust aside the foolish ramblings.

He moved out from behind his desk and walked toward her, and she immediately retreated, which was, of course, foolish. More than twenty long strides separated them and she wasn't easily roused to fear and…Her back thumped noisily against the door. "Mrs. Munroe," he drawled, as he came to a stop at the center of the room. "Do you intend to stand at my door all afternoon or will you sit?"

That deep, mellifluous baritone was a devil's tone, too. Smooth and refined, yet clipped and cool. There was nothing soft in that voice, either. "Sit," she blurted.

He gave a flick of his wrist and she followed that subtle movement to the leather button sofa, and then looked to him once more. Did his lips turn up in a smile? Surely she'd merely imagined that faint expression of amusement? A coolly aloof, lofty gentleman such as he did not smile. She peered at the marquess through her glass lenses but could detect no trace of humor.

The marquess studied her through thick, hooded, black lashes and the singular intensity of his focus jolted her into motion. Jane tipped her chin up and sailed over to the nearby sofa. She hesitated, detesting that in claiming the seat he'd be granted even more of an advantage over her. Her previous positions in the homes of those vaunted nobles had taught her that they'd take, regardless of whether anything was offered. A muscle leapt at the corner of her eye. And she'd not offer anything to those indolent, self-serving lords.

"Mrs. Munroe?"

Jane hastily claimed a seat and folded her hands upon her lap. And waited. After all, her recent dismissal from Mrs. Belden's had taught her the perils of her quick tongue. Surely for two months she might manage to be the proper, polite companion the marquess sought for his sister.

The Marquess of Waverly claimed the chair opposite her. He continued to examine her in that assessing way until she shifted under the weight of his scrutiny. She'd spent the better part of her life striving to remain invisible, to attract no notice. To be noticed was to be ruined, particularly for a young woman in a powerful nobleman's employ. Jane promptly dropped her gaze to her lap. The fire snapped and hissed from within the hearth, however, the roaring fire did little to warm her. *He knows.* She fought to still her quaking fingers. Of course he didn't know. How could he? She stole an upward peek at him. Or did he?

Ever the regal, polished nobleman, he reclined in his seat, elegant in repose. His long fingers rested along the arms of his mahogany armchair. He broke the impasse of silence. "Forgive me. I'd believed I'd been clear with Mrs. Belden that I would send around a carriage to retrieve you."

Jane curled her hands into a white-knuckled grip. She should truly be focused on that carefully ignored detail accounting for her hasty travel plans. *Retrieve her.* Instead, she fixed on those two insolent words. Retrieve her, the way he might an errant child.

"Mrs. Munroe?"

"Forgive me, I didn't realize yours was a question." His dark eyebrows snapped into a single line and she cursed her tongue. Jane managed a demure smile. Or at the very least attempted a demure smile. Alas, her mother had always said Jane had possessed more spirit than a ghost haunting his resting place on All Hallows' Eve. "Mrs. Belden knew your request was an urgent one, my lord." There, a safe response. After all, Mrs. Belden was long concerned with respectability and the powerful peers who entrusted their daughters to her care. She would have recognized any missive sent by the marquess as a matter of urgency.

The marquess inclined his head as though he'd found her answer satisfactory. Hope stirred within her breast as some of her misgivings lifted. "I trust Mrs. Belden has shared information with you about my sister?"

He may as well have removed the medieval broadsword from his office wall and drove it directly through the fledgling optimism. Of course the beastly headmistress would be expected to select a companion who, if not a former instructor, at the very least came to the marquess with knowledge of his sister.

"Oh, yes," she lied through her forced smile. Her mind raced as she considered all the ladies she'd known in her tenure at the finishing school. Dull. Proper. Exceedingly polite. Unfailingly and unflinchingly demure English ladies in every regard. "Mrs. Belden spoke with fond remembrance of your sister."

He stilled. "Did she?"

As those two words lacked any hint of emotion or indication of his thoughts, she gave a vigorous nod. "Ever so proper." Devoid of spirit. "Practical of nature, she evinces all ladylike skills the school is renowned for instilling." Did his lips twitch?

The marquess hooked his ankle over his knee, drawing her attention down to his leg. She swallowed hard and told herself to look away. It wasn't polite or proper or any of the other very ladylike words she'd spouted for his benefit. But perhaps she had more of her shameful mother in her than she'd believed, for Jane, who'd never done something as foolhardy as notice a man, particularly not a nobleman, stared transfixed at the thickly muscled expanse of his thighs, entirely too broad for any proper nobleman. Marquesses were supposed to be spindly and reed-thin from lack of physical exertions, not this…She fanned her cheeks.

"Are you warm, Mrs. Munroe?"

"Yes." Jane yanked her gaze up and found the faintest trace of amusement contained within his eyes, as though he knew she'd been staring at his legs, which was madness. Jane Munroe, bastard daughter, detester of men and their glib tongues, did not admire men. And then belatedly she recalled the frigid room. "No," she said quickly.

His brow dipped in confusion. That was preferable to any knowing on his part of the effect his impressive physique had upon her. "Forgive me," she said, proud of the stoic deliverance of those words. "You were saying, my lord?"

"I was not saying anything." Dry humor underscored that statement.

She furrowed her brow. "Weren't you?"

"We were speaking of my *polite* and *proper* sister."

Something in the slight emphasis of those two very important words gave her pause; set up a slight warning bell that suggested there was more at play. As soon as the thought slipped in, she thrust it back. Of course any prideful nobleman would speak of his sister's worth in their narrow-minded Society. "Yes, we were," she murmured.

"Do tell me," he drawled. "What else did Mrs. Belden say about my sister?"

Her mind went blank. Literally blank. Every single thought, worry, or hope fled with that question. Something in his tone suggested he sought a very specific *something* from Jane with that question. "Say?" She winced at that dreadful nervous tendency to parrot back another's words.

He waved a hand about and she followed that faint movement. "Surely she spoke more of my sister, Chloe?"

"Indeed." She had not. Oh, to someone the head dragon had surely said something, but it would have never been to Jane who, with her birthright, had been treated as lesser than the dirt upon the dull, black boots donned by the headmistress. The marquess sought specific information from her on his sister. She'd give him precisely the fal-sities craved by the heartless, self-aggrandizing members of the ton. She spread her hands wide. "I assure you, my lord, Mrs. Belden has thoroughly informed me about your sister, the esteemed Lady Chloe, who by her very nature aspires to an honorable, distinguished match."

That silenced the pompous lord. After all, Jane had merely spouted off what most members of polite Society hoped for; for their daugh-ters, sisters, and selves.

FOUR

The esteemed headmistress, Mrs. Belden, was either cracked in the head sending him Mrs. Munroe to oversee his sister Chloe or the woman knew her charges a good deal less than she was purported to.

Gabriel ran a critical eye over the rumpled woman in her drab brown dress. By the manner in which she'd drawn her blonde hair tightly back at the nape of her neck and the spectacles perched on the rim of her pert nose, Mrs. Munroe evinced a proper companion and she'd make some proper English lady a perfectly acceptable companion.

Just not his sister.

By Mrs. Munroe's admission, his sister aspired to an honorable, distinguished match. In truth, his sister would sooner lob off her arm than make any match. He bit back a curse of annoyance. His spirited, headstrong sister would devour a woman with Mrs. Munroe's awkward smiles and words of proper, polite ladies. No, if he allowed Mrs. Munroe the post of companion, his sister would remain unwed for yet another Season and Gabriel would be obligated, once more, to endure another Season and another year with her uncared for; his responsibility stretching on. He drummed his fingertips on the arms of his chair.

"I mean you no disrespect," he began. Because there really was no gentle or polite way to dismiss a woman from a position she'd not even fully stepped into. Time was of the essence.

With an unexpected show of spirit, Mrs. Munroe leaned forward in her chair. "I beg your pardon, my lord?" A frown marred her lips.

Gabriel opened his mouth to disabuse her of the notion that she'd be granted the position as companion but blinked instead. He fixed his gaze upon the too-full, bow-shaped lips. Odd a plain woman of her severity should possess such a tempting mouth that fairly begged to be kissed. Gabriel fisted his hands into tight balls. God help him, he was his depraved father's son. "I am afraid you will not do," he blurted. What madness was this, admiring the mouth of a servant who'd come to him seeking employment? He gave his head a disgusted shake.

Confusion creased her brow. "I will not do what?"

He was making a blasted mess of this. "You will not do as a companion." With a sigh, he came to his feet. "You are, of course, welcome to stay the evening and I will send you back to Mrs. Belden's with the use of my personal carriage." He sketched a bow and made to turn toward his desk when he registered the crystalline blue of her eyes. The endless depths made a man think of summer skies and unexplored waters. For all that was plain about the woman, there was a staggering beauty in those fathomless irises.

Mrs. Munroe met his stare with a staggering boldness. "Send me back?" For the lady's bravado, a hint of panic underscored her words.

The woman had a rather bothersome tendency of parroting back a man's words. He nodded. "I will also send you with a letter informing Mrs. Belden of your suitability." For anyone other than his minx of a sister. He strode over to the bell-pull, rang for a servant, and then stalked over to his desk.

Gabriel claimed his seat and tugged open the drawer. He removed a sheet of velum and reached for his pen...when his skin pricked with awareness. With a frown, he picked his head up. The young woman stood at the center of the room, her hands planted akimbo in a move that was not at all polite, proper, or spiritless.

"Did you just dismiss me?" A thread of steel underlined the lady's softly spoken question.

He opened his mouth to ask which manner of dismissal she spoke of, but considering he'd summarily dismissed her twice, wisely pressed his lips into a line. A faint muscle twitched at the corner of the lady's eye, hinting at her annoyance.

He set his pen down and leaned back in his chair.

Interest stirred. Odd, he'd taken the colorless creature as the cowering sort. This woman with her fiery eyes and frowning lips demonstrated more bravado than he'd credited. Still, by her words and actions to this point, she'd proven herself unsuitable for the post. "You are upset, Mrs. Munroe," he said patiently, adopting the tone he'd used on his injured mount when the creature had stepped on a burr during a ride through his country estates several months past.

She narrowed her eyes and took a step forward. "Are you speaking to me as though I'm a wounded pup?"

It had been his loyal mare, but by Mrs. Munroe's thinly veiled fury, she'd little appreciate that slight distinction.

The office door opened and they both looked as one to the entrance. His loyal butler, Joseph—who'd been with their miserable household since Gabriel had been a mere child, beaten and bloodied by his violent sire. "You rang, my lord?"

"Would you—?"

She planted her arms akimbo. "Are you dismissing me again?"

The lady's indignant tone cut into his orders. Had the insolent young woman challenged him—in the presence of his servant? He looked to his butler. By the smile pulling at Joseph's lips, the other man was thoroughly enjoying Mrs. Munroe's bold showing—at Gabriel's expense. He tamped down his irritation and gave Joseph a pointed look. The old servant wisely backed out of the room and pulled the door closed behind him.

Gabriel returned his attention to the companion.

She swung her gaze away from the door and over to Gabriel once more. "You intend to send me away." There it was again. That panic that flickered to life in the woman's eyes.

Remorse tugged at him. "I do." Still, his sister's well-being was far more important than this stranger's pride.

Mrs. Munroe's shocked gasp filled the room.

Life had instilled in him the necessity of blunt honesty. Those sentiments protected a person from being guided down a path of foolish hopes and weakness. Though he felt a modicum of pity for the instructor sent to him from Mrs. Belden's, he'd not be weakened by that useless emotion. Was the proud woman fearful of returning to Mrs. Belden's without the assigned post? Dread, desperation, and anger paraded across the expressive lines of her face. He braced for her to employ tears or her womanly wiles.

Which is why her calm practicality took him aback.

"But you do not even know me," she said with a far more steady tone than he believed her capable of in this moment.

Gabriel drummed his fingertips along the arm of his chair. She dropped her gaze to his hands. Annoyance flashed behind the young woman's eyes and he stilled the distracted movement. "You are determined to have this post, aren't you, Mrs. Munroe?"

She tipped her chin up. "I am. I came here to fulfill the role of companion and I'd see to that responsibility." Then she added as if more an afterthought, "Mrs. Belden would be disappointed if one of her instructors was rejected in the respective role."

Though he admired the lady's determination, her unsuitability could not be changed or helped. She merely did not suit. Long tired of the exchange, he shoved to his feet. "Mrs. Munroe, as I said, I am appreciative of your circumstances." She opened her mouth but then remained blessedly silent, allowing him his piece. "I will pen you a note, ensuring your position is secure at Mrs. Belden's, however," he continued over her when she made to protest. "My sister is entirely too spirited for you," he said with a bluntness that effectively silenced the companion. "I require her wed and the woman you spoke of," he gave his head a shake, "is not my sister and, therefore, it is necessary that I find a companion who will suit my sister's temperament," and who will see Chloe wed when she was determined to do anything but make a match. "Now," he said, inclining his head, "if you will excuse me?" He marched past the wide-eyed young woman. "I have business to attend to." He gave another firm tug on the bell-pull.

The door opened immediately and Joseph, with his blessed timing would see a raise in his salary by day's end, reentered the room. "If you would show Mrs. Munroe to the guest chambers for the evening and have a meal prepared."

Joseph motioned with his arm for Mrs. Munroe to follow him. With the fire snapping in her eyes, she appeared one more wrong word on his part away from marching over to the scabbard adorning his office wall and slaying him for his efforts. God spare him from any more angry ladies. At least this one, he'd soon be free of.

Then, with a remarkable poise that had likely landed the woman her post at Mrs. Belden's, she dropped a stiff, deferential curtsy. "My lord," she said in cold, crisp tones better suited to a queen than a delusional companion. With a final glower, she followed Joseph from the room. The soft click of the door closing behind the retreating Mrs. Munroe echoed loudly in the empty space.

By God he'd dismissed her. Not merely dismissed her. Why, the arrogant, emotionless lout had sacked her before she'd started. As Jane marched silently alongside the kind-eyed butler, she gave her head a bemused shake. This was certainly a first in her rather bleak employment history. A nervous laugh bubbled up from her throat and she nearly choked on the half-sob, half-giggle.

The butler cast a sideways glance her way. She braced for the sneering disapproval. Instead, concern filled his old eyes. Fortunately, he said nothing and allowed her the small trace of pride that remained. Their footsteps fell in unison as they moved down the long corridors, past familial portrait after familial portrait of distinguished kin, but for their powdered heads and dated attire, may as well have been the austere Marquess of Waverly for the coldness in their gazes frozen in time.

She fixed on the outrage coursing through her, for it prevented her from giving in to the swiftly rising panic that threatened to consume her. The marquess, of course, didn't know that returning to Mrs. Belden's was an impossibility for her because there was no post at the finishing school. Not for one of Jane's quick tongue. The irony of this moment did not escape her. The demmed marquess had taken her for a spineless, cowardly sort who'd be trampled by his too-spirited sister and that weakness of character touted by Mrs. Belden had seen

31

her sacked before she'd started. That was what happened to those who stole into a stranger's home and attempted to steal a position of employment.

Jane and the butler walked quietly up a wide, darkened staircase. They reached the landing. The stairs spilled out onto a darkened corridor. She followed the old servant down the hall and then came to stop beside him.

"I have taken the liberty of having your belongings installed in your room."

Ah, so the butler had anticipated she'd been given a room in the guest chambers. Had he also anticipated that she'd be effectively out of a position before she'd begun? "Thank you, Mr.?" She gave him a gentle look and he started.

A flash of surprise lit his eyes. "Joseph," he supplied.

Annoyance stirred to life in her breast once more. This was the manner of household that foul beast ran? One in which his servants were unaccustomed to those small courtesies and kindnesses? "Thank you, Joseph."

He pressed the handle and admitted her to her chambers. With a forced smile, she entered the rooms and closed the door behind her. The hum of quiet filled her ears, blending in blaring cacophony with the steady beat of raindrops upon the crystal windowpanes. Drawing in a shuddery breath, Jane laid her back against the door and shook her head slowly back and forth as a laugh worked its way up her chest. In all her fears of stealing into the marquess' home and commandeering the role of companion, she'd never once considered that she'd be turned out the moment she arrived. The insurmountable challenge had been orchestrating the travel arrangements and entering the marquess' home. She'd erroneously assumed that the challenges presented by her plan ended the moment she'd stepped into his room.

Filled with a restive energy, Jane shoved away from the door and took in the opulent space. The Marquess of Waverly's guest chambers were finer than any of the modest dwellings her illustrious father had set Jane and her mother up in. With tentative steps, she walked over to the vanity. She trailed her fingertips along the mahogany surface and absently picked up the pearl-encrusted brush. The smooth handle was firm and reassuring in her grip. Her gaze snagged upon the bedraggled, rumpled creature in the bevel mirror and she studied herself with a critical eye. With her wrinkled uniform and the flyaway curls that had escaped the tight knot at the base of her neck, was it any wonder she'd been judged and found lacking in a man whose home could surely rival the palaces of most kings? Her lips pulled in a grimace and she set the brush down.

Returning to Mrs. Belden's was not an option. There was nothing to return to. She removed her spectacles and pinched the bridge of her nose. She'd no sooner plead for her post at Mrs. Belden's than send 'round a request for assistance from the Duke of Ravenscourt. The Marquess of Waverly, in all his infinite coolness and icy disdain, had ordered her gone. Granted, he'd permitted her the use of his chambers—

A knock sounded at the door.

She stiffened, but then the handle turned and a small army of servants hurried into the room. Jane widened her eyes and shock slapped her as they carried forth an enormous bath. In short order, the contingency of the marquess' servants filled the porcelain tub with steaming buckets of water and then ducked from the room.

A lone young woman bearing a large silver tray of food entered on the wake of their speedy departure. The woman caught her eye and gave a smile. Another kindly servant. Despite the precariousness of her situation, Jane managed to return a grin.

"I am Cora," the young lady greeted as she set the tray down on the small secretaire. "Is there anything else you require, Mrs. Munroe?"

"Jane," she corrected automatically. She was not different than these people. In fact, she'd wager by her dependence upon her father's assistance in finding employment, she was inferior to any one of the marquess' servants who attained their posts by merit. "Please, just Jane, and no, there is nothing else I require." *That is unless you have any ability to drum up a miraculous position in a safe household for the next two months.*

The woman's smile widened. "Very well, Jane." With a slight curtsy, Cora took her leave, closing the door quietly behind her.

Steam poured off the top of the bath and beckoned Jane over. She sank to her knees alongside the porcelain piece and rested her arms along the side. He'd turn her out. He would send her back to Mrs. Belden's, having judged her worth on a conversation not even fifteen minutes long. Jane skimmed the tip of her fingertips along the smooth surface of the water. Her determined visage reflected back in the shimmering ripples. He believed her spiritless and easily cowed? He thought to send her away in the morn? Well, the ostentatious nobleman would find out tomorrow just how spirited she, in fact, was and then let him try to turn her out.

FIVE

Seated behind his office desk, Gabriel consulted the neat, meticulous lines of the open ledger. He dipped the tip of his pen into the crystal inkwell, marked an additional column, and then tossed his pen down. The landholdings had proven far more successful under his careful attention. He rolled his shoulders, even as his lips pulled up in a hard smile. His father would have been pleased. Such a thought was enough to make a man let all that carefully crafted success go hang.

Yes, he'd like to see all legacies left by his evil sire rot and all the while he would revel in that destruction. If it weren't for the siblings who'd been dependent upon them.

A knock sounded at the door and he raised his gaze to the doorway. "Enter," he barked.

His butler appeared. "My lord," he greeted, a serious set to his weathered face.

Gabriel frowned. The man had been in his family's employ since his youth. He'd stayed on, loyal and, on occasion, scuttling his depraved employer's children off and shielding them. Yet, Joseph refused to quit his post. "Did you see Mrs. Munroe received my note this morning?" he asked, climbing to his feet.

"Er, yes, my lord," he said and stepped out of the way as Gabriel took his leave of the office.

"And you had the carriage readied?" he asked as the man fell in to step alongside him. He recalled the lady's crystalline eyes, the most interesting part of the bland creature, snapping with fury.

Joseph inclined his head. "I did, however—"

"I take it Mrs. Munroe was less than pleased with being sent away."

The old servant scratched his brow. "I would venture you are correct, my lord. However, there are several matters I would speak with you on." They turned right at the end of the corridor and moved toward the breakfast room. "It is Lady Chloe."

Those four words jerked Gabriel to a halt. He swung his gaze to the loyal servant. "What is it?" he asked, his tone harsher than intended, knowing before a confirmation of his fears even left the man's mouth what plagued Chloe.

"She has another of her megrims, my lord."

The muscles of his stomach clenched and unclenched. With a curse, he quickened his steps. "Have—"

"I've taken the liberty of having Dr. Talisman called," Joseph interrupted.

Dr. Talisman. The irony of that old doctor, who'd also served the Edgerton family through the years, did not escape him. How often did he come attending Chloe, who suffered frequent headaches from the abuses of their past?

The old butler hastened his stride to match his pace. Mindful of the exertions, Gabriel slowed his step. "I want to see Talisman as soon as he attends her."

"Of course, my lord. But there is something else I'd speak to you about."

They turned at the end of the corridor and continued walking down the long hall. "What is it?" The hint of light or sound exacerbated his sister's suffering, so he'd not visit her when she descended into one of her megrims, but he often set himself up outside her chambers in the event she called for him. According to Chloe, only the dark and absolute still of silence brought her any semblance of comfort. Except she never called. The chore of that was too great.

"It is Mrs. Munroe."

Bitterness lanced his heart. Nor should Chloe call for him. Why would he be the brother whose support she sought? It was little wonder she preferred Alex and detested him. No, he did not begrudge any of his siblings their resentment. Then the servant's words registered and he cast a sideways glance at Joseph without breaking his stride. "Mrs. Munroe is not my concern. I've sent her letter and sent her on her way. Her position with Mrs. Belden is secure and my obligations to that woman are concluded."

The muscles of the man's throat bobbed up and down and he drew to an abrupt halt. He stole a frantic look at the breakfast room. "My lord, as I mentioned, there was an additional matter of concern I'd speak to you on." Worry creased the man's face.

Gabriel cast a backward glance at the frowning butler, who tended to shuffle back and forth when distraught and then looked to the end of the hall. He released a long sigh and started back toward Joseph. "I take it the young woman was displeased." He recalled the icy cold of her words as she'd fought for a post in his household.

"Er..." Joseph shot a pained glance over Gabriel's shoulder. "She—"

Impatient, Gabriel pressed him. "She what?" He had Chloe to attend to and didn't care to think on the young woman sent him by Mrs. Belden whom he'd promptly sent back. Then an unexpected guilt pricked at him for his callous disregard for Mrs. Munroe. The lady's faults were not her own, nor did he wish her ill. He merely wished his sister properly cared for. Impatient with Joseph's silence, he turned on his heel.

"She is here," Joseph blurted.

A frown formed on Gabriel's lips. Seventy if he was a day, Joseph's vision had begun failing him two decades ago. Now it would seem the man's mind was to follow. Gabriel cast a glance about. "Who is here?"

Joseph tugged at his cravat. His wide eyes bulged in his face. "Mrs. Munroe," he said on a whisper that was not at all a whisper. He jabbed a finger toward the breakfast room.

Gabriel followed that frantic movement and then with a narrow-eyed gaze on the entrance of that room, strode forward. He stepped into the room and froze at the threshold of the door. Sure enough, Mrs. Munroe, as bold as the lady of the house herself, buttered a crusty piece of bread. He eyed her plate heaped with cold ham, eggs, kippers, and bread.

Then, as though she'd not heard every loudly damning word he'd uttered in the hall, she looked up from her plate. "Oh, hello, my lord." The less rumpled, bespectacled lady climbed to her feet and dropped a curtsy. Without awaiting permission, she reclaimed her seat and resumed her buttering efforts.

He opened and closed his mouth several times and then cast a perplexed gaze about. Joseph had wisely fled, leaving Gabriel the unenviable task of dealing with the obstinate woman. "Mrs. Munroe?"

She paused and looked up. "Yes, my lord?"

"What the hell are you doing here?"

A wide smile wreathed her lips. "I believe it should be fairly obvious, I'm breaking my fast."

He started at the unexpected discovery that, for the severity of her coiffure and the paleness of her cheeks, the lady really was quite stunning when she smiled. Then her words registered. "I see that," he snapped and her smile dipped. She made to take a bite out of her now well-buttered bread. "Why are you here?"

Mrs. Munroe froze, her lips slightly parted, Cook's flaky bread but a hairsbreadth from her mouth. "Would you have me take my meal someplace else, my lord?"

He'd have her take it wherever she blasted well pleased—but not his home. "I'd have had you break your fast and left several hours ago," he said, glowering at the insolent miss. By God, what game did she play here?

Then she bit into that damned bread. Her lips closed over it and had she been any woman other than this displeased, oft-frowning instructor from Mrs. Belden, he'd have believed the innocently erotic gesture, deliberate. He groaned.

Mrs. Munroe leaned forward in her chair. "Is there something wrong, my lord?"

"My chair."

She cocked her head. "Beg pardon?"

"It is my chair."

Four little creases indicated the lady's confusion as she glanced about. "Where is your chair, my lord?"

Oh, blast and bloody hell. Tired of Mrs. Munroe and her delayed departure and furious with his sister's debilitating condition, he strode over and towered over the young woman until she was forced to crane her neck back. He expected fear to light those expressive eyes. Instead, an eager glint lit their blue depths. By God, the insolent slip was enjoying herself. She'd orchestrated this entire exchange.

"Yes, my lord?" She arched a golden eyebrow.

"What are you still doing here, Mrs. Munroe?" he snapped.

"Break—"

"And do not say breaking your fast." She closed her lips and then reached for her cup of coffee. Silence marched, punctuated by the slow draw of her sipping from the contents of her glass. Now she'd gone silent? He closed his eyes and prayed for patience. "Mrs. Munroe?"

"Yes?"

He'd long prided himself on his unflinching control. "Do you have nothing to say?" Did that harsh growl belong to him? All that control had been shattered by this slip of a woman more than a foot smaller than him and so narrow-waisted a faint wind would likely take her down.

Mrs. Munroe lifted her shoulders in a slight shrug. "You advised me against mentioning that I was breaking my fast and so I did not." Then with long, slender fingers, she held up her partially filled glass for his inspection. "Now I am drinking." To prove that very point, she took a small sip of her coffee.

Gabriel took in her bow-shaped lips pressed to the rim of the porcelain and a sudden need to take her mouth under his sucked all logical thought from his head. He blinked rapidly. What in blazes? He gave his head a firm shake, dislodging his desirous musings. Yesterday, when he'd first met the quiet, stammering, wide-eyed companion he'd immediately dismissed her as unsuitable for his spirited, unconventional sister. Chloe required a companion who'd not be dragged along on his sister's madcap schemes, with the steely resolve to convince her of the rightness in making a match with a good, honorable gentleman. This more colorful, more insolent, and vastly more infuriating version of Mrs. Munroe, however, would not do for any number of different reasons. He'd go mad with one such as she in his home.

He steeled his jaw. "Explain your presence in my home now, Mrs. Munroe."

For all Jane's false bravado, her heart thumped hard enough that she marveled His Lordship could not see the frantically pounding organ against the wall of her chest. The forced smile on her lips threatened to shatter her cheeks. She'd have to be deaf as a dowager to fail to hear the thin thread of rage underscoring the marquess' question. She'd wager a powerful, commanding lord such as he was unaccustomed to having his orders gainsaid. Yet for all her unease, she clung to the furious annoyance of the dismissive words he'd uttered in the hall. The fact that he cared not at all for her security, post, or in any regard beyond those should come as little surprise. All the noblemen she'd had the displeasure of knowing had seen her as a lesser person there to serve, there to see to their pleasures, or, in some instances as in the case of her father, see her not at all.

"Mrs. Munroe?" he snapped.

Jane started and hurriedly set down her tepid coffee. She placed her hands on her lap, out of his vision, shielding the faint tremble that would demonstrate how unnerved she was by his massive, towering form standing above her. Marquesses had no right to look the way this man did. A muscle-hewn frame and sun-bronzed skin, he might as well have been any honorable man who worked with his hands in the Kent countryside that she and her mother had called home.

In an attempt to demonstrate some mastery over the tenuous situation, Jane dusted her palms together. He followed that movement and then looked at her through dark, impenetrable slits. "You see, my lord, you unfairly dismissed me. You judged my suitability by a brief conversation and nothing more." Which in fairness was his right. In a world where she was powerless, subject to the whims and desires of her employers, she chafed at the total lack of control over her circumstances. "You believed your sister and I would not suit."

He leaned down and shrunk the space between them. "I believed you would not suit," he said with a bluntness that deepened her frown.

Oh, the lout. "Precisely," she said with a vigorous nod.

Only, that slight movement brought him down further, so mere inches separated their faces. The slight cleft in his square jaw ticked in a telltale indication of his annoyance. Fury emanated from his eyes. "I beg your pardon, Mrs. Munroe." And God help her, she really shouldn't note anything beyond his high-handedness and easy disregard for her future, she'd have to be blind to fail to appreciate the chiseled planes of his face that may as well have been carved of stone.

"You believed I would not suit your sister, but you can't know that. Not truly." He pierced her with his intense stare and she rushed on before her courage fled and her feet followed suit. "If your sister is as spirited as you proclaim—"

"She is," he bit out.

"Then surely the lady should have some input as to my suitability." Which was the desperate plan she'd crafted somewhere between the glorious, hot, soothing bath last evening and the hours of being unable to sleep. It was a sorry day indeed when a woman hung her hopes upon a post she'd hoped to steal and the benevolence of a spirited noblewoman.

The marquess straightened. "You would have me allow my sister to decide as to whether you will suit as a companion?"

Jane gave a terse nod. She braced for the mocking insolence she'd come to expect of men such as he who saw women as weak-willed and robbed them of a voice in all matters. Instead, a mocking smile turned his lips upward. The first indication that the brilliantly hatched scheme concocted in his guest chambers had proven a faulty one.

"Very well, Mrs. Munroe. I shall allow my sister to decide on your suitability as her companion."

She eyed him warily. "You will?" The lords whose homes she'd resided in had made decisions for their wives and daughters. Those same men had only and always acted with their desires placed before anyone else's. There had to be more at play where the marquess was concerned.

He ran a fierce stare over her. "I will, and when," not if but rather when, "my sister decides you will not do as her companion, I expect you to take your leave immediately."

Jane balled her hands into fists. "*When* I meet her and *if* she decides we do not suit," his eyes narrowed all the more until nothing more than the blacks of his irises were visible. "Then I will leave." Not before then. Being turned out by Lady Chloe Edgerton was not an option.

The marquess straightened and, with one final hard look, started for the door.

A cowardly surge of relief coursed through her and she hopped to her feet. "My lord," she called out. He froze at the threshold of the door and spun back to face her. He eyed her in stony silence. "When can I expect to meet Lady Chloe?"

He flexed his jaw. "My sister is now indisposed."

"Indisposed?" she repeated.

For a long moment he said nothing and she expected he intended to allow that question to go unanswered. After all, it was not her right to put questions to him. Then, she'd never done what was expected of her where Society was concerned. Her lips twisted in a dry smile. That strong-willed aspect of her character had inevitably found her in this now impossible position with the Marquess of Waverly.

He spoke at last. "She suffers megrims, Mrs. Munroe."

A twinge of guilt struck her. "I am sorry," she said automatically.

The marquess gave a terse nod and then took his leave. Jane's shoulders sagged and she gripped the back of the shell chair, borrowing support from the mahogany wood. Each day she was permitted to remain closeted away here, the closer she was to the freedom provided by the trust settled upon her by the duke. She would have claim to that money entitled her and then never again would she rely upon the Duke of Ravenscourt connections, the benevolence of strangers, or the whim of a nobleman. She would be free. Free when her mother had been reliant upon her protector's generosity.

After days of the dark gloom of rain, an unexpected ray of sun filtered through the crack in the gold brocade curtains. The light danced off the crystal candelabras and threw a rainbow of color about the room. She stilled. As a girl, her mother had filled Jane's ears with tales of legends and fables and fairytales. The first time Jane had ever seen one of those elusive rainbows, she'd been a girl of six. Her mother had told the tale of all great fortunes found at the end of that colorful masterpiece. All one had to do was battle the devilish leprechaun for those riches.

A smile played about Jane's lips. It appeared her rainbow emptied out into the Marquess of Waverly's home and, at the end of this particular battle, she'd have her riches—and then she'd be done with her father, the marquess, and any other arrogant, commanding nobleman.

"Mrs. Munroe?"

A gasp escaped her, and she spun around. The butler stood at the doorway. She relaxed. "Joseph," she greeted, and with her momentary victory over the marquess and his intentions to send her off, embarrassment crept in at the boldness in commandeering the marquess' breakfast room.

"As you will be a member of His Lordship's staff, would you permit me to show you about the townhouse?"

If the marquess had his way, there was little reason for Jane to familiarize herself with any part of his lavish townhome except for the black front door with its dragon knocker. "I would be appreciative," she said, instead.

He inclined his head, and then without waiting to see whether she followed, started from the room. Jane hurried after the older servant. Joseph moved at an unexpectedly quick clip for one of his advanced years. Every so often, his left leg hitched. That halting movement allowed her to fall into step beside him.

He grimaced as though in pain.

A twinge of sympathy tugged at her heart, and with it an equally strong loathing for the marquess, who'd not permit this man a deserved retirement. She opened her mouth to assure Joseph that she was not in need of an escort, but then he shot her a challenging glance. Jane promptly closed her mouth. Too often she'd been the object of people's pity. She'd not subject the kindly servant to that emotion.

She would, however, use the opportunity to find out more of her employer and his willful sister. "You have been in the marquess employ long, Joseph?" she asked as they moved down the thin-carpeted corridors.

"I've been in service to the marquess and his family for forty years, Mrs. Munroe."

Was it loyalty to the man's father that kept him here? Periodically, Joseph motioned to a room—a parlor, a study—acquainting Jane with her new, temporary, but hopefully not *too* temporary residence. "And His Lordship requires you to continue at your post?"

He shot her a sidelong look. "The current Marquess of Waverly has offered me my retirement. I choose to continue in my role," he murmured. Before she could ask the questions that sprung forth to her lips, he motioned to a closed door. "The library, Mrs. Munroe."

It did not escape her notice that he sought to divert her questions away from the Marquess of Waverly. Hmm. The man inspired loyalty in his servants. She furrowed her brow and considered how such a rigid, unbending, and unfeeling man could rouse anything but fear and annoyance in a person. It mattered not. The person who would ultimately decide her fate was none other than the gentleman's sister. As they turned at the end of the corridor, Jane put another question to the servant. "And what of Lady Chloe?" she asked. "Is there anything you might tell me of Lady Chloe?" Anything that would prove useful in winning over the likely spoiled, young lady.

A frown tugged his lips downward. The kindly gentleman grew a good deal less kind when presented questions about his employer or the man's kin. "She is an honorable, spirited young lady."

Spirited. There was that word again. And honorable. Together, two unexpected words assigned any of Mrs. Belden's former students.

As they moved through the house, Jane committed the long halls and corridors to memory. Having been employed in the homes of other powerful nobleman, she'd learned to appreciate possible paths of escape. What seemed an interminable amount of time later, they reached Jane's chambers. "His Lordship would likely afford you the use of the rooms, Mrs. Munroe." She highly doubted that. Not when he was likely plotting, even now, the most efficient way to have her removed from his home.

With a murmur of thanks, Jane stood staring down the hall, long after Joseph had taken his leave, wondering at the austere nobleman who commanded such loyalty.

SIX

G abriel stood at the corner of the darkened library, his gaze turned out to the quiet streets below. The half-moon that hung in the sky cast a soft glow upon the cobbled roads, illuminating the deep puddles left after days of cool, London rain. He looped his hands behind his back, following a lone, slow moving carriage as it rattled past. His sister still lay abed, incapacitated with her megrims. Oftentimes, the episodes would last the course of a day. In rare cases, they would last longer. Through each, he suffered the blame that came from his sister's suffering.

He laid his forehead against the cool windowpane and took each lash of guilt. What manner of brother did not stop vicious attacks upon a mere child? The honorable one, the younger one, nearly took their father apart with his bare hands. What had Gabriel done? Nothing that mattered. A hungering thirst for a drink filled him, consuming and desperate. He strode over to the sideboard, made his selection, and decanter and snifter in hand, he then carried them to the leather winged back chair set up in the corner of the room. Gabriel claimed a seat and shifted the burden in his hands. He filled his glass to the rim and set the decanter at his feet.

The door handle clicked and he stilled. Shrouded in the dark of the room, he peered at the entrance. A frown formed on his lips as the tart-mouthed, insolent Mrs. Munroe slipped into the room. He should excuse himself. At the very least, he should announce himself. Instead, he remained immobile and took in the companion sent from Mrs. Belden as she stole a quick glance about the library. Then, she closed the door behind her and stopped. With the moon's pale glow, he studied her. She caught her too-full lower lip between her teeth as though warring with herself over the decision to remain, but with a slight shake of her head, moved to the long row of shelving.

The amber contents of his glass forgotten, he continued to study the woman who, even after his dismissal, had challenged her way into staying in his home. She trailed the tips of her fingers over the leather volumes and paused on a black book. Gabriel squinted but the title was lost to the darkness of the room. Interest stirred as the young woman hesitated, tugged a book free, and then opened it. Head bent, with her attention fixed upon the tome, he used the opportunity to study her. What did one such as Mrs. Munroe read? And who was she? Stammering, fearful miss? Or bold-spirited, insolent minx?

With deliberate movements, he took a slow sip of his drink. All the while, the woman with her nose buried in the pages continued reading, unaware of his presence. For if she were, she'd have likely fled long ago. He'd wager she favored books about propriety and decorum and all things proper. After all, what else interested a woman who served as a stern instructor at an esteemed finishing school? On the heel of that was another question: How did a woman enter into such a position?

"Good evening, Mrs. Munroe." He found an inordinate amount of enjoyment in her startled shriek. She flung her arms up and the volume sailed from her fingertips and landed at her feet.

"Ouch."

Or more precisely on her feet.

He set his snifter down on the side table and stood. Despite the darkened room, crimson blazed upon Mrs. Munroe's pale cheeks. He resisted the urge to smile as she hopped up and down on the uninjured toes in a move that was not at all proper and certainly not fitting behavior of one of Mrs. Belden's distinguished instructors.

The lady chose that inopportune moment to glance at him. She narrowed her eyes. "Do you find enjoyment in another person's pain?" she snapped.

Her words swiftly killed any of his earlier humor. A man who still bore the scars upon his back, he could never delight in another's pain. "Forgive me. It was not my intention to laugh at you."

"What was your intention, then?" she challenged. He gave his head a wry shake. Spiritless, indeed. "I was struck by the honesty of your reaction."

The lady could have, and likely should have, taken those words as an insult. She peered at his face a long while and then shocked him with her slow nod. "I thought I was alone." Ah there, the faint accusatory edge, words that danced around a reproach, but remained just shy of an insult.

Yes, pairing this one with Chloe would be dangerous for all manner of reasons. Fortunately, he'd wager all his holdings when presented with the option of retaining one of Mrs. Belden's dragons or being spared a companion, if even temporarily, she'd choose the latter.

Poor Mrs. Munroe did not have a hope. As one who'd ceased believing in hope long ago, he recognized as much. The bespectacled miss, however, clearly still retained that useless sentiment. "Are you enjoying your stay, Mrs. Munroe?" *Your very brief stay.* He'd delight in packing this one up in a carriage, any carriage, closing the door, and having her ride off to Mrs. Belden's where she belonged.

The color deepened on her cheeks. "Joseph indicated I might visit the library. I…" Her words trailed off. "Forgive me. I will take my leave." She turned to go.

"Mrs. Munroe?" The quietly spoken words halted her retreat. She stiffened and turned back.

"My lord?" She darted the tip of her tongue out and traced the seam of her bow-shaped lips.

He followed that innocent, yet maddeningly erotic gesture. An agonized groan built in his chest. God help him, he was noticing plain, drab-skirt-wearing Mrs. Munroe.

"Of course you may use the library, or any other room, for as long you are here."

"Thank you," she murmured and dropped a curtsy, heightening the awareness of the station difference between them.

48

Gabriel studied her, this contradictory creature. One moment, hissing and snapping like a cornered cat in the kitchens, the next shy and hesitant. Having lived his life erecting barriers, he recognized Mrs. Munroe—the woman without a Christian name had crafted a carefully constructed facade. "How did you come to be an instructor at Mrs. Belden's?" It was hard to say who was the more shocked by his unexpected inquiry—he or Mrs. Munroe with her gaping mouth.

She wet her lips and cast a quick glance about. "I'd venture the way any woman comes to find herself in such a post."

The deliberate vagueness of her response didn't escape his notice. It did, however, rouse his curiosity. "And how is that?" he asked the question of a genuine desire to know, even as he could not sort why it mattered that he knew—just that it did.

Mrs. Munroe scoffed. "I thought you didn't care?"

He cocked his head and a frown formed on his lips. The woman possessed a deep cynicism for one so young.

She waved a hand about. "Oh, come," she said. "Surely you'll not feign any concern on my account, my lord."

Gabriel folded his arms at his chest and winged an eyebrow upward. "I assure you, Mrs. Munroe, I do not feign interest on any-one's account."

"It is, as you said," she lifted her shoulders in a slight shrug. "I am not your concern. After all, you've given me a letter and sent me on my way. My position with Mrs. Belden is secure and your obligation is concluded."

Those words casually tossed out to his butler, and overheard by this woman, roused guilt in his chest. How must Mrs. Munroe have perceived those words? He'd spent the course of his life caring for, nay worrying about, the survival of his siblings and mother. "I meant no insult," he said at last. However, there was no room within the deliberately small circle of those dependent upon him for anyone else's happiness. But how should that truth appear to this woman?

She tipped her chin up at the mutinous angle he'd learned upon meeting her meant she prepared for verbal battle. "There was no insult there, my lord. There was a lack of feeling. Regard. Decency."

"On what do you base your charge?" That terse question silenced her. Tired of her allegations that would paint him as a self-absorbed nobleman who cared about no one, he took a step toward her, and Mrs. Munroe retreated. "You would cast aspersions upon my character and for what? Because I met you, interviewed you, and found you wholly unsuitable to care for my sister?" He continued walking and with each movement, she backed away. Did she believe he intended her harm? At that truth, fury roiled all the deeper within his gut for altogether different reasons than the unfavorable opinion she'd developed of him. He abruptly stopped. "Should I have placed your pride in your capabilities as a companion above all else? Including that of my own sister's needs and interests?" A mere handbreadth separated them and he expected her to retreat.

Instead, she remained rooted to the floor, her chest heaving. With fear? Anger? Desire? Where would *that* thought come from?

Then he dipped his gaze lower to her fathomless, blue stare and, God help him, if her eyes were water he'd gladly lose himself within their depths. He swallowed reflexively and urged his feet to carry him away from her but made the mistake of lowering his eyes further to her lush, full lips. No companion should have a mouth such as hers. With a pained groan, he lowered his head, praying she'd slap him in fury, but hoping more that she allowed him to explore the soft contours of her perfectly bow-shaped lips.

But as he touched his mouth to hers, she remained still. A slight, shuddery intake of her honey-scented breath hinted at her desire. Encouraged by that breathy sigh, he deepened the kiss.

She stiffened, and for an agonizing moment he thought she'd wrench herself free of his embrace but then she angled her head and accepted his kiss with a tentativeness that hinted at innocence and belied the *Mrs.* before her name. He moved his lips in a slow, determined path, brushing his mouth over the corner of her lips. "Surely you have a name?" How did he not know her name? How, when he knew she tasted of honey and smelled as though she'd been traipsing through fields of lavender?

"J-Jane," she rasped and tipped her head back to aid him in his quest.

At the satiny softness of her long, graceful neck, Gabriel's heart thundered in his ears. Or was that her wildly beating pulse under his lips? "Jane," he repeated back, exploring the taste of her name. Short and yet, strength melded with the faintest hint of softness to that one syllable. "Perfect," he whispered, taking her lips once more. It suited her in every way. He folded his arms about her, drawing her close and taking her lips under his again. A startled cry escaped her. He stiffened and drew back just as Jane punched him. Her fist connected solidly with his nose.

As the lady stumbled away from him, Gabriel touched his nose. He winced. By God, too many counts in a ring against Gentleman Jackson himself and never broken, but then with one dangerously wicked right jab, the lady had broken his nose. Belatedly, he registered the sickly warm trickle of blood. Gabriel yanked his kerchief from his pocket and pressed it to his nose glaring at Jane over the rapidly staining fabric. The lady continued retreating, her pallor white. "Bloody hell." He winced at the pain of his own touch. What companion learned to handle herself in that impressive manner? If he'd not already sworn to have her gone, and then violated the unspoken vow to never dally with those in his employ, he'd have hired her on as a companion if for no other reason than the certainty that Chloe would be well-cared for in her capable, if violent, hands.

Jane pressed her hands to her lips. Her well-kissed lips. Oh, bloody hell, she'd hit him. The marquess withdrew a kerchief from his pocket and then snapped open the stark white linen. Horror filled her as a splash of crimson stained that immaculate fabric. "I—" That strangled word caught in her throat, as she recalled the last man she'd hit and the consequences of that violent, but deservedly violent, outburst. She'd been cast out of her employer's home and scuttled off to Mrs. Belden's. But this was altogether different. This circumstance, however, was *vastly* different. The marquess had not forced his attentions

51

on her. Instead, she'd pressed herself against him like the shameful harlot her mother had been and eagerly returned that kiss.

From over the rim of his handkerchief, he studied her. The faintest amusement glinted in his emerald green eyes, which was impossible. A powerful, commanding nobleman would not take to being dealt a facer by a member of his staff. And certainly not a woman who was merely a member of his staff because she'd laid siege to his breakfast room and refused to leave until she met and made a plea to his sister.

"A simple no would have sufficed," he said drolly and experimentally tested the soundness of the bridge of his nose.

"Oh, God, have I broken it?" It would be the very worst shame for that aquiline nose to be forever crooked because of her involuntary reaction.

"I'm merely afforded a 'my lord' from the title marquess. I assure you, I'm no god," he drawled.

How could he affect that droll, dry humor? How, when she'd hit him as she had? She backed into a rose-inlaid side table and the fragile piece of furniture shifted sideways, upending a porcelain shepherdess. The white and pink piece tumbled to the floor and exploded in a spray of splintered glass. She stared blankly down at the mess she'd created and then swung her gaze back to the marquess. "M-my lord. Forgive me," she said, detesting the hoarseness of her tone; that weak, spiritless quality which had convinced him of her unsuitability for the post as companion to his sister.

He waved his free hand. "It was inappropriate for me to kiss you." Heat spiraled through her at those uttered words that made the memory of his embrace all the more real. The marquess lowered his handkerchief and she let out a small sigh of relief at the halted blood flow. He gave her a wry smile. "And considering that kiss, I'd venture it is entirely appropriate for you to refer to me by my Christian name."

She blinked. It would never be appropriate for her to refer to him or any other nobleman by his Christian name. And yet, she angled her head, hopelessly wanting, nay needing, to know the name assigned to a broadly powerful figure such as the marquess.

"Gabriel," he supplied.

Gabriel. One of those seven archangels, a warrior of the heavenly armies. Strong, powerful. It perfectly suited him. "It wouldn't be appropriate." She warmed at that belated, half-hearted protestation.

"No. It would not, *Jane*." His thick, hooded, black lashes shielded all hint of emotion within his eyes. There was the faintest and yet, she'd venture, deliberate emphasis on that, her name. A statement from a man who, with his aura of power, could command a kingdom, that he'd noted her regard for propriety and gave not a jot.

She fisted her hands. But then, wasn't that a luxury permitted one of his lofty station? Jane stiffened as he bent down and retrieved something.

He held up her fragile, wire-rimmed spectacles. "Your spectacles?"

Jane touched her naked face and anxiety pounded at her chest as she flew across the room and, in the most undignified manner, plucked them from his fingers. How could she have not recalled dropping them? The hideous and *useless* frames she'd donned after her first post as a companion to an aging countess "Thank you." The woman's devoted son, with his wandering hands, had taught Jane her first important lesson on those of the nobility who saw in her, and every other woman of her station, someone there for nothing more than their pleasures. She hurriedly opened them and jammed them on her face. Jane smoothed her palms over the front of her skirts. "I would apologize again for hitting you, my lord."

"Gabriel."

"Gabriel," she amended. After all, when one was pleading for one's post, it wouldn't do to argue.

He took a step toward her. "And I've already said there is nothing to apologize for."

"But there is." Putting one's hands upon a nobleman, a punishable offense that, at least, merited being turned out immediately. She held her palms up. "I'd ask that you not dismiss me outright, but allow me to remain on so that I might meet your sister."

The ghost of a smile hovered on his lips. "And you still believe that my sister will agree to you as a companion?" There was a faint trace of humor there that gave her pause. He was so very confident that she should be turned out by his sister, and the experience Jane had working with Mrs. Belden's students should have very well supported his opinion, and yet something gave her hope.

The long-case clock struck eleven and she started. A slow smile tipped her lips at the corner at that slight, but very obvious, sign. "I do believe you'll not be rid of me as quickly as you wish, my—Gabriel," she corrected at his pointed look.

"Is that what you believe?" He arched an eyebrow. "That I am eager to be rid of you?"

"Aren't you?"

"I'm merely trying to see my sister properly cared for." The serious set to his face hinted at a sadness to him and gave her pause. She recognized that sadness because she carried that painful sentiment within her and she hated that she'd seen a like emotion from him. For it was far easier to challenge and loathe a man for his high-handedness. It was quite another to confront a gentleman who genuinely cared for his sister and wore a cloak of sadness about him. That made him real in ways that were dangerous to her well-ordered thoughts. "I have to leave." She winced. *Should* leave. She *should* leave.

He inclined his head, but made no move to stop her. Instead, he stepped aside, opening the path to the doorway. Jane forced her legs to move.

Gabriel called out. "Jane?"

She stopped and cast a glance back at him.

"Have you forgotten something?" Her common sense, her logic and clear thoughts. He motioned to the lone book, startled from her hands a short while ago lying indignantly upon its spine.

Jane rushed over and claimed the forgotten volume and with the black leather book pulled protectively against her chest, she hurried from the room, desperate to put distance between herself and the suddenly very human marquess.

Gabriel.

SEVEN

The following morning, Gabriel sipped coffee from his cup. His lips pulled at the familiar but still bitter bite of the black brew. Periodically, he glanced at the empty doorway. Jane, the feisty companion with a powerful right jab, had occupied his thoughts from the moment she'd fled the library. With her parting, he'd sought out his chambers. Alas, sleep had eluded him. Instead, alternating emotions—desire, a hungering to explore her mouth once more, and a nauseating guilt had gripped him. Gabriel didn't go about kissing those in his employ.

He tightened his grip on the fragile glass in his hand. He'd spent the better part of his life distancing himself from the man the previous marquess had been. He'd dedicated himself to never adopting any part of his father's ways. Yet, drunk with the scent of lavender and honey, he'd kissed her. Sleep had eventually come and when he'd arisen from that restless slumber haunted by the wide-eyed companion, he'd gone through his morning ablutions resolved to be free of any thoughts of Mrs. Jane Munroe. Her presence here only roused the dark similarity between him and his bastard of a sire who'd taken his pleasures where he would—with ladies of the *ton* and servants in his household.

He stared into the contents of his cup and then took another slow sip. Except—was she a Mrs.? Was the lady, in fact, a young widow dependent upon her own skills to survive in a society that gave few options to those very women? He frowned at the empty doorway and then shifted his cup to his other hand and consulted his timepiece. Jane had broken her fast at this time yesterday morn. At the prospect of seeing the companion, an odd excitement stirred in his chest.

With a groan, he set down his cup and scrubbed his hands over his face. What manner of madness was this, his thinking of the woman with anything less than annoyance? The sooner the tart-mouthed, yet kissable, lady took her leave, the better he'd be. He didn't require distractions in the form of stiffly proper companions with a veneer of ice and a coating of molten heat underneath. But now that he'd tasted Jane's fire, God help him if he didn't burn for her.

The soft tread of footsteps sounded in the hall and he glanced up, a nonsensical eagerness stirred within, and then died a thankfully swift death. His sister stood framed in the entrance. "Oh."

Chloe softly laughed. "It is lovely to see you as well."

Gabriel blinked and then registered her presence. "Chloe." He sprang to his feet and the wooden legs of his chair scraped noisily along the floor. "How are you feeling?" Guilt chafed at his insides. He'd been so fixated on Mrs. Jane Munroe he'd not given proper thought to his sister's well-being.

Chloe waved a hand about. "I am rested and well," she said with a smile. As though to prove as much, she moved with energized steps to the sideboard. She favored a nearby servant with one of her patently sincere smiles and proceeded to fill her plate. She carried it over and then claimed the spot beside him, and then froze. "What happened to your face?"

His face. As in his blackened eyes. He'd arisen with the underside of his eyes painted purple and blue for Jane's efforts. And as he couldn't very well admit to kissing a stranger fighting for the post as companion and then being dealt an impressive facer for those efforts, he said the first words to form on his lips. "I don't know what you're talking about." He winced as soon as the lie left his mouth. His tenacious sister would not release her talons from this juicy morsel.

Chloe leaned up and touched the bruise. He winced. "This. I'm referring to this." With a moue of displeasure on her lips, she adopted the disapproving tone used by their mother too often. "You do not fight, Gabriel." No, he disavowed all violent endeavors. Having been the victim of too many fists of fury rained down upon him, he'd vowed to never raise one to another, except if it was to defend himself or his kin.

And so, with his sister staring pointedly at him, he did what any gentleman who'd been kissing his sister's companion would do. "I was visiting Gentleman Jackson's." He lied.

"Oh." The slight nod indicated she approved of that endeavor. "Well?" she prodded as she sat.

Would she not let the matter rest? "Well, what?" he asked, reclaiming his seat.

Chloe carefully diced a piece of cold ham. "Has she arrived?"

Ah, she spoke of Mrs. Munroe. Gabriel cast another look over at the door. "She has."

"And?" she popped the breakfast meat into her mouth and chewed.

His mind drew a blank. What was there to say about the woman who was a spitting mad vixen one moment and a quiet-mannered, proper young woman the next?

Chloe pointed her eyes to the ceiling. "Do not be deliberately obtuse. Regardless, I must politely reject your plan to tie me to one of Belden's dragons for the remainder of the Season."

The floorboards creaked and they swung their gazes to the entrance of the room. The determined Jane Munroe, who should have taken her leave two days ago, stood at the threshold. Hesitant, hovering, and uncertain, she bore traces of the woman who'd first shown up on his doorstep.

He climbed to his feet, a grin on his lips. "Chloe, may I present to you one of Mrs. Belden's *instructors*." His sister had the good grace to blush. "This is Mrs. Munroe." After all, there was little doubt that Jane had, in fact, heard the unfavorable words leveled at her.

His sister stood. "Mrs. Munroe," she murmured.

Jane executed a flawless curtsy. Her gaze strayed momentarily over to Gabriel and then she swiftly returned her attention to Chloe. "My lady, it is a pleasure."

Chloe warily eyed her, as though she feared one wrong word and the woman would drag her back for another year of finishing school. Ah, Jane, who'd been so very confident of her persuasion that she'd commandeered his home and boldly rejected his plans of returning her to Mrs. Belden's. Amusement filled him and Gabriel felt himself grinning as he reclaimed his seat.

Chloe returned her attention to her plate. From over the top of her head, he caught Jane's gaze and lifted his cup in silent challenge. She narrowed her gaze, and then with stiff footsteps made her way to the sideboard. The lady heaped eggs, kippers, ham, and bread atop her plate. His lips twitched at the healthy portion for the trim young woman. His skin pricked and he glanced over at his sister who paused, her fork midway to her mouth, and studied him.

Silence descended upon the breakfast parlor, which with his usually garrulous sister was a rarer occurrence than a solar eclipse. Jane slid into the vacant chair beside Chloe and a footman helped push the chair forward. She gave a murmur of thanks and then, head bowed, proceeded to butter that warm, flaky bread just as she'd done yesterday morn.

Gabriel settled back in his seat and cradled his cup between his hands. He eyed Jane over the rim. In the two days with which to develop a proper entreaty to put to his sister regarding Jane's suitability as a companion, she was now silent. He broke the impasse. "I trust you've had several days to resolve yourself to the necessity of a companion, Chloe. As you are in the market for a husband, it is essential you," *we*, "have a proper," at his sidelong glance, Jane's frown deepened, "companion."

Chloe finished her bite and then dabbed her lips with the edge of her white napkin. "There is no need for a companion." She paused. "I've resolved that your presence will suffice." She cast a sheepish glance at Jane. "I mean no offense, Mrs. Munroe. I simply do not need you." With those six words, she severed Jane's connection to his household.

Jane politely inclined her head in acknowledgement. For a moment, panic flared to life in those expressive, crystalline eyes, and the depth of emotion there froze him. The fear and desperation there went beyond mere pride. She opened her mouth, as though prepared to launch a defense, but then her lower lip quivered. The muscles of his stomach clenched and he hated he'd noted that slight tremble, but there it was. And it could not be unseen. Through the young woman's tumult, Chloe attended her breakfast, unknowing that she'd ultimately decided Jane's fate.

The matter of Jane and her position as companion to Chloe was at last settled. As he'd demanded from the onset, Jane would board his carriage and return to her post at Mrs. Belden's. So why did that prospect cause this odd, empty, bereft feeling in his chest? Where was the earlier victory? The elation? He stared at the contents of his plate.

"Despite your hopes and expectations for me," his sister spoke, bringing his head up. "I am not in the market for a husband." Those words were said to both of them. With the same show of defiance she'd practiced since she was a mere girl, she pursed her lips and favored Gabriel with a glower. "I've no intention of marrying."

From the corner of his eye, he saw Jane sit forward in her seat, as though intrigued by his sister's bold pronouncement.

Oh, bloody hell. He fought back a groan. Chloe would have this discussion again. Jane forgotten, Gabriel finished his coffee and set the cup aside. He waved off the servant who rushed forward to refill his cup and settled his elbows upon the table. "Chloe, you are one and twenty, nearly two and twenty," he continued when she made to speak. "With several days in which to consider our last exchange, surely you see the necessity in securing a husband. I have already assured you, the man chosen will be honorable, caring, and considerate."

"The man chosen?" His sister gaped at him.

What was it with young women and parroting back a person's words?

Jane hopped to her feet so suddenly, the crystal clattered noisily on the table.

He spared a distracted glance for the young woman whose kiss had stolen his logic and, for that maddening loss of control, a reason he needed her gone. For a moment, he thought she intended to do precisely that. To turn, abandon the table, collect her valise, and then be gone. Forever. A vise squeezed his lungs. He tugged at his cravat. The blasted fabric was too tight, was all.

Instead, she made for the sideboard once more. He cast a glance down at her untouched plate and the impressive mound of breakfast meats and pastries and eggs she'd assembled.

"And I've told you, I do not want that."

Gabriel jerked his head around to look at his sister. He really should do a better job of attending. Yes, Mrs. Munroe could not be gone soon enough.

"Do pay attention, Gabriel." He winced as Chloe rapped him in the knuckles. "If you are going to speak on a matter of import, such as my marital state, then at the very least you can pay attention to me while I speak."

Ah, yes. The business of finding her a husband. As he'd seen few results in ordering her about over the years, now he gentled his tone and appealed to her sister's reason. "All I ask is for you to trust me and allow me select your husband as I did Philippa."

By the fury lighting Chloe's eyes, she appreciated his calming tone as much as Jane had two days prior. "I've already told you…" Her words trailed off and Gabriel followed her stare.

Jane marched over with an empty plate and thrust it under his nose. He eyed the porcelain dish and then gave her a perplexed look. What was she on about? She shook it at him. "Well, take it."

And *that* was likely the clipped tone that had earned this woman and every other at Mrs. Belden's the moniker of dragon. He quickly accepted the dish. "And what would you have me do with this plate, J—" His sister's eyebrows shot to her hairline and he swiftly amended, "Mrs. Munroe?"

Chloe's eyes formed perfectly round moons as she alternated her stare between him and Jane Munroe.

A steely glint lit the silver flecks of Jane's eyes. She lowered her voice. "With such a total lack of faith in your sister's decision-making on the matter of her future and the man she'd wed or not wed, perhaps you should begin selecting her choices for meals as well."

Gabriel widened his eyes. By God. Had she just given him a public dressing down? Jane wheeled around and strode toward the door, nothing at all ladylike or Mrs. Belden dragon-like about her pace or furiously frantic movements. *And* she'd dismissed him. How had he ever taken her for a weak-willed, spiritless creature?

Jane stopped suddenly and spun back to face them. Color heightened her cheeks and he braced for her apology. "Forgive me, Lady Chloe." Chloe? What of his apology? "I am sorry we did not suit and I wish you the best of luck." She shot a glare in Gabriel's direction. "With that one." This time, without a backward stare, she stomped from the room.

The footmen at the back corner of the room shifted back and forth. By the tightly compressed lines of their mouths, they fought off humor.

With a curse, Gabriel grabbed his cup and raised it to his lips. His damned empty cup. He slammed it down with a loud thunk. How dare she enter his home and question his care and regard for his sister? By God, he'd failed his siblings in the past and, as such, he'd committed his life to righting those wrongs, and seeing to their happiness. Now this stranger, with her damned ugly spectacles and her painfully tight chignon, should challenge him for caring?

And then he registered a small laugh. He snapped his gaze toward Chloe, pleased that one of them should find Jane's antics entertaining. There was solace to at least be found in knowing she was even now packing her hideous brown skirts and apron and preparing to join the other dragons. A growl rumbled from deep within his chest. He grabbed his knife and fork and with a gleeful delight, carved the ham on his plate.

"Gabriel?"

He looked up.

A smile lined his sister's face—mischievous and coy—and as life had taught him, all things dangerous. "I rather like her a lot." He stilled. The wheels of his mind turned with a staggering slowness and then roared to life, spinning wildly out of control. Those words. Her enjoyment. *Oh, blast, damn, and double-damn.* "In fact," *Do not say it. Do not say it.* "Mrs. Munroe will do splendidly as a companion."

With that, she popped up from her seat and took her leave. Laughter trailed in her wake. Gabriel dropped his head into his hands. What had he done?

EIGHT

Jane marched through the house. What madness had possessed her to not only return the kiss, but also *crave* the kiss of an insufferably arrogant, condescending, pompous lord such as Gabriel? With each step that carried her away from the breakfast room and above stairs to her private chambers, the more her fury and annoyance grew. This position posed one hope for freedom, and yet, how could she ever dare live beneath the roof of a man who'd disparage the beliefs and hopes of his sister, believing he knew what was right for her? Though if he truly knew, he'd realize that any and all gentlemen were nothing more than priggish, domineering louts who—

"Mrs. Munroe!" The breathless cry brought Jane up short and she stumbled.

She came down hard on her palms and grunted. Pain shot out from the palms of her hands.

"Oh, my!" Chloe Edgerton cried out. "Do forgive me."

Jane's cheeks burned with a blend of annoyance, embarrassment, and remembered fury. She sat back on her haunches when the young lady held her fingers out. She eyed her fingertips a moment and then accepted the kind offering. "Thank you," she said shakily. She'd never possessed the grace that would have earned her a position as companion if it hadn't been for her father's insistence.

"Where are you off to?"

Intelligence sparked in Lady Chloe's eyes, and yet surely, the young woman knew precisely where Jane was headed. Unless this lady, like so many before her, merely toyed with Jane the way she might a bothersome rodent "I was just returning to my chambers," she said cautiously eying the young lady and braced for a heavy dose of gloating from the woman who no more desired Jane's presence than Jane did the company of the shrewish Mrs. Belden. When Lady Chloe still remained silent, she added, "If you'll pardon me, I must see to my belongings." *And either swallow my pride and contact my father or, well, was there really another option?* She couldn't very well live on the streets of London. Her gut churned at the prospect of humbling herself before the stranger who'd sired her. She made to step around the young woman.

Gabriel's sister stepped into her path. "You are not a dragon."

She cocked her head.

"I daresay you overheard me in the breakfast room. I referred to you as one of Mrs. Belden's dragons and yet…" She leaned close and peered through squinted eyes, until Jane recoiled under her scrutiny. The young woman gave her head a slow shake. "And yet, I do not believe you are truly one of those dragons."

Jane thought of the other instructors who'd honorably earned their posts at the finishing school. Always frowning, grim, and determined to train the joy and free-thought out of a young lady's mind.

"May I walk with you?" Lady Chloe did not wait on a response. She looped her arm through Jane's. "That was a rather splendid showing."

Jane cast a glance back at the carpeted floor she'd stumbled upon.

The young lady squeezed her arm. "Not your fall." She wrinkled her nose. "A fall, which was very much, in fact, my fault. Rather, your exchange with Gabriel, my brother," she said almost as an afterthought.

She needn't clarify. Jane knew precisely the gentleman referred to. She'd kissed him quite eagerly in the dead of the night. "It was not my intention to put on any type of show for anyone," she said quietly as they turned down the corridor and then came to a stop beside the first door—her chambers. Or now, her former chambers. "I—"

"Merely spoke the truth." A wide smile wreathed Lady Chloe's heart-shaped face. "My brother is unaccustomed to women who speak their opinions."

The domineering marquess, who'd first greeted her and summarily dismissed her, slipped into her mind. "I gathered as much," she muttered.

Lady Chloe tossed her head back on a loud, and a not at all lady-like, laugh that would have made Mrs. Belden cringe with horror. "Oh, you are delightful, Mrs. Munroe." She leaned around Jane and pressed the door handle. "May I speak to you for a moment?"

"I—" The young woman sailed past her. *Of course, you may.* Jane closed the door behind her and froze.

A determined gleam lit the young woman's soft blue eyes. "Mrs. Munroe—"

"Jane," she offered. Lady Chloe Edgerton was not a young lady who'd not yet made her Come Out. She was a woman of one and twenty years. Jane had not been hired as a governess, but rather a companion. Or rather, she had been, before the whole business of being sacked by first the marquess and then his sister.

"You must call me, Chloe." Gabriel's sister settled her arms akimbo. "And you're not leaving," she said with a firm resolve that increased the beat of Jane's heart.

Life should have taught her the perils of foolishly dreaming and yet that blasted corner of her heart still filled with optimism and innocence clung to the fragile hope. "I'm not."

"Oh, no," Chloe gave a firm shake of her head. She caught her lower lip between her teeth. "Well, at first, I'll admit, when I learned you were coming from Mrs. Belden's, I was glad to have you gone." She claimed Jane's hands in her own and gave a squeeze. "Now, I would have you stay."

What would the lady say if she were to discover the nasty headmistress had, in fact, turned her out? Likely she'd name her a forever friend. Since that numbing day in Mrs. Belden's office, when she'd been sacked from her post and then subsequently stole off and lied her way into Gabriel's home, terror gripped her. "Thank you," she said softly.

The young woman applied a gentle pressure to her hands once more and then released her. "He means well. Gabriel," she clarified and stepped away. She wandered a distracted path around the opulent ivory guest chambers and paused beside the small, mahogany table stacked with Jane's books. Her lips pulled in a grimace. "He'd have me wed."

And when that was the goal and expectation for any and every lady in Society, this woman would not. "You would remain unwed, then?" Jane asked, studying the young lady's distracted movements as she ran her fingertips over the aged and cracked leather volumes.

Jaw firmed with determination, Lady Chloe gave a brusque nod. "I will. Despite my brother's expectations."

Despite everyone's expectations. Having lived a life where her mother was nothing more than a plaything to a powerful duke, Jane had vowed to never surrender her happiness or independence to a man. Curiosity tugged at her. What accounted for this young lady's like sentiments? Something quelled the question on her lips. A knowledge that it wasn't her right to know; an understanding that it was a truth Lady Chloe would impart if or when she felt Jane was deserving to know.

"You are quiet," Chloe observed.

She smiled wryly. "I suspect that is why your brother believed I would not suit."

Chloe's eyebrows shot up. "He didn't?"

Jane bit the inside of her cheek at revealing that fact about her employer.

A small laugh bubbled past Chloe's lips. "Oh, come. I assure you, you've freedom to speak candidly with me." She dropped her voice to a conspiratorial whisper. "Particularly about my domineering brother."

Odd the word choice ascribed by his sister was how Jane, too, would have described him. And yet…"You are fortunate that he at the very least cares." Unlike her, who was the shameful, dirty secret of a lofty duke.

"I don't doubt he loves me," Chloe whispered, the words spoken more to herself. She fanned the pages of the top volume. "However, in his love for me, in his desire to see me protected, he would take upon himself finding a gentleman who'd suit." With a snort she slammed closed the book. "Only, he doesn't realize I don't want any gentleman." She beamed. "Why, I'm quite content to become the eccentric spinster who doesn't give a jot for Society's opinion."

With that handful of words that revealed so very much of the young woman she'd serve as companion to, Jane came to the swift realization—she liked Lady Chloe Edgerton a good deal. A smile pulled at her lips. "I can only imagine how Mrs. Belden would have responded to such an opinion."

Chloe wagged her eyebrows. "Poorly."

A burst of laughter escaped her and she stifled it with her fingers. "Never tell me you told her your hopes for your marital state." Or lack thereof.

Chloe gave a vigorous nod, a devilish sparkle in her eyes. "I told her quite often."

At last Gabriel's dismissal made sense. Any one of Mrs. Belden's instructors would have come here staid, proper, and determined to help Lady Chloe coordinate an advantageous match.

Some of Chloe's amusement lifted, replaced instead with a contemplativeness. "My brothers and friend, Imogen, are quite insistent that I'll one day wed and," she gave a wry smile, "fall in love." The droll edge to her tone indicated Lady Chloe Edgerton was not one of those romantic sorts, with hopes of a powerful match and the dream of love all rolled perfectly together.

Clearing her throat nervously, Jane then filled the quiet. "Are you familiar with her works?" she asked, nodding to the pile as Chloe proceeded to leaf through the books. All the books in question were the products of Mrs. Wollstonecraft, the unwed philosopher and mother with two illegitimate children. With her scandalous thoughts, she'd hardly be a favored figure in polite and, most times, impolite Society.

The young lady shook her head.

Well, if he'd not sacked her already, Gabriel would likely do so for this. And yet, she had an obligation to Chloe that moved even beyond the security Jane craved that would come at the end of these two months—if she could behave.

Alas, she'd never properly behaved.

She gestured to the stack of books. "Mrs. Wollstonecraft was an English writer." Interest sparked in Chloe's pretty blue eyes, and she then picked up the book she'd been toying with earlier and skimmed the cover. Her lips moved silently as she read the title.

"Mrs. Belden, your brother, Gabe—" Chloe whipped her head up and Jane's cheeks heated at her inadvertent error. "The marquess," she substituted lamely. "They will urge you to make a match, all the while trusting they know who will *make* you a good match." Gabriel's face flashed behind her eyes. "Perhaps he will be powerful," she added. Her lips still burned with the imprint of his kiss. "He'll have wealth and status, and Society thinks they know what you want, because Society believes you can't yourself know what you want." As Jane spoke, Chloe stilled, frozen, with her silence giving no indication as to whether she approved, disapproved, or worse, was indifferent, to Jane's words. Regardless, Jane pressed forward. "Mrs. Wollstonecraft didn't believe women were inferior. She believed we are uneducated and through that forced ignorance, we are treated as less than logical, rational people."

The hum of silence met her words. Treasonous ones, Mrs. Belden had claimed. Then a slow smile turned Chloe's lips upwards. "Mrs. Munroe—"

"Jane."

"Mrs. Munroe, I quite like you." She eyed the book in her hands a long moment and then set it down. "Are you certain you were one of Mrs. Belden's instructors?"

Not for the first time since she'd slipped into Gabriel's household did she feel the pinpricks of guilt sticking at her conscience. "I was." She curled her fingers tightly into her palm. It wasn't wholly a lie. Chloe had spoken in the past tense and Jane had once held one of those distinguished posts.

"You are not at all like any of the instructors I'd known." A small sigh slid past the young woman's lips. "What a very different time I

68

would have had at Mrs. Belden's had you been my instructor." She wrinkled her nose. "Trust Mrs. Belden to do something as contradictory as hiring smiling, kindhearted and clever instructors such as you only after I'd left."

"You may rest assured that Mrs. Belden still is in possession of her stern set, drumming lessons of propriety and properness into each and every lady," she said dryly and then silently cursed at her quick tongue.

Except—Chloe burst out laughing. Her narrow shoulders shook with the force of her mirth and she dashed back tears from her cheeks. "Well, I am very glad she sent you to us." With that she all but sprinted to the door, but then paused with her fingers on the handle. "Mrs. Munroe—Jane," she self-corrected. "I believe we are going to get on very well." One more smile, a jaunty wave, and a rapid snap of her skirts later, Chloe hurried from the room.

Jane stared at the closed door. With the trusting, kindhearted young woman's faith in her and her worth, the weight of guilt magnified, pressing down on her like a boulder being applied to her chest. Before, she'd lied to strangers who believed her inferior. Gabriel, the austere nobleman, and his sister, the spoiled, indolent lady, had represented a path to freedom. Now, they were more. Gabriel was a brother who loved and loyally protected his sister. Chloe was a woman with dreams and hopes that existed beyond the strictures polite Society would impose.

She closed her eyes. Could she remain here under the guise of being sent by the harridan, Mrs. Belden, and violate Gabriel's trust, while all the while strengthening a friendship with his sister?

Then, what choice did she have?

NINE

"We must visit the modiste. We are in need of gowns."

Seated behind his desk the following morning after his sister had gone and upended his carefully ordered world with her insistence on keeping Jane on as companion, Gabriel glanced up from the open ledgers upon his desk.

"Gowns," Chloe repeated as though he one, didn't know what a dress was, or two, as if there was something wrong with his hearing, which there certainly wasn't. He was just two and thirty years, hardly one of those doddering old lords.

Either way, "*You* want to go shopping?" What would come next? She'd be hoping for suitors and eagerly planning her wedding? He snorted. Horses would likely fly above Tower Bridge before that day came.

"Not for me." She clapped her hands together once in what he expected was a clue indicating he was to stand. He remained seated. His sister frowned. "For Jane." Jane? As in Mrs. Munroe? The strait-laced, bespectacled woman whose kiss still haunted his waking and sleeping thoughts? "Now, do hurry." With another clap of her hands, Chloe spun on her heel and started from the room.

He blinked, slowly processing that pert announcement. "Chloe?" he barked.

At once, she poked her head back inside his office. "Yes, Gabriel?"

How many years had he taken his brother, Alex, as the indolent, shiftless rogue? Gabriel swiped a hand over his face. Now, he appreciated that with his care of Chloe over the years, he'd spared Gabriel

70

from a good deal of her scheming. He folded his hands before him and rested the interlocked digits upon the desk. "Just what does Jane," his sister narrowed her eyes. A flush heated his neck. "What does Mrs. Munroe require new gowns for?"

With a beleaguered sigh better suited a bothered mama, she reentered the room. "Have you seen Jane?"

The bespectacled, plain young woman with her dull skirts slipped into his mind but as she'd been with her glasses knocked to the floor and the captivating blues of her eyes, her full lips swollen from his kiss. Unable to force out any words, he managed a nod.

"Well, she is perfectly lovely."

Lovely. Jane's was an understated beauty made all the more intriguing when challenges flew from her lips. He gritted his teeth at the wandering direction his thoughts were taking him down. "Chloe?" he bit out, his tone heavy with impatience.

"Yes, right." Chloe flicked a hand about. "She is perfectly lovely, however, she cannot attend Societal functions in her dragon skirts."

"And you'd have me fit her for a wardro—ouch," he winced as she pinched him.

"Do not be a pinchpenny." She furrowed her brow. "Unless your estates are not prospering in which case, then, we really should all consider adjusting our—"

"My estates are just fine," he snapped.

A triumphant gleam lit Chloe's eyes and he bit back a curse at the second cleverly laid snare he'd stepped into. "Perfect. I shall collect my cloak, then." She skipped to the door and disappeared out the entrance.

He dug his fingertips into his temples. "Chloe," he called. Not for the first time wishing his sister, Philippa, had the patience to wait until the Season was concluded before seeing to all the *enceinte* business.

"Yes?" She stuck her head inside the room once again, an impish grin on her face.

Gabriel folded his arms at his chest. "I have matters of business to attend. Important matters." Ones that did not include squiring her and Mrs. Munroe to modistes and milliners. When she opened her mouth, he continued, speaking over her. "And furthermore, you have Mrs. Munroe to accompany you about town."

She dropped her eyebrows and, by the darkening of her eyes, he knew he'd made a faulty misstep.

"Oh, so you've foisted all of your responsibilities off on Mrs. Munroe, have you?"

Oh, bloody hell.

He tugged at his cravat, which only drew his sister's attention to that guilty action. Gabriel immediately stopped and laid his hand back to the desktop. "I am not foisting you off on another." Not *entirely*.

She brightened. "You aren't?"

Well, perhaps he was. "Of course not."

A pleased smile turned her lips. "Splendid." She gave another annoying clap of her hands. "Now, do hurry." With that, she dismissed him and rushed from the room.

Oh bloody, *bloody* hell. On a groan, he dropped his head into his hands. Knowing his sister as he did, Chloe had every intention of making him miserable for saddling her with a companion. Yet again, he'd stepped neatly into one of her traps. Lord Wellington himself would have admired Chloe's masterful plotting.

Abandoning his plans for the morning, he came to his feet. Gabriel took his leave of his office. He walked at a quick, clipped pace through the corridors to the foyer. As he stepped into the marble foyer, he came to a sudden, jarring stop.

Jane stood at the center with her back arched and her neck tipped back at such an impossible angle it was a wonder she remained upright. Those tempting, red lips, that had made him forget the vows he'd taken to never be the dissolute lord to dally with his staff, were parted as though in wonder. She stared transfixed up at the towering ceiling above. The air left him on a slow exhale and it was a physical hungering to know what should so move this usually stoic, often frowning woman to such awe. It was a physical effort to tear his gaze from her moist lips.

He followed her stare upward to the mural painted on the high ceiling and frowned. He'd long detested the heavenly scenes captured by his ironical father, the devil who'd delighted in those tableaus of cherubs and angels. They adorned nearly every blasted room. When he had been a boy of nine years and his father had forced him to sit at his knee while he imparted all the dealings that would one day be Gabriel's, he'd allowed his mind to wander. In those dreams, he'd crafted his revenge. On the darkest days, after his brother and sisters had been battered by the birch rod, Gabriel had gleefully plotted all the ways he might kill the bastard. On other days, he'd scheme up ways in which to destroy the marquess' legacy—having those murals painted over had been one promise he'd made to himself. And yet he'd never gotten around to it.

Seeing the wide-eyed awe stamped upon the heart-shaped planes of her face, he was glad he did not. For then he'd never have witnessed Jane, riveted in silent wonder. What manner of madness possessed him? He kicked dirt upon his fanciful musings. "Jane," he greeted with an icy calm.

She shrieked. Her slippered feet slid out from under her and she flailed her arms.

Gabriel closed the distance between them in three long strides and slid his arms under her slender frame and caught her. He braced for a stiff, polite "thank you".

She blinked up at him. "Hullo," she said her voice a breathless whisper that carried up to his ears. In the four days he'd known Jane Munroe, he should have learned she never did what was predicted.

With a forced nonchalance he inclined his head. "Jane." But then, he made the mistake of looking down and his gaze snagged upon her bow-shaped lips once more. And the sight held him as transfixed as the sight of her moments ago, head tilted back in awe. Gabriel hurriedly set her upright on her feet. He cast a desperate glance about for Chloe.

"I was admiring your paintings," Jane continued. Did she know the effect she had on his senses? Where in blazes was his sister? He didn't need to be alone with Jane Munroe. The unpredictable minx was dangerous to his senses, threatening calm, order, and logic. The folly of agreeing to this outing reared its head with a renewed vigor. "It is lovely."

You'll know the goddamn difference between a painting and a mural... "Mural." The black memory long buried slipped in as they occasionally did at the most random moments.

Jane looked to him perplexed. Some of the light dimmed in her eyes. He balled his hands. She thought he corrected her. Gabriel gestured to the ceiling. "My father," he squared his jaw, those two words like vitriol upon his tongue. "Took great pleasure in instructing me as to the difference."

She eyed him a moment. He wagered the lady's curiosity warred with pride. In the end, her need to know won out. "What is the difference?"

No different than that moth lured by flame, he shifted closer, so close she was forced to tip her head back to meet his stare. Honey and lavender filled his senses until he was nearly drunk on the fragrance of summer and innocence. Ah, God help him. What hold did she have over him? Why, he didn't even like her. She was mouthy and insolent and defied his orders. And...Gabriel pointed up at the emerald green pastures captured by the artist. "You see, the architectural elements are harmoniously incorporated into the work." Jane craned her neck once more and followed his point, skyward. By the parting of her lips and the softening of her eyes, it was as though she were seeing the angelic tableau painted upon the ceiling for the first time.

In the honesty of her reaction, there was an innocence, a softness, he'd not imagined her capable of. A golden strand pulled free of her tight chignon and involuntarily he reached to brush it back, when her words froze him.

"It reminds me of my childhood." It also harkened him back to the days of his own youth.

He let his hand fall to his side. There was a wistful, far-off quality to her words that gave him pause. A hint of sadness, nostalgia, but also the faintest trace of happiness. What was Jane's story? "Does it?" His quiet question called her attention from the mural.

Color bloomed on her cheeks. Was it her body's awareness of him? Embarrassment to be caught not once, but now twice awestruck over the pastel oils upon the ceiling? Unable to resist the lure, he captured the single blonde strand between his thumb and forefinger. He intended to tuck it back behind her ear in an entirely bold move he'd no right to. Not as a gentleman. Not as her employer. He intended to release the lock immediately. But then he registered the smooth feel of spun silk and was loath to release the satiny soft strand. She wet her lips and he followed that subtle movement, hungering for her kiss. "Wh-what do you see?"

His throat worked. The sun's rays collected. Beauty. Perfection—

"When you see the painting. Th-the mural." That breathlessly stammered whisper yanked him from the moment and he released her with alacrity. He blankly followed her stare.

Hell. Torture. Agony. "I also see my childhood."

"There you are."

They both started. Gabriel stepped away as his sister strode forward. "Forgive my delay, I was distracted by…" At the stilted silence, Chloe looked back and forth between them.

Gabriel cleared his throat. "We should be going." Several servants rushed forward with their cloaks. As Gabriel shrugged into his cloak, he studiously avoided looking at the tempting Jane Munroe. He held out his arm to his sister.

Joseph stepped forward and opened the door. Where in blazes had the old servant been a moment ago? The other man possessed an eerie ability to dissolve into the shadows and appear when needed. Heat burned his neck in thinking of the other man observing Gabriel fawning over his sister's companion's loose curl.

"Would you please slow down," his sister chided and pinched his arm. "I'd say you are trying to leave Jane behind with this ridiculous pace you've set."

He slowed his steps and kept his gaze trained forward on the waiting carriage. A servant pulled open the carriage door and held a hand out. The liveried footman handed Chloe into the carriage. Jane came to a stop. She smiled at the young servant and then the smile died as she looked to Gabriel.

And once more, the defensive walls put up between them were firmly in place. He was her employer. She was his sister's companion.

The servant helped her inside and Gabriel followed in, claiming the bench alongside Chloe.

Jane sat tucked in the corner, her hands folded primly on her lap. Had he merely imagined the smiling, innocent for a moment woman who'd spoken too briefly of her childhood, a childhood he'd wager both his arms had been a good deal more pleasant than his own? The carriage rocked forward, and he continued to study her, suddenly wanting to know about her formative years.

Which was, of course, neither here nor there. It mattered not to him. Gabriel yanked back the red velvet curtain—the shade of blood and evil—and directed his attention at the passing London streets.

For a moment, she'd believed Gabriel intended to kiss her.

And for an even longer moment, she'd wanted him to. Jane sat in the corner of the carriage, focusing on the rattle of the carriage wheels as they rumbled through the busy London streets. All the while, Chloe prattled on and on, a cheerful smile on her face, unknowing that in her absence, Gabriel had revealed with his solemn looks and serious eyes a glimpse of more than a harsh, unfeeling nobleman. No, having known pain and heartache, Jane easily glimpsed those sad sentiments within him.

And she hated it. For with each passing moment spent with Gabriel, he ceased to be a stranger, which was dangerous to her plans for security and her hope of a school for women such as her. Her intentions were good, honorable. Then, hadn't Brutus said the same? Were her intentions *truly* honorable? Were they, when there was Chloe lauding her as a good, worthy companion, and Gabriel, a brother who fiercely loved his sister enough to entrust the final decision of a companion?

Brother and sister said something, and their laughter filled the carriage, driving deeper the knife of guilt until she wanted to clamp her hands over her ears and blot out the sound. But she could not. This was to be her punishment; to bear witness to their sibling bond—a closeness Jane would have traded her left, lonely, index finger for, growing up the bastard child of the Duke of Ravenscourt. Emotion clogged her throat as from the crystal pane she viewed brother and sister. They chatted amicably. Occasionally, Chloe would point her eyes skyward and Gabriel's chest would rise and fall with laughter. Such a loved sibling would never be cast out, scuttled from household to household, a lost soul. For Gabriel's high-handed words at breakfast yesterday morn, the man that he was, would not, even if his sister believed it, ever dare select the man Chloe would wed.

Jane knocked her head against the windowpane as with each moment this family threw her into tumult over the deception she practiced.

"Mrs. Munroe?"

Gabriel's concerned tone cut into her tortured musings, twisting that blade once more. The emerald greens of his eyes moved a path over her face.

"We're here!" Chloe called out as the carriage rocked to a blessed halt.

The door opened and Chloe hurried past her brother and, with the help of the driver, stepped down. Gabriel lingered a moment and she swallowed, not wanting any probing questions because she feared in her weakness this moment she'd confess all—and then be promptly dismissed. He exited the carriage and reached back inside.

Dropping her gaze to his long, outstretched fingers, she recalled the manner in which he'd caressed one of her strands of hair. Cheeks afire, Jane hurriedly took his hand and let him hand her down.

"I must confess, Jane," he confided so quietly those words were nearly lost to London's street sounds. "I have a desire," her breath caught, "to know what has you go silent one moment and prickly and feisty the next."

For the span of a heartbeat, she thought to pretend she did not hear that question. But then she detected the challenge in his eyes. "Bold employers," she tossed back and started forward to where Chloe stood in wait at the shop front. The young lady smiled and then sailed through the entrance.

Jane hurried after her, desperate for much needed distance from the marquess.

He called out. "And are you accustomed to bold employers?" His words brought her to a slow halt. There was a lethal edge to his question, as though he'd do battle should she utter an affirmative.

No one had cared about her or for her in so very long. Even to her mother, Jane had merely come second to the Duke of Ravenscourt's scandalous use of her. "N-no," she stammered and made to enter the shop, but Gabriel blocked her path.

"You're lying."

He couldn't know that. Not truly. She shook her head once more. "I'm—" Her breath caught as he dipped his head lower. Jane's heart thumped erratically and she should be horrified by the curious stares being shot their way by passersby, but instead only knew the intoxicating scent of sandalwood threatening to drown her senses.

"Do you know how I know you're lying, Jane?" He didn't allow her a reply. "Because a woman of your spirit would not accept the charge of liar being ascribed to you, unless there was, in fact, merit to my claims."

"I worked at Mrs. Belden's Finishing School. There was hardly a worry where gentlemen were concerned." She forced a droll humor to her tone, praying it would distract him from the intimate understanding he'd show of both her temperament and circumstances. "I assure you, Mrs. Belden would not countenance a gentleman within her proper walls." She flicked her stare over his person. "Even if he was a marquess." A duke, however, would be granted certain freedoms. Jane slipped past him and entered the shop. Such as taking on that powerful nobleman's by-blow.

Gabriel fell into step beside her. "And were you long at Mrs. Belden's?"

"Yes." A year was a long time for some.

"What of before that?"

She gritted her teeth, as all the tender awe of his early concern was replaced with annoyance. Questions were dangerous. Particularly when all the answers brought them back to the truth of her lies. "Before that I was employed as a governess."

"A governess?" he asked with some surprise.

"Yes, a governess." To a spoiled, nasty, and not at all pleasant sixteen-year-old lady who'd quite enjoyed the day Jane had been sacked without a reference.

"Jane?"

They looked to the long table at the back of the shop littered with bolts of fabric. Chloe stood beside a plump, graying woman of indiscriminate years. Grateful for the young lady's timely intervention, Jane all but sprinted in that direction. Her skin burned with the feel of Gabriel's gaze on her person.

"Ah, there you are, Jane," Chloe said. She motioned to her. "Madame Clairemont, this is my companion."

"A pleasure." The woman peered down her very un-French nose at Jane, indicating her opinion on the acquaintance.

Jane stole a backward glance at Gabriel. He stood off to the side, leaning against the wall. With his arms folded against his broad chest and his hooded gaze upon her, he was elegant in his repose. She quickly snapped her gaze forward.

"...An entire new wardrobe...something vibrant...pink...Jane?"

She blinked, suddenly aware by the questioning stares trained on her that something was required of her. Pink. Pink. "Pink is a splendid selection, my lady." Had there ever been a time in Jane's life where she'd spent her days on frivolous pursuits, permitted luxuries?

Madame Clairemont hurried around the side of the table with a piece of shimmering pink fabric. Jane stiffened and looked questioningly at her, but the woman's lips moved silently as though she recorded her thoughts. Jane swung her attention back to Chloe. "What—?"

"Well, I do not need new gowns, Jane." A familiar sparkle lit her blue eyes. "You, however, are in dire need of something more than your dragon skirts."

Jane jumped and knocked into a table of fabric. She hurried to right the items. "Oh, no." She held her palms up and glanced about for help. "I'm merely a companion." Who wished to blend as much as possible with the other companions and hired help. Long ago she'd learned the perils in being noticed. "There is no need for a gown."

A determined glint replaced Chloe's earlier enjoyment. "There is every need for a gown." She shot a look over Jane's shoulder. "Isn't that true, Gabriel?"

Jane's heart thumped wildly and she turned and cast a hopeful look at him. He stood several feet away. How did a man of his impressive height and strength move with such a stealthy grace?

"I daresay it would be impolite of me to agree," he drawled.

A panicked giggle worked its way up her throat. Where the other gentlemen whose employ she'd found herself in had showered her with words of praise and other nauseating compliments, Gabriel was hopelessly honest. She preferred that honesty, and yet it also proved dangerous for its appeal.

He flicked his gaze over her; this was a coolly impersonal search of her person. "It is decided."

With little help from the marquess, Jane whipped around. Nothing was decided. "I am extremely grateful." What was one more lie atop the mountains of mistruths she'd constructed? "I do not," she held up her hands warding off the other woman's efforts. "Require any gowns."

Chloe ignored her and continued with the modiste. "In two nights, we will be attending Rossini's premiere and Mrs. Munroe must have a gown prepared."

The woman's slight frown bespoke her displeasure. "Eez impossible to have a gown readied. I am a veery busy woman with many orders for—"

"My brother," Chloe motioned to Gabriel, "will pay you quite handsomely for the one." She smiled. "Well, all of them." She squared her jaw, all hint of meek, polite miss gone. "But for this evening we require the one."

"Oh, no." Jane gave her head an emphatic shake. "I will wear my Sunday dress. I do not need—"

"Don't be silly," Chloe scolded. "Tell her not to be silly, Gabriel."

Jane looked imploringly to a stoic Gabriel. He gave a slight shrug of his broad shoulders. There was little help coming there. She returned her entreaty to Chloe. "I cannot." Not when she'd already lied her way into the man's household. She'd not add lavish gowns to her crimes. She looked pleadingly to Gabriel, but he remained stoic and unmoving as he'd been since their first meeting several days earlier.

Alas, not one of the present trio appeared concerned with what Jane wanted.

At the mention of a hefty purse, the sneering modiste turned smiling. "Of course, I can have one prepared." The woman with a suddenly very English-sounding accent hurried over and took Jane by the shoulders. "*Oui, mademoiselle.* You are in need of gowns. Let Madame Clairemont help you. With but a little help, you will be very nearly pretty."

Chloe shot her an apologetic look and despite the fast-spreading panic, an unexpected laugh bubbled up her throat.

Having clearly sensed capitulation, Chloe clapped her hands and then took Jane by the hand. "Come along." She waved to Gabriel. "Off you go, then. We must keep Jane a surprise for y—" she quickly cut the words short, a blush on her cheeks. "Yes, very well. Off you go."

Jane looked to Gabriel once more, desperately wishing the coolly aloof gentleman who'd turned her out after a brief meeting would point out that there was no need for such a purchase—not on behalf of his sister's companion.

He sketched a quick bow and, with a heavy dose of relief stamped on the angular planes of his face, he hurried from the shop.

Coward.

Though—she eyed the front door he disappeared out of enviously, tempted to race after him.

"What of this color, Jane?" Chloe held up a soft pink fabric.

Alas, Gabriel's sister had altogether different plans for her. With a sigh, she allowed the two women to drag her forward to be fitted for something more than dragon skirts.

And the unexpected thrill that went through her was not excitement.

Jane sighed. Then, she'd proven herself a liar just by joining Gabriel's family. She was the very tiniest bit excited.

TEN

Lady Chloe Edgerton marched with a military precision Lord Wellington himself would have admired. She neatly steered Jane through the crowded streets, while keeping her gaze fixed determinedly ahead of them.

Gabriel followed his sister's stare to the black and gold sign: Harding Howell and Co. An involuntary groan escaped him. He and Jane spoke in unison.

"Not another blasted shop."

"Surely, we've completed our shopping for the day."

Granted, his sister's companion's words were a good deal more appropriate than his. Jane shot him a sideways, commiserative glance, an apology there. He inclined his head. It was hardly Mrs. Jane Munroe's fault that his sister had set her mind on the day's activities.

"We must bring Jane to Harding's."

"No," Jane said firmly with a shake of her head. "No, you do not. Please," there was an entreaty he'd not imagined Jane Munroe capable of. "You've been overly generous. There is nothing else I require."

His sister slowed her determined steps and steered Jane to a halt. She jabbed a finger in the air. "Fans."

"Fans," Jane and Gabriel parroted.

And all of a sudden, Chloe, who'd detested any and every trip to the modiste and milliners, had discovered a love of fashion. She nodded her head vigorously. "Yes. A fan. You require a—" She glared at Jane when she opened her mouth to speak. "And do not say you are just a companion. Is that clear?" With that, she took Jane by the hand and yanked her inside the shop.

Jane cast a desperate glance over her shoulder. Despite the havoc wrought by the infernal closeness to his sister's tart-mouthed companion, a grin turned his lips. She narrowed her eyes, as though she'd followed the exact direction of his thoughts. He knew her but a handful of days and yet knew her enough to know precisely how to needle the young woman. Gabriel winked.

Her eyes flew wide in her face. Whatever furious response she likely planned with blistering words were effectively quelled by his determined sister. Chloe motioned to the back of the expansive shop. "At the very least, you'll require one fan." With that, she marched down the rows draped in fabrics, passed by other shoppers, onward, to the rear of the establishment.

Jane shot a long glance over her shoulder at the door, as though contemplating escape. Gabriel wandered close, closer than was proper or appropriate and attracted assessing stares from the other patrons. "A woman who'd boldly challenge me with an empty plate in my own breakfast room wouldn't be so cowardly as to run from a fan."

She shoved her spectacles higher on her nose. "There is sizeable conceit to a charge from a gentleman who ran from the modiste as though his heels were on fire."

A bark of laughter escaped him. The boisterous sound of his mirth earning all the more attention.

Jane's cheeks pinkened to a soft pale hue. "Must you do that?" she said from the corner of her mouth. "You are earning whispers." Without awaiting his reply, she made her way down the aisle. She moved past the furs and the muslins without sparing a glance for any of the expensive fabrics.

He'd long ago ceased to give a fig for what members of *polite* Society thought. "I don't give a jot about whispers or gossip." It was hard to respect or trust a lot who'd revered the previous Marquess of Waverly.

She gave him a reproachful look. "Some of us do not have the luxury of being permitted the opportunity to thumb our noses at Society."

Her words gave him pause, as he was momentarily humbled by the proof of his own conceit. Of course a young woman whose station and safety in life was inextricably intertwined with her moral appearance would indeed worry. With two long strides, Gabriel moved ahead of her. He planted himself before her, effectively ending her retreat. "Forgive me."

Her eyes formed round circles. "You apologized," she blurted. Was her opinion of noblemen truly so low? Or was it men in general who'd earned the lady's wariness? He knew the ugliness of man. That she also knew some manner of ugliness dug at him.

"Despite my pomposity, I am not a total boor in terms of manners."

"I didn't say you—"

He dipped his head close. "I was teasing, Jane."

"Oh." A golden curl popped loose of her hideous chignon. She brushed the strand back, but the tress refused to comply. Gabriel took in that strand he'd caressed a short while ago. He peered past her spectacles and that painfully tight coiffure. By God...if one looked past the dragon skirts and severe hairstyle, Jane Munroe really was—by God, she was quite captivating.

"What is it?" she asked, still warring with that loose strand, a strand he gladly wished to see her lose. Those curls should not be smoothed straight but rather worn in their natural way, tight spirals that hung loose about her shoulders.

Reluctantly he released his hold on her silken blonde tress. "I don't know another woman who would not revel in the purchase of fabrics and fans and fripperies."

"You do your sister a disservice with your assertion."

Goodness, she was a loyal thing, or she was adept at steering even the hint of compliments away from herself. Another protective measure? "You are indeed, correct. But for my sister, I do not know another, then. Aside from you." That truth, the evidence of her character, a person who, presented with limitless garments and fripperies, should protest and fight at every turn, spoke volumes of who she was.

Gabriel expected another curt response. Instead, she picked up a strip of satin fabric and rubbed it between her fingers. He studied that subtle movement, hating himself for envying a slip of fabric. "I don't desire fabrics and fripperies as you call them because there is little worth in them."

He eyed the fine French fabrics that would put broke a lesser lord attiring his sister's companion.

"I do not refer to monetary value," Jane explained, accurately interpreting his musings. She let the satin fall and it landed in a soft, noiseless bounce atop the pile. "I am sure these fabrics together cost more than my earnings at Mrs. Belden's." Those words from any other young woman would have been intended to elicit sympathy. From Jane, however, they came out matter-of-fact. "A lady's gowns and garments do not define her, my lord." Unrestrained emotion filled her eyes and Jane pressed a hand to her chest. "It is who she truly is—her actions, her thoughts, her beliefs. That is what truly defines a woman."

How many women aspired to the material and desired status? By the passion in Jane's eyes and the fervor of her tone, she longed to be seen for more. Her quick-wit, coupled with her calm pragmatisms, was enough to rob a man of logic. Then he made the mistake of dropping his gaze lower, to her pert nose, ever lower to those tantalizing lips, and, God forgive him for having accused his brother of being a rogue, but Gabriel moved his stare downward to the modest bodice of her dress. There was nothing the least captivating or alluring about the drab brown dragon skirts as Chloe had referred to them. Yet, staring at Jane with the thrum of other patrons milling about the shop and a humming in his ears, he appreciated the extent of his own depravity. He momentarily closed his eyes. And he hated himself for it.

"My lord?" Jane whispered. It was a spark in her eyes and the parting of her moist lips.

Gabriel swallowed hard. She too felt this pull between them. "Yes."

"Will you step aside? Lady Chloe is motioning to me."

He tripped over his feet in his haste to get away. A humiliated heat climbed his neck and as Jane rushed past him, Gabriel tugged at his cravat. There was something quite humbling in being so dismissed. Then, he'd never possessed the heavy dose of charm of his younger brother or any of those other rogues so favored by the ladies.

Yet, standing there amidst the aisles of fabric, with his gaze trained on Jane's swiftly retreating frame, she paused to cast a final glance at him.

He grinned and favored her with one more wink—

She crashed into a table of hats. Several toppled over and fell silently to the floor. Once again, the other ladies present peered condescendingly at the young lady. "Forgive me," Jane apologized and hastily fell to her knee to rescue the handful of creations at her feet. Her apologies were met with further sneers. His sister's companion made quick work of picking up each bonnet, one at a time. The faintest, almost imperceptible tremble to her fingers hinted at her quiet shame.

A powerful, consuming rage manifested in the form of a low growl in his throat. He strode forward, detesting a world in which lords and ladies saw her as a stranger and for that, an interloper in their existence.

Chloe raced forward. She skidded to a halt beside Jane and dropped to a knee beside her. "You needn't worry, Jane," she said on a whisper loud enough for all nearby busybodies to hear. "They are just bonnets. No more or less important than any of the other pieces here." She directed those words at a plump matron who had the good grace to blush and then hurry on her way.

Jane gave a weak smile. "Thank you."

Gabriel stopped beside them. He held a hand out first for his sister and then Jane. She hesitated a moment and then placed her gloved fingertips in his. A shock of awareness penetrated the thin kidskin of the fabric, searing his palm. She smiled and, with her murmur of thanks, conveyed how wholly unaffected she was by him.

Good. Her response was the safer one. Any other passionate kisses and desirous looks would weaken him in ways he'd never allow. He'd never allow himself to be vulnerable.

As Jane followed Chloe to the display of fans, shame consumed her. She'd spoken to Gabriel of actions and thoughts and a person's worth, and in actuality, there was no more dishonorable person than she. For *Mrs.* Jane Munroe, none other than *Miss* Jane Munroe, bastard daughter of the Duke of Ravenscourt, was a liar. She was here accepting his sister's kindness and gowns and garments that she had no right to.

"Jane?"

She looked up.

Chloe snapped open a pink satin fan with a wooden frame. She handed it over.

Jane tossed her palms up in protest. "My lady—"

"Chloe."

"Please, I cannot—"

Gabriel's sister thrust the frame into her hands. "Here."

Jane gave the piece an awkward wave and then made to hand it back. She wanted nothing more in terms of this family's generosity. "It is lovely."

A beaming smile lit Chloe's face. "It is yours then." She waved over the shopkeeper. "We shall take the pink fan."

The older woman took the delicate piece, far lovelier than anything Jane had ever possessed, and rushed to wrap it.

Chloe slipped her arm into Jane's. "May I speak candidly, Jane?" She didn't allow her a response. "I've known you but two days and yet there are things I know about you." Jane bit the inside of her cheek hard. For everything Chloe believed she knew about her, she comprehended a good deal less. She guided Jane down the next aisle and then cast a glance about. Jane followed her stare to Gabriel, who strolled at a safe, deliberate distance. "Do you know what I believe?"

Jane's mouth went dry under the sudden fear that her secret had been discovered and she'd now be publically decried by this woman who'd been only kind before now. She managed to shake her head. "What is that, my lady?"

"Chloe." She released Jane's arm and captured both of her hands. "You do not want to be noticed."

At the unerring accuracy of that admission, Jane stilled as panic threatened to overtake her. Were her efforts at concealment very obvious to everyone?

"I recognize that in you, as someone who also doesn't want to be noticed." A somber glint lit Chloe's expressive eyes. "Do you know what else I've realized?"

Jane shook her head once more.

"The best way to escape notice is to blend." With a quick flick of her hand she motioned to Jane's skirts and spectacles. "And you, with your dragon skirts and spectacles do not blend."

Understanding dawned. The young woman's almost desperate efforts to appropriately attire her. Chloe saw in Jane part of herself—a part she'd protect. Emotion swelled in her throat as the guilt grew. "Thank you," she whispered. *Thank you, when I do not deserve your kindness. Thank you, when I'd steal my safety from your family.*

As they made their way down the row and toward the front of the shop, Jane resolved to repay Gabriel and his sister. When she acquired those precious funds from the duke, she would pay for every last expense.

"Come along, Jane. Now, to the milliner."

She suppressed a groan. With Chloe's lavish spending, Jane doubted there would be funds enough left for her school come the end of this two months with the Edgerton family. Such a thing would not have mattered only a handful of days ago. But now she knew them as people. Guilt spiraled through her and settled like a stone in her belly. She would repay them what she could.

Then, she'd learned long ago that trust, devotion, and loyalty meant a good deal more than a fat purse. Her father had showed her that.

As Jane entered the milliner to meet the smiling Chloe, the stone became the size of a boulder.

ELEVEN

That evening, instead of seeing to his brotherly responsibilities and obligations, Gabriel gave his sister a reprieve. Nay, he'd given himself a reprieve and proven himself to be the coward he always was. However, this time it was not the towering, hulking frame of his now thankfully dead father he avoided, but a thin slip of a bespectacled woman.

Gabriel sat at his table at White's, with his back presented to the crowded club. He stared at the bottle of brandy upon the smooth, mahogany surface and, with a quiet curse, grabbed it. The sound of crystal touching crystal was lost in the din of the dandies and lords who also avoided polite *ton* gatherings in favor of the betting books and fine brandy. He took a sip of his drink. For after accompanying Jane to milliners and mantua makers, he'd rushed out of his townhouse and sought out his clubs where he now sat nursing the same half-bottle of brandy he had for the past five hours. He shifted in his seat, his lower back numb from the position he'd set up on the mahogany seat.

"Waverly, what are you doing here, now?" He stiffened at the familiar drawl but remained seated as his only friend, the Earl of Waterson, pulled the chair out and availed himself to a seat. "I believe you have a sister still to wed o—by God what happened to your face, man?"

Yes, he'd earned quite a few curious stares for Jane's handy work. "A go in the ring with Gentleman Jackson." The lie came easily.

"Ah," the earl said, disappointment laced that one word utterance, as though he'd hoped for something more interesting from his friend.

Gabriel motioned to a servant who rushed over. The liveried footman set down a snifter and Waterson took the bottle. He proceeded to pour himself a glass of brandy. "Visiting your clubs? Trips to Gentleman Jackson's? However will you see your sister wed with such inattentiveness?" His friend chuckled.

Gabriel frowned and then opened his mouth, prepared to tell Waterson just what he thought of his jesting…but then stopped. He drummed his fingertips along the table. Chloe must marry—to a good, honorable gentleman. *Hmm.* He eyed Waterson a moment with renewed interest.

His friend choked on his drink. "Do not look at me in that manner. I've already said your sister and I would not suit."

With a frustrated sigh, Gabriel sat back in his seat. "Yes, you have said as much." Six times now. Had the rejection come from any other gentleman, he'd have been deuced insulted. Alas, Waterson and he had been friends long enough that the other man was well aware of Chloe and her madcap schemes. He rolled his shoulders. "Even if you would do me a tremendous favor in wedding her."

Waterson chuckled. "Waverly, if you believe you are going to control the gentleman your sister weds or does not wed, then you're corked in the head."

A growl of frustration stuck in his chest.

"You've hired a companion." Interest underscored the other man's words.

He blinked as, with those four words, thoughts of Chloe's unwedded state were replaced with the reminder of Jane. "I have." Gabriel tightened his grip upon his glass. "What do you know of it?"

Waterson took a small sip. "Merely that she's a pinch-faced, frowning young widow your sister is being forced to drag about town."

Pinch-faced? Gabriel scowled. Is that how the cruelly condescending lords and ladies saw Jane? Then, isn't that how he himself had? But that had been before her awe-struck appreciation of the mural, and their kiss, and…"What matter is it to the *ton*?" Nor would he bother pointing out that Chloe had been the one insistent on keeping Mrs. Jane Munroe.

The earl lifted a shoulder in a slight shrug. "You know the way of it, Waverly. Polite Society makes all matters, their matter. And your sour, ugly companion has earned some attention."

At his friend's casual, throwaway words, fury snapped through him. "Shut your mouth," he bit out. "I'd hardy call her ugly." At first he'd thought her plain but never ugly.

"Oh?" Waterson inquired, arching a single brown eyebrow. There was a layer of questions to that one word utterance.

"Do not be ridiculous. The lady is in my employ."

Waterson gave a half-grin. "I didn't say anything."

Christ. He gritted his teeth at his unwitting revelation. He gave his head a shake and instead focused not on the lovely Mrs. Munroe, but rather the fact that she had somehow found herself an object of gossip. Inherently reserved and exceedingly private, Jane would detest knowing that Society discussed her. He'd have a care to keep that information from the lady.

His friend planted his elbows on the edge of the table and, with his glass in hand, leaned forward. "Is there perhaps something I should ask about the lady whom you'd hardly call ugly?"

Fortunately, Gabriel had become a master of disguise in terms of emotions. "There isn't," he spoke in the clipped, cool tones his father had drilled into him with the edge of a birch rod. His friend wisely said nothing, but instead took a sip of his drink. "The lady comes from Chloe's former finishing school."

Waterson spit out his drink, spraying the table with liquid. He yanked out a handkerchief and covered his mouth. A servant rushed over to wipe down the table. Only after the waiter had left did his friend manage to speak without laughing. "You hired one of her former instructors?"

It had been no secret that Chloe had been the bane of Mrs. Belden's Finishing School. A brother to two sisters himself, Waterson well knew the trials and tribulations of caring for those younger ladies. That had been just one of the other ties that bound them and Gabriel had spoken freely to his friend about Chloe's lamentable years there. "Ja—," he flushed, "Mrs. Munroe," he amended at his friend's pointed look. "Was never Chloe's instructor." Now he wished he was a good deal less loose-lipped.

"Regardless," Waterson gave a mock shudder. "My sisters are exasperating enough to drive me to Bedlam and still I'd never force one of those harridans upon them."

It spoke volumes of the man's regard for his sisters. It was also one of the main factors to recommend him as a husband for Chloe. If the two of them would just bloody relent, it would solve all manner of difficulties. Waterson and his obligations to the earldom. Chloe and her need for a good, honorable, decent chap. "No."

"Are you—?"

"I'm certain."

He sighed. Deuced bothersome this elder brother business. He'd always been rot at it. The dark, ugly visage of his father slipped into his mind and a chill stole over him. Even all these damned years later, just the memory of that fiend could turn him into a silent, cowering, quivering bastard. Gabriel finished his drink in a quick swallow. He welcomed the fiery trail it blazed down his throat and then reached for the bottle. With a slight shake to his fingers, he poured another snifter teeming to the rim. He took another sip. This one slower, more practiced. And then he registered his friend's concerned stare trained on him. All earlier amusement fled.

Waterson looked from Gabriel's face to the drink held in his hand. He repeated his study in that recriminating way. But for his siblings, only Waterson knew of the hell Gabriel had suffered through, and even then only the glimpses he'd shared with the man. Suddenly, the topic of Jane was immensely more appealing and far safer. "Mrs. Munroe is a proper and perfectly acceptable companion. Her physical appearance has no bearing on her ability in the role." It did have bearing on this unholy claim she'd laid to his thoughts. "Now," he set his glass down hard with a thud. "If you'll excuse me."

"Of course," Waterson said with a slight incline of his head.

Gabriel shoved to his feet, and then with a short bow, took his leave. With each step, he battled the demons of his past. Only, time had proven that once his father dug in, Gabriel remained in his grip—which was as strong now from the grave as it had been when the monster lived.

When Jane had been a small girl, she'd always admired her mother's satin and silk skirts. She would brush her fingers over the smooth, cool fabric and dream of the day she'd be draped in such vibrant gowns. With a child's innocence, she'd not given thought to where the beautiful dresses came from. She only knew they came in great big boxes with velvet ribbons and when they did, her mother's oftentimes sad smile would turn a bit happier, and she'd don those skirts and Jane would sit in wide-eyed awe at such beauty.

It wasn't until she was seven, the first time she'd met her father that she understood just where those gowns came from and the significance of those great big boxes with their velvet ribbons. So that had shattered her innocence as the once revered dresses were beautiful no more. For at that moment, Jane learned why nursemaids had shuttled her off and why the village children had whispered and stared and why she was, in fact, different than the others…and it was also why she vowed to never wear a stunning satin gown.

Until today. When at the insistence of Chloe Edgerton, she'd allowed a modiste to layer those luxuriant fabrics to her body. Each scrap had touched her skin like a lash with ugly reminders of her past and the shameful truth of her existence.

Jane removed the useless wire-rimmed spectacles from her nose. Seated on the leather button sofa in Gabriel's library, she sighed and set the delicate frames on the rose-inlaid table beside her. For as much as her mother had loved her father and the lavish, albeit secret, lifestyle he'd allowed her, all those material comforts, all those gowns and jewels had ultimately meant nothing. They'd not brought her happiness. They'd not brought her respect. No, they'd merely degraded her before a cruel Society. In that weakness, for the love of a man she could never have and empty, meaningless possessions that only brought a fleeting and very empty happiness, Jane resolved to never become her mother. A woman who even at her death four years ago of a wasting illness had lain abed waiting for a man—who'd never come.

That was love.

A man who would abandon the woman who'd given all for just a scrap of his heart.

A woman who would choose that selfish cad above her own daughter.

Her lips twisted with bitterness. Love was cold and empty and selfish, and Jane wanted no part of it. After she had the three thousand pounds her father had settled upon her when she reached her twenty-fifth year, she could retreat from the reminders of satins and silks and use those funds for something that mattered. Except, since she'd entered Gabriel's home, how often had she thought of her plans for a school different than the Mrs. Belden's Finishing Schools of the world? Instead, she'd kissed Gabriel of her own will and desires, and worse, still dreamed of that embrace.

Jane drew her knees close to her chest and dropped her chin atop the coarse, brown, and comfortably safe fabric. Being here as hired companion to his sister was a matter of necessity; safety, even. And yet nothing seemed safe anymore, now knowing the coolly aloof nobleman. For God help her, she'd tasted in his kiss the weakness that had so consumed her mother that she'd tossed away all for the pleasure of it. Jane rubbed her chin over the fabric of her gown. She must take care around Gabriel. For this awareness of him moved beyond the physical and into dangerous territories that involved emotion and—

The press of the door handle echoed like a shot in the dead of night and she stilled, knowing with an intuitiveness that terrified her who stood on the other side of that door. Heart pounding, she looked up as Gabriel stepped inside and closed the door with a soft click. He paused at the entrance of the room and blinked several times, as though accustoming himself to the dimly lit room.

And then he located her with his stare. "Jane," he murmured.

Jane immediately lowered her legs to the floor. "My lord." She hopped to her feet, but he waved her back down. Reason warred within her—abandon this lavish space that was his, a world in which she was merely an interloper and worse, a thief. Hesitantly, she reclaimed her seat.

He stalked forward with the lethal grace of a panther, and she stiffened in a breathless anticipation, but he continued past her. She followed his movements as he strolled over to the sideboard and with crisp, concise movements poured himself a snifter of brandy.

Lord Montclair, with his wandering hands and hard eyes, had favored brandy. Yet, as Gabriel carried his glass over and claimed the leather chair opposite her, she acknowledged that this was not a man who'd force his intentions upon a woman. No, most gentlemen would have sacked the woman responsible for those faint purplish-blue marks he still wore and yet, Gabriel had responded without even the faintest hint of anger to her punch.

"You do not sleep at night." His was an observation.

Since her mother's death four years earlier when she'd been thrust upon the world with not a single skill to recommend her but only the benevolence of her father, she'd tasted the fear of her circumstances. "No." He peered hard at her face a moment and then looked into the contents of his drink. The haunted depths of those fathomless eyes spoke of a deep pain. "Nor do you," she said softly.

His broad shoulders tightened the expert cut of his sapphire coat sleeves. "No." The usual smoothness of his tone was now gravelly and harsh.

He too had fears. She dropped her gaze to her lap. What fears would a powerful nobleman such as he know? Then, she lifted her gaze back to him and his white-knuckled grip upon his glass. Suffering and pain were not reserved to a single station.

Suddenly, the intimacy of this moment, the view of him as more than a marquess and merely a man hammered home the folly in her being here, alone with her already weakening defenses. She made to rise.

"Did you enjoy yourself today?"

His words froze her. *He doesn't want to be alone.* For his cool nonchalance and his veneer of icy strength, he craved company. She knew, as only one who'd lived a solitary life could, that need in another. Retreat was wise and yet compassion kept her at his side. Jane settled back in her seat. "Which part of the day did you refer to?" *The stolen moment when you captured my curl?* "Our trip to Bond Street?"

Some of the tension seeped from his shoulders. Relief that, even as she should have taken her leave, she'd, in fact, stayed.

Jane studied him, this stoic stranger who would have tossed her out after their first meeting, but now spoke to her in the privacy of his library. What did he think of, even now?

And more…what was this hungering for her to know his unspoken thoughts?

Tonight, the demons of his past haunted him. They came at the most unexpected moments, triggered by a scent, a sound, and a memory. He'd prided himself on effectively squashing the memories of his father's abuse and yet he'd never truly be free of them. None of them would.

This evening it had been Waterson's unassuming statement about Gabriel's role as brother that had plunged him into the turbulent horrors of his youth. It was what had driven Gabriel to abandon his clubs and seek out the solitude of his office. Except, as he'd wandered down the silent corridors, the faint flicker of candlelight from under the doorframe had beckoned and with it a need to see the occupant of that room, knowing intuitively the woman who'd be on the other side of the door.

After years of striving to be different than the foul, rotted bastard his father had been, Gabriel, staring at Jane Munroe, came to the unpleasant realization that he was more like that monster than he'd ever dared believe.

For in the faintly lit library with just he and Jane for company, he hungered to know the soft, bow-shaped contours of her lips once more. He clenched the glass between his hands and burying his disgust, Gabriel downed a long sip. The familiar burn of the fine French spirits did little to dull his senses.

He wanted her still; this woman with her frowning lips and proudly held frame. Curiosity struck once more—a desire to know just who this angry one moment, smiling and teasing the next young woman was? He swirled the contents of his glass and eyed her over the rim. How did she come to find herself a companion? As it was safer to feed the desire to know more than the need to lay her gently curved frame upon the leather button sofa and take her as he longed to, Gabriel fixed on the need to fill in the pieces of Mrs. Munroe's story, for the unknown bits of her were far safer than the detailed pieces of his own that could never be forgotten.

As though unnerved by his scrutiny, Jane shifted back and forth. With a slight tremble to her fingers, she fanned the pages of the book in her hand.

"How did you come to be a companion?"

She stilled and her fingers ceased their distracted little movement. The book fluttered closed with a soft thump. "My lord?"

As a young boy, his safety had become dependent on an ability to gauge his father's actions and reactions. He'd become adept at detecting the subtle nuances of a person's every movement. Jane frowned and "my-lorded" him when unnerved. He frowned. What secrets did she keep? He shifted and hooked his opposite ankle across his knee. "Surely mine it is not a question that should merit surprise?"

She wrung her hands together. "Do you find me an inadequate companion to Lady Chloe? Do you intend to send me away?"

Send me away. He paused. Not back to Mrs. Belden's. Rather *away.* She preferred being here. Why should such a fact matter? And yet, it did. An inexplicable lightness filled his chest. "I assure you, I'm pleased with your services, Jane." Even if she infuriated him with her insolent words and tone. He admired her spirit. "I do not intend to send you back." And had admired those of brazen courage, since his own failed childhood as the scared, cowering boy beat for his father's cruel enjoyments.

The tension left Jane's shoulders and her expression softened. By the lady's reaction, he may as well have handed her a star. "Thank you," she responded. She dropped her gaze to the book in her lap

97

and, for a long moment, he believed she would ignore the question he'd previously put to her. "There is a remarkable lack of options for a young, unwed woman."

He'd have to be deafer than a doorpost to fail to hear the thick resentment underscoring her response. Regret filled him, as well as a heavy dose of shame. He'd dedicated his life to seeing his siblings contented and yet he'd never given thought to the precariousness of others—such as Jane. "What of Mr. Munroe?" It was an improper question he had no right to ask and certainly no right to an answer.

She picked her head up. "Mr. Munroe?" she asked, brow furrowed. Then belatedly appeared to recall her mistake. "O-oh," she cleared her throat. "I t-take it you refer to my husband?"

He took another sip of brandy. She'd been no more wedded than Gabriel himself. "Yes. Was there another?" Yet, the lady was a companion and Mrs. Belden, one of the most revered, feared, and stern headmistresses in the entire kingdom, would never hire into her employ a woman who was not widow or spinster.

Jane shook her head so hard she dislodged several of those blonde tresses. "Of course not." She caught her lower lip between her teeth. "Mr. Munroe's father, I suppose, could have been the other Mr. Munroe you referred to."

Poor Jane and her rather deplorable attempt at smoothing her lie. From the previous bitterness in her tone when she'd spoken of the *remarkable lack of options* for young women, the lady had carefully built a world as Mrs. Munroe, as opposed to Miss Munroe as a means of protection. He took pity and turned his questioning to truths about the lady and not these weakly constructed lies. "How did you come to be at Mrs. Belden's?"

"Much the way most instructors come to be at Mrs. Belden's."

Which was how? "And will you return to Mrs. Belden's employ after you complete the terms of your service here?" His gut tightened at the prospect of her gone. He'd had too many spirits this night. There was no other accounting for this irrational response.

"Where do you believe I might go?" Ah, her question with a question.

At her deliberate evasiveness, annoyance blended with amusement. Gabriel finished his drink in one, long, slow swallow and then set his snifter on the mahogany side table. He unfolded his leg and leaned close. "Who are you, *Miss* Munroe?"

She stilled at that deliberately emphasized word. He expected her to look away. Then, he was fast learning Jane never did or said the expected. She tipped her chin up and held his gaze with an unflinching directness. "I'm just a—"

"Do not say you are just a companion," he said with a growl of annoyance. Suddenly, her repeated words coupled with Waterson's disparaging remarks snapped his patience. The lady, through her work, demonstrated character and strength. How many women would or could take on the employment? "What if I say my questions have nothing to do with my role as your employer?" Jane stared unblinking at him. He angled closer. "What if I say I want to know about you?"

"Why?"

Why, indeed? Why when he'd committed himself to never worrying after the cares and desires of anyone outside the knit of his family's fold? Because, after an evening of burying the memories in a bottle, he'd confronted the truth—he was lonely. In the light of a new day, such a fact would not matter. It would even bring him solace and comfort and the assurance that he'd not be indebted to another soul. Yet now, with just him and the guarded Jane Munroe, he craved this momentary connection, one that he'd comfortably sever come morning.

"I enjoy reading."

That brought his attention up and he started at her unexpected admission.

She held the book in her hand aloft. He tried to make out the title, but Jane swiftly lowered the leather volume to her lap. It did not escape his notice the manner in which she hurriedly flipped it over, shielding the title from his scrutiny. His intrigue redoubled. "What do you read, Jane?"

"Anything," she said quickly. "Everything."

"As a companion do you have much time for reading?"

She gave her head a shake. "I do not."

"Do you have any family?" With his question, he craved an answer that set her apart from his own tortured childhood. It was a desire to know that when he'd been subjected to hell, she'd known the comfort of a predictable familial life.

"You have a good deal of questions, my lord." He gave her a long look. She sighed. "As a child, there was only my mother and me. I knew no siblings and my mother," she slid her gaze off to a point beyond his shoulder. "My mother was whimsical and fanciful while I craved practicality."

Even as a child? A familiar pang tugged at his heart. Then with the sobering reality of his own childhood, had he been at all different than Jane in that regard? There was bitterness in her tone that steered him away from questions of her family, a confirmation that hers was not the easy childhood he had hoped. "What did you read?"

"I used to read fairytales." Another one of those wistful smiles played about her lips. "Not all fairytales. Only those silly ones of love and happily ever afters." An image flickered to life. A small, bespectacled young Jane with her nose buried in a book about princes and princesses and unending love. The idea pulled at him with an inexplicable appeal that fought the decade's worth of disavowing those tiny beings, susceptible to hurt, who'd only bring him greater responsibility and ultimately failure.

Then two of her words registered, driving back the musing. *Used to.* Some hard, indefinable emotion twisted in his stomach. "At what point did you cease believing in the dream of love?" She was entirely too young to also have given up on happiness.

She clasped her hands in front of her. "It is not that I do not believe in love, my lord." Ah, it was to be *my lord,* again, was it? So the lady was uncomfortable discussing matters of the heart with him. "I do believe in love. I've witnessed the power of that emotion." Witnessed. But not experienced? Her lips turned up in a wry smile. "I've no desire to turn myself over to its hold."

He passed his gaze over Jane's heart-shaped face. Gabriel did not speak on matters of intimacy with anyone. Not his kin and not his

TO LOVE A LORD

lone friend in the world. However, he suspected the end of Chloe's
naiveté had come very early on at the brutal hands of their sire. But
what of Jane? The bitter young woman who'd only known a mother?
She shifted under his focus. "When did you stop believing in fairytales?" Again, a terribly bold question given life by too many spirits and
the early morn hours.

"When I realized—" Jane closed her lips tight, ending whatever
that revealing piece of herself she kept close. She jumped to her feet.
"I should seek my chambers," she confessed, eying him as though he
were the wolf mingling with the unsuspecting sheep.

"Yes," he concurred. He remained frozen, with his stillness convey-
ing her safety.

Jane lingered. She met his gaze with her own. "You needn't worry
that I will encourage flights of fancy in your sister. I will not fill her
head with fairytales and romantic hopes."

"Because you do not believe in them?" he shot back.

"Because I am practical and logical enough to know the perils in
entrusting one's heart to someone unworthy of that precious gift."

She'd had her heart broken. Why did a wave of jealousy roll
through him at that revelation? In their earlier discussions, he'd sur-
mised that Mr. Munroe had been nothing more than a fictional figure. Now, he was presented with the ugly possibility of some bounder
who'd forced Jane to adopt a false married title. Gabriel swiped his
empty snifter from the side table. With glass in hand, he rose in one
fluid motion and carried it over to the sideboard. He poured himself another drink and turning back, held it up in salute. "For all
we've disagreed on, Jane, we are of a remarkably like opinion in this
regard." After years of protecting himself, there was nothing left of
his heart to give anyone.

"Yes," she said softly. "It does appear that way." She took a step
toward him. "I venture someone has hurt you, Gabriel." There had
been. The someone who sired him.

Something passed between them. A bond unwittingly forged by
two people who'd both learned at some point to be wary of love and
leery of all sentiments that involved in anyway caring.

101

He recoiled as panic, potent and powerful clamored in his chest. This unfamiliar connection he had with no one. Not his brother who'd despised him through the years. Not his sister, Philippa, who was polite and soft spoken to all, not Chloe who saw him as more bother than brother. Jane took another step toward him and his feet twitched in an involuntary need to take flight. He did not want a connection to Jane or anyone. Those bonds only brought responsibility. Responsibility brought disappointment and that disappointment brought pain. His heart pounded hard as he tried to reclaim control from the stranger who'd stolen into his sanity. He schooled his features into a hard mask. "Jane?" he said quietly when she continued her advance.

She came to a slow stop. "Yes?"

Jane Munroe was dangerous to his ordered world. "Regardless of your beliefs on love, hope, and happiness, I still wish for my sister to aspire to more. As such, I'll ask that you do not impress your own cynical thoughts upon my sister." And he could not afford to be weak. Not again.

Jane stiffened. "My lord?"

How was it possible to both mourn and embrace the shattered bond between them? "Chloe requires a husband and I'll not have you fill her head with your own bitterness." Inwardly, he flinched at that charge he'd stolen from his meeting with Waterson at White's.

If looks could burn, he'd be a pile of charred ash at her feet. "With my bitterness?" she gritted out between clenched teeth. In this barely suppressed rage she bore no hint to the cowering young woman who'd first stood before him. Jane closed the space between them and in an entirely un-companion-like manner, jabbed him in the chest, hard with her finger. "I am not bitter. I am realistic." As was he. They made a sorry, dreary pair, the two of them. "Furthermore," he winced at another sharp jab. "I'll have you know you do your sister a disservice if you believe I, you, or the king himself could control, manipulate, or override her opinions." With a toss of her head, she marched from the room.

Why did he feel all the worse with her gone?

TWELVE

The following morning, bleary eyed with exhaustion, her mind dulled with fatigue, Jane sat in contemplation of her meeting with Gabriel. How could she have been so very foolish as to believe there was anything warm, good, or kind about Gabriel, the Marquess of Waverly? The memory of that blasted kiss had thrown her logic into disarray. It had forced her to see past the curt, condescending lord to the *man*. In that, she'd seen warmth and pain and a gentleman who would not force his attentions upon her—a man who saw her as a person that mattered, regardless of her station.

What a fool.

And yet for the restored order of her thoughts about him, why could she only focus on one particular truth of that meeting in the early morn hours? He'd had his heart broken. There was no other explanation for his cynical grin and his emotionally flat words on the matter of love. Jane plucked at the pages of her book—the same poor, forgotten volume she'd muddled her way unsuccessfully through the prior evening. Lords and ladies didn't know broken hearts and pained regrets. Their station protected them from hurts and uncertainties. Only, that is what she'd naively and foolishly believed.

Seeing Gabriel as he'd been last evening, a man haunted by his past and demons he'd likely never share with anyone, had torn asunder that erroneously drawn conclusion. It had also shaken her enough to see his icy indifference as a façade to protect himself. As one who adopted a disguise every day of her life, she easily detected it in another. In this case, it was Gabriel. Even as she wanted to hate him and consign him into the same detested category as every other lord. She could not.

"You are quiet, Jane."

Jane glanced up and flushed. Gabriel's sister occupied the chair opposite her. The young lady peered at her over the top of the book in her hands. "Forgive me. I was r—" She ended the lie. The closed volume on her lap was testament to that.

Chloe gave her a gentle look. A kind warmth filled the young woman's eyes and all but begged Jane to share that which troubled her. To do so, however, would be both folly and scandalous. There was no place for Jane to know anything more about Gabriel, the Marquess of Waverly, her employer. Soon, her time here would be at an end. Perhaps sooner should her deception be uncovered. Her belly twisted in knots.

"What is it?" Chloe rested her book on her lap and leaned closer. The young woman was nothing if not persistent. Then her lips tightened on a moue of displeasure. "Is it my brother? Has he been rude to you? He's ever so stodgy and commanding."

"No." The denial burst from her lips. Her cheeks warmed at that emphatic reply. "No. Your brother has been nothing but polite and proper." The memory of his kiss burned across her mind.

Chloe snorted. "That is an apt description of my eldest brother."

Jane shifted her gaze to the closed parlor door and then back to Chloe. She'd not inquired about the marquess. Why, Gabriel's sister herself had ventured forth details about the powerful nobleman. Surely, there was no harm in politely asking a question about the young lady's question? "Has he always been so very—?"

"Dull?" Could anyone truly find the powerful young lord to be dull or stodgy as alleged by his sister?

"No." She opened her mouth, but Chloe cut in, once again.

"Inflexible."

A grin formed on her lips. Yes, a man who'd gauge her suitability in her role based on one meeting alone would certainly be at the very least considered, inflexible. "Serious," she supplied instead, recalling him as he'd been with the brandy in hands and dark thoughts in his eyes. "Has he always been so very serious?" Some of the light dimmed from Chloe's eyes and Jane bit the inside of her cheek at the shame in pressing the young woman for information about the marquess. "Forgive me," she said hurriedly. "It was not my place to—"

"He has." Chloe's quiet words interrupted her apology. "Gabriel has long been the serious one. Alex, my other brother," she said by way of explanation, "has always been the carefree, charming one." A twinkle lit her eyes, driving back the earlier solemnity. "The papers purported he was a rogue."

"Is he?" She'd too many times found herself the recipient of those carefree, charming rogues. She vastly preferred Gabriel's dry humor and more reserved self.

"Alex is wed now," Chloe said with a smile. "And quite reformed." Jane doubted that. Once a rogue, always a rogue. "He wedded my dearest friend, Imogen." Her grin dipped. "Which is why I find myself alone and unattached." Some of her earlier cheer restored. "Though, I must admit, I expected this to be a lonely Season, Jane. I never expected I should find a companion who both reads philosophical books and would become a friend."

Emotion suffused her heart. "A friend," she whispered. In the course of her four and twenty years she'd never had a friend. As she'd said to Gabriel last evening, hers had been a solitary childhood and only all the more lonely the older she became.

"Yes, a friend." Chloe gave her a look that could only come from another woman who herself had known if not the same, at least a similar solitary existence. She winked. "Even if you are one of Mrs. Belden's dragons."

Reality raised its ugly head. The truth of her deception, the lies she'd built her relationship with Gabriel and this young woman upon, shook, shaming her not for the first time with her being here under these false pretenses. She shifted on her seat and dropped her gaze to the book on Chloe's lap.

A relieved sigh escaped her when Gabriel's sister moved the conversation to safer topics. She held her copy of *Thoughts on the Education of Daughters* aloft. "I must confess I've been quite devouring your Mrs. Wollstonecraft."

Jane would bet the whole of the trust coming to her in two months that the Marquess of Waverly would sack her faster than she could utter "scandalous teachings" for introducing Chloe to the philosopher. "Mrs. Belden would not be pleased," she muttered to herself. After all it had been a sackable offense.

Chloe tossed her blonde head back and laughed. "Yes, I daresay the mother of the dragons would not tolerate such reading material." Then some of her amusement slipped. "Though, I confess to my disappointment with Mrs. Wollstonecraft."

"In what way?" Jane prodded when the young woman fell silent.

Chloe shrugged. "She is scandalous in her thoughts and beliefs on women and their role in Society and yet here," she lifted her book once again. "Here she encourages women to wed." Disappointment turned her lips down. "She suggests with her words that the only way a woman can contribute to Society is through that wedded state." She tossed the book down on the table between them and caught her lower lip between her teeth. "Do you agree with that, Jane?"

Jane hesitated, knowing there were many ways in which to answer the question. The one in which she dutifully confirmed her ascent as Gabriel would likely wish. In that lie, she'd guide Chloe as he so wished, toward that estimable state of matrimony to some proper, powerful lord.

Or the truthful one.

She held Chloe's gaze. "It matters not what I think but rather what you believe, Chloe."

A wistful smile played on the young lady's face. "You are the only one of Mrs. Belden's instructors, my siblings, my mother, of *anyone* to say as much."

What a confining world they both lived in. Jane lifted her hands up. "Society, your family, they think to protect you—us," she amended. "They think to guide us to the perfect marital match." Her first meeting with Gabriel reared in her mind. "Ultimately trusting that we should be cared for and they are wiser to know what we need. All the while they fail to see the truth."

The young woman stared at her, frozen, hanging on to each word. She shook her head.

"The truth is we know our hearts and, more importantly, our minds. If a dog snaps and snarls at you, you'd not reach out to pet the thing. Even as Society thinks you will, without the proper guidance."

An unexpected bitterness lined the young woman's face, chilling in its rawness. It aged her beyond her twenty-one years. "Then, wouldn't it be wiser to avoid all those creatures to avoid being snapped and snarled at?"

Someone had touched her in violence. A spasm of pain squeezed Jane's heart and the breath left her on a slow exhale. Of course. It was why for Society's expectations and her brother's determination, she disavowed the marital state. The young woman had known pain and by the telling of those handful of words, hers went beyond the emotional hurt Jane herself had known. Instead of replying, she answered Chloe with a question. "When I arrived you'd already formulated an opinion of me. You wanted to turn me out. Did you not?"

"Oh, I—"

Jane waved off the contrite apology in the lady's eyes. "You looked at my gown," she looked pointedly down at the skirts unaffectionately termed dragon skirts by the lady. "And you decided I was the same as every other instructor you'd had or known." The truth was those women were far more honorable. Jane was a mere liar. Guilt knifed through her once more. She gently took Chloe's hands in hers. "I will not guide you or force you to an opinion on marriage, as your brother and Society wish. I will only gently encourage you to realize that just because one is dressed as a dragon does not make them one." Jane gave her fingers a slight squeeze.

The muscles of Chloe's throat worked and she gave a nod.

"Do you know what I believe?"

Chloe gave her an encouraging look. "What is that?"

"You can spend your life avoiding all dogs because you'd been bitten in the past, and yet to do so wouldn't truly be to live and then, he...," she amended. "That dog," *whoever the nameless, faceless monster is who so scarred you.* "Would win." Did Gabriel know his sister had experienced this pain? The powerful, unbending man he was would likely have taken apart that fiend if he did. "You mustn't allow your fears of the past to control your future. After all, the beginning is always today." Even as the familiar words left her mouth, the absolute hypocrisy of simply uttering them stuck at the corner of her mind.

The young woman widened her eyes. "That is lovely, Jane."

She managed a sheepish grin. "Alas, the credit belongs to our Mrs. Wollstonecraft." Who, God help her, if Gabriel learned was being taught of in his household, would unhesitantly turn her out *sans* reference.

"You mustn't worry," Chloe said, giving her a pat on the knee. "I daresay Gabriel will not mind." The mischievous glint lit her eyes. "As long as he doesn't know of it."

"As long as I don't know of what?" A familiar voice drawled from the doorway.

Jane and Chloe jumped in unison. Jane scrambled to her feet and hurriedly set down the book in her hands. Alas, Chloe had far more years of prevaricating around the astute nobleman. She trilled a laugh. "Do not be a boor, Gabriel." The slight scowl gave hint of a man who chafed at his sister and Society's opinion of him. She sailed over to her brother and wrapped him on the knuckles. "Nor should you go sneaking on ladies. It is not at all polite."

"I'm here at your bequest," he said, his voice dryer than autumn leaves. He slid his gaze over his sister's shoulder and settled it on Jane.

She warmed under his intense scrutiny but retained his direct stare. In a handful of meetings, he'd become more than her employer. He'd become a man with similar fears and thoughts on love. And a man whose kiss she craved and...She suppressed a groan. What manner of madness had befallen her? His hot, assessing stare indicated he knew very well the path her thoughts had traversed.

"Regardless," Chloe said, as though instructing a small child. "You should have, at the very least, announced yourself. Isn't that right,

Jane?" They both jumped guiltily. "I thought a walk was in order. The sun is shining and I have tired of shopping." At last. Though in the lady's defense, she'd not purchased an item for herself. "I'll return in but a moment." With that she raced over to the door. Gabriel stepped aside to allow Chloe her exit and then strolled deeper into the room. All the while his gaze remained trained on her.

A wild fluttering danced in her belly and she wanted to attribute the sensation to discomfort from their previous meeting, and yet she could not. Not without lying to herself. "My lord," she greeted when he came to a stop several feet away. She backed up a step and his intelligent eyes took in that hasty movement.

"I expected you'd be in a temper this morning, Jane." Expected or hoped?

She folded her arms across her chest in a protective manner to shield herself from any further weakening. "Is that why you were boorishly rude last evening, my lord?"

"I wanted to apologize," he confessed.

"Apologize?" She furrowed her brow. Noblemen did not apologize. They took their pleasure where they willed it and hurt without thinking.

"It was wrong of me to call you bitter."

Yet, this man, regardless of his lofty title, took ownership of his words and actions. And she preferred him as the safe, predictable lord with his censorious eyes and clipped commands. That man she could relegate alongside the other nobles she'd known before. This man she knew not what to do with.

"Will you not accept my apology?"

Yes, she supposed some response on her part was in order. Jane's breath caught as he brushed the back of his hand along the curve of her cheek. Under the power and heat of his touch, her lashes fluttered closed. "Y-you needn't apologize, my lord." His had been a protective measure, and more, there had been truth to his charge. She was bitter and she detested that she'd become so consumed by her own regrets and resentments. "I a-assure you," she whispered when he continued to run his hand along her cheek. "I would never i-impose my own thoughts or beliefs upon your sister."

No, she'd only steal from him and lie her way into his household. God forgive her.

✍

What maddening hold did Mrs. Jane Munroe have upon him?

When he'd arisen this morning and gone through his morning's ablutions, he'd reconciled himself to reestablishing order between him and the young woman in his employ. There would be no more private meetings or talks of their families and pasts. He would be the cool, proper marquess his father had beat him into becoming.

And his life could resume its normal course.

He let his hand fall to his side. Jane blinked as though bereft over the loss of his touch. "Before my sister returns, we should speak." He took several steps away and then clasped his hands behind him.

A panicky fear lit her eyes. "D-do you intend to send me away?"

Again, with her almost desperate question. He frowned. He might have kissed her and violated all manner of appropriate and honorable behaviors where his staff was concerned, but he wasn't a total bastard. "I have no intention of sending you away, Jane. You are effectively stuck with my family until Chloe is wed. At which point you will be free to return to your post at Mrs. Belden's." Her eyes darkened. "Or whatever other post you desire." The muscles in his stomach went taut at that imagined, but inevitable parting.

She gave a little nod. "Thank you."

How very polite and deferential she was. It was as though nothing else had transpired between them. He started. Which was, of course, for the best. It was the very reason he now spoke to her. Gabriel began to pace. "It occurs to me that I've been wholly inappropriate and improper where you are concerned." Why was that one kiss not enough?

"Gabriel?" she cocked her head at an endearing little angle.

TO LOVE A LORD

"We've spoken on matters that have little bearing on my sister," he paused mid-stride and looked at her. "Matters that have nothing to do with your tenure here. For that I make my most humble apologies. Going forward, I pledge to honor your role on my staff." She winced. He silently cursed at the pomposity of such a statement. His lips pulled in a grimace, as he wished not for the first time that he possessed the effortless ability to speak to and with a lady. He pressed ahead. "The kiss," *has haunted my waking and sleeping thoughts*, "was a mistake," he finished lamely as he yanked his gaze away from the hurt expression stamped on the delicate lines of her face. Except, there was nothing in her reaction that conveyed regret.

"It was but one kiss, my lord," she said in flat tones. "Nor was it forced upon me." She clasped her hands before her and studied the interlocked digits.

Forced upon me. The second hint that there had been others before him who'd taken advantage of her. He balled his hands into tight fists so that his nails left marks upon his palm. *It is not my place. It is not my place.* He'd already reestablished the boundaries between them. Or at the very least, he hastily constructed them now. To ask questions about her past had no bearing on her future here, or those barriers he sought to cast up. "Who?"

She did not pretend to misunderstand that lethal whisper. "It matters not."

He'd shred the man apart with his bare hands were he to discover his identity. "It matters to me."

"Why?" Jane raised her gaze to his. "You are correct, my lord," *My lord.* His chest throbbed with regret as he longed to hear the three syllables of his name once more on her lips. Except, he'd resurrected the walls of the station between them. "I am here in your household with a very defined role. There is little need for you to know anything of my past." She tossed her head back. "Unless you'd turn me out for those pieces, in which case you are deserving."

He blanched. "I would never." Did she believe he'd be so callous as to set her from his employ for actions that were no fault of her own? Did everyone truly have such a low opinion of him? He thought back to heated exchanges he'd had with his younger brother, Alex, who with his disgust of Gabriel, would have readily concurred with Mrs. Jane Munroe. Then, had he truly given anyone reason to believe better of him?

Jane's chest rose and fell with a slow, steadying breath "Very well." She dropped a polite, deferential curtsy. "Then, if there is nothing else you'd wish to speak with me on, I should fetch my cloak before your sister returns." She took several steps toward the door and his mind raced, filled with a desire to stay her retreat.

"Mrs. Munroe?"

She stilled and wheeled slowly back to face him.

"We are to attend a ball this evening." A flash of panic lit the blues of her eyes. What was it she feared? Entering polite Society? Or something else? Something more? She gave a nod and then made her escape. Gabriel stared after her. With a curse, he raked a hand through his hair.

"Did you just curse?"

"Bloody hell."

"Again?" His sister stood framed in the doorway, her hands planted on her hips and a displeased frown on her lips.

"No."

"And lie?"

Lying, cursing, kissing lovely members of his staff? With each day he descended deeper and deeper into his father's vile ways. Perhaps he'd been wrong and he could not purge the evil running through his veins from the blood he shared with that old monster. "Let it rest, Chloe," he said tiredly.

Alas, she stalked across the room a blazing ball of fury. "Whatever did you say to Jane?"

His heart kicked up a beat. "I said nothing—"

"Oh, come. She was running through the house in a bid to be free of this room."

"I reminded her that we would be attending a ball this evening." That much was at least true. Guilt flared.

"Well, that would be enough to frighten any young woman," Chloe muttered. He grunted as she jabbed a finger in his chest. "I like her a good deal, Gabriel, and you are not," he winced as she stuck her gloved fingertip at his person once more. "I repeat, are not to drive her away." What was it with young ladies and their tiny but impressively powerful digits?

"It is not my intention to drive her away but rather—"

"Good." A final thrust of her finger. "Then do not." She gave a toss of her blonde ringlets. "Now, if you are quite through here." If *he* were quite through? "It is time for our walk at Hyde Park." With that she spun on her heel and marched from the room.

Gabriel swiped a hand over his face. An afternoon with an angry, putout Chloe and a hurt, annoyed Jane Munroe? It was fitting punishment he supposed for his outrageous behavior since Jane had entered his household and upended his world.

THIRTEEN

Standing in the corner of the ballroom alongside two other companions, Jane kept a careful eye on Chloe, never more grateful for her modest Sunday dress and spectacles that offered a modicum of protection. Though what she'd expected in taking on the position as companion to a lady, other than attending lavish *ton* events, she did not know.

Just then, Lady Chloe, entirely too forgiving, by half, and in that way, naively trusting, stood beside Gabriel and a tall, slender gentleman. While she conversed with the two men, Chloe darted her gaze about the room and then her stare collided with Jane's. Gabriel's sister pointed her eyes to the ceiling, letting Jane know precisely what she thought of the marquess' matchmaking.

An unexpected bark of laughter escaped Jane, and she promptly clamped her lips together. Alas, she'd already earned censorious stares from the companions beside her and curious stares from nearby lords and ladies.

Blend in. Meld with the walls.

Blast and double blast. How many years had she attempted to perfect that very feat? And how many years had she failed? Every single one of them. Jane smoothed her palms over her satin skirts, the smooth, cool fabric luxuriantly soft against her hands. She'd long ago committed herself to remaining unseen, and yet with her sharp tongue, and bothersome golden curls, she'd never quite successfully managed to do so. No, she'd not wanted the attentions of those self-serving nobleman with their wandering stares. Until Gabriel. Unbidden, her gaze found him once more. His sister, now gone, escorted onto the dance floor by the gentleman whom she'd previously spoken with, he stood off to the side, skimming his hard gaze over the heads of the twirling dancers.

Her breath caught. With his midnight black coat and stark white cravat, he really was quite magnificent. So very different than the fops and swains in their vibrant, satin knee breeches and slick oiled hair. What was it about Gabriel, the Marquess of Waverly, that so commanded her notice? She continued to study him. He sipped from the crystal flute in his hands. With her eyes, she took in those hard, firm lips once pressed against hers, touched to the rim of his glass. Oh, of course with his chiseled cheeks and thick, midnight black hair, he possessed a remarkable beauty lauded about by artists. But there was more. His solemnity, his devotion to his sister plucked at the strings of her heart. For he'd proven that not all men were, in fact, self-serving and living only for their own pleasures. He lived for his sister. Jane's throat worked. And in a world where no one had ever lived for her, there was something potently addictive about a man capable of that regard and love for a person other than himself.

As though feeling her gaze on him, Gabriel looked out across the crowded dance floor, and then their stares collided. She should look away. She should politely avert her gaze and turn to the other women at her side. Yet again, however, she proved herself remarkably like her audacious mother, for she continued to boldly study him as he drained the sparkling contents of his glass. Fear pounded away at her chest, pressing down on her like a boulder and threatening to cut off her airflow. This hold he had upon her was dangerous. He'd been abundantly clear in her role in his household and yet for that vital reminder he'd given, she could not set aside the thought of him. He presented folly of the worst sort, only heightening her weakness as a woman. Jane drew in a breath. She should be fixed on the ruse that had brought her into his life—a reprieve until she secured the funds settled on her by her father. Yet, how often had she thought of the goal that had driven her all these years? Once? Twice? Always as an afterthought and a matter of guilt.

A couple stepped into her line of vision and immediately broke the charged energy between Jane and Gabriel. The young gentleman, with his too-long, nearly black hair had an air of vague familiarity to him, but it was the captivating crimson-haired creature at his side that commanded attention. The elegantly attired couple spoke with a relaxed ease, motioning and laughing, and the faintest softening occurred on the harsh planes of Gabriel's face, a genuine appreciation of the two before him.

And once more, Jane was as she'd always been—an interloper on life. She touched her hand to the Scamozzi column and stood, a voyeur to the happy exchange. For years she believed all she wanted, all she needed was her school, a place to give her purpose. Yet, a witness to Gabriel's world, she craved more. She longed for something she'd never, ever believed or would have dared to believe—companionship.

She closed her eyes a moment and fought to suppress a panicky giggle, the irony not lost on her. The hired companion longed for companionship.

"Tsk, tsk, why, it is Jane Munroe. Never tell me you don a pair of spectacles and think you could remain hidden?"

Her eyes flew open as that loathsome voice slapped into her consciousness. Shivers of loathing ran along her spine as she confronted the grinning, unrelenting visage of the Earl of Montclair.

"What nothing to say?" he taunted, when she remained silent.

Panic consumed her and she registered the curious and disapproving stares trained on her by the other companions.

Jane shot her gaze about the crowded ballroom and found herself invisible to all those lords and ladies present, a feat she was never more grateful for. She located Gabriel still locked in conversation with that unfamiliar pair.

The earl angled his body in a way that cut the marquess off from her line of focus. "Ah, you are looking for someone? Your latest protector perhaps?"

An unholy rage to plant him another facer, here in the midst of the ballroom filled her so strongly she had to fist her hands to keep from burying her fist in his nose. "You were never my protector," she said on an angry whisper. He was merely the demon who'd haunted her.

"Ahh," he dipped his head closer and the familiar tinge of heavy spirits that clung to him slapped at her senses, offensive and overpowering.

"There you are, Jane."

At the unexpected arrival of Chloe, Lord Montclair straightened.

And coward that she was, she sent a silent prayer skyward as Chloe appeared before her, a five foot five inch savior. The young woman glared at the Earl of Montclair and then presented him with her back.

Montclair schooled his features and inclined his head. For a moment, dread ran a rampant course through Jane's being at the idea he'd shame her before this woman who called her friend, and with his admission, proving her unworthy of the role she'd stolen into. For all his brazenness this night and the night she'd been dismissed from his father's household, he maintained a proper gentlemanly façade for the *ton*. "Lady Chloe Edgerton," he murmured. "If you'll excuse me?" he said quietly with a deep bow. Then, with a slight bow and a final glance for Jane that promised this was not the last of their meetings, he took his leave.

As his loathsome form disappeared into the crowd, Jane's shoulders sank with a quiet relief. Her relief was short-lived.

"Do you know Lord Montclair?" A muscle ticked at the corner of the young lady's right eye.

"No," she said quickly.

Too quickly by the narrowing of the other woman's intelligent eyes. "Was he bothering you?" She didn't allow Jane to respond. "If he was," Chloe said in hushed tones, "you need just say something to my brother. Gabriel would—"

"No," she said loudly, once again attracting those curious stares. She drew in a calming breath and lowered her voice. "No." Suddenly, the deception she practiced upon Gabriel and coupled with Montclair's reappearance in her life, was too much. Her feet twitched with an involuntary need to take flight. "Will you pardon me, Chloe?" she pleaded. She was the veriest coward, but the din of the ballroom, combined with the high heat threatened her senses. "I require a moment."

Concern flared in Chloe's eyes. "May I come with you? I—"

Jane gave her head a shake. "I'll be but a moment." Then, in a bid of attempted humor, she forced a smile. "I daresay your brother would be none too pleased with me if I stole you away from the evening's festivities." She waggled her eyebrows. "What manner of companion would that make me?"

"A perfect one," Chloe admitted, and with those words she roused an honest, unrestrained laugh from Jane.

Oh, how much this young lady had come to mean to her. Another twinge struck her heart with the truth of the briefness of this stolen interlude with Chloe and her family. As she dropped a curtsy and sought out a moment of solitude, she acknowledged that, at the very least, life should have conditioned her to the inconstancy of relationships and happiness.

What the hell was Montclair doing with Jane? With Alex and his wife, Imogen, before him carrying on about God knew what, Gabriel remained fixed on the young, slender siren at the corner of the room. The healthy color of Jane's cheeks faded and even with the distance of the ballroom between them, he detected the flash of terror in her eyes. He'd end the man if he'd insulted her. He snapped the stem of his champagne flute. A servant hurried over to collect the remnants of his glass and to sweet up the crystal.

"Whatever is the matter with you?" his brother drawled sounding more amused than concerned. "You've gone all red in the face. Aren't I right, Imogen?"

"Do hush." His sister-in-law, the logical young lady who'd managed to tame his rakish brother, swatted her husband's arm. "You're insufferable."

Alex grinned.

At that thankful moment, Chloe interrupted Jane's exchange with Montclair. "Nothing is the matter." Bloody hell, what had come over him that he'd be so demmed hot-headed, wanting to exact violence against Montclair for all manner of imagined slights?

His brother followed his stare and furrowed his brow. "Who is that?"

At one time, they'd shared everything from dreadful wishes for their evil sire to hopes for the future. He flicked an imagined piece of lint from his sleeve. "That is Chloe's companion." There had been a time when no two souls had been closer than he and Alex. All of that had been forever changed at the altar of their father's abuse. Alex had never forgiven him for allowing those beatings to carry on. Now, they each held their own secrets. Which was only right. Gabriel had never forgiven himself.

His brother chuckled. "You've hired another companion."

"I didn't hire you," he pointed out with a frown.

"Ah, yes. That is correct," Alex said, inclining his head. "You threatened me." He gave a wry grin. "You are still foisting off that role on anoth—oomph." The words ended as his wife buried her elbow into his ribs.

"Do you have a problem with that role you'd been assigned?" Imogen arched a single, fiery eyebrow.

"Not at all," Alex replied automatically.

And the silliest, most hapless grin marred his brother's lips that Gabriel shifted on his feet, feeling like the worst sort of interloper on the loving couple's shared moment. Had he not demanded Alex escort Chloe about Society, then he'd not, even now, be married to Imogen, Chloe's best friend.

Odd, he had spent the better part of his life disavowing those shared sentiments with another human being, and yet standing here, he was filled with an unholy envy for his younger brother's happy existence. Gabriel worked his gaze over the dance floor and located Chloe. Alone. He silently cursed and quickly scanned the room. "Where in hell is she?"

"She is beside the column," his brother put in, pointing his finger.

Gabriel wrinkled his brow. "No, she's—" Chloe. He clamped his lips tight. His brother erroneously believed Gabriel even now sought out their headstrong sister. Which if he was a good, worthy brother, he should be, and yet time had proven how very inadequate he was. "Ah, yes." He coughed into his hand. "If you'll excuse me. Imogen, Alex." He sketched a brow and then started after his sister. If anyone would know where Jane Munroe had taken herself off to, it was Chloe.

Not that he should be concerned with his sister's companion. After all, by nature of her role, Jane was just that—a companion. She didn't require a companion. And yet, with each footfall that carried him closer to his sister, his ire grew. Jane couldn't be more than a handful of years older than Chloe. Regardless of her station or status or wedded state, a woman of her young years was deserving of the same care and protection as any other young lady. He stopped beside his sister. "Where is your companion?"

Chloe shrieked and slapped a hand to her heart. "You startled me."

Yes, the shriek had suggested as much. He looked about once more for Jane. For a moment, his gaze lingered on the Earl of Montclair, the same charming rogue who'd been engaged in discussion with her a short while ago. And he wanted to kill the man all over again. The lady was not with Montclair. Some of the tension thrumming through his frame left him. "Mrs. Munroe?" he gritted out, careful to keep his tone low from possible listeners. "Where is she?"

In an exasperating manner that had driven him mad as a youth, Chloe directed her gaze to the chandelier. "I'm not Jane's keeper. If you want Mrs. Munroe watched, you should assign the lady a companion."

He bristled at having been both caught and called out, by his young sister, no less. "Not watched," he groused, and resisted the urge to tug at his suddenly too-tight cravat. "I'm not suggesting you are her keeper. I, oh blast and damn," he groused.

Chloe's eyes formed wide moons. "Did you just curse?"

Again, cursing.

"No." Her eyebrows shot up. *"And lying?"*

Jane Munroe was a deuced bad influence. He should stand here beside Chloe until she returned. It was, at the very least, the brotherly thing to do.

"Chloe!"

He gave silent thanks as Imogen and Alex descended upon Chloe, effectively relieving him of his responsibilities. An excited squeal bubbled past his sister's lips and with little regard for Society's rules, she flung her arms about the other woman. "Oh, how I have missed you. I daresay I never imagined when I performed matchmaker for you two, that you'd abandon me to my own devices."

Chloe's teasing words roused sheepish expressions from the recently married husband and wife.

Taking advantage of the sudden, and much welcome, diversion, Gabriel sketched a bow. "If you'll excuse me?" he remarked, and then without awaiting permission, or allowing questions, went in search of Jane.

He wound his way through the throng of guests and strode from the hall. With the din of the crowd at his back, he glanced first down one corridor and then another. Where in blazes had she gone off? With an impatient curse, he moved at a brisk clip through one hall. All the while, Jane Munroe occupied his thoughts. Where did he always find the lady in his own home? He paused and narrowed his gaze. *Of course.* Then with purposeful strides he made his way past door after door in search of the library. The memory of Jane and Lord Montclair, the notorious rogue, grew increasingly strong in his mind. With each opened and closed door, fury expanded...and the fury should be reserved for Jane having abandoned Chloe, but instead, a dark, niggling emotion that felt very much like jealousy slithered inside him like a venomous serpent.

There had been a familiarity to Jane and Montclair's exchange—the position of their bodies, the furtiveness of their meeting. And he intended to find out just how Jane Munroe knew the gentleman. He shoved open another door. The library. It took his eyes a moment to adjust to the dimly lit space. He peered into the expansive room and then located her almost immediately, tucked against the wall, as though she sought to make herself invisible.

"G-Gabriel," she stammered. Her cheeks whitened and with unease stamped in the graceful planes of her face, the niggling grew and expanded as the ugly possibility took root and grew within his mind.

Gabriel entered the room and closed the door quietly behind him. Her gaze followed his every movement, as he turned the lock. He leaned against the frame and folded his arms at his chest. "I believe you have some explaining to do."

Jane's mind raced. Oh, she had some explaining to do, all right. The question was, which bit of explaining did Gabriel reference? Life had taught her patience. Inevitably, people revealed themselves and their inner-thoughts.

He shoved away from the door and made his way across the quiet library.

Alas, in this instance, life proved wholly incorrect. Gabriel, stoic and somber as always, gave no indication as to his thoughts. She wet her lips. "My lord?" she began tentatively.

Could one go to prison for stealing a missive and securing oneself employment? And would he have her thrown in Newgate if it was a punishable offense? With his love for his sister, she didn't doubt he'd ruin Jane, if he believed she'd compromised Chloe's well-being in any way.

He stopped before her and dipped his head close. His champagne-scented breath wafted about her senses and her lashes fluttered. How was it possible the scent of spirits upon this man's lips should fill her with a heady desire that drove back the ugly thoughts of another's brutal attack? Her heart beat an erratic rhythm and she leaned up to take Gabriel's kiss. "Are you here meeting someone?" The crisply spoken question brought her eyes flying open.

Jane stared at him. "My lord?" What was he going on about?

His gaze darkened. "There is nothing honorable that would have a lady alone in her host's library, when she should be attending her responsibilities as a companion."

She choked. "Y-you think I am here on a liaison?" His silence stood as affirmation. Jane gave her head a frantic shake. "Oh, no. Never. Never." She'd sooner dance through the flames of hell than meet any gentleman for a clandestine meeting. To do so would consign herself to the same ranks as her mother.

"And yet you are here," he persisted, relentless.

"I needed…" To escape the memory of Montclair. "A moment of quiet," she finished knowing even as the excuse left her mouth how lame her response sounded. "I grew overheated from the crush of the room."

He narrowed his eyes. "I saw you conversing with Lord Montclair."

Her heart dipped. Of course he did. A man who so closely attended to his family and responsibilities saw everything—particularly the actions of a stranger residing under his roof. She'd only hoped he had failed to note Montclair's approach. Her mind raced and for the span of a heartbeat she considered telling him all. As soon as the thought entered, it fled her mind. What reason did he have to believe her, a stranger? So when presented with the bold demand of that statement, she did the only thing she'd done to him since she'd entered his house. "I dropped my spectacles." She lied.

"Your spectacles?" he repeated, with heavy disbelief underscoring that question.

She nodded. "My spectacles." She removed the wire-rimmed pair from her nose and showed him the frame. "He was so good as to rescue them." Jane detested giving the loathsome letch even a hint of praise for imagined acts. The vile monster was deserving of nothing good.

Some of the fury receded from Gabriel's taut frame and he reached for the pair. He eyed the delicate lenses bent at the rims with a wary caution. "They are bent," she said needlessly. Ruined from the man's attack more than a year past. They'd never been the same since and she'd never spared the funds to have the merely ornamental disguise replaced or repaired.

He handed them over to her slowly and she quickly snatched them from his hand. "You should return to the ballroom, Jane," he said hesitantly.

Jane nodded. "Of course." She placed her spectacles upon her face and started for the door.

"Jane," he called out, staying her movements.

She stopped and turned back to face him.

"If I find you have lied to me and if you, in any way through your presence here, harm my sister," he paused and lowered his voice. "I will see you ruined." His words contained the satiny edge of steel, a lethal threat that drove the beat of her heart into an even more frenzied rhythm.

She managed to incline her head. "Is there anything else you require, my lord?"

He shook his head once and she, with forced calm, opened the door and took her leave of him. She did not doubt if he were to discover all the lies she kept, he'd attempt to see her destroyed. Alas, he didn't realize, it was impossible to ruin someone who'd already been born ruined.

FOURTEEN

Jane stood frozen before the bevel mirror. The young woman with some curls held in place with butterfly combs at the base of her neck and the other tresses hanging freely down her back, stared back, a stranger. She took in the pale pink of the satin creation selected by Chloe and with trembling fingers, ran her palms down the smooth, soft French fabric.

It was just a silly scrap of material. In the bearing of a woman's worth and capabilities, it had neither here nor there to do with her value, as she'd maintained to Gabriel just two days earlier. Her throat worked. Yet, it was by far the loveliest garment she'd ever donned. Tears filled her eyes and she blinked back the useless weak droplets. God forgive her, but five days in the Marquess of Waverly's household and she'd proven the ugly, sorry fact that she'd spent the better part of her life convincing herself otherwise of—she was her mother.

With her desire for the kiss of a man who saw her as a member of his staff and yet attired her in lavish gowns, she proved that blood held true. Jane closed her eyes, detesting the resemblance to the woman who'd given her life and chosen another. A woman who'd passed her weakness on to her daughter.

The door handle clicked and she stiffened at the soft tread of footsteps. "Jane, are you—?" Chloe's words ended on a gasp. The mirror reflected the shock stamped on her face. She blinked like an owl in the night. "You are beautiful," she whispered. Awe, shock, and wonder filled those three words.

And if Jane weren't so blasted miserable and terrified and panicked she would have found humor in that shock. She gave a small smile. "Thank you."

Chloe walked a small circle around her while assessing her in that contemplative manner of hers. She captured her jaw between her thumb and forefinger and continued to study her as though she were an exhibit at the Royal Museum. Then, she stopped suddenly and rocked back on her heels. "Why, you don't require spectacles." No, those clear, crystal frames however had detracted notice. She gestured to her hair. "And your hair is, why, it is gloriously curled." Gloriously bothersome. Those loose tresses had been what had lured the lecherous Lord Montclair. He'd tangled his wandering hands in her hair until she'd vowed to never wear even a single strand free about her shoulders.

She thrust back the memory. "It is too much."

"Do not be silly." Chloe's smile widened. "You are absolutely splendid."

Jane gave her head a forceful shake. "I do not need to be absolutely splendid." Quite the opposite. She fixed an accusatory stare on the young woman. "Your intention was to have me blend with Society." A companion in satins with diamond encrusted hair combs woven throughout her hair would earn her all manner of inappropriate attention.

A beleaguered sigh escaped Gabriel's sister. "Yes, yes I did. Unfortunately, Jane," she moved her gaze from the top of Jane's head to her toes. "You are incapable of blending in."

Panic cloyed at her chest. "No, I'm not." With her gaze, she desperately searched for her spectacles.

Chloe was across the room in four long strides and intercepted her efforts. "These," she held them up, "do not make you blend in. They attract notice. Your dragon skirts," she pointed to the offensive garments in question, "also earn you notice, for entirely different reasons." With careful movements, she set the wire-rimmed spectacles down on the table beside Jane's bed. "You spoke to me of not judging all dogs by the ones who snapped and snarled." She held Jane's gaze. "Do not hold all members of polite Society in judgment for those unscrupulous ones you knew in your past."

Shock went through her. How could this woman she'd only just met see so easily through her? With a sound of impatience, she took a step back. "This is different." The words exploded from her lungs.

"It isn't," Chloe said matter-of-factly.

A bitter laugh bubbled past Jane's lips and she stalked over to the corner of the room. She peered out the floor-length window down into the streets below. For as good and intelligent and all things kind Chloe Edgerton was, she'd been born to an altogether different world than Jane. As the daughter, and now sister, of a marquess, she didn't bear the shame Jane knew for her illegitimate beginnings. She pressed her forehead against the cool windowpane. Chloe was firmly settled in her world, whether she wished it or not. Jane, on the other hand, straddled two very different worlds—the glittering Society she'd never belong to courtesy of the fraction of blood given her by the Duke of Ravenscourt and also that shameful, scandalous world of an actress-turned mistress. There was no belonging for her. There was only the hope of leaving everything and reestablishing something that mattered.

Her school.

From the crystal windowpane, the harsh smile on her lips reflected back at Jane. A finishing school she'd not given proper thought to because she'd been so very consumed with Gabriel's touch and the connection they shared.

She started as Chloe's visage pulled into focus behind her. The young lady settled a soft hand on her shoulder. "I do not know your story." Which story did the young woman refer to? The lies of her birth? Or the lies that brought her into this household? "Nor is it my place to know." In the glass, she searched Jane's face with her gaze. "Unless you wish to tell me."

Gabriel's lethal promise last evening snaked about her. She closed her eyes. *Tell her. Tell her, not in the hope she'd understand the desperation that brought forth this deception.* But tell her so she could be freed of attending this ball and any other...and Gabriel.

127

"It does not have to be now," Chloe said softly with a slight squeeze of her shoulder. "Come along, we are off to your first performance." She made to leave.

Jane could not do this. Not anymore. The ruse had been different when they were cold, calculated strangers. Now they were people; loyal brothers, loving sisters. These people she could not deceive. "I was not sent here by Mrs. Belden," she said quietly. The words echoed damningly in the quiet room, and yet Chloe continued forward, as though they'd never been uttered.

At last her words registered. Chloe turned back, her brow furrowed in consternation.

With a painful breath, Jane dropped her gaze to the tips of her slippers. Slippers she would one day pay for with the funds given her by the duke. Would it matter to Chloe and Gabriel if she paid for those stolen gifts—gifts she did not want nor desire? Gabriel deserved the truth. Her throat swelled with emotion. Both Chloe *and* Gabriel, but mostly the man who'd flagellated himself with guilt for kissing a member of his staff. When in truth, she'd never been a member of his staff. She was a liar. A charlatan. A pretender of the worst sort. Guilt stabbed at her heart.

A thousand questions filled Chloe's eyes. "Jane?" The perplexity in the young woman's eyes only deepened the guilt rolling through Jane in waves.

Before her courage deserted her, she continued. "I *was* an instructor at Mrs. Belden's."

"Was."

Jane nodded, and too cowardly to focus on that emotionless utterance, pressed ahead. "I was there for a year but deemed unsuitable." The Duke of Ravenscourt's very legitimate daughter flashed to her mind. With her cruel smile and taunting words, the young woman had hated Jane for no fault that was her own. "She did not take to my sharing Mrs. Wollstonecraft with the young ladies." Did she imagine the smile on the other woman's lips? "I was turned out for it, without a reference." Jane folded her arms at her chest. "There was a note," she forced out the most shameful part of her truth past numb lips. "From your brother. A request for a companion."

"And you pilfered the note?" Shocked outrage would be preferable to the gentle question there. There was no recrimination. Just a desire to understand and those dratted tears filled her eyes. She blinked them back.

"I did. Your brother requested a companion for you, for two months' time. In two months I will—" She flattened her lips.

Chloe searched her face. "What will happen in two months, Jane?"

Except for the lies and deception she'd practiced upon the Edgertons, at the very least she could provide this small truth. She drew in a breath. "Funds were settled on me, by my father." Surprise lit the young woman's eyes—the first outward reaction from the collected young lady. Guilt twinged at the likely erroneous assumption drawn that presented Jane as a lady, an assumption she did not bother to correct. "In two months I will receive funds which will be mine to use as I wish."

"What will you do with your funds?"

"I will set up a school. A finishing school," she said softly. "It will be different than the schools run by the Mrs. Belden's of the world," she spoke on a rush at the frown that formed on Chloe's lips. Jane lifted her palms up. "It will be a place where young women," who dwelled on the fringe of respectability, like her, "will be encouraged to use their minds and trust their judgments. I am so, so sorry about the lies between us." *You and Gabriel.*

Her revelation was met with a long stretch of silence, made more powerful by the tick-tock of the ormolu clock atop the fireplace mantel. At last, Chloe spoke. "If you are determined to establish a school for young ladies," Not necessarily ladies by Society's standards. "And that is what has brought us together, then," she collected Jane's hands. "Then that is why we're together. Your secret is yours, Jane." She frowned. "Is your name in fact, Jane Mun—?"

"Oh yes. Though I was referred to as Mrs. Munroe at Mrs. Belden's." She lowered her gaze. "I am not married, nor have I ever been."

Except, this understanding between Jane and Chloe could not be so very simple. The secret was a deception she'd practiced not only on Chloe, a woman who after just several days considered her a friend, but also Gabriel. "Your brother deserves the truth."

Chloe's eyes went wide and she gave her head several sharp shakes. "No. No. No. No." She slashed the air with a hand. "Gabriel sees the world in absolutes." Her heart spasmed. "He sees only the white and black but never the gray between."

Yes, the coolly aloof lord who'd so kissed her and who, even for just several stolen moments had felt connected to would never understand. And yet—"Perhaps, but he is deserving of the truth." All of it. With absent movements, she retrieved her spectacles and then toyed with the useless pair. Regardless of how a nobleman would view a young woman turned out for having struck the son of an earl who'd put his hands upon her person. Even as the thought entered, she thrust it aside. Gabriel was a good, honorable man. He'd not hold her guilty for crimes of another. She drew in a shuddery breath. He'd only hold her guilty of the crimes that were hers.

Chloe gave her a gentle smile. "Now come," she took her free hand. "Gabriel is waiting below."

Her heart tripped a beat. "The marquess." She flinched. Was there another?

A mischievous twinkle set the young woman's blue eyes aglow. "I do concur. It would be a good deal preferable if my charming, affable brother, Alex, were to accompany us. Alas, we are to be with Gabriel's miserable self."

"He is not miserable." Those words escaped her and she curled her toes into the soles of her slippers at that revealing defense.

Chloe, however, gave no outward reaction she'd noticed anything awry. "That is good of you." She slipped her arm into Jane's. "You are loyal," she said as she steered her from the room. They fell into step down the quiet corridors. "But he really is quite miserable, you know." Chloe waved a hand. "Very high-handed."

Yes, he'd proven himself to be that on numerous occasions since she'd entered into his employ. Annoyance stirred in her belly. Still— "You are fortunate to have his support." Life was a good deal harder with no support.

Chloe snorted. "I'd appreciate him a good deal more if he accepted my resolve to remain unwed and ceased treating me as a woman in need of his guidance. Ah, here we are," she said as they came to a stop at the top of the stairwell.

Gabriel paced the white, Italian marble foyer. His elegant black cloak whipped about his long legs and Jane stood frozen, stilled by his masculine perfection. With his midnight black, unfashionably long hair and broad, powerful shoulders, he was that first man—virile and strong. "Where in blazes are they?" That impatient question carried up the marble stairs.

Her lips twitched at that reminder of how very real and human he was. He was no marble God. He was just a man. Who happened to curse.

The butler glanced up the stairwell and caught her eye. His eyes glittered with amusement. "They are above stairs, my lord."

"Yes, I know as much," he said, his tone heavy with impatience. "I'm wondering—"

"He means we are here, Gabriel," his sister called down.

Her words startled him into a stop and his cloak snapped noisily. "At last," he complained.

Gabriel's words ended on a soft hiss of shock.

His sister stood at the top of the stairwell, and yet it was the stranger alongside her who commanded his attention, captured his notice and he was ensnared all over. He blinked. Jane Munroe? Surely not? Where were the spectacles and the severe chignon and…

Then she wet her lips, a nervous gesture on her part.

By God, Jane Munroe. There was nothing plain or bitter or ugly about this woman, gossiped about by Society. She was the goddess Aphrodite, rose from the sea foam, to torment with her beauty. He opened and closed his mouth several times, but could not manage one single utterance. At his notice, color blossomed on her cheeks and God if he did not want to go back on every honorable pledge he'd vowed where she was concerned and make her his.

Chloe urged the young lady forward. They stopped before him and waited. His sister stared pointedly at him. His mind raced. There was something expected of him? Words? Actions? Unscrambled thoughts? With a deliberate cough, Chloe tipped her head in Jane's direction.

"Where are your spectacles?" he blurted.

A becoming blush stained Jane's cheeks as she hastily placed the wire rims in their proper place. By God, they did nothing to detract from her beauty. She was still more striking than Aphrodite, Goddess of Beauty. How had he failed to see it from the moment he'd first met her?

His sister coughed into her hand.

Gabriel remembered himself. He sketched a jerky bow. "Mrs. Munroe." *Jane.* She could only be Jane, in this moment.

She dipped a curtsy, holding his gaze with a boldness he admired. "My lord."

It was a sin the name belonging on her lips went unuttered. *Gabriel. My name is Gabriel.*

Several liveried servants came over and saved him from making a cake of himself any further with his gaping mouth and lack of words. The footmen helped the young women into their cloaks and then Joseph rushed forward and pulled the door open. Arm-in-arm, Chloe and Jane filed out before him. He drew in a deep breath and lingered at the doorway, taking a moment to appreciate the gentle, seductive sway of Jane's hips.

"My lord?" Joseph drawled with such dry amusement, Gabriel flushed.

"Er, yes. Very well." He tugged at the lapels of his cloak and set out after Jane. And his sister. Jane Munroe was a companion and nothing more.

What a bloody liar. As he walked to the carriage, he remained with his gaze fixed on Jane. She was a blasted beautiful woman. Just then, she placed her fingertips in the servant's hand and with a murmur of thanks that made the young man's cheeks flush, allowed him to hand her into the coach.

At the momentary flash of masculine appreciation in the man's eyes, Gabriel balled his hands into fists. With a growl, he stomped the remainder of the way. As though feeling Gabriel's burning gaze trained on him, the servant glanced at his employer. His throat bobbed and he backed quickly away. Gabriel pulled himself up into the carriage and paused.

The two young women, seated side by side gave him no choice but to claim the opposite bench. He slid onto the seat and, a moment later, the coachman closed the door. The carriage rocked into motion.

In a bid to not openly stare at Jane, Gabriel tugged the red velvet curtains open and peered out at the passing London streets. Jane's visage, however, reflected back in the crystal pane and he used the opportunity to study her in ways he shouldn't notice her. Yet, how had he failed to appreciate the heart-shaped contour of her face or the long, thick, golden lashes that shielded her crystalline blue eyes? In the windowpane, their stares collided and she hastily averted her gaze. He frowned. How could she remain so indifferent to him when she'd so upended his righted world?

His sister, ever the consummate talker, filled the quiet. "Have you ever attended the opera, Jane?"

Over the years, his sister's inquisitiveness had proven the bane of his existence as she'd asked improper and impolite questions she had no place knowing an answer to. In this moment, however, he found himself grateful for his sister's bold questioning.

Jane shook her head. "I have not."

What a travesty. A woman of her grace and beauty should be performing the intricate steps of the waltz at some ball or soiree, with her golden hair awash in candlelight. Except, on the heel of that came the image of her in the arms of some nameless, faceless stranger. A growl climbed up his throat and stuck there.

Two stares swung in his direction; one concerned, one curious. "I am fine," he gritted out.

Chloe returned her attention to Jane. "The opera is a good deal better than attending some ball or another." Her lips pulled into a grimace. "At those events one is expected to dance." She gave Jane a wide smile.

An awkward pall of silence descended over the carriage and Gabriel settled into his seat. For the first time, he truly wondered about the young lady in his employ. Before, it hadn't mattered being the context of her references or the role she would fulfill, but this evening he was filled with a desire to know who, exactly, was Mrs. Jane Munroe? She spoke with the elegant, refined tones of a young lady, which indicated a woman who'd received a proper education. Yet, how had she come to this moment where she served in the role of companions and governesses to other English ladies? Up until this moment, she'd been quite tight-lipped with details about her past, neatly stepping around his inquiries.

It was just an evening at the opera. He'd faced far greater trials and tribulations, most of them right in this very household, than attending one performance by Rossini with a woman who'd wreaked havoc upon his senses. He closed his eyes a moment and drew in a deep breath.

How bloody difficult could that be? His gaze met Jane's. Bloody impossible.

An interminable carriage ride later, they drew to a stop before the crowded theatre. As the ladies shuffled ahead, he trailed at a safe distance. "You've never been to the theatre, then." His sister's words reached back to him.

Jane had said as much at breakfast. Could his sister not remember the excited sparkle in her companion's usually guarded blue eyes? They entered through the theatre doors and he kept his gaze on Jane's proudly held shoulders. The hall resonated with the booming laughs and loud whispers and conversations being had about the space. Jane paused and his sister continued on several feet.

Jane, the blonde temptress, remained frozen with her head tipped back at an impossibly awkward arch as she stared up, just as she'd done in the foyer of his home, with her lips parted in a silent awe at the ceiling. He froze mid-step, his gaze trained upon her, For the remainder of his days, when he was old and at the end of his life, alone for a decision that had been his, he would remember her in this moment— innocently wide-eyed and awed by a mural of Adam and Eve in the Garden of Eden with an apple between them.

Much like Jane, a veritable Eve, tempting, enticing, taunting Gabriel with his desire for her.

"Jane?" his sister called, and then she made to take a step forward.

He should let her go and maintain the careful distance. He should pretend he'd not noted her gawking at the ceiling.

Then, he'd spent the whole of his life doing exactly what was expected of him. He quickened his stride and fell into step beside her. She startled at his appearance and cast a desperate look at his sister. Chloe, however, marched ahead, moving at an unladylike clip that would have scandalized their mother. "You were admiring the painting," he said with a gentle teasing.

She stole a glance at him. "The mural," she corrected with a smile.

About them, leading members of Society stared openly at him conversing with his sister's companion. And he would have had to be blind to not see the manner those condescending matrons peered down their noses at her.

He fisted his hands. Had he ever been so self-absorbed that he'd failed to note the disdain shown to people the *ton* took as interlopers? *You don't care. Isn't that the person you've perfected through the years? One who tends his familial obligations and nothing more?* Shame turned in his belly. Yet Jane, with her strength and courage in making a life for herself, without the assistance of anyone, was far stronger than he or any other member of the whole damned peerage.

They reached his private box.

"Imogen and Alex will be in attendance," Chloe prattled. She claimed the seat at the right of the box as she was wont to do. "I do so wish they'd share our box." A beleaguered sigh escaped her. "Alas, they are wedded." She wrinkled her nose.

Jane hesitated and then slid into the far left seat. As Gabriel sat, Chloe's chattering filled the tense quiet. "Does your excitement for the evening's festivities meet your expectations?" She gave a cynical tilt of her chin, motioning to the theatre below where lords and ladies craned their necks about, shamelessly taking in the other peers about them.

"I daresay, the real reason for my excitement would be for the performance itself." As Jane spoke, she cast an eager look about the expansive hall.

Chloe leaned past Gabriel and held Jane's gaze. "No one attends for the performance."

"How very sad," Jane lamented as the orchestra thrummed their haunting strands of Rossini's work. "One should not cease to find joy in something just because…" She paused. Her brow wrinkled.

He leaned closer, intrigued by the confusion in her eyes. "Just because what?"

She met his gaze. "Because there are unpleasant others about." Her eyes reflected surprise at her own words.

Whatever his sister would have said was lost to the increasing tempo and beat of the orchestra's tune. From the corner of his eye he took in Jane as she returned her attention to the stage and studied the performance below with an uncharacteristic softness in her expression.

Attending the theatre was no different than attending a soiree or ball or dinner party. Each affair bore the same social obligations. They were events in which lords and ladies went through the motions of life focused on the power and wealth that drove their relationships. Since he'd left university and fulfilled the responsibilities thrust upon him as the Marquess of Waverly, he'd gone through the proper motions of Societal life. All the while knowing there would be nothing more for him or of him, and that had empowered him. For it was a decision in which he'd reclaimed his life after years of abuse and shame.

Seated beside Jane, with a cynical eye he looked out to the stage, at the actors and actresses, as they performed Rossini's *La Cenerentola* with the theatre abuzz in loud whispers of gossip. These affairs were as contrived and tedious as any ball or soiree attended by members of the *ton*. Surreptitiously, he peered at Jane. Her wide eyes formed round moons and her lips were parted, as she stared at the stage with the kind of awe worn by Adam when he'd first seen Eve with that succulent apple in her temptress' fingers. He glanced down at the stage and then back to her. Had he ever been so innocent as to find pleasures in events such as these?

"Are you enjoying the performance?" he drawled quietly. It was a foolish question. The lady's appreciation was stamped in every delicate plane of her heart-shaped face. And it was there on her quivering mouth—that mouth he'd kissed so recently and dreamed about since.

Jane started and then glanced about to ascertain whom he spoke to. A small frown formed on her lips. "I am." She returned her attention to the stage below.

Ah, the lady was displeased with him. He should leave the stilted relationship between them as just that—disapproving and combative. He spoke on a hushed whisper. "You have an actress' soul, then."

A crimson blush stained her cheeks and all pleasure faded from her eyes. Regret cut into him. She angled her chin up a notch. "My lord?" There was a challenge there.

He waved a hand. "Do not allow me to distract you from your pleasures, Jane."

Her frown deepened at the use of her Christian name and she stole a glance at Chloe. Had the young woman heard that bold familiarity? When she returned her gaze to Gabriel's, there was a fiery challenge in her eyes. "Are you having fun at my expense, my lord?"

A flush burned his neck. "Is your opinion so low of me?" Or was her opinion so low of any gentleman? His breath stirred the loose curl that hung over her eyes and it took a physical force to keep from brushing back that silken tendril. "You came to enjoy the theatre."

"I came as your sister's companion," she pointed with a pragmatism that made him grin. She peered around Gabriel and cast a glance over at Chloe. He followed her stare. For all his sister's protestations to the contrary, she studied the stage below with a similar excitement he'd spied from Jane.

Gabriel and Jane fell silent and the lively orchestra's song filled the theatre with the contralto Cenerentola soaring through the enormous ceiling.

"Despite what you believe, Jane, I did not make light of you," he whispered quietly against her ear. She stiffened at his side but remained silent. In an effort to restore the lightheartedness to her earlier expression, he asked, "Do you speak Italian?"

She tore her gaze from the stage below and gave her head a slight shake, eying him warily. What man put that guardedness in the eyes of a lady so young? Then, weren't his own sisters scarred by life in a way that should have shown him that age had little impact on experience?

"Once there was a king who grew tired of being alone. He searched and he found three who wanted to wed him."

"What did he do?" That whisper was pulled from her as though she warred within herself to maintain the walls she'd erected between them and her own curiosity to know more of the play.

"He despised show."

"Who did he choose then?" With her words and eyes she urged the answer.

"Ah, but you have to listen," he whispered once more as the contralto's soaring lyrics filled the massive theatre, drowning even the whispers of gossip to a dull hum. "He chose innocence. Innocence and goodness."

And God, for all his vows these twenty years, with Rossini's words, he understood the seductive pull of those gifts—innocence and goodness.

FIFTEEN

With Gabriel's innocuous translation of those seductive lyrics, desire flared to life once more, potent and strong. "You should not," she said, her words pleading to her own ears.

"I am merely translating the words, Jane." His husky whisper invaded her spirits. "Listen to their song." She closed her eyes and lost herself to the seductive trance cast by each word translated. "My heart is pounding." As was hers. In a desperate rhythm for him. "Why is my heart pounding so?" Because it, too, possessed the same madness as her own heart? Which was madness. With the exception of his kiss, he'd been quite clear in his feelings for her. He liked her not at all. And she liked him not at all. And...She was the very worst liar. "How lovely that smile." His breath fanned her cheek; the hint of brandy, once ugly and vile, a sign of sin and evil, filled her senses until the power of those spirits threatened to make her drunk with a desire for life and him. "That smile. It enters my heart and brings me hope." He shifted close and his powerfully muscular thigh brushed her leg and crushed her satin skirts.

Was that subtle movement deliberate? The weighted feel of him against her burned her through the fabric of her gown, touched her skin, and went deeper into her blood, heating it so it coursed through her body and threatened to set her ablaze. *I want him. I want him in ways I've never wanted, or wanted to need, a person.* She longed for his touch in ways that marked her as her mother's daughter. Jane pressed her eyes closed.

The hall surged with a crescendo of applause as the orchestra concluded act one of Rossini's latest masterpiece and it brought her eyes flying open. Jane blinked away the befuddlement woven upon her senses by Gabriel's innocent translations and careless touch.

"It is splendid, isn't it?" Chloe's cheerful voice piped in.

It was a blasted disaster. Jane nodded jerkily. "Yes." Her skin pricked with the burn of Gabriel's gaze upon her person.

Chloe dusted her gloves together and scanned the crowded theatre as the lords and ladies present rose from their seats to take in the real show—the one occurring about them in respectable theatre boxes. Jane welcomed the young woman's distraction and used it as an opportunity to bring sense to her muddied thoughts, and to set Gabriel firmly from her mind.

And focus on the whole disliking him business.

He stretched his legs out in front of him and hooked them at the ankle, wholly elegant and so unaffected it was impossible to not admire him and the figure he cut.

She groaned. Whatever was the matter with her? A harlot's heart through and through.

"Are you all right, Mrs. Munroe?"

Gabriel studied her with that familiarly veiled expression. She swallowed hard. "Fine. I—"

He leaned close. "It appeared as though you groaned."

Chloe swung her attention to Jane. "Oh dear, are you ill, Jane?"

"I—" Am utterly humiliated. Sick with embarrassment. Though she didn't suspect that qualified as any type of illness.

The red velvet curtain fluttered and she gave thanks for the sudden interruption.

A tall gentleman with black hair and familiar chiseled cheeks filled the entrance. At his side stood a crimson-haired lady with a wide smile on her face. Gabriel stared unblinking at the couple a moment.

Chloe emitted a small shriek and leapt to her feet. "Imogen, Alex."

This was the roguish brother spoken of by Chloe, and his beloved wife.

Jane hesitantly climbed to her feet and took in the reunion between the young ladies who spoke with such rapidity, her head spun. Through their animated greeting, she hugged the edge of the wall in an attempt to make herself as small as possible from the intimate exchange. The two women gesticulated wildly. Wide smiles wreathed their faces as they alternated between soft laughter and excited chatter. Jane fisted the fabric of her gown. How long had she been alone? She'd given up on the dream of even a friendship as a child. Yet just now, seeing the two so effortlessly communicate, that age-old longing she'd thought firmly buried came rushing back. There was something so very bittersweet in the happy exchange that she forced her gaze away to Gabriel and his brother.

Seemingly forgotten by the Edgerton women, the two brothers took each other in with a guardedness that was belied by the close, animated greeting between sister and sister-in-law. She used their quiet meeting as an opportunity to study Gabriel alongside his brother. With their midnight black hair and chiseled features, they might be taken for mirrors of one another. And yet, there was whipcord strength to Gabriel's lean frame that bespoke an understated power.

What was it about Gabriel that so fascinated her? By his own admission and his brusque manners, he was, as his sister pointed out, nothing charming in the way of those roguish sorts. Yet, she preferred the sincerity of him to the—

Gentlemen now looking openly at her.

She flushed as she became aware of the four pairs of eyes trained on her person.

"Hullo," the red-haired young lady said with a gentle smile.

Jane bit the inside of her cheek. Why did the woman have to smile and be kind? Why could this new Edgerton lady not be the cold, callous, and calculated peers Jane had encountered before now? "Hello," she replied and dropped a belated curtsy.

Lady Imogen Edgerton looked between Chloe and Gabriel in an apparent request for an introduction.

"Oh, of course," Chloe said, pointing her gaze to the chandelier overhead. "Allow me to introduce you to my new companion, Mrs. Jane Munroe."

Silence met the young woman's pronouncement as Lady Imogen Edgerton and Lord Alex looked on with questions in their eyes; those silent queries landed on Gabriel. Unflappable as ever, he gave no indication he'd noted or cared about the inquiries from any of his kin.

"Mrs. Munroe," Lord Alex drawled. A half-grin formed on his lips and he sketched a polite bow. "I daresay, I hope you're being well compensated for the task of going about with these two." His words ended on a grunt as Chloe buried her elbow into his side.

"Do hush. I'll not have you run off Jane. I quite enjoy her company."

Emotion balled in Jane's throat. No one enjoyed her company. Her existence had been an unwanted and unwelcomed one that had only ushered in years of being that same unwanted and unwelcomed person. Chloe was merely being polite, but the fact that she'd even uttered those words wreaked havoc on her orderly emotions. "If you'll excuse me a moment?" she said, hastily. She skirted the edge of the marquess' private box, aware of his gaze following her movements. "I—If you'll excuse me," she repeated dumbly, and then before questions could be asked by the ever inquisitive Chloe, Jane slipped from the box and set the curtain aflutter once more.

Her heart pounded as she walked with quick strides through the corridors. Lords and ladies in their evening's finery still filled the hall. Jane kept her gaze trained forward, avoiding the interested stares that flicked over her person by those who'd clearly identified her as an outsider in their glittering world. She dimly registered the orchestra plucking the strings, signifying the beginning of act two, and she welcomed the exodus of the lords and ladies curiously peering at her as they returned to their seats. Jane continued on in the opposite direction. No purpose to her movement in mind, merely an escape from the kindness of that family whose trust she even now violated.

She was an interloper. A liar. A—

A shriek escaped her as a figure stepped into her path. Heart thudding hard, she pressed a hand to her chest. "Forgive m…" Jane swallowed the rest of that apology and choked on the remaining syllable as the loathsome figure she'd hoped never to see again leered at her. The same man whose vile soul and ugly touch had haunted her dreams.

"Jane Munroe," Lord Montclair murmured. "We meet again." His breath still stank of brandy. It slapped her face and sucked the breath from her lungs and assailed her senses. How could that scent be so potently seductive when Gabriel had cradled his snifter, and not inspire this revulsion that turned in her belly?

Jane backed up a step. He would never go away. He was relentless. "What do y-you want?" She detested the faint tremor to her tone. She cast a glance about. If Gabriel discovered her now, he'd turn her out without a backward glance.

By the triumphant glint in his eyes, Lord Montclair delighted in her fear. That victorious gleam forced her feet to stop moving. Observers or not, she'd be damned if she allowed him to cow her. Not again. He'd already cost her the post within his father's household and too many evenings of rest. She'd not allow him to steal her pride, as well.

She made to step around him.

He matched her movements, effectively blocking her retreat.

Her heart pounded hard in her ears, and she hid her shaking fingers in the folds of her skirts, lest he see the effect he had on her. He'd relish in her fear. He always had. "What do you want?" Her chest heaved with the force of her emotion. Of course, she'd known entering London Society it was possible their paths would cross, but she'd believed her role as companion would have kept her along the edge of ballroom floors and out of notice. From within the auditorium *La Cenerentola's* aria soared through the rafters and carried to the hallway.

"Is this any way to treat the man you set out to seduce?"

Rage melded with fear and threatened to blind her. She bit down hard on the inside of her cheek and tasted the metallic hint of blood. "I did not seduce you," she said, proud of the steady deliverance of those words. "You forced your attentions on me."

His eyes became thin, impenetrable slits of displeasure. He shot a hand around her wrist and lowered his head close to hers. "I do not force my attentions on anyone, sweet Jane." The heavy liquor scent on his breath slapped her face. Nausea churned in her belly. How very different than when the hint of spirits clung to Gabriel's breath.

In an attempt to dislodge Montclair's hold, she yanked her hand. He maintained his manacle-like grip upon her person. "Remember yourself, my lord."

"Remember myself?" he chuckled. "You are no lady, Jane. Society would find nothing untoward with my advances on a whore's daughter."

Her heart dipped at his accusation. She dug deep for the deserved indignation at his vile words, but shock and years' worth of those very same charges being leveled at her flooded forth with a potency that robbed her of a suitable response.

Lord Montclair captured one of her loosely arranged tresses. "Come, nothing to say now? Did you think I didn't know the truth of your birthright?"

Her mind raced. How had he discovered...?

"It took nothing to figure out who'd sent you to my father's household and who continued to scuttle you about," he supplied, correctly interpreting her unspoken thoughts.

"Let me go." She yanked her hand once again, managing to wrest free. She took a step backward. "Whore's daughter or kin of the queen, I would never sully myself by taking one such as you to my bed," she spat.

Rage mottled his cheeks and for one moment she suspected he intended to hit her, but then his gaze moved past her shoulder. She followed his gaze to the tall, commanding, and, more importantly, familiar figure just several paces away. Eventually, when Montclair was gone, there would be the implications of Gabriel's arrival and inevitable questions. A man who loved his family as he did and pledged to ruin her if she brought shame to his family would turn her out in a moment. For now, however, her shoulders sagged in relief at his unexpected, but timely, arrival.

Montclair inclined his head. There was a faint mocking sneer on his lips. "Waverly."

Gabriel moved that cool, crystalline stare between her and Montclair, and ultimately settled that hard gaze upon the earl. "Montclair," he drawled. A lethal edge of steel underlined that one word greeting.

For one horrifying moment, Montclair gave Jane a prolonged look, and she believed he intended to reveal all to Gabriel, here, now, in this public way. But then, he dipped a bow and gave her a lingering glance. At the determined glint in his eyes, gooseflesh dotted her arms. He stepped around the marquess and made to take his leave. Some of the tension left her, but then he suddenly froze.

She fisted her hands at her sides as Lord Montclair looked Gabriel up and then down. What game did the calculated lord even now play?

"With your regard for your sisters, I would expect more care in the selection of their companion." Jane went taut; her body so brittle she feared if she moved in any way she'd splinter apart. "Surely a woman with Miss Munroe's past is unfit company for your sister." She flinched at his deliberate use of her title miss. Then, the earl shot her a condescending grin and left.

With the earl gone, stilted silence stretched on between her and Gabriel. The lively strains of the string instruments from *La Cenerentola* mocked the volatility of the moment. She shifted on her feet. "We should return to your sister."

He narrowed his gaze all the more. "That is all you'll say?" That same unforgiveable tone fit more with the stranger who'd first ordered her from his home than the gentleman who'd shown her more kindness than she'd known in the course of her life.

At the unrelenting gleam in his eyes, Jane wet her lips. "Er, yes?" The silver flecks of fury in his eyes threatened to ignite. She skittered her gaze about. No, it was too much to hope he'd simply ignore the meeting he'd stumbled upon. Gabriel took a step toward her and took her by the wrist in a manner similar to Montclair's, and yet, so entirely different. For the power of his hold, there was still a gentleness, a care to not harm her. Blasted emotion clogged her throat once again, but then she met his gaze squarely and there was nothing warm or caring in the green of his eyes. A startled squeak escaped her as he pulled her into a nearby alcove. The curtain settled about them, shrouding them in darkness. She blinked several times in an attempt to bring his face into focus. When she did, she wished she'd left the veil in place.

Fury, outrage, and questions stamped the harsh, angular planes of his face. "How do you know Montclair?" His touch, however, remained gentle and for that, she knew he'd not harm her. His words contained a wealth of questions that as a gentleman he was too proper to bluntly speak.

"Ask the question you truly wish to ask," she spat out. "Am I his lover?"

Gabriel relinquished her so suddenly, she stumbled back. The thick, crimson fabric rustled in protest. He folded his arms about his broad, muscular chest and shrunk the space between them. "Well, madam?" His thick, black lashes swept low, veiling his eyes. But not before she detected the flash of fury there.

She bristled. Granted, she was a liar and a thief by the manner in which she'd entered his household, but she'd not be intimidated by him and treated as though she were a mere child. Jane angled her chin up. "Does it really matter whether…?" Her attempt at bravado slipped as he lowered his brow to hers. Of course it mattered. Even she, an outsider to Gabriel's world, knew that.

"Madam, you try my patience." A muscle ticked at the corner of his right eye. "You have five minutes, Mrs. Munroe."

He could gift her five hundred minutes and it wouldn't be enough. "You have already found me guilty. What matters what I say at this point?" Those words dripped with bitterness that came from years of scorn by polite and proper gentlemen and ladies.

"Your first minute is up," he said, coolly unaffected.

Did you expect him to be kind and concerned? Not when he loved his siblings as he did? Still, for Jane's indignation at Gabriel's high-handed treatment and the fury in his tone and words, he was not undeserving of those sentiments. Not when she truthfully looked at the circumstances that had brought her to this moment and to his life. And now, she wished she'd handled everything so very differently. Wished that the truth she'd given to Chloe, she'd given to him before the likes of Montclair had robbed her of choice— once again.

"You are rapidly approaching the end of your second—"

"You asked if I know Lord Montclair," she said tiredly. "And I do." Her sudden admission cut into his warning. Unable to meet his probing gaze, Jane slid hers to the curtain. "Not in the way you…" Her skin warmed. "N-not in the way you alluded to," she attested.

Gabriel's eyes narrowed, but he said nothing. Finding courage in his silence, she continued. "I served in his father, the Marquess of Darlington's employ as the governess for his youngest sister." As vile as Lord Montclair had been, that was as kindhearted as his sister was. She and Jane had not had the close relationship that Jane knew with Chloe, but still the young woman had been kind and for that she would be eternally grateful. She stole a glance up at Gabriel, and though there was none of the warmth she'd known from him these past days, neither was there vitriol in his green eyes. Not wanting to relive the horrors of Montclair's touch, she shifted the conversation to safer, more comfortable topics—other lies. "I do not need spectacles," she blurted, in a desperate bid to slow the admission that she must give. Jane plucked the metal-wired frames from her face and fisted the delicate pair. "Chloe, Lady Chloe," she corrected, "insisted they earned attention for the wrong reasons, and yet, when I did not wear them, I found far greater difficulties." She clasped her hands together so tightly, the rims of her spectacles dug into her palm. Her skin burned at the intensity of his gaze trained on her.

At last, Gabriel broke his silence. "What manner of difficulties?" he asked through stiff lips.

That night in the Marquess of Darlington's parlor flashed to mind. The door closing. The click of the lock. Terror churned in her belly, and even knowing she was safe and out of Montclair's clutches, the vile remembrance of his hands upon her rolled through her as though it had just happened.

"Jane?" he prodded, and had his tone been cold and aloof she could have found the strength to conclude the telling. Yet it was so gentle and soft that a single teardrop rolled down her cheek.

She angled herself away lest he see that crystalline sign of her weakness. "Lord Montclair decided I was..." Her tongue grew heavy with embarrassment. She discreetly rubbed at that lone tear on her cheek. "There for his enjoyments." Glasses in hand, she folded her arms and attempted to rub warmth back into the chilled limbs. She jumped as Gabriel settled his hands on her shoulders, angling her back around. Lethal fury emanated from his frame, potent and powerful, and oh so comforting that another blasted drop squeezed past her lid. Jane swiped it away.

"Did he put his hands upon you?"

Her skin crawled with the memory of his lips, hard and punishing on her skin, as he'd worked his wet, ruthless mouth over her neck. Her lips still throbbed in remembrance of his vicious kiss. She gave a jerky nod.

A black curse escaped him and echoed around the alcove. If she were a proper young lady, the ugliness of that obscenity would have stung her ears, and yet she'd been born to a different station and heard things no polite lady would have ever heard. She continued on a rush, desperate to have this admission complete. "I did not want him to." Her fingers tightened reflexively so hard about the frame in her hands, she snapped the fragile metal. She stared dumbly down at the spectacles rendered useless. "He said I'd given him reason to believe that I did." She drew in a shuddery breath. Her lips twisted up in a mirthless smile. Then since she'd come into Gabriel's home she'd panted and sighed after him like the whore's daughter she was.

"I will kill him," he whispered.

His words brought her head up. "No," she said matter-of-factly. "You won't." Yet, her heart skipped several beats at the rage etched in the chiseled planes of his face. He would do that for her. No one had ever dared defend her. Her father had shuffled her off from one position to the next, but that had been a mere obligatory responsibility for the by-blow born to his mistress. It hadn't truly been of any real caring or affection. Would he still defend her when he discovered the origins of her birth? Knowing the man who cared for and defended his kin, she suspected he would. Because that was what honorable men did. She'd just always believed that none of those men existed.

She forced words past a tight throat. "I didn't seduce him." The admission came out as a raw whisper. Desperately craving space between them, she backed up. Jane knocked into the alcove wall. She braced her hands on the hard plaster at her back, seeking the strength to stand. "For his insistence that I did, entice him, that is," she rambled. "I did not. Nor would I ever…" She bit her lower lip. For her mother's blood in her veins, she still didn't have any more idea on how to seduce a man than a sister taking her orders. What reason did Gabriel have to believe she didn't simply go about kissing or enticing her employers? "I expect given our…" Her face heated all the more. "Our exchanges," His eyebrows dipped. "That you would believe Montclair, but I…" Her words ended on a startled gasp as he closed that slight space she'd placed between them.

"You think I would believe Montclair?" His breath tickled her face, soft, like a gentle caress and with the faint hint of mint, so very different than the earl's from a short while ago. He cupped her cheek and she stiffened as his touch had the same entrancing effect upon her senses.

What hold did he have upon her?

SIXTEEN

When Gabriel had been a boy of seven, he'd realized that in his father's presence, he'd clenched and unclenched his hands at his sides. The reflexive action had been borne of a desire to wallop his sire, but more, a fear that he'd sought to hide from the heartless beast.

As he'd come upon Jane and the Earl of Montclair, a thick haze of red had coursed through him, a sentiment that had felt a good deal like jealousy. She'd clenched and unclenched her hands at her sides. And he'd seen the movement that bespoke her unease and then the terror in her eyes. It marked the rakish Montclair a liar before the man had opened his mouth and uttered his vile charges about her.

Even now, a burning fury coursed through him, a desire to take Montclair apart for having put his hands upon Jane…

He noticed me.

That slight imperceptible pause spoke volumes of Montclair's notice and called up the legacy of violence he carried in his blood.

He steeled his jaw. "Montclair is a snake." Had he sung in praise of her beauty, she could have not been more captivating in her appreciation. Her lips parted on a soft moue of surprise and then she darted the tip of her tongue out and trailed a path over the line of her lips. He followed that movement, hating himself for being no different than Montclair and wanting her. Despite what she'd just shared.

She glanced away from him and looked to the tiniest gap in the curtain. "Why are you here?" Her words emerged ravaged and breathless.

Why am I here? Why had he taken a hasty leave of his family and left Chloe alone with Alex and Imogen to follow after Jane—a companion in his employ who was mature enough and capable enough to care for herself? But then, was that entirely true? He'd seen how Montclair had eyed her like the last ice at Gunter's and he with the intention of laying claim to it. He'd never been one to prevaricate. "I worried after your sudden flight." He tightened his mouth. "And seeing Montclair, I had good reason to be concerned."

Jane sucked in a shuddery breath. "Why can you not be the arrogant, domineering lout I'd first believed you to be?"

His lips twitched and some of the tension left his frame. Gabriel cupped her cheek, bracing for her to pull away. She angled her head and leaned into his touch. "Would you have me believe Montclair's charges for no other reason than the station of his birth?"

The muscles of her throat moved with the force of her swallow and she gave another nod. "Y-yes. Y-yes, that is just what I'd expect you to do."

Was that what every other gentleman had done before him? Never had he resented his station in life more than he did in this moment. Those snide, hypocritical members of the *ton* who'd look down upon the Jane Munroe's of the world, while lauding the late Marquess of Waverly, a man who beat his children, for no other reason than his status at birth.

Jane pressed her fingers against her temple and rubbed. "What are you doing?"

"I told you, I—"

"Not here," she cut in on a soft cry. "With your Italian words and your—" A delicate, pink blush stained her cheeks.

"And my what?" he prodded. He'd have everything between them. The lies hinted at by Montclair. *All* of it.

"Your kiss," she said on a harsh whisper.

Gabriel stilled. He opened and closed his mouth several times.

"And, not that you've kissed me of late." Even as he'd dreamed of it, every day since. "Nor should I think of you as I do. I should forget your kiss and your touch." And it would destroy part of him if

those embraces meant nothing to her. Not when she'd been the first—
"But…" Her spectacles fell from her grip and landed on the carpeted
floor with a soft thump. She covered her face with her hands. "What
are you doing to me? Why can't you be the condescending, judgmen-
tal man you first showed yourself to be instead of this seductive, gentle
person I do not know what to do with?"

Not once in the course of his thirty-two years had he been
accused of being a rogue. He'd taken great pains to distance himself from the image crafted by his father and, in many ways, adopted
by his brother. With gentleness, he encircled her wrists in his hands
and lowered her arms to her side. "I was not seducing you." Shame
and embarrassment added a gruff quality to his tone. Guilt turned
within his belly. "You likely see me no different than Montclair." A
man whose residence she'd shared, who should have respected her
station within his father's household, and had instead forced his
attentions on her.

"You are nothing like Montclair," she said tiredly. "If you were, it
would be a good deal easier."

Her words gave him pause. He should not press her for answers on
that statement, but he could no sooner quell the question on his lips
than he could shake free this link to his father's blood. "What would
be a good deal easier?"

Jane dropped her gaze to the floor. Why should he be shamed,
when he'd been the one to take her lips under his? Why, when he still
wanted her, now just a curtain away from a theatre full of potential wit-
nesses to their scandalous actions?

He brushed the backs of his knuckles down her cheek and that
gentle caress brought her lashes fluttering once more. "I am not a
rogue, Jane," Those grounded words brought her eyes open. "I am not
a charming gentleman with easy words around ladies as my brother."
He'd prided himself on that for the better part of his life. Now he
wished he possessed even a trace of Alex's capabilities for then he'd
have the words to muddle through this exchange. He brushed his
knuckles along her jaw. "I would never force my attentions upon you
or deliberately set to seduce you with words or actions." *I would want*

you because you desire me as I desire you. "When I shared Rossini's words, it was so you might know everything about the opera you'd looked forward to."

Jane leaned up on tiptoe and shrunk the distance between his tall, and her much shorter, frame and kissed him.

Gabriel stiffened and then with an agonized groan, he devoured her mouth with his. There was nothing gentle or sweet about the exchange. It was an explosive meeting of two people who both wanted one another and who'd fought that longing for too long. "I want you," he whispered as he dragged his lips down her neck.

As he gently sucked at the sensitive skin, a moan slipped past her lips. "I w-want you, too."

Her words had a maddening effect and a low moan rumbled from deep within his chest. He drew her close to him. Gabriel dropped his attention to the exposed flesh of her décolletage and of their own volition, her hands came up and she anchored him close.

Ah, God damn his soul. He was his father's son and there was no escaping that crime. Gabriel rucked the skirts of her gown up higher, higher, ever higher and exposed her limbs. Then with desperate movements he ran his hands over her hips then lower. He stroked the expanse of her thigh and drew it about him, testing her against his form. His aching shaft pressed against the front of his breeches and another groan rumbled up from his chest and stuck in his throat.

The orchestra's distant music, muffled by the pounding of his heart, faded altogether. "We should stop." *Please do not agree.*

"We should." She dropped her head back, allowing him access to her neck once again. He groaned and released her skirts, shifting his search of her body higher.

She whimpered as he returned his attention to her neck. Jane pressed herself against him and drew his head forward. He stumbled and pulled his mouth away, attempting to right her. To no avail. She tipped and crashed backward onto the thin-carpeted hall. Gabriel caught himself on his elbows, above her. The red velvet curtain fluttered and danced damningly about them.

He registered the three pairs of feet in front of his gaze. Two pairs of slippers and a gleaming set of Hessians to be precise. Gabriel swallowed hard and forced his stare upward.

Chloe and Imogen stood with their mouths rounded in like circles while Alex's green-eyed stare gleamed with the faintest trace of amusement.

"Gabriel?" Alex's slightly bored drawl jerked him back to the moment. He held a hand out to assist him to his feet.

Bloody hell. This night could not possibly get any worse. Then Lady Jersey with Lady Castlereigh arm-in-arm stepped into the corridor. Their gazes collided with Jane and Gabriel's prone forms, and as one their eyes formed round moons. He bit back a curse.

He'd been incorrect. The night had just worsened.

Positioned between Lady Imogen and Chloe, Jane hurried through the theatre. Her skin pricked from the burn of Gabriel's gaze on her back and the stare of the two Society matrons who'd chosen the most inopportune time to slip from the performance and enter the corridor and see—

She closed her eyes a moment. The matrons saw her twined with Gabriel's form like a vine of ivy around a powerful tree. Jane swallowed a humiliated groan and quickened her stride. Had there been any doubt before this moment, there was none now—she was her mother's daughter. A shameful, wanton harlot who'd kissed a man and been discovered before his family and two ladies of the *ton*. She pressed a hand to her mouth and buried a moan.

Chloe shot her a sideways look. Concern filled the young woman's overly kind eyes. "I say, it was a splendid performance, don't you think, Jane?"

Tears pricked behind her lids. Why would this woman be so kind? Why, when she'd shamed her and Gabriel's entire family as she had? Chloe slid her arm into Jane's and patted her hand. "Alex will have secured the carriage by now," she said with swift assurance.

They made their way down the stairs, through the quiet hall, and outside to where, as Chloe predicted, Lord Alex stood beside the waiting carriages. A surge of relief slammed into her; a desire to hide within the black lacquer walls and hope that those two women failed to glean her identity and—

She thrust aside the futile wish. Society matrons made it their affair to know the affairs of others. Even now, the scandalous exchange between Jane and Gabriel was likely circulating through the theatre fodder for the gossips and no black lacquer carriage would shield her from that.

Jane accepted the assistance of the coachman and allowed him to hand her inside. Chloe followed, and for one moment she believed Gabriel should take a carriage with his brother and for one longer moment, wanted him to and spare her the humiliating agony of sitting beside him and Chloe.

Alas, the fates were uncooperative this evening. Gabriel climbed inside and the wide space of the carriage grew smaller under the power of his frame.

A moment later, the servant closed the carriage door and the conveyance rocked forward. The rumble of the carriage wheels along the cobblestones filled the quiet, punctuated by the beat of her heart in her ears. She gripped the edge of the seat and replayed each horrid moment of this evening.—Montclair's presence. Her wanton kiss. The discovery.

And worse, the lie between them still remained. She stole a sideways glance at Gabriel. He sat, white lines drawn about his tightly held mouth. A faint muscle jumped at the corner. What was he thinking?

"Did you enjoy the performance, Gabriel?" Chloe's hopelessly bad question broke into the stiltedness.

Jane peered at the young lady who wore a wide smile on her heart-shaped face.

The muscle twitched once more. "Chloe," he bit out.

The young lady pointed her eyes to the carriage ceiling. "Gabriel has always enjoyed the opera."

Jane stared at Chloe. Had the young lady gone mad? Did she not comprehend the implications of this evening's debacle? For all of them.

"I thought it was a lovely performance." Apparently, *not* by the cheerful pronouncement. "I—"

"That will be all, Chloe," Gabriel snapped with such rigidity to his tone that Chloe went instantly and uncharacteristically quiet.

The carriage rattled along the remainder of the infernal trip, in absolute silence for which Jane was grateful. It gave her an opportunity to try and sort her tumultuous thoughts and put to rights some of her confounded emotions.

She could not stay here. That much was clear now. Her presence only posed a risk to Chloe's reputation and ability to make a match. She'd given her the truth, though in actuality it was Gabriel who'd been deserving of the details that had brought her into his household. Instead, she'd infringed upon his family's kindness and left disaster in her wake, as she was wont to do.

She dimly registered the conveyance rocking to a halt before the stucco façade of Gabriel's townhouse. He didn't wait for the carriage to come to a complete stop before he shoved the door open and leapt to the ground. He reached back and handed his sister down. Chloe frowned up at him and opened her mouth as though she wished to say something, but with the glower he trained on her, wisely remained silent and sprinted ahead. Gabriel turned back to the carriage and held his hand out.

Jane hesitantly eyed it, and then avoiding his gaze, allowed him to hand her down. She scurried ahead.

"Mrs. Munroe?" he said quietly, momentarily halting her retreat.

She froze.

"Await me in my office."

This was to be her sacking. They all began with a call to the nobleman's office. And this time, like the others before it, there would be no reference. Jane gave a jerky nod and then raced ahead. What household would retain her for their daughters' care—she a woman, discovered with her employer atop her, with her skirts rucked about her lower legs, her lips swollen from a kiss? A sob escaped her lips as she sailed through the entrance, avoiding Joseph's gaze and made her way through the house to Gabriel's office. She turned the corner and collided with Chloe.

The young woman caught her about the shoulders and steadied her. "Forgive me," she insisted. "I do not have much time." She glanced about. "I suspect Gabriel will arrive any moment to speak with you."

To sack her.

She claimed Jane's hands and gave them a gentle squeeze and met her gaze with a seriousness she'd not before seen in Chloe's eyes. "He will do right by you." What did that mean to a woman such as her, a whore's daughter? Then Chloe clarified. "He will not see you ruined."

"Ruined?" she parroted back. A sad smile turned her lips. She'd been ruined at birth. "I am long past that."

A momentary flash of pity lit the young woman's eyes.

Uncomfortable with that show of support and that useless, unwanted emotion, she gave a smile. "I believe I saw to that all on my own, Chloe."

The soft thread of boot steps sounded down the corridor. Chloe gave her hands one more squeeze and then darted down the hall. Jane turned quickly and pressed the handle. She slipped inside the darkened room and took in the space she'd stood, pleading for her post not even a week ago, feeling remarkably as though she'd come full circle.

She'd required sanctuary for two months. She'd managed to steal but a week. And for that theft, she'd sacrificed the Edgerton family's good name.

Jane stilled, sensing with an intuition that only came from her body's inexplicable awareness of his presence. She turned in the middle of the room and folded her arms about her person.

Gabriel stood framed in the doorway, watching her with an inscrutable expression.

She wet her lips, and he followed that slight movement a moment and then closed the door behind him with a soft click. Jane clenched and unclenched her hands at her side. In that assessing manner of his, he dropped his gaze to that distracted movement. When he met her stare once more, a frown marred his lips.

Then, wordlessly, he strode past her and made for his sideboard. He swiped the nearest decanter, poured two snifters of the amber brew, and returned. "Here." He thrust the glass at her.

Jane held her palms up. "No. I…" Something hard in his eyes silenced those words. She accepted the glass and cradled it in her hands. Of all the households she'd been employed in, every last man had drunk the dratted spirits. What was it about the favored spirits that called to a man? Perhaps the ability to make a person forget? Jane raised the glass to her lips and took a tentative sip. Her lips pulled in a grimace and she exploded into a fit of coughing. She glared at him. "Th-that is horrid." She'd never understand men. There was no accounting for their interests and tastes.

Some of the hardness left Gabriel's mouth and that ghost of a smile hovered on his lips. He took a sip of his drink and then carried it to his desk. With a casualness she marveled at, he propped his hip against the edge. Then, being a male and a marquess no less in their Society permitted one that effortless ability in all regards. And just like that, all hint of warmth was gone, replaced with that frozen impenetrableness so that she wondered if she'd merely imagined any softening.

Unnerved, she dropped her gaze to the liquid contents of her glass. "I am sorry," she said quietly and then grimaced at how useless those regrets were.

"Do you think I hold you responsible for what transpired this evening?" That terse question brought her head up.

Jane stared unblinking, back at him. "I kissed you." And then she darted her stare about the room, half expecting interlopers to charge forward with their accusatory fingers pointed. She raised the glass to her lips, took another sip, and then promptly choked. "It really is horrid stuff. Utterly awful."

He took a long swallow and then set his glass down on the desk beside him. "I am sorry," he said without preamble.

Jane cocked her head, but otherwise remained silent.

"It was not my intention to seduce you at the theatre."

"Yes, you've said as much." Three times now.

"We will marry," he continued as though she'd not spoken.

Her heart fluttered and she touched her chest. Her reaction made so very little sense. Why should she have this odd lightening when she'd never before even considered marriage and to a powerful nobleman no less? Surely she'd heard him incorrectly. Though, there had never been anything wrong with her hearing. Or at least she didn't believe there was. And yet it had appeared he'd said...

He nodded. "Marry." Gabriel shoved away from the desk and stalked over to his sideboard. He poured several fingerfuls into his snifter, and then seemed to think better of it. "As in wed." And then added another splash for good measure.

As in, she had heard him correctly.

"Wed?" Gentlemen like him did not wed women such as her. *But then, he doesn't know who I really am.*

He gave a brusque nod. A flash of horror glinted in his eyes, the first indication as to just what Gabriel Edgerton, the Marquess of Waverly, felt about the prospect of marriage to her. Her heart dipped back into its proper place and resumed beating a steady, unaffected rhythm. She studied him as he downed the contents of his drink in a single, long swallow. "Of course, given the state of..." He tugged at his cravat. "Our discovery." He was as awkward at picking his way through this discourse as she. Was there a gentleman in the whole of the kingdom less interested in sealing his marital fate than Gabriel? "There is no recourse except marriage."

Except there was. There were the funds settled upon her and her finishing school and a life free of a gentleman's interference in her life. Where was the joy in those prospects that had once given her hope?

Her mother had depended on a man and it had cost her all. Yet in this moment, there was something sweetly seductive in the prospect of being wanted for her. She clasped her hands to her throat. "You would marry me?" Guilt twisted in her belly and she fisted the glass so hard, her knuckles turned white. She was undeserving of his apologies and his generous offer. "You would marry me, when you don't even know me?" In a world with men who'd take their pleasures where they would, when they would and how they would, this was the kind of man Gabriel Edgerton, the Marquess of Waverly, was. He'd wed her, a stranger, to protect her. *Or is it to protect himself,* a suspicious voice needled. Was Gabriel so very committed to being the responsible gentleman that he'd marry her and sacrifice his own happiness in the process?

He rolled his shoulders and took it, however, as a question. "I see little choice in the matter." She winced at those emotionless words, hating that they grated on her heart.

To give her mind something else to fix on, Jane took another sip. She dissolved into a sputtering fit of coughing. No, she could not do it. She set the glass down hard. Foul, stuff the spirits were. They did have a dulling effect upon her senses that at least drove back the edge of anxiety that had dogged her since her and Gabriel's discovery at the opera.

"I'll obtain a special license in the morning," he said, with all the wariness of a man who'd been saddled with the weight of the world upon his shoulders.

Despite the disarray of her own life and her inevitable ruin, her heart tugged with regret. Poor Gabriel. He cared for his sisters and his brother. Would he take on Jane, a stranger, to appease his misplaced sense of guilt? Never would she steal a person's freedom, not when she so craved it for herself. She gave her head a slow shake. "I cannot," *will not,* "wed you." Not in good conscience. Not when she'd long disavowed marriage to a nobleman. And most certainly not to a nobleman who appeared more eager to march the steps to a guillotine than find him wed to her. His reaction should not matter, and yet, oddly, a pang struck her heart. She could not maintain the lies between them. Not any longer.

Gabriel froze with his drink midway to his mouth. "Of course you—"

Before her courage deserted her, she cut across his defense. "The Earl of Montclair was not wholly wrong about me, Gabriel."

SEVENTEEN

From the moment he and Jane had tumbled from the alcove at the London Opera House, horror had attacked his senses over the inevitability of his fate—he had no choice but to wed. He, who'd vowed to never take a wife, or bring offspring into this world, had lost self-control, and as such, had confined himself to a life with everything he'd disavowed. That horrifying prospect had occupied his thoughts— until now.

Jane shifted back and forth on her feet and wrung her hands before her.

The Earl of Montclair was not wholly wrong about me...

The other man's allegations rushed to the surface. "What are you on about?" he bit out.

She cleared her throat. "I told you I was employed by the Marquess of Darlington," she said over him when he made to speak. "I did not explain what happened after I'd been," she wrinkled her nose, "relieved of my responsibilities from that post."

Glass in hand, Gabriel stalked over to Jane. "Continue," he snapped, impatient at her unfinished thoughts.

"Er, yes. Right. You see." He didn't really see anything this night. "I was given employment at Mrs. Belden's. I served as one of her instructors." Dragons as Chloe referred to those other women. "For nearly a year." Jane ran the tip of her finger along the fabric of the sofa in a distracting manner and when she spoke, her words came fast and furious. "One of the *ladies*," Bitterness laced that word. She slashed the

161

air with a hand. "She spoke to the headmistress about me and I was turned out. I discovered your note."

"My note?" By God, she hadn't! Gabriel set his glass down hard on a nearby side table. Liquid splashed over the rim.

Jane's color heightened. She peeked up at him. "I didn't steal it," she said defensively. "It was left on the edge of Mrs. Belden's desk and I…" She let her words trail off. He studied her through narrowed eyes trying to make sense of that pink color on her cheeks. Was it guilt on the lady's part? Regret? "And yet, I did steal it, didn't I?" she whispered, more to herself. "That, and everything else."

Impatient with that confession which really answered nothing, he tipped her chin up and forced her gaze to his. "I do not understand," he bit out. "Explain yourself, madam."

"I am a liar." She flinched. "An impostor."

He let his hand fall to his side, momentarily robbed of words and thoughts. An impostor? A chill stole through him. "What are you on about?" he prided himself on the steady deliverance of those coolly spoken words, while disjointed questions spun through his mind.

"I intended to tell you. And then your sis…" She colored. *His sister.* He narrowed his eyes. What secret did Chloe withhold from him about her mysterious companion? Jane cleared her throat. "That is, *I* resolved to wait until the right moment to tell you." She furrowed her brow. "Though in hindsight there never would have been a right opportunity. Not truly."

Her incessant prattling snapped his patience. "Jane?" he demanded in clipped tones.

"I was not sent by Mrs. Belden as your companion. I stole the missive and presented myself before you in the respective role." The long column of her throat worked. "But I am not that woman, Gabriel. And you deserve to know that."

Shock slammed into him; froze him immobile. Surely she jested? And yet by the agonized glimmer in her blue eyes and the sheen of tears she blinked back, these were the only true words she'd spoken. He took a step back, and then shook his head, as he desperately tried to make sense of her admission. "I do not understand." Gabriel winced, knowing he must sound like the greatest lackwit, gaping at her.

Silence met his confusion.

Despite his intentions to turn her out on the day they'd met, she'd wheedled her way into his thoughts and household. With her deception, she'd involved his sister Chloe. Fury thrummed through him. He took in this interloper into his household, a mere stranger, a woman he'd not known at all. Jane must have seen something terrifying in his eyes, for she took a quick step back. He shot a hand around her wrist, halting her retreat. Gabriel raked an icy stare over her slender frame. "Explain yourself, madam," he seethed.

Jane pulled free and held her palms up in an entreating manner. "I did," she said quickly, "at one time work for Mrs. Belden, that is. But then she…" She blushed. "She let me go. I'm really rather deplorable at maintaining employment, which I understand reflects ill, and I could maintain that it was not my fault…" She captured her lower lip between her teeth and worried the plump flesh.

All the while, Gabriel tried to sort up from down. A dull humming filled his ears. This woman had entered his home, slipped into his employ and, despite his early misgivings about her suitability, had refused to leave. He captured her wrist in his hand once more, in a hard, relentless grip. By God, he'd put his sister's care into this woman's hands? "Who are you, Mrs. Munroe," he hissed. Self-loathing filled him for risking his siblings' well-being once more. "If that is even your name."

"It is," she said and flinched.

He lightened his hold but did not release her. How was he to believe the words of a stranger who'd lied her way into his home?

"My name is Jane Munroe," she said quietly. "I have served as a companion and governess as I said." He searched her face for the truth of her claims, wanting to believe her—to believe *in* her. "However, I lost my post at Mrs. Belden's and discovered your letter." Her cheeks blazed red. "You required a companion for your sister—" Jane's words ended on a gasp as he stuck his face close to hers.

Gabriel relinquished her wrist and she hurried to put distance between them. "And you lied your way into my household?" For that, she'd robbed him of his freedom, the vow he'd taken long ago, and sealed his fate. A black curse escaped him.

Jane backed up a step, tripping over herself in her haste to be free of him. "It was just to be for two months." Now it would be forever.

He stepped around the couch and stalked toward her. "And lied to me at every turn."

"Not all lies," she said futilely. She continued her retreat.

He was unrelenting, advancing forward. "And you risked my sister's reputation?" That was by far the most egregious affront. For it was Chloe's happiness and security he'd resolved to protect.

She compressed her lips into a flat line. There was no rebuttal to that accurate charge.

By God, how indignant she'd been when he'd questioned her suitability. Lies, all of it. Then the ugly truth slipped in. "Did you intend to trap me?" he asked, coming to a stop just a handbreadth away.

She opened and closed her mouth several times. "Trap you?" Jane shook her head hard. "Egads, no." By the horrification etched in the delicate planes of her face, the lady appeared as eager to marry him as he did her. Then she widened her eyes. "You think *that* is why I am here?" He bristled at the horrified, mirthless laugh to escape her lips. Those lips he'd kissed not even thirty minutes ago, and longed to kiss, even despite her deception. What a weak fool he was. "Oh, no. No. No. Not at all, my lord."

So, he was my lord again. Unknowing why her dismissive response should chafe, he folded his arms at his chest. "Madam?" he demanded pointedly.

"I am trying to assure you I have no designs upon your title." She gave her head an emphatic shake. "I cannot wed you."

There it was again. Cannot. An ugly, niggling of a possibility took root and grew in his imagination. "You are married," he said, his voice garbled. Even as her marriage would have preserved his vow and freedom, the idea of her belonging to another twisted at his insides.

"Married?" she squawked. "Me? No!" She smoothed her palms over the front of her skirts. "I am…" She hugged her arms to herself. "That is to say, I am illegitimate." There was a slight catch in her voice and she coughed into her hand.

He stared blankly at her. "Illegitimate?" he repeated, dumbly. That was the lady's secret? The origins of her birth?

Jane nodded. "A bastard."

Something in the matter-fact deliverance of that harsh term grated on his nerves. Gabriel scowled. "I know the meaning of the word illegitimate, Miss Munroe."

"Oh." She dropped her gaze to the Aubusson carpet and made a show of studying the pale threads interwoven upon the fabric. "Yes, of course."

Gabriel took in the forlorn sight of her. Why, she'd taken his displeasure as a sign of disparagement. Annoyance built in his belly, coupled with some other odd tightening he didn't care to evaluate, for it hinted at a weakness for this woman, a desire to erase the hurt that stemmed from years of likely rejection.

She clasped her hands before her. "So, as you see," she said when the silence stretched on. "There really is no need for you to offer marriage." *To me.* Those two unspoken words hung on that sentence. A viselike pressure squeezed at his heart. He tried to imagine Jane Munroe going through life as an object of ridicule and rejection for circumstances that had nothing to do with her, a stigma that had followed her and forever would.

He detested the idea of her, not many years older than Chloe, and the same age as Philippa dependent upon herself, serving as a companion and governess to spoiled, unkind English ladies. "What will you do?" A resourceful woman like Jane Munroe who'd served as companion and governess, had likely put thought into what she'd do after she left. His gut tightened. At the prospect of her gone from his life. At the prospect of her alone.

An unfettered smile turned her lips. How could she smile? "Oh, you see." Once again, he didn't see anything in this murky world she'd thrust him into. "My father settled funds upon me. When I reach my majority, I will attain the money and then I will no longer be…" She pressed her lips into a tight line. Dependent upon others.

Her father had settled funds upon her. That handful of words far more telling than anything else she'd uttered to this point. "Who is your father?" he asked quietly.

Jane snapped her attention upward. "My father?" She eyed him with a sudden wariness. "It does not matter."

And yet it did. It mattered because he wanted to know those details about the young woman before him with her thousands of secrets and unspoken truths. Her response set off the first stirring of warning bells. For the man to have settled funds upon her, he must be a member of polite Society. "Is he a nobleman?" Was it a man whose events he'd attended or spoken with at his clubs? He gripped his glass so hard, his knuckles turned white, as the need to know took on a lifelike force. "Jane?" he demanded with a touch of impatience.

Except, she'd proven herself incapable of being cowed. At his gruff command, she frowned and walked the perimeter of the sofa, ultimately putting distance between them. "It matters not, Gabriel. I will have my funds and you," she gave a slight, nonchalant shrug. "And you are, of course, free of any obligations or sense of responsibility for me."

Very well, she'd remain deliberately evasive. He relented. "And you'll retire to the country and live a quiet," *unwedded,* "life." There was a crime in knowing that a woman of her beauty and spirit would remain forever alone, on the fringe of living.

Then, what was the alternative? Her married to a man who'd take her to his bed and give her children and—he growled.

Jane jumped. "I will establish a school," she said quickly, likely interpreting that harsh sound as a show of his impatience. "A finishing school," she clarified. "For young women." She set her chin at a resolute angle. "A school different than Mrs. Belden's and those others attended by young ladies. It will be for women such as—" She fell quiet.

Her. For women such as her.

Gabriel dragged a hand over his face. Her school would be a place for the young women who straddled the peerage and impolite Society.

He hated that she hovered on the fringe of both. Despised it when she was worth more than most members of the peerage together. He let his hand fall to his side. "When do you attain your funds, Miss Munroe?"

"In two months," she replied automatically. "One month three weeks and two days, to be precise," she clarified, more to herself.

Two months. The length of time he'd required a companion for Chloe. He bit back a curse. And also one month three weeks and two days until she had access to those funds. Which posed the question— what would Jane do in the interim? "Who is your father?" he repeated. For the man would surely care for his daughter until then.

She hesitated and for a long moment he expected her to maintain that great secret. Then she squared her shoulders and met his stare with an unrepentant boldness. "The Duke of Ravenscourt."

Christ. She was one of the Duke of Ravenscourt's illegitimate issues. He swiped his glass from the table and stalked over to the window.

"My father's identity changes nothing," she said, hurrying over to him. "I will not wed you simply because my father is a duke." She paused. "He is not truly a father," she said softly. "Nor will he expect anything of you where I am concerned. None of Society will."

No, the man was no father. A callous, heartless, self-indulgent nobleman who'd allow his offspring to take post after post in the households of other callous, self-indulgent noblemen was no different than the Marquess of Waverlys of the world. Jane, through the years, had been without protection and care. Just as Chloe and Philippa. He clenched his eyes tightly closed.

And yet, if he did not wed her, he'd be no different than any of them. "There is no choice but marriage, Jane," he said tiredly. The decision had been made long before her admissions. Rather, it had been settled in a small alcove at the London Opera House.

A soft cry escaped her. "What you are proposing is madness, Gabriel." And just like that, he was Gabriel again to her. "I will not wed you so you might be assuaged of unnecessary guilt. You've nothing to be guilty of."

He spun around so quickly, she stumbled back. "I have everything to be guilty of," he barked. "In my advances, I am no different than

167

Montclair. No," he gave his head a sad shake. "There is no recourse but marriage."

The sadness and unease lifted from her eyes and a familiar spirit and fury ignited within their blue depths. "You would be high-handed with your sister and you think to be high-handed with me. I am not yours to look after or care for." Did he imagine the trace of regret in those words? "You would wed me to do the honorable thing." She planted her arms akimbo. "I do not want you to do the honorable thing. I want my freedom. I want my school." Her chest moved with the force of her emotion.

Jane's message could not be clearer—she did not want him. Where was the sense of relief in avoiding that institution he'd sworn to never enter into? Surely, it would come later but for now, only regret churned in his belly. He managed a stiff nod. "Very well, madam. It is not my place to force your hand. I will speak to your father in the morn." He made to step around her.

She stepped into his path. "My father?" She flattened her mouth into a hard line and gave her head a brusque shake. "You do not need to speak to my father."

"Don't I?" he arched an eyebrow. "You'll not wed me." Her stony silence stood as testament to that. "And if you'll not remain here as my wife, then you cannot remain here. Where will you go for the next two," one month, three weeks, and two days, "months' time?"

She jutted her chin up, but by the flash of unease in her eyes, the young woman knew she was without options.

He flicked an imaginary piece of lint from his sleeve. "Now if you will excuse me, Miss Munroe, I bid you goodnight."

With that, he turned on his heel and left.

EIGHTEEN

The following morning, with a meeting scheduled with the Duke of Ravenscourt, Gabriel sat in his office. He glanced across the room at the long-case clock and frowned. Where in blazes was he? He'd sent a missive around last evening and had been quite clear in—

A knock sounded at his office door. At last. "Enter," he barked and tossed his useless pen down.

Joseph opened the door.

His brother, Lord Alex Edgerton, once rogue, now notoriously infatuated, thoroughly besotted, and hopelessly in love husband, stood at the entrance.

"I sent around a note late last evening," Gabriel said without preamble, as he shoved back his chair and stood.

Alex, consummately unaffected, raised a dark eyebrow. "Do you mean a summons? You sent 'round a summons." Those eerily reminiscent words flung at him not even two months ago, when Gabriel had worked at putting Alex's disordered life to rights, raised a dull flush on his face.

The butler's lips twitched as he pulled the door closed behind him and left the two Edgerton brothers alone.

A groan of impatience climbed up Gabriel's throat as he reclaimed his seat. "I do not have time for games," he said tersely, adopting his most coolly, distant tone.

An inelegant snort escaped his brother as he strode over to the sideboard and helped himself to a brandy.

"Isn't it a bit early for a brandy?" he asked with an automaticity that came from years of scolding and lecturing his brother, and then from the corner of his eye registered the nearly empty glass upon the corner of his desk. With a silent curse, he placed himself in front of the snifter and hid it from his brother's line of focus. Then, with the time he'd had of it since Jane's appearance in his life, he'd taken to drinking a good deal more brandy, at all godforsaken hours of the day.

Alex paused mid-stride and wheeled around. A half-grin formed on his lips. "I daresay with the time you had of it last evening you could benefit from a strong glass of spirits as well." He resumed his march to the sideboard. "And I recommend beginning with the consumption of that snifter at the edge of the desk before you move on to your finer spirits," he drawled without so much as a glance back.

His neck heated and with his brother's attention on the crystal decanters before him, Gabriel removed the snifter from the mahogany surface and carried it around the desk. In a bid to reassert the order and logic he'd perfected over the years, he claimed the familiar chair behind the mahogany piece that had once belonged to their father.

*You are a weak, fool...*The sneering, snarling visage slipped in, as it often did, and he thrust back the memory of his father. When he looked up, he blinked several times and registered Alex in the seat opposite him, staring expectantly back at him. "Er, yes, right," he began and took a long sip of brandy.

"I didn't yet speak," Alex said with the same droll humor he'd always adopted.

He set his drink down hard and launched into the reason for his brother's presence. "I expect you know why you're here. I had also expected you earlier this morn." There was, after all, his meeting with the duke.

A hard, humorless grin turned Alex's lips and he leaned forward. The office resounded with the soft thunk of his snifter settling on the surface of Gabriel's desk. "You do realize it is you who is responsible for this latest scandal," he drawled. He rested his palms on the edge of his chair and drummed the arms in a grating rhythm. "Would you not say *you* are the one in dire need of a lecture on proper behavior and responsibility?" This time.

The truth of Alex's accusation ran through him. Gabriel took a deep breath and rubbed his palm along his forehead. "You are indeed correct," he said, tiredly. With last night's scandal, he'd jeopardized Chloe's name and fueled gossip about a woman who'd already been scorned since birth.

"Feeling something does not make you weak, Gabriel," his brother said quietly, all dry mirth gone from his expression and words. "It makes you human."

Human. To be human meant to be weak and broken and battered. It meant one hurt and he wanted no part of any of it. "Regardless," he infused an edge of steel to his words. "My actions with Ja..." His brother gave him a pointed look. "With Mrs. Munroe, last evening were unpardonable."

"I daresay you are permitted the use of Christian names with last evening's..." Gabriel's lips twitched. "Er, activities."

Annoyance stirred. How could the other man be so casual and amused by the muck Gabriel had made of the Edgerton name...and Jane?

Alex leaned forward once more and rested his palms on his knees. "I have never, in the course of my life, known you to be anything but devoted and loyal to the Edgerton name."

Recently, those words would have been a stinging accusation from the younger brother who'd blamed him for failing their siblings. And rightly so. Now, however, with a recent understanding reached between them, they'd moved into an easier peace. Oh, their friendship would never be fully restored to the uncomplicated, wholly loving one they'd known before their father's influence. But they had rekindled a friendship and, in a world where Gabriel was remarkably without anyone but Lord Waterson, he'd have his brother's friendship.

Gabriel swiped his glass and took another sip. "Regardless, I've dishonored the Edgerton name." He didn't give a jot about the name that could burn in hell with his father's vile soul for all he cared.

"Do you truly expect me to believe you care so very much about the marquisate?" There was a gentle prodding there that hinted at accusing Gabriel of being the liar he was.

He gave a brusque shake of his head. "No, you are correct." Alex had proven correct about far more than he'd ever credited through the years. He drew in a breath. "I care about Chloe's opportunity to make a match."

Alex frowned. "And what of your Mrs. Munroe?"

"She is not my Mrs. Munroe." He would have had her as his wife to do the honorable thing and right his wrong. But the lady had been abundantly clear in her feelings of that prospective state. He'd never before met another soul who disavowed marriage in quite the same manner—perhaps they suited better than he'd ever credited.

His brother snorted and leaned back in his chair. "I daresay a woman who makes you forget yourself, in the midst of an opera hall, before all Society, is at the very least something to you." He looped an ankle across his knee.

"Do not be preposterous," he scoffed. "It is not possible."

"And why is it not possible?"

His mind went blank. "It...because..." He closed his mouth. "Because it just isn't," he managed to force out. Bloody hell, he felt like a blasted green boy. Gabriel tugged at his suddenly too-tight cravat. A relationship with Jane was as preposterous as...well, he wasn't sure just what it was as preposterous as, just that it was.

His brother continued relentlessly. "I expect being wedded to the lady will at the very least result in...er...more, at some point."

That brought Gabriel blessedly back to the reason for Alex's presence. He squared his shoulders and regained control of his tumultuous thoughts. "That is why I've asked you to come. We will not be marrying."

Alex opened and closed his mouth several times, looking like a fish plucked from the sea. "What?"

He waved a hand dismissively. "We will not be marrying."

His brother's eyebrows dipped. "Alas, if you've brought me by with the intentions of righting your wrong, my marriage to Imogen prevents any such assistance," he said in ill jest.

Contained within the depths of his green eyes, there was so much disappointment and disgust that Gabriel shifted. It should not matter what his brother believed or didn't about Gabriel and yet, it did. He'd not have this man whom he'd just reestablished a connection with, believe he'd not at the very least try and do right by Jane. "It is…I offered," he bit out.

"And she said no?" Shock underscored Alex's question.

He nodded once, recalling Jane as she'd been last evening, bold and proud and wholly uninterested in marriage to him. "And she said no, which is why you are here." Gabriel slid his gaze to the closed door and then returned his focus to Alex. He found his brother watching him with curiosity with eyes that may as well have been a mirror of Gabriel's as similar as they were. "The lady has no interest in marriage." *To me.* An inexplicable pressure squeezed his chest. Why should that matter?

"I would say the lady is a bit past that decision."

And yet, it did.

"I never expected you to become this proper gentleman," he said with droll humor.

"I know." Alex grinned. "Love does peculiar things to a fellow."

In an unexpected moment of camaraderie, they shared a smile. Then Gabriel recalled what brought him by. His grin slipped. "I need you to take her."

His brother cocked his head.

Gabriel sighed. He was blundering this. "I need you and Imogen to allow the lady to remain with you until I speak to her father."

Alex stilled and then a sharp bark of laughter escaped him. He slapped his hand upon his knee and laughed so hard tears seeped from his eyes. "Th-the lady's father? You've gone mad."

Gabriel bristled. At least one of them could find humor in anything after last night's disastrous turn of events. "She is the Duke of Ravenscourt's daughter," he bit out on a tense whisper.

That brought an immediate cessation to Alex's laughter. He snapped a white handkerchief from his pocket and wiped off his cheek. "Beg pardon?"

What was so really difficult to follow about the admission? He glanced about. "She is…" He frowned, torn between explaining why he required Alex's support and protecting Jane's secrets. "She is illegitimate." A memory flashed to mind of her, as she'd been when she'd made that very admission, embarrassed, braced for his disdain. Gabriel took another long swallow of his drink.

Dawning understanding lit Alex's eyes. "Ahh."

An overwhelming urge to knock his brother on his bloody arse for that single syllable utterance filled him. He planted his elbows on the edge of his desk. "What?" he snapped.

Alex held his palms up. "I did not say anything."

"He has settled funds upon her," he continued on, opting not to debate the telling "ahh" Alex had uttered. "The lady desires her independence. She can no longer stay here." As it was, she should have never returned home with him and Chloe. However, the world had been so topsy-turvy last evening the rights and wrongs of her being here had been lost to confusion.

Liar. *You did not want to send her away.* Now, he had no choice but to send her away—for her protection. For Chloe's. For his. Every moment they spent together jeopardized the order and calm of his world and his very existence.

"I see," Alex, said, suddenly all seriousness. And by the understanding glint in his eyes, he did very well see.

"She requires but a temporary place." Gabriel consulted the long-case clock once more. "I have a meeting shortly with the duke and will inform him," *that I ruined his daughter. That she has nowhere to go. That she will not have me.* "That she requires his assistance." He shoved back his chair and stood.

Alex took that as his cue to leave for he came to his feet. "I will, of course, assist in any way you require."

He flexed his jaw, uncomfortable with the emotion from his brother who'd treated him with nothing more than icy disdain through the years. "Thank you," he said stiffly.

Alex gave him a gentle smile. "You still have not realized it, have you?"

He looked questioningly at his younger sibling.

"We help those we love. There is no chore in that." He gave a slight bow. "I will send my carriage around to collect Mrs. Munroe."

"Thank…" At Alex's pointed glance, he allowed those words to go unfinished. He inclined his head. "If you'll excuse me. I'm to speak to Jane before my meeting with the duke."

"Mrs. Munroe." Alex winked.

Perplexed, Gabriel glanced about for the lady in question.

His brother chuckled. "I suspect you care a good deal more than you would admit to even yourself," he said and pulled the door open.

Jane stood at the entrance, her fist poised to rap on the wooden panel. And for the hell of last evening and the uncertainty of today, a lightness filled his chest at seeing her there, wide-eyed like a night-owl frightened from its perch.

Effortlessly charming as he'd always been, Alex sketched a bow. "Mrs. Munroe. It is a pleasure to meet once again." He stepped aside, permitting her entry.

However, Jane, wholly unlike any other woman he'd ever before known, only eyed Alex with a healthy dose of suspicion. "Lord Alexander," she greeted as she fell into a deep curtsy.

Then, those of his and Alex's stations had given her little reason to trust. Her father, Montclair….how many others?

Alex slipped past her and left. Which also left Gabriel and Jane— alone. They stood there a long moment studying one another with her framed in the doorway, the panel open at her back. He cleared his throat and motioned her inside. "There are matters we should speak on, Mrs. Munroe."

NINETEEN

She'd received his summons early that morning. Jane had spent the better part of two hours since, both dreading the exchange and looking forward with an inexplicable anticipation of seeing him again. She told herself that after the chaos of last evening's scandal, he was familiar. He was the one constant in this cold, uncertain world she'd entered. Yet, in this instance, standing across the large, wide space of his office, with him looking at her through those hooded, black lashes, she was Mrs. Munroe.

Of course he should refer to her as Mrs. Munroe. Or Miss Munroe. But never Jane. So why did she, hovering at the edge of his office, miss hearing her name uttered in his mellifluous baritone?

"Mrs. Munroe?" he prodded gently.

She jumped and entered his office. "Forgive me," she said hurriedly. "My lord?" She dropped a curtsy.

A frown toyed at the hard line of his lips. Did he, too, crave the once familiar uses of their Christian names?

Gabriel strode across the expansive space, his large-legged stride ate away the distance between them and he came to a stop in front of her. His gaze fell to her lips and then slowly he reached an arm out. For a maddening moment she thought he'd kiss her. Her breath caught as she tilted her head back, but he merely closed the door behind her. Disappointment swirled inside, proving yet again she was her mother's daughter. "I will not take up your time, Mrs. Munroe," he said with an aloofness she only remembered from their first handful of meetings.

She shifted back and forth. "My lord?"

He stalked back to his desk and motioned her forward. "Please, sit."

How could he be so dispassionate following everything that had transpired? After he'd had his hand upon her thigh, his lips upon her skin? She wet her lips and took a cautious step and then another but did not take the proffered seat. Instead, she hovered at the leather winged back chair at the foot of his desk. "I prefer to stand, my lord."

He snapped his dark eyebrows together with a slight scowl on his face. Good, so he was not unaffected. He was just far more adept at maintaining falsities than she, the deplorable, caught-in-a-lie companion that Jane was. "Very well," he said from behind his desk. "Your trunks are being readied. I have spoken with my brother. He and his wife have agreed to allow you to visit until," he waved a hand about, "this situation has sorted itself out."

This situation. That was all she'd ever been. To the mother who'd loved a duke. To the duke who'd no need of illegitimate issue. Now to Gabriel. Why did this one hurt the most? Her throat worked with the force of her swallow. Then his words registered. "You are sending me away." She flinched at how very pathetic those words were.

Gabriel tugged out his watch fob and consulted the timepiece. "I have a meeting with the duke shortly, at which time I shall speak to him of your funds. In the interim, it is best for all," For Chloe. His innocent, unwed sister was the one requiring protection. "If you remain with my brother and his family." He stuffed the intricate gold piece back into his waistcoat pocket.

"Of course," she said stiffly. She smoothed her palms over her skirts. "Is there anything else you require?"

He shook his head. "That is all. I will visit following my meeting with the duke."

The duke. Her father. The same man who'd had to deal with the scrapes Jane had landed herself in through the years by shuffling her about to various posts, at her inability to hold whichever one he'd secured through his influence.

From the moment she'd stolen the missive from Mrs. Belden's office, this parting had been inevitable. Gabriel's magnanimity in light of her deception and the trouble she'd brought to his family was far more than she deserved. Yet, there was an agony of regret in knowing she would leave—Chloe—*him.*

But there would be her school and that would fuel her and sustain her. It would give her purpose and be the constant in her life. She pulled her shoulders back. "I would thank you for your kindness, particularly with my," her cheeks warmed. "My lying to you." She prided herself on the stable deliverance of those humiliating words.

He rose and came around the desk so she was forced to crane her neck back to look at him. "You need not thank me, Jane," he said gently.

She blamed dust for the sudden tears that popped behind her lids. Which was, of course, silliness. The marquess did not have dust. Not in his well-tended home. But then, why would she be crying? "But I do." He dropped his gaze lower, to where she fiddled with her skirts.

Jane stopped the telling gesture that had long been a sign of her discomfort. She lifted her eyes to his. "In my deception, I've brought difficulties to you, your sister, and your entire family." As much a burden now as she'd been since her birth. "And I am sorry," she said, knowing as the words left her mouth how hopelessly inadequate they were. "So very—"

He pressed two fingers to her lips, ending that weak apology. "Stop," he ordered on a whisper that was both gentle and hard all at once. Her heart thudded at the intimacy of his naked hand upon her mouth. "It is done." And yet, he did not draw back. Worse, she did not want him to.

Gabriel worked his gaze over her face, lingered upon her lips. He dipped his head lower and she leaned up to receive his kiss when he froze, his mouth a hairsbreadth from hers. "I should go."

"Yes." He should. There was his meeting. But more, they'd established this was wrong. Yet, there was this irrevocable pull between them. An awareness she'd never known of anyone. And it terrified the blazes out of her.

Either he had far more strength than she, or his desire for her was far less consuming, for he let his hand fall to his side, and then without another word, turned on his heel and left.

At the echoing of silence, her shoulders sagged. This was just another post, and he was just another man, and soon she'd have her freedom. Freedom that would soon be arranged and secured by the Marquess of Waverly—a mere stranger in the real scheme of life. Why, she'd known him less than a week and a handful of hours, yet, it felt as though she'd known him far longer.

"Gabe—"

A startled cry rang from Jane's throat at the unexpected intrusion. She wheeled around, a hand at her breast. "Chloe," she said.

The young woman's smile widened. "Jane. Good morning. I did not see you at breakfast this morning."

With last night's catastrophe, the prospect of food had left her belly churning with nausea. Unable to explain her absence, she said nothing.

Gabriel's sister glanced about. "Have you seen my brother? I needed to speak with him."

This was safer. Questions that required answers she could handle. "He has gone out on a matter of business."

"He is always attending to business." Chloe wrinkled her nose. "The stiff, starchy marquess, as usual."

"He is not—" The other woman looked to Jane's rapid defense with a question in her eyes. "He is not here," she amended. It wouldn't do to reveal more in terms of Jane's relationship with this young lady's brother.

Chloe wandered over to the window and pulled back the curtain. "The servants are readying the carriage and trunks."

Jane fisted her hands at her sides. He'd wasted little time in ridding himself of her. His household. Ridding his *household* of her. Chloe looked back with a frown. She cleared her throat. "I am to go to reside with your brother, Lord Alexander, and his wife."

The curtain slipped from Chloe's fingers and she stared at her. "What?"

Her lips pulled in a grimace. How very pathetic to be shuffled about and for her shameful ruination the evening prior, no less. "I cannot remain in your residence," she said with a matter-of-factness

179

she did not feel. She'd never had a right to be here and it had been the height of foolishness to accept the young woman's friendship.

"You cannot leave," the young woman said with a firm shake of her head. "I forbid it."

Warmth unfurled in her chest at this undeserved show of support and kindness. "I must leave," she said with a gentle firmness that merely brought Chloe's shoulders back.

Then her eyebrows shot to her hairline. "Why, he is sending you away." Before Jane could respond, a shocked gasp filled the office. "He will not do right by you."

"That is not—"

"I never expected this of him." Chloe, who'd apparently already made up her mind as to the circumstances, began to pace. "He is proper and polite and all things stuffy."

Surely, the other woman did not even now speak of her brother, Gabriel? A man who kissed with his passion could never be considered any one of those things.

"A man such as he would always do right by you." No, most gentlemen of his lofty station would not. Only, Gabriel had been the first nobleman who'd seen beyond her bastardy. He'd known of her birthright and offered for her anyway. She slid her eyes closed a moment. That defining piece of her life had mattered so much to everyone and yet he'd not allow that fact to keep him from marrying her. Her heart swelled with some dangerous emotion she didn't care to examine.

"Well, this will not do," Chloe muttered to herself as she increased her frantic back and forth pattern upon the carpet. "My mother will assuredly gather what has transpired and return posthaste."

The horrifying possibility of the distinguished marchioness returning to right a wrong that only Jane was responsible for jerked her to the moment. "He did offer." She drew in a slow breath. "I politely declined."

Chloe stopped mid-stride with such alacrity her satin skirts snapped noisily about her ankles. She spun to face Jane. "What?" The young woman's mouth formed a round moue of surprise.

"I could not in good conscience trap your brother. Not when I should never have joined his employ in the first place."

"Yes," Chloe said with a nod. "Yes, you should have."

"Why?" She turned a question on the young woman. "To preserve a name that doesn't require protection?" Gabriel's sister did not know the circumstances of her birth. But it was only a matter of time before the ugly truths were whispered about drawing rooms, spread by Montclair and anyone else who would hear the tale of the Duke of Ravenscourt's high-handed bastard. A question shone in Chloe's eyes. "I am not a lady," she settled for.

Chloe pursed her lips. "By whose standards?" She slapped her fingers upon her open palm. The sharp noise reverberated in the office. "And so you will not wed him, for *them?*"

A niggling at the back of her mind took root. The outing to the modiste. The pink gown. "I will not wed him for me," she said. "There is my school," she put in, interrupting Chloe before she could speak.

"But what of Gabriel?"

"Gabriel?"

"My brother." Chloe clarified unnecessarily.

All the times Chloe had left Jane alone with her brother to see to her friend, or some other such business. The young lady had been matchmaking for her brother. Oh, Chloe. Sweet, loving Chloe, who swore off marriage and yet would try to arrange that same blissful state for her eldest sibling. Surely, she'd had greater expectations for her brother's eternal partner than a liar such as Jane? "I daresay your brother will wed," a woman of his station and rank. "It just will not be to me." With that truth, an ugly, green emotion slipped inside and twisted like a snake, spreading its venom. An emotion that felt a good deal like jealousy. "If you'll excuse me," she said, in a desperate need to be free of Gabriel's office, his sister, and anything and everything connected to the Edgerton family.

She reached the entrance of the door when Chloe spoke softly, staying Jane's retreat.

"I wanted it to be you."

Jane turned slowly about.

A sad smile wreathed Chloe's cheeks. "What will you say? I knew you but a week?"

Yes, there was that.

"You have spirit, Jane. You are not afraid to go toe to toe with my brother. And you don't think he is stuffy or stodgy."

Her lips twitched. "No, no I do not."

"You see, he's been very stuffy and stodgy for so long, I'd ceased to believe he could feel anything. With you, he smiles and laughs, and is...*alive.*" At the passion in the young woman's eyes and response, Jane's throat moved. "Those things matter, Jane. He hasn't smiled in the twenty-one years I've known him and he is smiling now, and that is why one week matters so very much."

And without any suitable reply, Jane turned once more and left with Chloe's haunting words trailing after her.

TWENTY

S eated in the dark office finished in Chippendale furnishings, with the ormolu clock ticking away the moments, Gabriel stared at the Duke of Ravenscourt. He had her eyes. The crystalline blue depths with silver flecks. They were the eyes of a man who'd not even the courage to claim his daughter and protect her. Gabriel tightened his grip upon the arms of the seat he now occupied.

The duke, of advancing years, sat back in his desk chair. "Waverly," he said in clipped tones. "There was a matter of business with which you'd wished to speak with me."

A matter of business.

Even as he'd penned those words last evening, it had felt like a betrayal of sorts. Seeing Jane with her hope for a finishing school and her wide, blue eyes as a matter of business. And yet, that is what she was. "I am here about your daughter," he said without preamble. He'd never been one to prevaricate or waste time with pleasantries and niceties. He'd not begin now for this man. This *was* a matter of business.

The duke arched a blonde eyebrow. "My daughter?" His tone dripped the frozen austerity reserved for the handful of dukes in the realm.

Gabriel gritted his teeth. He'd read the gossip columns that morning and well knew he and Jane's names were being bandied about. The other man did not necessarily yet know of the gossip and, if he did, that the young woman in question was, in fact, his daughter. "Jane Munroe. I am referring to Jane Munroe," he said with the same cold, emotionless tone he'd adopted early on. The duke was not the only one who'd perfected icy rigidity. Eager to have this matter discussed, addressed, and, at last, done, he continued. "You are likely unaware of," Shame twisted in his stomach and he resisted the urge to tug at his cravat. "Of a scandal," he settled for. "Last evening." For the other man's disregard for Jane through the years, he was still her father and Gabriel had compromised her beyond redemption. "Between myself and Jane...Miss Munroe. Your daughter," he finished lamely.

"I am a duke, Waverly." The implacable lines of his face gave little indication as to his thoughts. "I am aware of everything as it might pertain to me."

In short, he knew Gabriel had Jane's skirts rucked about her legs with said actions discovered by Lady Jersey and Lady Castlereigh. "Er, yes." He placed his palms on his legs and drummed his fingers. "That is what brings me 'round then."

Jane. And her future and her happiness and her school, and then restoring his world to rights. That latter one proving to be more important.

The duke winged an eyebrow upward. "You do not believe I'd expect you to wed the lady."

Gabriel cocked his head and tried to sort through those callously spoken words. "Your Grace?" he said tersely, certain he'd misheard the man. Yes, Jane was illegitimate but certainly, as his daughter, still deserving of the man's protection.

Her father flicked a hand about. "Oh, come, I knew your father quite well, Waverly. We frequented the same..." A hard grin turned the man's lips up at the corners. "Clubs, and got on quite well."

He froze, as the blood coursing through his veins turned to ice. This was the man who'd sired Jane. A friend of his thankfully dead father. Odd, how he and Jane had both failed to realize their shared connection to vile, depraved monsters.

"Her mother was a whore, Waverly. Surely, you don't think I'd expect you to wed the gel?" With a wholly undukelike manner, he snorted. "It is enough I've had to shuffle the girl about from household to household after she'd lifted her skirts to any and every employer she's had."

A black haze of rage descended over Gabriel's vision. In all the years of his father's abuse, never before had he been consumed with this urge to reach out and choke a man by his throat the way he did in this moment. He concentrated on his steady, even breaths and when he trusted himself to speak, said, "She is your daughter."

"She is possibly my bastard," the other man said simply.

Through the late marquess' depravity and vileness, Gabriel had believed himself long ago immune to any shock where a person's parentage was concerned. He'd been wrong. His fingers twitched with the urge to bloody the man's pompous face. "I offered her marriage." He wanted him to know the truth. That Jane was a woman of strength and courage and convictions. "She did not accept my offer." And she was far nobler than Gabriel and the duke could or would ever hope to be.

A momentary flash of surprise lit the duke's eyes.

"She wants her freedom." And seeing the life of ill treatment she'd known with men of Gabriel's station, he now knew why. He didn't much like himself in this moment for no other reason than for having been born to the same gender and station as Ravenscourt and the Montclairs of the world.

"Oh?" the duke asked, his tone mildly curious.

"She wants the three thousand pounds you settled upon her," he said bluntly. Three thousand pounds when she was deserving of so much more.

The Duke of Ravenscourt furrowed his brow.

A pit settled in Gabriel's stomach; an intuition that was born of years of learning to rely on his instincts alone, and so he knew before any words were spoken, knew by the confusion, and the reprobate's previous, heartless thoughts about Jane Munroe.

"Three thousand pounds? I did not settle anything upon her."
Christ.

The air left him on a loud hiss. "The lady said you had—"

"I understand what the young woman might have said, Waverly," the duke interrupted. "But there has never been, nor will there ever be funds for Miss Munroe." He slashed a hand through the air. "If I began settling thousands of pounds upon any young woman professing to be my offspring, how many more do you think would come crawling from whatever whorehouse or hell they dwell in?"

Disgust tasted like a bitter acid in his mouth. "You knew her mother," he said slowly. The man had admitted as much just moments ago.

"But neither can I be sure I was the only one who knew her. You probably understand that, Waverly. Especially being your father's son."

If he remained any longer, with his fists he'd prove just how much his father's son he, in fact, was. It was too much. Gabriel shoved back his seat so quickly it scraped along the wooden floor. Fury, rage, and hurt for Jane made his movements jerky. The duke looked at him, a question in his eyes.

Jane's eyes.

Gabriel settled his palms upon the edge of the man's immaculate desk and leaned across the broad surface and shrank the space between them. "You sit upon your chair, condescending and calculated. In truth, you are a vile, pathetic excuse of a human being the world would be better off without." But then there never would have been Jane. The thought of that slammed into him.

The duke's eyebrows shot to his hairline. "How dare—"

"How dare I?" he asked on a lethal whisper. "How dare you? Your daughter may be illegitimate, but she has far more worth and strength than you or any other member of the nobility." Gabriel straightened and with the man sputtering behind him, started for the door. He reached the entrance and with fury thrumming through him, wheeled back around. "And I am nothing like my father," he bit out. With that, he yanked the door open and took his leave, with but one question rattling through his mind.

Now, what?

So it was, a short while later, with the question of what to do with Miss Jane Munroe in mind, Gabriel entered the hallowed doors of White's. The din of conversation came to an immediate cessation as all pairs of eyes in the distinguished club swung to him. With his gaze trained on his back table, he strode purposefully through the club, daring anyone to ask questions or utter one damned word about him and Jane last evening.

He reached his table and waved off a servant who made to pull out his seat. With a growl he yanked out the chair and then sat. He'd wager everything that was unentailed there was already some form of wager or another that involved his name, in that famed book at the center of the club. The irony of that was not lost on Gabriel, in the least. He'd studiously avoided scandal or any shameful behavior that could or would link him to his sire and had condemned Alex for being a consummate rogue...and yet he should be the one in that blasted book, with every occupant at White's presently looking at him.

A servant appeared at his shoulder and set down a bottle of brandy and a crystal snifter. With curt thanks, Gabriel pulled out the stopper and poured himself a healthy measure. He raised the glass to his lips—

"Waverly," his friend's amused greeting cut into his solitude. Then was there truly any real solitude at White's?

Gabriel took a sip and looked over the rim at Waterson.

Waterson snorted. "Will you not invite me to join you?"

He wasn't even permitted an opportunity to formulate a reply as his friend tugged out the chair across from him and sat. At the amusement in the earl's eyes, Gabriel directed his attention to his drink and glared into its contents. He'd not take the carefully laid bait. Not today. Not in light of the scandal he'd caused with Jane and her father's subsequent rejection and he finished his drink in a long, slow swallow. He reached for the bottle. He had every intention of getting completely and utterly soused, for then perhaps he might have some answer to... Jane.

"Well?" Waterson questioned as a servant came over with an empty glass. He accepted it and then took the liberty of pouring himself a healthy drink.

Do not ask. Do not ask. Do not... "Well, what?" he gritted out and then downed his brandy.

Waterson swirled the contents of his drink and reclined in his seat. "Do you know with your absence at the clubs these past days—?"

"I was here but three days ago," Gabriel felt compelled to point out.

"*I* had attributed it to brotherly devotion," Waterson continued over him. The demmed annoying grin on his lips widened. "Not that you are not the most devoted of brothers, you are."

"Shove off," Gabriel commanded as he picked up the bottle. He splashed several fingerfuls into the glass, thought better of it, and then poured it to the rim.

The earl widened his eyes. "Oh, you are in a bad way, my friend."

Do not ask. Do not ask. He swallowed the dry bite. "In what way?"

The room echoed with Waterson's thunderous laughter, earning them curious stares. "And now lying?" He made a tsking sound and then glanced about, seeming at last mindful of the attention being shown them. When he returned his attention to Gabriel, a mocking grin pulled his lips up in the corners. "I say, don't you have brotherly obligations to see to? Attending Lady Chloe and all that?" he asked, with a wave of his hand.

Except the knowing glint in his friend's eyes indicated that Waterson knew precisely why Gabriel was here. Waterson knew. Hell, everyone knew. Following his meeting with the duke, he was in ill-humor and didn't have time for the always-affable Waterson's games. "Say whatever it is you intend to say," *and be done with it.* There was Jane's situation to sort through. He tightened his grip upon his snifter so hard, his knuckles turned white. The same agonized disquiet that had besieged him since his meeting with the duke coursed through him and he took a much-needed sip of brandy.

Waterson set his glass down and then folded his arms at his chest. "I just thought, considering our friendship, you would speak on anything new or that might be of import to your life. Oh, say, that you've been so ensnared by a lady you'd ruin her at Drury Lane."

"The London Opera House," he muttered under his breath.

Waterson leaned across the table and angled his head. "Beg pardon?"

"I said, oh, go to hell," he finished as Waterson exploded into another round of laughter. "I am not ensnared by the lady," he said at last when his friend managed to get his hilarity under control. *No, you only think of her kisses and dream of the satiny softness of her skin and...*

His friend guffawed. "Regardless, you are now thoroughly trapped."

Not even his only friend in the world knew of Gabriel's sworn disavowal of marriage. Waterson, just like the rest of the world, saw a marquess so devoted to his title that he'd put responsibility before all else. How little they knew. Jane, however, had seen that glimpse of truth he'd hidden from all—that he had fears and desires. His heart sped up. And that she knew him as she did, terrified the hell out of him.

For now, with the duke's rejection and Jane's absolute lack of funds, there was no recourse as they'd both believed.... Hoped? Other than marriage.

Marriage.

A dull humming filled his ears and sucked the breath slowly from his lungs. He dimly registered his friend's mouth moving as he spoke, but for the life of him could not string together a single clear utterance from the other man. Horror and terror sucked away all logical thought and robbed him of speech.

Concern replaced the amusement in his friend's eyes and cut across his rapidly expanding panic. "Waverly?"

Incapable of anything else, Gabriel managed a jerky nod. This is how the legendary King and Queen of France had surely felt on their final day. Waterson spoke of marriage to Jane and in this, the earl was indeed correct. There was no other recourse. The slender, sometimes insolent, always passionate young woman as his wife. Forever. For that was, after all, what a wife was. A person he would be eternally bound to for the remainder of his days. He shoved back his chair and leapt to his feet.

"Waverly?" his friend looked up at him, worry stamped on the lines of his face.

"Fine, fine," he said and moved out from behind the table. Only he was not fine. Nausea twisted in his belly. He had no choice but to wed her. Society saw her as a companion—beneath him in station. She was illegitimate and, by their vile standards, they'd found her unworthy of entry into their world. "If you'll excuse me." He sketched a bow and before his friend could utter another word, Gabriel started through his club and to the exit.

With each footfall, he recognized, in light of his meeting with the duke, those were also the reasons he had no choice but to wed Jane. A woman of her origins, shamed and scandalized, would never find respectable employment. *You can provide her the funds,* a voice whispered. *Tell her they are from her father, put her aboard a carriage, and be done with her forevermore.* He braced for the rush of relief at the prospect. Except...he slowed his stride. Jane would never be able to retreat to any corner of England to set up her finishing school. Which families, noble or not, would entrust their daughters to the care of a woman with her history who'd also been discovered locked in a man's embrace at the Opera House? And she would still be alone.

The noose tightened all the more. He'd spent his life trying to care for others but now, there was not another person more in need of his protection than Jane. That ugly idea of her dependent upon the Montclairs of the world entered once more and drove back his own selfish fears. What other course would she have?

An image flitted through his mind. Jane lying with some other man, her golden curls draped in a curtain about her silken, naked frame—Rage slammed into him and sucked away all reservations.

When presented with the possibility of turning her out with no one to care for her, there really was no other option. He reached the front of the club and a servant hurried to the open the door. Gabriel strode through the exit, grateful to be free of the whispers and stares.

His friend, for all the nuisance he'd made of himself, had been unerringly accurate in this. There was little recourse but for him to wed her. And with their union, she would become one more person whose happiness and safety he was responsible for. Gabriel scrubbed his hands over his face. There would be the expectation of children, just additional tiny human beings who would also become figures who would forever look to him. More people to fail.

God help him.

For with one moment of weakness in an alcove with Jane in his arms, he'd consigned himself to this eternal hell that forever reminded him of his previous failures. With wooden movements, he accepted the reins of his horse from a waiting boy in the street. Now, it was a matter of convincing Jane.

TWENTY-ONE

J ane sat at the edge of the window seat and looked down into the streets and scanned the quiet cobbled roads below. Her open book lay at her feet. The dark clouds of night had ushered out the afternoon sun.

She'd expected him hours ago. Of course, that idea had only come from her own opinion. Gabriel had not told her when he intended to meet with the duke or when he'd visit. She'd just assumed. And now, she sat, a stranger in a new world, the ruined lady taken in by his benevolent family.

Gabriel had no obligations where she was concerned and yet, even so, had met with her father in attempts to secure her funds and had enlisted the help of his family to protect her. In the crystal pane, her lips twisted in a melancholy smile. He seemed to be the only one who believed she merited protection.

She stiffened as her benefactress, Lady Imogen Edgerton, appeared in the doorway. Jane swung her attention around. "Lady Imogen," she greeted. She glanced past the woman's shoulder and some of her eagerness dipped.

"No need to rise," she assured as she strolled over. "And please, just Imogen." She came to a stop at the edge of Jane's seat and peered around her shoulder into the streets below. "I daresay you're wondering where Lord Waverly is?"

She mustered a smile. "Have I been so very obvious?" After all, she'd closeted herself away in their parlor with her book and claimed the very same seat by the window for the past nearly six hours.

A light twinkle lit the other woman's kindly eyes. "Just a bit." Some of the gentle teasing lifted and she sank into the seat beside Jane. "For my friendship with Chloe and my marriage to Alex, I do not know the marquess, hardly at all. I venture no one truly knows Lord Waverly." A loose tendril escaped her neat chignon and she brushed back a crimson curl from her cheek. "He's a rigid, formidable gentleman who invokes fear, but a loyal brother."

Rigid, formidable, a man who invoked fear. Is that how the world viewed him? But for that last, very important, telling statement by Lady Imo—*Imogen*, she rather suspected it was. How could they not look past the rigidity and coldness to see the person she'd known these past seven days?

Imogen plucked at the fabric of the window seat. The other woman wished to say more. That much was clear. Alas, Jane had spent too much time with her own company and could not fill the uncomfortable voids the way Imogen, Chloe, or any other lady of their respective station might. Gabriel's sister-in-law stopped suddenly. Jane followed her gaze to the book beside them. "May I?" the woman inquired. However, she'd already retrieved the small leather volume of Mary Wollstonecraft's work. She trailed her fingers over the gilt lettering.

Jane stared blankly at that poor volume, forgotten more times in this past week than the course of her life. For years those words had filled a void. They'd given her a belief in a world she thought she desired for herself. It was a world in which she was dependent upon no one and found contentment in her own accomplishments. And though there was the dream of a school for women such as herself, there was all this never before confronted desire for more—a family, a connection. She closed her eyes a moment—love.

"It is a cruelly harsh world oftentimes for young women, isn't it?"

"It is," she said softly. Until Jane had slipped into the fold of the Edgerton family she would have scoffed at Imogen's words. What did lords and ladies know of the trials and uncertainties that came in being born on the fringe of their glittering, opulent world of perfection? But it wasn't perfect. Gabriel and Chloe's life spoke to the same struggles known by so many and, in that, Jane's unfair lumping of all the peerage into one self-absorbed category had proven incorrect. If she'd been so very wrong about that, what else had she been wrong in?

The young lady fanned the pages of Jane's book. "I once believed the *ton* was horrible and cruel and all things unfair where young ladies are concerned."

She recalled Montclair's tepid breath against her lips. "Aren't they?" she asked, unable to keep the bitterness from creeping in.

Imogen stuck her finger on a random page of the book and looked down at the words. "Yes, yes they are often that," she said matter-of-factly.

They. She'd not consider herself a member of the world to which she rightfully belonged?

Gabriel's sister-in-law placed her hand on Jane's and she started at the unexpected contact. "I was…" She wrinkled her nose. "There was a scandal that involved me," she substituted.

"Oh." For what really was there to say, with realization after realization she was not as unlike these people as she'd believed. Once more, it was harder than ever to resent the whole of them for the crimes of a few.

"You won't ask me about that scandal."

"Never." She shook her head. "I've been gossiped about by too many," she said with a bluntness that brought the young woman's eyebrows shooting up. "Most of the things whispered about me were untrue." She thought of her father, the powerful duke, and then the scandalous discovery of her and Gabriel last evening. "But some of them are not. I would not ask you to share the stories which belong to you."

The woman gave Jane's hand a slight squeeze and a gentle smile wreathed her cheeks. "I would not have volunteered unless I wished to share." Which was, once again, all the more terrifying. "My betrothed jilted me for my sister."

She blinked several times.

"I swore to never wed for any reason but stability and order, to a gentleman who inspired no grand sentiments. Do you know what happened to that pledge?"

Jane recalled all of Chloe's words about her brother, Lord Alex—
the infamous rogue. "I do not," she said for politeness sake.

The gleam in the woman's eye indicated she knew as much. "I fell
in love." How often had Jane scoffed at that emotion that had so weakened her mother? And yet, there was nothing wrong about Imogen, or
Lord Alex, or Chloe, and Gabriel and the entire Edgerton family who
loved so passionately. "So, there are scandals," Imogen said bringing
her to the moment. "And they are awful when they are happening, and
some of them are disastrous and horrible in every way, but sometimes,
just sometimes, good comes from them. As it did for me." She touched
her neck, as though searching for something. Then, she let her hand
flutter back to her lap. "And I suspect as it will be for you."

Of course. The lady believed Jane would wed Gabriel. Even with her
own scandal, Imogen had not disavowed marriage. She'd merely sought
to avoid a match based on the volatile emotions that Jane herself feared.
A lump formed in her throat and she swallowed several times. "Why are
you being so nice to me?" she asked, desperate to understand why these
strangers were so different than all others she'd known. They'd shared
parts of their lives with her, an outsider, an interloper, and thief.

"Mrs. Munroe—"

"Jane," she corrected.

"Jane, kindness costs us nothing, but brings us everything." She
squeezed Jane's hand once more. "And you must call me Imogen."

Footsteps sounded in the hallway, calling their attention to the
front of the room just as Gabriel stepped in. His brother, Lord Alex,
stood at his side. He favored his wife and Jane with one of those charming smiles that had likely earned him the reputation of rogue and then
looked to his wife.

Imogen jumped to her feet. "Gabriel," she greeted with a smile
and sailed across the room in a flurry of skirts. Jane rose and a thousand questions sprung to her lips about his meeting. She bit the
inside of her cheek to keep from blurting any one of them out.

He stepped into the room and sketched a polite, proper, and perfectly formal bow. "Imogen," he said. All the while, his gaze remained
on Jane. "Mrs. Munroe."

His family was too polite to draw attention to the great hypocrisy in him referring to her so very formally when they'd been discovered *en dishabille* at the opera. Instead, Lord Alex held his hand out, and his wife walked the remaining distance, and then slipped her fingers into his.

Jane studied that sweet, intimate moment as he clasped his larger palm around Imogen's much smaller one and a sudden hungering slammed into her—a desire to know even just a sliver of that connection to another person. She stared after them as they took their leave, until only she and Gabriel remained.

He fully entered the room and closed the door quietly behind him.

Yes, with her already non-existent reputation in tatters there was no need for a chaperone and apparently closed doors were permitted, too. She glanced down at the tips of her slippers.

He spoke without preamble. "I spoke to your father."

His words brought her head up. Her father. Had the duke truly been a father? He'd sired her, yes. But she'd only seen two glimpses of the man in the course of her existence. "Thank you," she said. She pressed her palms together.

It was done. He'd secured her funds, then. She would have her freedom and security. The Edgerton's would be nothing more than a reminder of a family who'd proven themselves different than all others. His thick lashes dipped. He may as well have been carved from stone for all the reaction he gave. She scooped up her book and pulled it close to her chest. "I—"

Gabriel held up a hand. He took a step toward her, his expression darkening. "There is, however, something we need to speak on."

He'd spent the better part of the afternoon and evening grappling with just what to do with Jane Munroe—the woman who wanted to wed even less than he wanted to be wed.

The truth of her father's betrayal had tumbled around his mind since he'd taken his leave of his club. He'd turned around and over and through all possible answers. Jane was, of course, deserving of the truth about his meeting with her father and yet…he could not tell her. To do so would shatter her dream and end her security. He could not do that. Not and live with himself.

Jane picked her way carefully toward him and then paused with the gold upholstered sofa between them. She had a white-knuckled grip on the volume in her hands. "What is it?" Concern darkened her eyes and he was struck once more by how very much alike they were. Life had given them reasons to be wary.

He cleared his throat. "I spoke to the duke," he corrected from earlier. For the monster who'd given her life, more alike than different from his own sire, did not deserve the distinction of parentage. "There is a condition of your acquiring the funds." For that was the only resolution he'd come to in his own mind.

Jane cocked her head. "A condition?" she repeated back dumbly, as she set her book down on the sofa.

A niggling of guilt pebbled his belly and he forcibly thrust it back. He'd ruined her. He would do right by her and compromising the pledge he'd taken as a boy was the very least sacrifice he could make for ruining her. *What right do I have to make that choice for her?* He took a step away and wandered over to the window seat she'd occupied moments ago. The small leather volume on the upholstered seat snagged his attention and he dropped his gaze to her beloved book. The book she had in her possession whenever he came upon her. The book that had served as her motivation all these years to establish her finishing school.

"Gabriel?" she asked. Unease laced that one word—his name. And just like that, he was Gabriel again to her and the decision was made.

He swiped Mrs. Wollstonecraft's work from the seat and welcomed the comforting weight of the book in his hands. "I will speak bluntly, Jane," he said as he turned to face her.

A wry smile formed on her lips. "I'd prefer bluntness to this stilted silence."

He returned her smile with a faint one of his own. "I have never been the one with ready words. That skill has been reserved for my brother."

"I'd have you be sincere to filling that quiet with platitudes and false cheer." False cheer.

"Your three thousand pounds is dependent upon our marriage," he said on a rush, before the wrongness in his decision cemented in his mind or before his own courage to move forward in this uncertain marital state registered.

Jane opened her mouth and closed it. And then tried again. "What?"

"Marriage," he supplied, though he far suspected that she very well heard and understood. "To me."

She furrowed her brow and then shook her head slowly back and forth. "I don't understand." Her whisper-soft statement may as well have thundered about the room for the absolute still of the parlor. "Marriage?" She paused. "To you?"

Was the prospect of marriage to him really so unpalatable to the lady? He bristled, feeding the indignation which was far safer than any other more dangerous sentiments that could or would suggest there was any other reason to care about Jane's response. He set aside her book. "As I said, you will receive the funds for your school if you wed me."

She gave her head a forlorn shake and then looked away. "I see." By her flat, emotionless tone he suspected she saw nothing at all.

"Marry me."

Her gaze shot to his. "Are you asking me?" She squared her shoulders at that same high-handed order he'd made just the prior evening.

Gabriel nodded. "Marry me?" he said again and this time the words were a question.

Jane eyed him with a wary confusion. "But you don't want to marry me."

No. He didn't wish to marry anyone and especially not a woman who roused these tumultuous sentiments within him that he didn't recognize or care to identify.

"Why?"

It took a moment for him to register her question. "Why?"

She nodded. "Why would you wed me to help me secure my funds? What benefit is that to you? You will not have a proper wife, a *lady* as your hostess."

Why, because there was little choice except marriage. He opened his mouth but then immediately pressed his lips closed and searched for a suitable response that would not offend a woman who was now presented with marriage to him. Gabriel forced a wry grin. "I expect it is fairly clear why we should wed." *I want you…* No, that is not what now drove his offer. It was the protection and security of his name. *That* was the impetus behind his proposal.

"No, it is not clear, Gabriel," she said slowly, as though picking her way through a conversation in Latin when she only spoke French.

He strolled over and stopped before her. "Very well," he said and brushed the back of his hand along her jaw. Like silk. Who knew satiny soft skin could be so very erotic?

Jane tipped her head at a slight angle, leaning into his touch in a trusting way that jerked him back to the perils of her.

"You are ruined." She went taut and drew slightly back. That movement forced his hand down to his side. He grimaced. "That is you are unmarriageable." Was there really a difference between the two? He thought not and, by the dangerous narrowing of Jane's eyes, she also thought not. He'd spent his life scolding and passing judgment on his rogue of a brother. Now he'd have traded his left hand for a handful of charming words to help him wade through this quagmire with Jane.

"You would marry me because of…" Her cheeks pinked. "Because of what transpired." What transpired? That was a good deal more polite than referencing the passionate exchange that had found her with her skirts up about her delicious lower limbs and her skirts wrinkled. "All so I could secure my funds?"

He bowed his head. "I would," he said solemnly. Through the years, he'd failed Chloe, Philippa, and Alex. He'd not fail another. "Marry me," he repeated. "You'll have your school."

A small smile played about her lips. "You cannot help but command, can you?"

Gabriel closed his mouth. "No." The need to be masterful and decisive had been ingrained into him from the moment Alex had beat their father within an inch of his life. At his younger brother's side, he'd gleaned the strength and power that came in possessing control—over all.

Jane studied her palms a long moment, and when she looked to him again, there was that wary mistrust he'd come to expect of her etched in the delicate lines of her face. "I'll have my school," she spoke that part as though to herself. "And what will you have?" Her cheeks flamed red like a summer strawberry. "I expect you'll require heirs."

Heirs. Children. Those small, dependent people who required caring for and protection. Figures who, until this moment, had been murky shadows who would never be, but now with her words, Jane had conjured up the delicious act of taking her to his bed, laying her down, exploring every crevice of her skin, tasting her scent…He groaned.

"Gabriel?" she asked, questioningly.

"There will be no children," he said harshly. Never before had he resented the vow he'd taken. Before it had been there to sustain and protect. Now the prospect of having Jane as his wife and not knowing every part of her body threatened to destroy him. "There will be no children," he repeated, this time for his own benefit.

She scratched her brow. "But you are a marquess." Her tone held all the befuddlement of one trying to divine the answer to life.

"Ours would be a marriage of convenience," he said. "You will have your funds and your school—"

"And what will you have?"

"A companion for my sister—"

"With the circumstances of my birth and our discovery at the opera house, I will be a dreadful companion."

He went on as though she'd not interrupted. "—You will serve as my hostess while my mother is away with my sister—"

"I know nothing about being a hostess."

"You will learn."

"But I don't want to learn."

He frowned.

Jane lifted her hands up. "I thank you for your offer." She'd thank him for his offer as casually as though he'd laid his jacket across the street so she might avoid a muddy puddle. "But there would be no benefit in your marrying me." She wrinkled her nose. "Nor do I expect you'd gladly accept your wife establishing and running a finishing school."

No, most gentlemen would not. Other noblemen committed to their lines and titles wouldn't even entertain an idea of their wife doing anything other than serving as hostess and becoming mother to their heirs. Gabriel folded his arms at his chest. "I don't believe I've been clear, Jane."

She nodded. "Yes. I would agree with that much."

"I am not looking for a wife."

The furrow of her brow deepened.

"I do not want a wife. Or children," he added as an afterthought.

"But you require a wife and child," she blurted with the same shock he'd expect from his now thankfully dead father. "Children," she amended. "Heirs and spares and issue to carry on your line." She gesticulated wildly as she spoke.

Gabriel propped his hip against the edge of the sofa. "As we are entering into this state—"

"We are entering into no state," she interrupted with a hard frown on her lips.

"If we are to enter into this state," he amended. "You should know that ours would be a marriage in name only. You will be, after your responsibilities to my sister are seen to, free to take yourself off to the country. Your three thousand pounds will be yours to establish a school and see fit the running of it. All you must do is marry me."

TWENTY-TWO

Gabriel spoke with a calculated, methodical precision about her life and his. Their future, which would really be no future together.

All she must do is marry him.

She would have her school. He would have…a very unsatisfactory end of the proverbial bargain. And there would be a husband, but not truly a husband.

The deal he put to her was generous and a week ago would have been the impossibility she'd never dared dream of—freedom. Until now. Now, with the perversity of her own internal weakness, something in his offer was missing. For both of them. How could he fail to see it?

Her skin prickled with awareness under the intensity of his gaze upon her person. Needing some space between them, Jane wandered to the cold, empty hearth and stared into the grate. When she spoke, she directed her attention there. "By your admission, all you require is a companion for Chloe. You would see her married, with me acting as your hostess." Her lips pulled in an involuntary grimace. "When she is wed, what then?" She cast a glance over her shoulder.

Gabriel remained propped at the edge of the sofa, coolly elegant and refined in his masculine perfection—his powerful height, his broad muscles rippling in the fitted contours of his expertly cut jacket. He lifted his shoulders in a slight shrug. "Then, it is as I said, you will have your freedom and I shall have mine."

A chill stole through her at that detached acceptance of an empty existence. "I do not understand. You have an obligation to your title."

All the noblemen she'd ever known had put that great lineage before all else.

"I have an obligation to those I care for and beyond that, the title can go hang."

Care for. Not love. And yet, she'd wager her soul to the devil that he loved more deeply than any other. Then his flat, emotionless words registered. She blinked several times. "Why?" Why, when the cold, calculated members of the *ton* prized that hereditary line more than anything, should he be different? Jane ran her gaze over him, searching for answers to solve the complex riddle of Gabriel, the Marquess of Waverly.

His thick lashes swept downward, shielding all hint of emotion from his eyes. "My father was a monster. I have no desire to carry on that line."

That was it. Two sentences emotionlessly delivered. Fourteen words meant to convey all about why he'd wed her and why he'd given up on his line and the possibility of a family for himself.

She opened her mouth to ask a question, but the words died in her throat as he suddenly shoved back from his relaxed pose and stalked over. Jane's feet twitched with the urge to flee but remained fixed at the hearth as he came to a stop beside her. "I venture you have your secrets," he admonished. She'd had her secrets. He now knew more than anyone else. "I ask for the privacy of mine."

Her throat went dry at the clipped request. She managed a shaky nod and then drew in a deep breath. "Surely, sacrificing your life is not worth the cost of a companion. Your mother—"

"Do you know where my mother is?" he cut in.

"Chloe explained she retired to the country for your sister's confinement."

"My sister has developed complications that have put at risk her life and the life of her baby."

Her heart throbbed. "Oh. I..." Her useless apology faded.

He ignored her. "I will not have Chloe know that."

In light of their circumstances, Jane really should be attending the question of her fate, marital state, and finances, and yet annoyance stirred in her belly. "You would keep that from her?" She could not keep the incredulity from creeping into her question.

Gabriel rolled his shoulders and she gritted her teeth at the infuriating nonchalance of him. "What good is there in her knowing? Is there anything to be done to change Philippa's circumstances?"

"No, but—"

"Should she retire to the country and worry, all the while being unable to change Philippa's circumstances?"

Jane nodded briskly. "Yes. Yes she should. That is what she'd want." She braced for him to question her brash insolence in knowing what his own sister wanted after only a week of each other's acquaintance. It spoke volumes that he did not.

"My family's circumstances aside, what will you do?"

A panicky laugh worked its way up her throat and stuck there. *What will you do?* With such harsh precision, there would never be the worry over either of their hearts being engaged. Gabriel, a man who made decisions for others and commanded as though he was born to it, a man who did not want issues or really a wife, would be safe in ways that mattered. Yet, for his devotion and his goodness to his entire family, and now her, he deserved more. "I cannot marry you," she said softly. "Even for my school. You will someday want a woman for your wife who is more than a companion for your sister, a woman you d-desire." His eyes grew more shuttered and an increasingly familiar heat burned her cheeks under his veiled scrutiny.

He shot a hand out and folded it gently about her neck. She stiffened at the unexpectedness of his touch. Shivers radiated at the point of contact and warmth spiraled through her as he angled her closer. Her lashes fluttered as he dipped his face close. His breath fanned her lips. "Is that what you believe? That I do not desire you?"

All she need do was reach up on tiptoe and their lips would touch. A little moan stuck in her throat. "I—"

"Surely, you know the effect you have upon me." Those last few words, spoken in that husky, powerful baritone cascaded over her senses and washed away reason.

"Then why?" she managed when she trusted herself to speak. Except the words came out garbled and thick.

He rubbed the pad of his thumb over her lower lip. "Why will I not have children with you?"

Those words conjured an image of she and Gabriel locked in an embrace, bound by marriage, and suddenly that binding did not seem so very unappealing. She wet her lips and told her throat to bob up and down.

A slow, seductive grin pulled at the corners of his lips. "I do not want the responsibility that comes with a wife or family, Jane," he said and then he let his hand fall to his side.

Her skin went cool at the sudden loss of his touch and she mourned the absence of his caress. "But you will have a wife," she reminded him, infusing as much strength as she could into those handful of words. She'd long ago sneered at any future that involved a gentleman in it and therefore, by all intents and purposes, should be of like mind in terms of a cold, empty union, if there must be any marriage at all.

Gabriel touched a finger to her lips and they parted as her belly stirred with a need for him. "Ah, yes, but you will have your school."

Her school. She blinked back the haze of desire he'd cast over her eyes and with an almost agonized pain at the loss of his body's nearness, she drew back and retreated. Yes. Her school. The beacon of hope she'd had all these years. The thought that had sustained her. Now, it was within her reach.

And yet, she wanted more.

Jane folded her arms at her chest. What choice did she have? The funds settled upon her by the duke would be lost if she did not do this thing. Yet, still…she hesitated.

Don't be a ninny. You will have everything. And more, she would, if not have Gabriel's affection or warmth, be a member of the Edgerton family. That was a heady thought, indeed. She drew in a breath and turned back to face him. "Very well," she said and stuck out her hand.

He eyed it a moment, as though he'd never before been presented with a lady's fingers. "You shall have a temporary hostess." Explaining that she knew nothing in terms of being a hostess or even the most rudimentary aspects of balls and soirees and such would likely only convince him of the madness in his offer. When he still did not accept her extended fingers, Jane grabbed his hand and gripped his palm, forcing a shake. "And I shall have my school."

Gabriel folded his hands about hers and she gasped. Would she ever grow immune to the heat of his touch? Hands weren't supposed to feel like his. They weren't. They were functional and used for all manner of mundane activities. So why did his fingers leave her with this breathless longing? He raised her knuckles to his lips and dropped a kiss upon the top of her naked hand. "It is settled."

It is settled. Never were there words less romantic or heartfelt than those. Then, why should there be? He'd been clear in his aspirations for her as his wife and she...well, she'd long ago sworn to never care for, or about, a nobleman.

Only in this short time, Gabriel had become more than a powerful marquess. He'd become a person who'd care for those around him, who'd forgive her deception and give her the protection of his name, anyway.

He released her suddenly. "We will wed tomorrow morn." *Tomorrow?* "If you'll excuse me?" With that, he started for the door.

Panic pounded hard in her chest. She raced after him. "Tomorrow?" She flinched at the desperate edge to that one word.

He stopped so quickly she skidded to a halt to keep from slamming into him. Her skirts, another gift given her by him and his sister snapped noisily about them. Gabriel fished around the front of his jacket and withdrew a thick, ivory folded velum. "I took the liberty of securing a special license."

That's where he'd been all this day.

She'd become so accustomed to making any and every decision that impacted her life, she didn't know what to do with a person who took on that role—and so boldly as Gabriel. "You were so very certain I would say yes?"

He grinned that crooked half-smile that made her heart flutter. "I was," he said with an arrogance that made her point her eyes to the ceiling. "Do you know how I knew?"

Jane pursed her lips. "How?"

"I know you well enough after just a week," Seven days. "To know that your school matters more than anything else, and as long as you have that, you'd be content." With that, he pulled open the door.

She mustered a smile as he dropped a bow and then left. When he was gone, her smile died. He spoke of knowing her so very well. And yet, if that were true, then he'd know, in this moment, with his request and offer of marriage, she wanted far more than her finishing school—she'd wanted a family.

Gabriel's skin pricked with the burn of Jane's gaze on his retreating form. He increased his stride, desperate to put much needed distance between them. She'd accepted his offer. Of course she had. There had been little choice. No recourse really, for the lady.

He turned the corner and froze. Yet, in the moment when presenting her with the terms of their marriage, for one span of a heartbeat, he'd read a desire for more in her eyes. Dangerous sentiments had swirled within her gaze and filled him with terror at the prospect that he'd merely been staring into a reflective pool of his own thoughts and feelings.

"You don't have the happy look of a man about to find himself wed," Alex drawled from beyond Gabriel's shoulder.

At the amusement underscoring his words, Gabriel stiffened and turned slowly to face his ever-grinning brother. "Alex," he said tersely. How could the other man smile through life so effortlessly and easily as he did?

His brother strode down the corridor. He narrowed his eyes. He'd wager Alex had not been far from the parlor where he'd just spoken to Jane. The idea that he had heard their exchange grated. "Were you listening to my conversation with Jane?" he snapped.

His brother chuckled. "Despite what you believe of me, I ceased listening at keyholes for some time now." He winked. "At least a year."

Some of the tension left Gabriel's frame. "Forgive me," he requested. Jane was wreaking havoc on every part of his world—most particularly the reason and calm he'd always valued. "I appreciate your allowing her to remain here with you and Imogen until…" He choked on his swallow. "Until…well until." Marriage. He would be married.

I will be married to Jane.

His brother looked at him for a long while and then tossed back his head and shouted with laughter. He laughed so hard tears seeped from the corner of his eyes and he dashed them back, not unlike Waterson earlier that afternoon.

"I am glad you should find amusement in my situation," he said with a frown.

Alex slapped him on the back. "I do not find amusement in your situation," he assured. He flung his arm around Gabriel's shoulders and guided him onward. "I find great irony in you, the man who'd taken such umbrage with my roguish ways through the years, not even being able to choke out the word marriage."

"I can say the blasted word," he argued as Alex steered him to his office.

"Oh," Alex drawled as they came to a stop beside the closed door. He quirked an eyebrow. "Then say it."

"I…" He tried once more. "Oh, go to hell," he growled as Alex launched into another round of hilarity.

"Here," Alex said and opened the door. With a hand between Gabriel's shoulder blades he shoved him inside. "I daresay a talk is in order."

"A talk?" As he stepped further into the room, he loosened his cravat. "I'm hardly a child requiring any kind of talk."

With the heel of his boot Alex shoved the door closed behind them. He stalked over to his sideboard and fetched a bottle of brandy. Decanter in hand, he jabbed a finger at the leather button sofa. "Sit."

Gabriel bristled, but then with the blasted day and previous night he'd had, the last thing he cared to do was launch into a childish debate about tones of voice and orders to sit. Especially not when Alex had been far more magnanimous than Gabriel deserved in not having a good deal more fun at the scandal at the opera house. He sat. The room filled with the sound of crystal touching crystal as Alex poured a drink. "I hardly see what there is to talk about," he said, grateful when his brother thrust a glass under his nose.

With his own glass filled, Alex claimed the King Louis XIV chair opposite Gabriel. He swirled the contents of his glass. "Oh, I suppose your Jane would be as good a place as any."

He sighed. It was too much to hope that the discovery, the offer of assistance, and the limited jests would be enough. "She is hardly my Jane."

Over the rim of his glass, Alex gave him a look. "That isn't quite true."

No, no it wasn't. Not when tomorrow morn, she'd belong to him forever. He wiped a tired hand over his face. "What in blazes were you and Imogen and Chloe doing wandering the corridors during the performance?" Then, it hadn't really mattered. Not when two of the most notorious gossips had also stumbled upon him and Jane locked in one another's embrace.

His brother frowned. "The Earl of Montclair visited our box." Bloody Montclair. "He indicated that you'd called for your carriage and advised me to escort Chloe to the entrance of the theatre."

He curled his fists into tight balls. A hungering to hunt down the man who'd quite adroitly destroyed his and Jane's life thrummed through him with a life-like force. "I'll kill him."

Alex rested his hands on his knees and leaned forward. "Montclair's machinations aside, you were, in fact, the one in the alcove with the lady." Some of the fight left him, replaced with a stinging shame. "Montclair should not be the matter of discussion but rather your marriage to Mrs. Munroe."

Oh, Christ. Gabriel took a long, fast swallow of his drink and welcomed the burn of liquor down his throat. Why did Alex have to be right in this regard? He expected more laughter from his affable, always in a good humor brother. Except when he looked at his brother, there was an uncharacteristic solemnity to him.

"All these years we've spent thinking we are nothing alike," Alex said quietly. "I was the rogue and," he motioned to Gabriel, "you were the responsible, always in control marquess." His lips formed a wry grin. "And yet, only now do we discover how very similar we are."

Gabriel stared into the contents of his glass. Alex had been the brave, indomitable one who'd put an end to their father's abuse. Gabriel had merely been the sniveling, cowardly, pathetic excuse of an older brother. "We are nothing alike," he whispered, and as those words filtered about them, he looked up hastily. His brother studied him through those mirror-like eyes of his own shade of green and Gabriel silently cursed. "I did not mean it as an insult." He'd mucked up his relationship with Alex long ago. Though they'd begun to reassemble the broken pieces, neither had they fully healed. Perhaps they never would.

Alex waved him off. "But we are. No matter your protestations and the cool mask you've donned. Both of us, all of us, have protected ourselves these years." He waggled an eyebrow. "Oh, you've done a rather impressive job of convincing me and likely most of the world that you don't care. But you do. We all do. We've just protected ourselves in different ways."

Gabriel gave his glass a swirl and looked down into the amber contents once more.

"Now, there is the matter of introducing Mrs. Munroe to polite Society." Gabriel tightened his hold upon his glass. The prospect of Jane facing down condescending lords and ladies twisted at his insides. He didn't give a jot for how the *ton* treated him, but by God if they hurt her…"There will be gossip." Alex frowned, likely remembering his wife's struggle in reentering Society after her own scandal involving her previous, and disloyal, betrothed. "We will of course help you. Once you are wed, I will enlist the aid of Lord Primly and Lord Wessex. They will help smooth her way."

Lord Primly. An unlikely friend to his brother. With a stammer and a kind disposition, the Earl of Primly would be a perfect ally for Jane. For *them*. Lord Wessex, however, a notorious rogue was the more *expected* company for his once roguish brother to keep. "Wessex?" he asked with a scowl. He'd rather the charmer nowhere near Jane.

"Yes, Wessex. A dance, perhaps. Just to throw his support behind the young lady."

Jealousy rooted around his belly. He nodded slowly.

"I'll speak to them after you're married."

Ah, God, there it was again. That word. *Married.* Gabriel shoved back his chair and jumped to his feet. He set his glass down. "If you'll excuse me," he said priding himself on the steadiness of those words.

"Of course," Alex said and came to his feet with the same calm he'd always exhibited through life.

Gabriel had his hand upon the door handle when his brother called out.

"I was certain I didn't want a thing to do with love," Alex's quiet pronouncement brought him back around. "I was certain I didn't need anyone. It was far safer to love none and depend on no one," *or be needed by anyone.* "Do you know what I ultimately realized, Gabriel?"

He gave his head a slight shake.

"Saying I didn't care and believing myself incapable of love, or being loved, well, that did not make it true." Alex took a slow sip. "Imogen showed me that."

An uncomfortable silence settled over the room; two brothers who'd been embittered against one another for too long, now talking about personal matters that gentlemen did not discuss. He cleared his throat. "Thank you for—"

"Do not thank me again for looking after your Jane."

"She is not—"

At his brother's arched brow, he closed his mouth, and then beat a bow. "I—"

"I know," Alex consoled.

And as Gabriel took his leave, he had the feeling that his brother did know a good deal more than he'd credited him with all these years which only left him to wonder—how many other things had he been wrong about all these years?

TWENTY-THREE

They were wed the following morning. Lightning slashed across the dark, London sky and a flash of blue light zigzagged outside the windowpane.

It was a sign.

Jane stood, frozen with her gaze trained on the opened curtains as panic built in her chest. It swelled and grew until breathing became impossible.

She could not—

Gabriel leaned down. "Are you all right?" he whispered in her ear.

She jumped and looked unblinkingly up at him. How could he be so calm and unaffected? He asked whether or not she was all right? Was she all right? She was a bloody mess. "Fine?" she said quietly for his ears. After all, what was one more lie in the scheme of their relationship?

"Is that a question?"

Well, yes, she supposed it was. "No. I am fine." She registered the expectant look on the aging vicar's face. He wanted something. What did he want? Jane looked hopefully out at the small, collection of guests present—a smiling Imogen and her grinning husband. An equally happy Chloe. Then there was the stranger she'd not met before. The Earl of Waterson, who'd eyed her with a deserved suspicion since he'd claimed his seat as witness. Panic threatened to overtake her. It ripped at her thoughts and robbed her reason. Why would everyone be so happy? And why was she staring back at them? She wrinkled her brow…

"Ahem." The vicar coughed into his hand and jerked her attention back.

"I believe this is where you recite your portion of the vows," Gabriel drawled close to her ear, his breath stirred a loose curl and she brushed back the bothersome strand.

How could he be so unaffected? How—"I Jane Madeline Munroe," she repeated after the vicar. "Take thee Gabriel—" her mind raced. *I do not even know his name in its absolute entirety.* Her mouth went dry at the absolute madness of a man who wanted nothing more from her than two months to see his sister wed and would then send her on her way.

Gabriel spoke in low tones. "Garmund Randolph Edgerton."

A long, distinguished name given to a respected, proper, nobleman's son. "Take thee, Gabriel G-Garmund," her mouth tripped involuntarily over the running of his name. "Randolph Edgerton, to my wedded Husband, to have and to hold," for two months' time. "From this day forward," she squeezed out on a tight whisper. "For better for worse, for richer for poorer, in sickness and in health…" The vicar stared expectantly back at her. Her throat worked in a reflexive swallow. She was not different than her mother. Oh, she would have a legal union and a lofty title, but in uttering these final words she'd sell herself for three thousand pounds and the dream of her school, to a man who'd never love her or cherish her or want anything more of her… than these two months.

She jumped as Gabriel touched the small of her back. Jane cast her gaze up to his and willed him to have the sense to end this façade even as she wanted it to continue on.

"Mrs. Munroe?" there was a faint entreaty in the vicar's tone.

For what she knew was expected of her, Jane could not call forth the remainder of her vows. She glanced back once more at the row of Gabriel's family members seated, with expressions that conveyed the first real doubt she'd seen until now that the marriage between Jane and Gabriel might not, in fact, happen.

Then Gabriel captured her hand in his and her skin heated at his touch. She looked to him. If he commanded her with his words or eyes, she'd damn the three thousand pounds her father had settled upon her to the devil. He angled his body in a way that shielded them from his family's stares. "I will be good to you," he pledged. "You will always be cared for."

The duke, her father had cared for her mother. But this vow made by Gabriel was not one founded on the sale of her body or pride. Jane drew in a steadying breath as calm settled over her. "I, Jane Madeline Munroe, take thee Gabriel Garmund Randolph Edgerton to my wedded Husband, to have and to hold from this day forward, for better for worse, for richer for poorer, in sickness and in health, to love, cherish, and to obey, till death us do part, according to God's holy ordinance; and thereto I give thee my troth."

And just like that the ceremony continued and then concluded in short order with Jane Munroe, bastard without a family, finding herself in the close-knit fold of Gabriel's kin. With a flurry of signing and hushed conversation in the background, she was now something she'd forever sworn to never be...or at least never imagined for herself—married.

"I have had Cook prepare breakfast for the occasion," Imogen said with the cheer Jane had come to expect of her. The collection of guests, along with the vicar, took that as their opportunity to depart the happy festivities, leaving Jane and Gabriel momentarily alone.

Alone.

Which wasn't altogether different than they'd been on many occasions. This, however, *was* altogether different. Now they were united in the bonds of marriage.

Gabriel brushed his knuckles down the ridge of her cheeks with such gentleness he brought her eyes fluttering closed. "I expect there are regrets for the cold union you've found yourself in."

At the softly spoken pronouncement, she snapped her eyes open. How could he speak so casually about their marriage? Then, it wasn't really a marriage. "What regrets should I have?" she said past tight lips. "I am, as you said, assured the protection of your name and will have security I've never been afforded before." She made to step around him, but he blocked her path.

"Your finishing school."

She stared confusedly up at him.

"You did not mention the funds you now have to establish your school."

Jane started. Why…he was indeed, correct. She hadn't. "Of course, there will be my finishing school." Though, now that they were wedded, it would really be his finishing school. She took another step around him and this time he did not block her retreat. She'd reached the door, when a question pressing on her all evening brought her spinning back around. "You would allow your wife, your marchioness to establish and run a school." The scandal of it would surely be gossiped about for years.

He walked over and then came to a stop before her. "I would."

"Why?" Was it because he, in some way, had come to care for her enough that he'd allow her that freedom?

"Because I think it is honorable, Jane. I think your efforts and goals are worthy and, for that, I don't give a jot for Society's opinion."

"I am a bastard," she felt compelled to point out. Bitterness tinged her words. She'd been reminded of that detail from the very moment she'd entered the world, as such, it was impossible to extricate herself from that distinction.

He pressed his thumb against her lips and rubbed the lower flesh. "My father was a monster," he said, jerking her attention up to him. "He beat my brother and my sisters…"

"And you," she finished when he let the obvious thought go unspoken.

"And me." He gave a terse nod. "Society would see him as a man of worth and value for no other reason than the title he was born to and the *noble* blood coursing through his icy veins." Suddenly, he stopped stroking her lip and she mourned the loss of that gentle touch. "The truth is, you have more worth than any bloody nobleman I've known, more worth than any person I know." He gave his head a sad shake. "You deserved a true marriage, to a man worthy of you. Not me. I'm merely a name."

Merely a name. That is all he believed himself to be? A sliver of her heart cracked away from the once whole organ and, in that moment, became his. No one had ever seen her worth beyond the circumstances of her ignoble birth. This man did. He might not want her in his bed or in his life, but he saw her worth. Selfishly, she wanted it all from him.

He offered her his elbow. Jane hesitated a moment and then placed her fingertips along his sleeve. The ripcord muscles rippled under her touch, hinting at a man who didn't only see her in terms of finishing schools and companionship for his sister.

They stood there, unmoving, with a room of his family and his closest friend, and the vicar who'd wed waiting. The room echoed with the noticeable intakes of her breath. Or was that his? She looked up and found his gaze trained upon her mouth. He dipped his head and then hesitated, as though warring with himself.

I want you, too. She willed him to kiss her as he'd done at the theatre, before they'd been thrust into this uncertain world as wedded strangers. Then with his hesitancy, she made the decision for him. Jane leaned up on tiptoe and touched her lips to his. He stiffened as she pressed herself against him but then, with a groan of surrender, he slanted his mouth over hers again and again. Lost was the restrained gentleman he'd been since the theatre two evenings ago. In his place was the man who'd wanted her.

Gabriel worked his hands down her body and settled them on her hips, dragging her even closer. She melted into him and opened to his fierce invasion. He stroked her tongue with his, over and over until a desperate moan escaped her. He swallowed that sound under the force of his kiss. Jane clung to him in a bid to stay upright, but he drove her back against the wall, anchoring her with the strength of his body.

She arched her neck and borrowed the support of the hard plaster. "What hold do you have upon me, Jane Munroe?" he rasped as he dragged a trail of kisses along the column of her throat. He nipped at the tender flesh where her pulse beat maddeningly for him and drew the skin into his mouth, suckling.

"Th-the same hold you have upon me," she gasped as her eyes slid involuntarily closed. Gabriel moved his lips down the length of her neck, lower, to the swell of her décolletage. She fisted her hands in his hair and bit her lip hard as he touched his mouth to her skin. "I never knew I could feel like this," she whispered as he continued to worship her with his searching caresses.

"Neither did I." His breath came in deep, gasping breaths.

He returned his mouth to hers and she gave herself over to the power of his kiss. Their tongues danced in a forbidden ritual of lovers, thrust and parry, thrust and parry. Gabriel cupped her breast, molding his palm to the full contour and she bit her lip to keep from crying out. She brought trembling hands to his hair, once again to hold him in place and never let go. Her lashes drifted closed and she, who'd fought this enigmatic pull he'd had upon her since their first meeting, let herself free to it—to him, to the possibility of them. "I love you," she whispered.

He stopped; his head bent over her breast. His rapid breath warmed her skin.

"I love you," she repeated when he still said nothing. She braced for the sudden rush of terror that making such an admission should cost her and yet it did not come. Days, weeks, or years, it mattered not how long a person knew another person; it mattered about the goodness of their soul and their hold upon a heart. Somehow, he'd shattered her resolve to protect her heart and live a life dependent upon no one but herself.

Gabriel's body went taut and he released her with such alacrity, she would have stumbled if the wall hadn't been at her back. Her chest rose and fell with the force of her breaths. He shook his head back and forth in a slow, repetitive manner.

She nodded. "I do," she whispered and held her palms up. "I love—"

"Do not." That harsh command cut across her declaration and killed the sentiments on her lips.

Her heart twisted at the horror stamped on the lines of his face. She managed a small smile and imagined it was a weak, pathetic attempt. "Not saying those words does not make them untrue, Gabriel."

He took a step away from her, and then another, and another, until his legs knocked against the chair. With fingers that shook, he raked a hand through his tousled dark curls. "You d—"

"Yes," she nodded. "Yes, I do."

"You don't even like me." There was an entreaty in those five words that if her heart weren't breaking even now at his response, would have brought her to laughter.

She pushed the door closed, and toyed with the handle a moment, fixating on the shiny gold metal. "Am I a whore because my mother was?"

"Do not even say that," he snapped out with a steely anger that stole the remainder of her heart.

Jane turned back to face him. "But isn't that the company I keep? By your own admission of your status and worth, shouldn't my value be weighed in a like manner?"

"It is not the same." He swiped a hand over his face.

"Isn't it?" She pushed away from the door and took a step toward him. "You cannot be a hypocrite and hold me above my birthright, and then not do the same for yourself."

"You don't love me," he said over her, not seeming to hear her words.

"I do," she said taking another step toward him.

A muscle jumped at the corner of his right eye. "You'd agreed to a marriage of convenience." He paused. "Not even a day ago." There was an accusatory bite to his words. "You are confusing gratitude with—"

She narrowed her eyes. "Do not even finish that, Gabriel Garmund Randolph Edgerton," she said, grateful more than ever for the entirety of that grand name.

He wisely snapped his mouth closed.

"I may love you, but you still infuriate the blazes out of me with your high-handedness." Jane took a deep breath and closed the distance between them. If he'd not already been prevented backward movement by the upholstered sofa, she'd wager all of her three thousand pounds he'd have retreated faster than Boney on his march through Russia. She placed her palms on his jacket and smoothed the lapels. His body went taut under her touch. "I know you do not love me." She paused for a fraction of a moment, hoping with a small tiny part of her soul she'd only just discovered existed that he'd issue a protestation.

But it did not come. The muscles of her stomach tightened painfully. Oh, God. In this loving a man who'd never return those sentiments, she'd become her mother. "I do not expect anything more from you than the security you provide." And with those words, she became more her mother than she'd ever dreamed herself to be.

Gabriel closed his eyes a moment. With Jane's nearness, the scent of lavender and honey that clung to her skin wafted about him until he was drunk on the fragrance of summer. Her hands upon his person coupled with her admission, sucked at his. She loved him. He pressed his palms over his face and drew in a slow breath.

What she asked, what she would inevitably expect would require a piece of him that he could not give. He wanted no part of caring for anyone else. *Except, now she is yours to care for, forever. Finishing school or no finishing school. Until death do us part...* "This is not what we had agreed to," he repeated those desperate words, ripped from deep within his chest. For with their vows sealed, the permanency of their decision registered.

And now there was love. Her love. With anything more of their marriage would come children and just more people to care for and more people to fail—"I cannot give you what you," *deserve.* "Hope for," he said. His thick tongue made words difficult.

Her hands fluttered back to her side. "I'm not asking you for anything."

In telling him, however, she did ask more of him. Expected more. Gabriel sidled away from her. His feet twitched with an involuntary urge to flee. "Jane, I will care for you, but I cannot," his mind balked at finishing those words.

"Love me," she said softly. A sad, little smile played about her bow-shaped lips. "Care for me?" she repeated those words back to herself. "Funny how one can care for a person while not caring about them."

Her words wrenched at his heart and ripped the blasted organ that had ceased to beat for over thirty years. She cleared her throat and took several steps away from him. He mourned the loss of her nearness. "We should join your family." Jane turned on her heel and started for the door.

Gabriel drew in a slow breath and then followed after her. How many other women would have spun on their heels and stormed off, indignant and making demands? Jane moved at a sedate pace and allowed him to reach her side. The synchronized footfall of his boots and her slippers echoed in the corridor, and as they drew nearer to the breakfast room, the cheerful peal of laughter and giggles punctuated the quiet.

They entered the room together and the small collection of his family and Waterson looked up in unison. Their laughter and discourse came to a screeching halt.

In apparent unease, Jane shifted on her feet and he imagined how hard this sudden change of circumstances was for her; a stranger to strange people, ruined and swiftly wedded and now part of his family's fold. God, she was brave. He reached for her hand just as Imogen shoved back her chair and sprinted over. Gabriel immediately let his hand fall to his side.

"Jane!" Imogen greeted and took his bride by the elbow and gently guided her to the table. His bride. A loud humming filled his ears and he took a frantic look about the table. His gaze collided with Alex's.

You can't even say the word...

The wry grin on his brother's lips indicated he even now had detected Gabriel's tumult.

"Do you intend to stand and stare at the door all day?" Chloe piped in, cutting into his musings. "Or will you join the breakfast?"

Jane cast a glance back at him and he gave her a slight nod, intending for her to know he was here, that these people were different than the beasts they'd both known. A servant pulled out the mahogany shell-backed chair and she slid into the seat. Gabriel hurried and sat beside her.

And just like that, the stilted awkwardness was replaced by the cacophony of discussion and laughter. He swiped his glass of wine and took a long sip. From the corner of his eye, he studied his wife. She spoke with a matter of fact shame about the origins of her birth, but for her strength and proud bearing of her frame, she had the regality of a queen.

She stilled, as though feeling his gaze upon her, and then looked up. He braced for the hurt and regret in her eyes, but there was merely the spirited glimmer he'd come to expect from the silver flecks. Jane leaned close. "You needn't worry, Gabriel. I will not have unfair expectations of you simply because I love you." *Simply because I love you.* His own siblings barely loved him and for very good reasons.

He was spared from formulating a reply, as servants rushed forward with platters of food, diverting her attention. Yet, as he sat there, he wished he could be everything Jane deserved.

TWENTY-FOUR

Having been the daughter of a duke's mistress, Society and servants alike surely expected that one such as she would have learned her mother's tricks and inherited her wanton ways.

Yet, with nothing more than Mrs. Wollstonecraft's book for company on her wedding night, Jane reflected with a droll amusement on the fact that she: one, didn't have an inkling as to what truly transpired between a man and woman on one's wedding night and two, that it didn't really matter, for hers would never truly be a wedding night.

With a sigh, she pulled her knees up and flipped open her copy of *A Vindication of the Rights of Woman* to the folded and marked page. She instantly located the familiar portion of text and mouthed the long ago memorized words.

> "…Whilst they are absolutely dependent on their husbands wives will be cunning, mean, and selfish, and the men who can be gratified by the fawning fondness of spaniel-like affection, have not much delicacy, for love is not to be bought, in any sense of the word, its silken wings are instantly shriveled up when anything beside a return in kind is sought.

She sat back in her seat and leaned against the wall. Those words took on an altogether new meaning. A love that was not bought, for if it was, the sentiment would shrivel and die. Her mother had been bought. And now so had she. How had she failed to see that? How, until Gabriel had kissed her in his brother's parlor, did she not realize that she'd sacrificed her future to secure her future? Her mother had shiny baubles and satin skirts. Jane would have her finishing school. Neither knew love, and she never would, by her husband's horror at her admission.

A knock sounded at the door and she glanced up. Her heart climbed, and then Chloe entered the room, and Jane's heart slipped all the way down to her toes. "Chloe," she said softly as she took in the usually cheerful woman's drawn features. She squinted into the dark at the ormolu clock atop the fireplace mantel. "It is late. Is everything all right?" She jumped to her feet. "Is it your head?"

Chloe pushed the door closed and waved. "No, it is not another of my megrims." She walked with a brisk clip over to Jane and then stopped before her. "It is Gabriel."

She looked about, her heart thundering hard once again.

"He is not here," the young woman said, interpreting Jane's question.

Sleep had eluded her, and since they'd returned from the lavish wedding breakfast thrown by Lord Alex and his wife, Gabriel had disappeared. Unknowing how else to respond, Jane merely uttered, "Oh." Of course he was not here. The office had been empty and quiet from the moment she'd retired for the evening.

Chloe gave her head a firm shake and pursed her lips. "You misunderstand me, Jane. He is not here. He is," she slashed the air with an angry hand. "He is gone out to his clubs or...wherever else it is gentlemen go," she said furiously.

Jane drew back to prevent from being hit by one of those wildly gesticulating hands. The young woman's words registered and pain knifed through her heart. It should not matter. Gabriel had already been abundantly clear that theirs was to be a marriage in name only. Yet foolishly she'd believed, nay *hoped*, there would be more...that there would be a real marriage and a wedding night and—

With a growl, Chloe planted her arms akimbo. "You are not to look like that."

She cocked her head.

"Dejected," Chloe supplied. "You should be livid. Why, it is bad enough he's allowed me to remain here so that you can't...be alone as husband and wife." Most young ladies would have been blushing red after having uttered those words.

A strangled laugh bubbled up and lodged in her throat. Oh, God love Chloe. She no longer knew whether to laugh or cry.

Chloe made a sound of sympathy and then patted Jane's shoulder. "Don't cry, please don't cry."

Jane smiled. "I was laughing."

The other woman snapped her eyebrows together. "Well, laughter is certainly not the appropriate sentiment."

She schooled her features. "Forgive me," Jane murmured. "I'm unfamiliar with the proper protocol for being abandoned by one's husband on one's wedding night."

Horror lit Chloe's eyes as she registered just how her bold words about Gabriel this night might affect Jane. She slapped her palm to her forehead. "I am such a ninny. Of course you are hurt."

Filled with a restive energy, Jane swept up her book and wheeled away from Gabriel's sister. She carried it over to the window at the opposite end of the room. "Ours is an arranged match, Chloe. Ours was formed because I was ruined and your brother had some misbegotten sense of loyalty to do right by me."

The snap of satin skirts indicated the young lady had moved. "As he should. Gentlemen do not go about ruining young ladies without then wedding those same ladies." With her strict expectations, Chloe would be far better suited to any post with Mrs. Belden than Jane had ever been.

She fanned the pages of her book. "The funds settled upon me by my father were contingent upon my marriage." She could not keep the bitterness from her words. After all these years, those three thousand pounds had represented the one thing her father had done for her that indicated he cared and worried for her future.

"What?" the young woman exclaimed, her tone that of one who'd been dealt a sharp jab in the belly.

She cast a glance back at Chloe. "Your brother offered to wed me so I might access those funds. He doesn't want a," her cheeks burned, "true marriage. He wishes me to serve as your companion until you are wed."

"I will not marry. But if I *did*," the young woman gave her a pointed look. "Which I will not. Ever—"

"Chloe," she prodded gently.

"Er, yes, right…if I did, I would not tolerate my husband abandoning me on my wedding night. The lout," she muttered that last part under her breath. She pointed a finger at Jane. "And neither should you. Furthermore," she went on. "All he has done is fueled more gossip where you are concerned. The lout."

"It matters not, Chloe. They will speak ill of me regardless."

"But he can protect you where he could." Those words burst from the young woman's lips. Her chest rose and fell with the force of her rapid breaths. "He wedded you to protect you? And you for what? Your three thousand pounds?"

It had begun as that. Or at least she'd convinced herself as much. Jane dropped her gaze to the tips of her toes. She'd proven herself a liar in every way, now.

"It wasn't truly about your funds though, was it, Jane?" her sister-in-law said with a maturity of one far older, who saw far more.

And because she'd grown tired of all the lies, she shook her head once.

"You love him." As the young woman's words were a statement, Jane remained silent, not trusting herself to speak.

She started as a small pair of hands settled upon her shoulders. Absorbed as she'd been in her own ponderings, she'd failed to hear Chloe's quiet approach. "Win his heart," Chloe urged softly. "He is afraid to love." She hesitated the fraction of a moment. "We all are. But Gabriel wants it. He just doesn't think himself worthy of that sentiment." She wrinkled her nose. "The protective, controlling man he's become, he likely blames himself for…for…just for," she finished lamely. "He's always been that way." A sad smile turned her lips up. "Since he was a boy."

A hungering to know more about who he'd been as a child filled Jane. She swallowed hard to keep from asking about his youth. She'd wager he would have been a serious boy with the weight of the world upon his little shoulders. "What was he like?" Alas, there was the whole business with her tongue having a will of its own.

"Serious," Chloe said automatically. "Alex was the smiling, laughing one. Philippa the obedient one. But as he was much older, I did not truly know Gabriel. I remember him to be the serious one of our family." She lifted her shoulders in a little shrug. "We all, each of us, learned to deal with the life we were given. Except, Gabriel, well, he took on the responsibility for what happened to us."

Agony lanced through her heart. Her life had been lonely and uncertain, but it had not been a violent one. "It was not his fault." Surely, all these years later, he knew that.

"Oh, I know that. But do you think a man of Gabriel's character could ever absolve himself of that misplaced guilt?"

A knot formed in her belly. "No," she said softly. For the person his sister had described would never cease to accept blame, nor could he not take care of others. That desire to protect at all costs was just one more piece of Gabriel Edgerton that she loved.

Chloe jabbed her finger once more and wagged it at Jane. "You are not to tolerate his loutish behavior. Is that clear?"

Jane managed a small smile, even as her heart was still breaking for Gabriel. "Abundantly clear," she assured.

Chloe dropped a kiss on her cheek. "Goodnight."

As the other woman took her leave, Jane sighed. *A good night, indeed.*

"Are you mad?"

Gabriel glanced up from his empty glass. Waterson towered over him with a bemused look on his face. "Waterson." He motioned to a chair. "Will you not join me?"

The other man frowned and tugged out the seat. "You abandoned your wife on her wedding night?" his friend asked without preamble.

Gabriel cast a glance about and found a sea of stares directed at them. He frowned. Rather him. After all, it wasn't every day that a proper marquess was caught with his sister's companion, at the opera, in dishabille, wedded, and then at his clubs in the course of a thirty-six hour span. "I did not abandon her," he said and shifted in his seat. "Furthermore," he said, dropping his voice to a hushed whisper. "Ours is a matter of convenience and the lady is far better off without me."

His friend snorted and swiped the bottle. "I will take that." He robbed Gabriel of his glass and poured a brandy for himself. He lifted the glass in salute. "If you believe that, friend, then you were the only one to see different at your wedding breakfast this morning." A servant started over with another glass, but Waterson caught the eye of the young man and gave him a look that sent him scurrying in the opposite direction. When he returned his attention to Gabriel, he wasted little time in getting to the heart of it. "I understand you did not want to marry the young woman," Was that wholly true? Everything was so blasted murky.

His friend continued "But your being here," he gave his head a shake. "Why, your being here does nothing to help Lady Waverly. It only complicates matters for the both of you."

Lady Waverly. Not his mother. But a new marchioness. A role he'd had no intention of filling. He reached for his drink and then registered the blasted thing in Waterson's hand.

The earl swirled the contents in a slow movement and stared contemplatively down into the glass before again speaking. "Of course, I do see why you would be regretful and prefer the presence of your clubs at this moment."

He frowned.

Waterson flicked a hand. "You've once again done the honorable thing and for that, you're married to the daughter of a who—"

Gabriel leaned across the table and grabbed Waterson by the collar. Liquid spilled over the rim of the other man's glass and splashed their fingers and wet the table. "Shut your bloody mouth or, by God, I will end you," he seethed. How dare the other man disparage Jane? She was worth both of them and every other blasted gentlemen of their acquaintance combined.

A twinkle of amusement glinted in the other man's knowing eyes and Gabriel released him with such alacrity, the earl fell back into his seat. He'd merely baited him. "Say whatever it is and be done with it," he snapped.

Only, he didn't need the other man to supply his thoughts to know precisely what he was thinking. Gabriel had no place being here. Not tonight. Not in light of the scandal and certainly not having deposited his new wife, at home. Now Society knew it as well.

"I've certainly heard the whispers about her—"

Gabriel fisted the arms of his chair. The whispers. *I am a whore's daughter....* That is what all polite Society would say about her. Fury hung like a black curtain over his eyes. "I don't want to hear about the damned whispers," he gritted out. The *ton* would not see the brave young woman with far nobler aspirations than most.

"I've been your only friend for nearly twenty years. Not once in the course of your life have you asked for, accepted, or appreciated any help being given to you. Mine or anybody's." Waterson held his gaze. "No man is an island, unto itself, and so you'll accept my blasted help whether you wish it or not. You will begin by going home and making love to your wife."

A dull flush heated Gabriel's neck, as with those words, Waterson roused seductive images of Jane, resplendent in her nudity, with her golden blonde tresses cascading in waves about them.

"And then you will accept that she is yours and you are hers, and that your marriage is final. Whether you wished it or not." The earl set his snifter, nay Gabriel's snifter, down, just beyond Gabriel's reach and then planted his elbows on the table. He glanced about a moment and then dropped his voice to a hushed whisper. "And when you are done with that, do not leave her side again or else condemn her to a life to which she'll never fully belong."

Gabriel sat in stiff silence and took in the other man's words. "I cannot," he whispered, unsure whether he spoke to himself or Waterson. He slid his gaze beyond the other man's shoulder.

His friend gave a wry grin. "Alas, my friend, you already have."

He looked about and his skin pricked with the pointed stares studiously trained on him.

"Why did you wed her?" Waterson asked bluntly, bringing his attention back. "To protect her?" he supplied before Gabriel could speak. "Then do so. Prepare her for Society and spare her from further gossip." He jerked his chin toward the entrance of the club. "Go," he urged.

With guilt twisting in his belly—that hated, too-familiar sentiment that had dogged him all these years—Gabriel stood. "Waterson," he said in clipped tones. "Th—"

"No thanks are necessary. Now, go."

Gabriel turned and started over the crowded floor of White's when a familiar, hated form caught the corner of his eye. The rakish gentleman with his Brutus curls tossed back his head and laughed at something the person opposite him said and then he froze. The Earl of Montclair shifted in his seat and a mocking grin formed on his lips. "Waverly," the earl called out, raising his glass in mock salute. "I understand congratulations are in order." Mockery tinged his words. Gabriel stared at the man's mouth as it moved, imagined that mouth on Jane's, hard and punishing, as she cried and fought for her freedom, then ultimately attained it. Only to be punished for resisting Montclair's vile assault. And then of their own volition, his legs carried him over to the table.

The earl looked questioningly up at him with a jeering glint in his eyes. "Waverly. You've come to join—"

He hauled the bastard who'd put his hands upon Jane up by the lapels of his jacket, up from his seat and buried his fist into his nose, relishing the crack of bone and an agonized cry rung from Montclair's lips. There was a triumphant thrill of revenge, a satisfaction of his bloodlust. Perhaps he was more like his father than he'd ever dared believe, for the sight of the man's suffering filled him with an unholy glee. Gabriel tossed the other man to the floor, a bleeding, whining mess and then ignoring the frantic whispers, continued his march to the front of the club. A servant, with his gaze carefully averted rushed forward with Gabriel's cloak and he shrugged into it. As he exited his clubs and accepted the reins from a waiting servant to his mount, he drew in a deep, steadying breath, filling his air with lungs. Then he swung his leg over the chestnut creature, Devotion, and guided it onward to his townhouse. To his wife. To his future.

His mount shifted under his legs, at the tension in Gabriel's, and he lightened his grip upon the horse. In the quiet of the London streets, he mulled his friend's words. He'd pledged to care for Jane. The minute he'd ruined her, she'd become his responsibility and he was shamed by the truth that by seeking out his clubs to avoid the woman who'd upended his world, he'd only brought greater difficulty, too. And more—he couldn't avoid responsibility. It was part of who he was and one he could not extricate himself from, no matter how much they might wish it. Nay, no matter how much he might wish it. Gabriel guided Devotion down the cobbled roads.

She professed to love him. And while he'd spent the better part of his life wanting nothing to do with that damned sentiment, when she'd uttered those words, she'd breathed into him the truths he'd buried deep down inside. Truths he'd kicked the dust of life upon and hid—even from himself—that damned longing to have someone. What she'd dangled before him preyed on his greatest fears, but also a desire he'd never known he possessed grew inside him.

The façade of his townhouse pulled into focus and he urged his horse forward. No sooner had he leaped to the ground than a servant rushed forward to claim the reins. With a murmur of thanks, Gabriel strode up the handful of steps and through the doors opened by Joseph. "My lord," the butler greeted. There was a reproach in his eyes that may as well have been a mirror of Waterson's sentiments at the club.

Gabriel shrugged out of his cloak. "Joseph," he said. He looked up the staircase and cleared his throat.

"Her Ladyship has retired for the evening." The servant had developed an uncanny knack to know precisely what Gabriel was thinking before he even spoke.

"Er, yes, right. Of course." He started the path up the stairs and reached the landing to the main living quarters when a figure stepped into his path.

He swallowed a curse as he nearly crashed into his sister. "What are you doing a—"

Chloe planted her hands on her hips and glared. "Do not finish that sentence."

It was the truth of his existence that he'd be ordered about by mouthy, bold, English ladies. With a sigh, Gabriel tugged out his time-piece. "Chloe it is late."

"Is it?"

"It is."

"I was being facetious, Gabriel," she said between clenched teeth. "Of course it is late. And you should have arrived home long ago."

First Alex, then Waterson, now Chloe. He should be expecting an opinion from Joseph on his marriage to Jane.

"Jane needs your support."

"I know that."

"She must do what Imogen did."

Perhaps it was the infernal hour or the brandy he'd consumed at his clubs, or mayhap it was just that his sister was deuced difficult to follow and always had been. "What Imogen did?"

Chloe pointed her eyes to the ceiling and her lips moved in what he suspected was a silent prayer. "Brave the scandal." A determined glint lit her eyes. "She is going to have to enter polite Society and only then, when they see she can't be cowed, will they move on." She wrinkled her nose. "Society is cruel and merciless, you know."

And Jane would have to brave that. At the idea of her facing down the condescending sneers and pointed looks, fury unfurled in his gut. "I know that." Gabriel curled his hands so tightly into the palms he nearly drew blood. "I've already, with Alex's help, arranged several *ton* functions for Jane to attend."

"And…" She blinked several times in rapid succession. "You what?"

Did his siblings think him wholly ignorant of what Jane must do and face? "Both Waterson and the Earl of Primly will throw Jane—us—their support. I've accepted an invite to the Duke of Crawford's ball." He firmed his jaw. Despite everyone's low opinion of him, he'd not see

Jane disparaged or shamed before Society. *Then abandoning her on her wedding night, aren't you already responsible for that crime?* Guilt knifed at his conscience. "I will speak to Jane in the morning. She will be presented to Society and I will stand beside her and—"

"Then you will send her to her finishing school."

His sister and Jane had spoken. He swiped a hand over his eyes. "Chloe, it is late."

"As you've previously stated."

With her in one of her tempers, it wouldn't do to tell his sister that the missing piece to her words was her inevitable marriage and *then* Jane's departure. "And I will not debate the terms of the contract I've entered into with Jane. Now, if you'll excuse me," he said with a firmness he'd usually reserved for Alex through the years and stepped around her. He made it no more than five steps when she called out.

"You think to protect everyone, don't you? You would protect Alex from himself and his once roguish ways. And you'd protect me and Philippa by seeing us wed to proper gentleman who would not abuse us." She paused. "You would protect me from the truth about Philippa's uncertain condition."

He stiffened and then turned back.

She arched an eyebrow. "Do you believe I would not know about Philippa and her unborn babe?"

"I..." What could he say? Any defense he'd make would likely be met with a thousand and one arguments of why he'd been wrong in shielding her from Philippa's complicated pregnancy.

"You what? Wished to protect me?" Chloe took a step toward him. "Don't you see, you protect people in the hopes of protecting yourself from caring." She motioned behind him to Jane's chambers. "To protect yourself from loving, but you cannot shut yourself off from feeling. No matter how much you may will it."

With that, his sister left him, as he'd been for thirty-two years—alone.

TWENTY-FIVE

One Week Later

One week after her marriage and her husband's subsequent abandonment, Gabriel had provided Jane tutors and dance instructors and gowns and well...everything, with the exception of himself. They broke their fast together, in relative silence, and took their evening meals together in even greater silence. For the times Jane had attempted to speak to Gabriel, he'd proven the aloof, distant figure she'd first met, so that she didn't know what to do with him. In fact, if it wasn't for the company of Chloe, Jane was certain she would have gone mad days ago with the tedium of her own company. Until now. Now, she thought she might go mad for altogether different reasons. *Is this to be my life?* This cold, distant relationship with a man who, despite of what they'd shared, had become more of a stranger than ever before?

Standing beside her sister-in-law, Jane stared wide-eyed down at her bed. "They are pink."

"Well, they are not *all* pink."

The "they" in question were in fact the gowns selected, ordered, and now delivered by the fashionable modiste once upon a lifetime ago. The color preferred by Jane's mother and a shade she'd detested for the endless packages sent by her father—or rather her mother's protector. She'd sworn to never don a pink dress. Then, she'd done all manner of things now that she'd sworn never to do.

Chloe picked up a satin creation. "See, this one is not pink."

233

Jane angled her head and studied the garment in the young lady's fingers with dubious eyes.

Gabriel's sister shook it. "It is mauve."

Mauve, which was very nearly pink. With a sigh, she brushed her knuckles over the soft fabric. "It is lovely," she conceded.

The young woman beamed. "See. You will look splendid at the Duke and Duchess of Crawford's upcoming ball." She dropped the dress atop the others and spun around. *A duke's ball?* "Of course, you'd look splendid in anything you donned," Chloe continued without breaking her stride.

"What ball?" Jane called out.

Chloe paused and turned around. "The Duke and Duchess of Crawford's. The duke and duchess attend few events and host even fewer. An invite to their ball is the most sought after." She paused. "Everyone will be there." Bloody wonderful. "Which will be the perfect place for you to confront the *ton*. All you must do is force a smile, dance a handful of sets with your husband, Alex, and Lord Waterson for support, and then we shall be on our way and the gossips are free to move on to their next victim." A handful of dances. She'd have as much luck in navigating through one set as she did having the circumstances of her birth reversed.

At the prospect of not only facing down the vultures of high Society but also dancing before them, Jane curled her toes into the soles of her slippers. "But…" Her mind raced. Of course she would have to be presented to the *ton*. Those were, after all, the terms of her arrangement with Gabriel.

Chloe looked at her expectantly.

"But…" But she'd not believed her introduction would take place so quickly. Montclair slipped into her mind, as he'd been at the theatre—cruel, relentless—then she imagined a ballroom full of the Lord Montclairs and the young ladies she'd known at Mrs. Belden's. "I can't…" *Go.* "I can't…" *Do this.* "Dance," she finished lamely. Jane drew in a slow breath and smoothed her palms over her skirts. "I still do not know how to dance." There had never been a need to master those steps reserved for ladies and gentlemen who'd flit from balls to soirees. Now, however, there was a need and she'd proven herself a rather poor study.

"I daresay it is Mr. Wallace's fault."

Poor Mr. Wallace who'd had his feet trod upon for the better part of the week. If he didn't end up with broken toes by the end of Jane's lessons, that would prove his greatest career accomplishment. "I hardly think it is fair to blame Mr. Wallace for my inadequacy."

Chloe smiled and patted her hand. "I do say that is why I so like you. You never shift blame to others as you should have done with..." *My brother.* The young woman cleared her throat. "Regardless, Mr. Wallace is likely waiting and we really should be off to your lessons."

Jane sighed as a determined Chloe took her by the hand and all but dragged her to the door, out of the room and down the corridor. This young woman hadn't needed a companion; she'd needed to *be* someone's companion. As they walked at a brisk clip through the corridors, they passed the occasional servant who shot her a sympathetic look.

She grimaced. Apparently, the servants had learned how poorly their new mistress was faring with the whole presentation before Society business.

"I have faith in you, Jane. Mr. Wallace will prepare you for the Duke of Crawford's ball."

Jane wasn't altogether certain who Chloe sought to convince, Jane or herself with that promise. "Yes, you said as much," she said weakly. "Perhaps another ball?" she ventured. It didn't have to be a duke's ball. After all, there was a kind of awkward irony in a duke's bastard making her entrance to Society at another duke's ball.

Yes, a few more days would allow her time to accustom herself to the idea of a public shaming. One would think after years of Societal condemnation she'd grow accustomed to such treatment. Alas.

"No," Chloe said forcefully. "It must be this one," she said as they reached the empty ballroom. "His wife is kind," she said as an explanation. A kind duchess?

Mr. Wallace, tall, frequently frowning, and always put out, stood at the entrance of the ballroom. With his chestnut brown hair pulled back in queue and his lean frame, he very well could have been considered dashing to some.

If he wasn't always frowning.

Jane repressed a groan as her sister-in-law shoved her between the shoulder blades. "Off you go." Then she dropped her voice a whisper. "I will be here."

As she'd been for the week since Jane had been abandoned. With a sigh, she started for Mr. Wallace.

He said something to the violinist assembled and then turned to Jane. A beleaguered sigh escaped him. "My lady," he said in cool, clipped tones her husband would have been hard-pressed to emulate.

"Mr. Wallace." Though there was something very real and appreciated in a person who disdained her not for the status of her birth but because of her dreadful habit of plodding all over his toes.

"We have but two days," he reminded her needlessly as he held out his arms. She really didn't require that reminder.

She knew precisely how much time she had. Jane settled her hand upon his shoulder and then he placed his upon her waist. "I do not see how this is proper," she muttered under her breath. A man's hands so intimately upon a lady?

Mr. Wallace winced as she stepped hard on his toes. "It is the waltz, my lady," he said, righting her as she stumbled.

"It is a one-two-three count," Chloe called from the side.

She didn't care if it was a one-count shuffle along the floor. She couldn't keep the beat.

"And it is all the rage. Brought over recently from the Continent." So, now it was to be a history lesson.

"Oomph."

"I am sorry," she said automatically.

His lips moved in what she believed was a curse, if the staid dance master did something as improper and impolite as curse. Jane stumbled—again—and he steadied her, catching her firmly about the waist and drawing her close.

"I fear your efforts are futile." She would not master the steps of any one of the blasted dances he'd shown her and certainly not in time for the duke's blasted ball.

"Gabriel!"

At Chloe's exclamation, Jane looked up swiftly and trod all over poor Mr. Wallace's toes once more. Her heart jumped as her husband's towering frame filled the doorway.

"Gabriel, you startled me," his sister said, a hand at her chest. "I was just speaking to Jane about the Duke and Duchess of Crawford's ball."

Gabriel stood at the entrance of the ballroom. He never removed his hard gaze from Jane. The intensity of that stare burned her with its heat. It sucked the breath from her lungs. Then he moved his focus to where Mr. Wallace's hands lingered on her waist. The moss green of his eyes darkened near to black.

Mr. Wallace abruptly relinquished his hold upon Jane.

Chloe continued to fill the silence. "Jane still does not know how to dance." She favored both Gabriel and the poor dance master with accusatory looks.

Gabriel blinked several times as though brought to the moment and then turned to his sister. "What is this?" A slight frown played on his lips.

She swallowed a groan. "*This* is nothing."

"Dance," Chloe explained and threw her arms out and demonstrated a step. Apparently Jane and Chloe were of a different mindframe on the importance of the nonsensical steps and Gabriel's need to know such information. "Even after Mr. Wallace's attempts, she still doesn't know how." The dance master's scowl indicated his displeasure at having his efforts called into question before his employer.

Jane shifted. In her defense it really had only been a week. Granted, she'd made little to no progress in the endeavor. "It's true, I fear. I'm really rather horrid." Chloe and Mr. Wallace's silence stood as confirmation to her admission.

"I am certain that is untrue," Gabriel encouraged, the consummate polite gentleman.

Her heart tugged. No one was ever polite and a gentleman where she was concerned.

"Oh, it is true," Chloe, said unhelpfully. She motioned to the violinist. "Allow Mr. Wallace to demonstrate."

"Chloe," Jane began. "I—oomph." Mr. Wallace put his hands upon her once more and forced her into movement.

Through the painfully awkward, and for Mr. Wallace, likely just painful set, Gabriel stood at the bannister, his arms folded at his chest as he took them in with a hard, dark gaze.

What was he thinking?

"Do pay attention, my lady," her instructor gritted out the command for her ears alone.

"I am trying," she said tightly. It was just particularly hard with her husband glowering in that menacing fashion at the dance master. What had poor Mr. Wallace done to merit—"Oomph." The aggrieved instructor steadied her again, tightening his grip upon her waist.

"That will be all," Gabriel barked. His loud baritone thundered from the marble floors and echoed throughout the cavernous space.

Mr. Wallace came to a stop as though he'd been granted the Queen's pardon.

"Chloe, Mr. Wallace," Gabriel snapped. "If you'll excuse me a moment?"

Chloe smiled widely and inclined her head. "Of course." Jane stared after her as unease warred with excitement at the prospect of being alone with her husband. Or bridegroom. She still couldn't quite sort out whether or not he was a blasted husband.

She fisted her skirts as being with this man, the same man who'd abandoned her on their wedding night, alone now, when they'd been alone before, became altogether different. Not that either of them had entered into the union believing it would be a marriage in truth. She released her grip upon her fabric. "Gabriel. You wished to speak to me?"

Gabriel wished to kill the bloody dance instructor with edacious hands is what he *wished* to do. The sight of the other man touching Jane had unleashed something primitive and primal from deep inside—a fierce, ugly part of himself he'd never known existed.

He clasped his hands behind his back as his sister and Mr. Wallace and the diminutive violin master he'd hired took their leave. Except, now that he'd gotten rid of the bloody instructor, he hadn't a blasted idea what to say to Jane—whom he'd studiously avoided for the better part of the week, torturing himself through meals with a glimpse of her, and then separating. He'd spent these past seven days trying to rebuild the walls he'd built about him for thirty long years. He needed distance from Jane and the longings she'd stirred within him. Yet, a week later, he'd only found he didn't need distance—he needed to see her.

"Gabriel?" she prodded once more.

He tried to put his disordered thoughts to right. Gabriel rocked on his heels. "Are you getting on all right?" Never more than this instance did he wish he possessed a modicum of Alex's affability. His brother always knew precisely what to say.

A smile twitched at her lips. "Er…did you perchance see the dance skills I've acquired?"

No, all he'd seen was another man with his hands on her, touching her waist, holding her flush to his frame. The body that he longed to take and make his in every way a man could mark a woman. He growled and quickly closed the distance between them.

"Are you all right—eep" Her words ended on a squeak as he settled his arms about her. "What are you—?"

Gabriel guided her hands to his shoulder and settled his upon her waist. "Teaching you to dance." *Holding you. Holding you when it makes it all the more impossible to extricate myself from your hold.* Then, with the invisible strands of the orchestra he guided her through the motions of the waltz.

Jane stomped on his foot. "I'm sorry." She caught her lower lip between her teeth.

He shifted her, angling her body closer to his and effectively shrinking the space between them. She tripped over his foot.

His lips twitched. She really was as horrid as his sister had indicated.

"Oh, do hush," she scolded and then stomped on his foot.

He winced.

"That was deliberate."

Gabriel wouldn't feel comfortable placing any such wager on that particular—

Jane jammed the heel of her slipper into his instep.

He arched an eyebrow. "And what was that for?"

"For doubting the previous misstep was not deliberate."

A chuckle rumbled up from his chest. The sound was rusty from ill-use these years and he stumbled.

"That was not my fault," she said tartly.

Yes, it was. "No." *You upended my world, so that I laugh and smile and tease.* He drew to a stop. His pulse pounded so loudly, it filled his ears with a dull humming. He released her with such alacrity she slipped, but then adroitly righted herself.

She wrinkled her nose. "You've given up a good deal before Mr. Wallace."

How could she be so casual, unaware or uncaring of the tumult she'd thrown his world into? "You need to be presented to Society."

"I know that," she said tentatively. "There is the matter of serving as Chloe's companion."

He fixed upon that. That was her role. That was why he'd wed her. That and to save her. "The sooner Chloe makes a match—"

"The sooner I can begin my school."

What was once honorable, now grated. He hated her damned school. He gave a nod.

Jane tipped her chin up at a mutinous angle. "I'll not be welcomed by the *ton*, if that is what you are hoping," she said with the same fire and strength he recalled from that day she'd refused to leave his townhouse.

His frown deepened. "Do not be preposterous. You are my wife." He'd ruin anyone who gave her the cut direct.

"Am I?"

He looked at her.

"A bride, yes. A wife, no," she took a step toward him. "Not as long as our union is…" Her cheeks turned red. "Unconsummated."

Gabriel choked at the boldness of her words as a sea of images flooded his mind. Of him taking her. Laying claim to her. Spilling his seed inside her. At that, he lurched backward.

"Gabriel?" She held out a tentative hand.

He gave his head a shake and her delicate fingers fluttered to her side. "I should not have left you," he said, his voice hoarse with emotion. "On our wedding night." *Any night.* Gabriel raked a hand through his hair. "I would—"

Several lines creased her brow. "What is it, Gabriel?"

"I would have you understand." He stared above the crown of her golden curls. Shame knotted his belly. "My father, as you know, beat me. He beat all of us with a staggering frequency. My sisters, my brother and me." A bitter laugh escaped him. "I was a bloody coward. I hid when I could, more concerned with my own survival than that of my siblings." He could not however, be a coward in this. He looked to her and held her gaze. Agony, regret, and some other host of emotions he could not identify filled her eyes. He held up his hands. "As their older brother, I had a responsibility to care for them, to see them unhurt. Do you know who put a stop to the years of abuse?"

She gave her head a jerky shake.

"My younger brother." He dragged a hand over his face as the memories of that long ago day flooded to the surface. "My brother stepped in when I was too cowardly. But the damage was done by then, Jane. Philippa, Chloe, Alex, they were all scarred. At that moment in my life, I knew I never wanted the care and responsibility of another to fall to me. I failed them." *And I will not fail you now.*

A single teardrop rolled down her cheek, followed by another and another. "Oh, Gabriel, you think yourself undeserving of love." Her words lanced through him with a shocking accuracy. "That is why you push everyone away." *That is why I push you away. I've never wanted another.* She took a step toward him and claimed his hand. "Don't you see?" He stiffened at her touch, wanting it and wanting himself free of all hint of her. "You didn't fail them. Your father failed them." Just as her father had failed her.

He went taut as she wrapped her arms around his waist and held on. His hands hovered involuntarily about the air, and then he slid his eyes closed and folded his arms about her and began to believe, for the first time, that perhaps, just perhaps, he could turn himself over to the power of caring.

TWENTY-SIX

Five hours.

Or 300 minutes.

And if one wanted to be even *more* precise, 18000 seconds.

As the carriage rattled along the cobbled London streets, Jane worked through the amount of time she'd be forced to smile and dance and well, mayhap not dance, but be present at the Duke and Duchess of Crawford's ball.

She drew back the curtain and stared out at the passing carriages. That was how long Jane had resolved she'd have to spend on the fringe of the glittering world of London Society that terrified her; a people whose world she didn't belong to.

From the opposite bench, Chloe gave her a sunny smile. "Alex and Imogen will be there, as will Lord Waterson. Imogen braved a scandal herself in a like manner. When you show Society you are unaffected by them, they move their attentions elsewhere. It's true. Isn't it, Gabriel?"

Jane looked to her husband. He gave a succinct nod but otherwise contributed nothing further to the discourse. She sighed. She would feel a good deal better if that lie was coming from the somber, stoic gentleman at her side. Their conveyance rocked to a halt in the long line of carriages and Jane's stomach plummeted to her toes.

They'd arrived.

The crush of carriages before the duke's townhouse delayed their arrival and with each painfully slow-moving moment, panic pounded away at her breast. It climbed up her throat and threatened to choke her.

A servant drew open their door and Gabriel stepped down first. He then turned back to her. She'd braved censure and disapproval throughout the course of her life. What was one more night? In front of hundreds of guests. Nearly all strangers. She drew in a steadying breath and climbed out of the carriage then paused to stare up at the pink façade of the impressive Mayfair townhouse. Her first event. She swallowed hard. She'd rather sit down to tea with Mrs. Belden after revealing she'd taken the woman's missive sent by the Marquess of Waverly.

A small hand settled on her back and she started.

Gabriel gave her a look. "It will be fine," he said with a stoic calm she resented from him in this moment. Of course he should be calm. This was his world. He'd been born and bred to live amongst these people. She had been scuttled away, a dirty secret kept, and by Lord Montclair's words at the theatre one week earlier—a poor secret, at that.

"It really will be fine, Jane," Chloe said quietly. She gave her a winning smile. "You have friends."

Friends. After a life alone, she had friends who cared for her and about her. She stared at Chloe's retreating back hating the blasted lump of emotion swelling in her throat. She didn't want to turn into a watering pot. Not now. Not ever. Showing emotion was dangerous. Particularly on this night.

He returned his attention to her. "I will not allow you to be ill-treated."

Poor Gabriel. She shook her head sadly. "You still do not know."

He gave her a look.

"You cannot prevent others from hurt just because you wish it. I have been given the cut direct before and do not doubt my status as your wife, given my circumstances, will not result in the same unkindness shown me by Society."

He passed a searching gaze over her face and appeared as though he wished to say more, but then glanced over at Chloe who stood at the entrance of the duke's townhouse. Gabriel proffered his arm and Jane slid her fingertips onto his sleeve.

A tall, frowning butler admitted them. Servants rushed forward to help them from their cloaks and then they were escorted through the lavish townhouse done in white Italian marble to the swell of noise from within the ballroom. From the top of the stairs, Jane surveyed the crush of bodies.

"You will do splendidly," Gabriel whispered against her ear. His breath stirred her ear and shivers of warmth ran along her spine.

The butler cleared his throat and announced them before the collection of guests. "The Marquess and Marchioness of Waverly and Lady Chloe Edgerton."

All conversation came to a stop. All eyes within the ballroom turned to them. Jane's heart fell into her stomach. Grateful for at least her boldly confident husband's presence at her side, she allowed Gabriel to guide them down the stairs to their host and hostess.

The chestnut haired, towering gentleman exhibited an austere power that marked him a duke before even introductions were made. The woman at his side, a wide-smiling, plump young lady, however, melted some of her tension. Jane dropped a curtsy as Gabriel performed the necessary introductions.

Jane greeted the powerful couple with the same deferential courtesy instilled in her from early on. "Your Graces."

"It is a pleasure," the duchess murmured and something in her kind eyes indicated that she did, in fact, believe it to be a pleasure, which was, of course, madness. Every other person present now eyed her like the sludge dragged in on the bottoms of their slippers.

Then the introduction was concluded and Lord Alex and Imogen rushed forward to greet them. The Edgertons set themselves up as a kind of sentry beside her. An unfamiliar gentleman stopped before their small collection of family. Tall, blonde, and lean there was nothing immediately remarkable about the man.

"Primly," Lord Alex exclaimed and slapped the gentleman on the back. "A pleasure as always. May I introduce you to my sister-in-law, Lady Waverly? Jane, the Earl of Primly."

She stiffened and tipped her chin up, braced for his rejection.

Then the earl smiled at Jane and someone who'd been unordinary a moment ago became someone quite remarkable. A friend. She dropped a curtsy. "My lord."

"A-a pleasure, m-my lady," he stammered and she relinquished her guard in identifying a kindred spirit. He motioned to her dance card. "Will you do me the honor of a s-set?"

She dimly registered the hard stare Gabriel leveled on her and the other man, the narrowing of his eyes as Lord Primly reached for her card and scratched his name. If she did not know better, she'd believe he was...jealous. Which was, of course, also madness. Gabriel would have to care in order to be jealous. "I must warn you, I am quite a dreadful dancer."

Chloe nodded. "It is true," she interjected. "Quite dreadful."

Lord Primly captured Jane's hand and raised it to his lips. "I-I b-believe it is worth r-risking my t-toes for the pleasure of your company," he said in a low tone that elicited another scowl from her husband.

"If you'll excuse me," Gabriel snapped. "I was going to claim the following set with my wife."

Lord Primly released her immediately. The small smattering of friends and family went silent at his snarling response. "E-er, yes. Very w-well then." He sketched a bow and with a hasty goodbye to the remainder of the Edgertons, took himself off.

Before Jane could reprimand her husband for his rudeness to the one, polite gentleman she'd met in the course of her life—with the exception of her now loutish husband—he dragged her toward the dance floor where the dancers were assembling for the first waltz. "What was that about?" she bit out as she placed her hand upon his shoulder.

"What was what about?" Gabriel guided his hand to her waist.

"You were perfectly horrid to that nice gentleman. Lord Primly."

The orchestra began to play the haunting stains of a waltz and he led them in the scandalous, yet equally delicious, dance. Gabriel lowered his face close to hers. Beneath her fingers, the muscles of his forearm tightened within his coat sleeves. "I did not like the way he was looking at you."

She stumbled and he quickly righted her, bringing her closer to his frame. Only this misstep had nothing to do with her horrid dancing skills as Chloe had called them and everything to do with her husband's stunning revelation. "Why does it matter how he was looking at me?" she asked curiously. "Why, if I do not matter to you?" She gave a vague motion to the dancers about them staring openly and whispering loudly. "What should it matter what they say about me? Why, if you don't care?"

Gabriel leaned ever closer, shrinking the space between them. "Because I do care, Jane."

Her heart started as she tried to sort through the significance of those words. "Because of your sister," she put forth tentatively. With his concern for Chloe and all of his siblings, of course, her actions and her reception amidst Society mattered for that very reason.

He lowered his voice. "Because of you."

Of all the admissions he'd made in the course of his life, those three words were the most costly ones he'd ever uttered. And yet, the onslaught of terror did not come.

Gabriel braced for the rush of fear, the sense of panic that admitting she mattered should bring. Jane was unlike any person he'd ever known. It mattered not the circumstances of her birth. For him it never had. It mattered she was so fearless as to take control of her life and shape it for herself. When others saw to their own comforts and security, Jane had carefully guarded her own dreams with the hope of helping other young women like her.

I need her. I want her. I…love her.

Gabriel staggered to a stop. A couple adroitly stepped out of his way to keep from tumbling over them.

"Gabriel?" Jane applied pressure to his arm. He gave his head a clearing shake and promptly picked up the motions of the dance once more.

For years he'd seen that emotion as weakening. It was a sentiment that would cement his connection to another and bring with it responsibility and through that, inevitable hurt, and he could not do hurt. Not anymore. Not because of his own failings. How humbling to realize the siblings he'd spent his life caring for had proven wholly correct in their warnings and urgings. The emotion of love had once represented a shackle and yet he'd shattered the manacles he'd wrapped about his heart and admitted—he wanted her love. He wanted to be loved. More importantly, he loved her. "Jane—"

She cocked her head and stared expectantly back at him.

"I—" Could not say it here. He registered the stares trained on them. She deserved this moment but away from the peering eyes of gossips and unkind lords and ladies. The music drew to a halt and they stopped. Couples politely clapped about them and he closed his mouth. "I will lead you back to my family," he said lamely.

Jane nodded. "Of course."

As Gabriel turned to lead her to the side of the dance floor, he froze. His gaze collided with a pair of familiar blue eyes—Jane's eyes. From where he stood at the opposite end of the hall, the man skimmed his bored, ducal gaze over the crowd, as though he felt Gabriel's frigid stare. And then their gazes collided.

He once believed he could never hate a soul more than that of his monstrous father. In this instance, he realized there was another. With every fiber of his being he detested the Duke of Ravenscourt who, with his pomposity and disdain, had forced Jane alone in a world in which she relied upon only herself. And for that, a seething hatred coursed through him and licked at his senses until it was all he could do to keep from storming the room and taking the man apart for his crimes.

"What is it, Gabriel?" Jane asked, concern in her voice as she followed his stare to the duke. She looked back to Gabriel. By the lack of recognition in her eyes, however, she did not know the man who sired her was just a floor's length away.

He steeled his jaw, and jerked his attention away. "It is nothing. My family is motioning," he lied. Wordlessly, they made their way back to his family and, of course, his sister paced relentless as usual. "You cannot keep the lady to yourself all evening," Chloe chided. "Lord

Primly is here to claim his set." She motioned to blasted Lord Primly who stood in wait.

Jane beamed as the earl sketched a bow.

Bloody hell. The ladies seemed to adore Primly. Granted, he was an easy-going, mild-mannered chap, but did his wife have to smile at him in that manner?

"M-my L-lady," Primly said with an arm outstretched.

With a last look for Gabriel, Jane allowed Primly to escort her back onto the dance floor. Gabriel stared after them as the orchestra struck up another waltz. His brother stuck a glass of champagne under his nose and he grabbed the glass. "Isn't there some manner of etiquette and rules in playing two waltzes together?" he groused and then took a sip while from over the rim he stared at Primly, with his hands upon Jane. And this was far worse than bloody Mr. Wallace whom she'd been all frowns for.

"I suspect there is," Alex drawled at his side. "But then, when one is a duke, I'm sure rules of etiquette in terms of dance sets do not apply."

"I heard the duchess has always loved to dance and adores the waltz," Imogen said with a softness in her expression. "And the duke orders orchestras to play those waltzes so they might be in each other's arms."

Gabriel shifted his gaze away from Jane and damned Primly with his...with his...*hands*, and glanced momentarily at the duke and duchess in question. Hard, unflappable and coolly aloof, nothing struck Gabriel as warm or sentimental about such a man. No, one would never take the aloof duke for the romantic sort.

Gabriel found Jane once more. His heart swelled. A loose golden tress wound down her back, the pink of her satin shimmered in the candlelight. But then, one would never say there was anything warm or sentimental about Gabriel...and he'd gone and fallen hopelessly in love with his wife, a mere stranger three weeks ago.

So, one never truly did know where matters of the heart were concerned. It had taken Jane to show Gabriel just how much he'd been wrong about in the course of his life. Just then Lord Primly said something that raised one of Jane's unfettered smiles.

A growl rumbled up his throat.

"Stop glaring at Lord Primly," Chloe scolded.

"I'm not glaring at him," he said from the corner of his mouth. If he was glaring, it was certainly permitted with the way the man had his hands upon Jane.

"No, not a glare," Alex said with far too much humor in his tone. "I'd say more a glower than anything else."

At that precise moment, Jane stumbled and Primly caught her to him. He said something that raised another smile, a smile that should be reserved for Gabriel. And he suspected would have been if he'd merely been honest with himself and her. But now there was smiling Primly. Jane laughed and even in the crowded room with the din of the orchestra, the bell-like sound carried over to him. He snapped the delicate stem of his champagne flute. A servant rushed over to attend to the mess. "What are they talking about?" he muttered to himself.

His brother leaned over and spoke in a low whisper. "If I know Primly it is entirely scandalous, inappropriate—"

Gabriel turned a glare on him and his brother dissolved into a fit of laughter. He found Jane once more. He was bloody pleased that everyone was having a good time at his expense, but blast and damn, this being in love business was as trying as he'd expected it would be.

She laughed once more and he curled his hands at his side. What were they talking about?

TWENTY-SEVEN

With Lord Primly's stammer and his easy nature, Jane came to an almost immediate conclusion—they related more than she'd ever expected she would with a peer.

"Th-they judge a person quite unfairly d-don't they, Lady W-waverly." His was more a pronouncement than anything else.

She grew guarded and looked up at the earl as they made their way through the waltz. "Er—"

He snorted. "D-do I take you a-as one welcomed i-into their fold?"

"No," she said automatically.

A slight frown played on his lips.

"You are too nice," she said honestly.

Her words raised a grin. How very blessed the Edgertons were. They had not only family, but also friends. It was wrong to begrudge people who'd given her everything, this special something, and yet, she'd trade a portion of her soul for such luck. "Thank you for your support. I imagine it cannot be easy to dance attendance with," a bastard. "One such as me."

He snorted. "D-don't be silly." Lord Primly jerked his chin. "Who would you rather me spend the evening with?"

She started with surprise at the steady deliverance of those words. Gone was the man's stammer.

"There is Lord Albertsley, rumored to be cruel to his servants." He motioned discreetly to a stout lord with a bulbous nose.

Jane frowned. "That is horrid."

He continued. "Or there is Lady McAtwaters, who won't speak to anyone who is less than a baron."

A shocked laugh escaped her. "Surely you jest?"

He winked. "Well, perhaps a bit. I'll not tell you what they say of Lady McAtwaters." Some of his lightness was replaced by seriousness. "Th-these people are not better than you. They might disparage you and treat you as less worthy, but you are not, and do not give them the satisfaction of thinking they are." Jane suspected the earl spoke to the both of them and the kindred connection between them grew. He cleared his throat. "M-more worthy that is."

He fell silent and Jane looked out at the dance floor once more, contemplating Lord Primly's words. The whole of her life she'd been told she was inferior because of her birth. It was difficult to shrug off years of those very reminders. Yet, in the time she'd spent with Gabriel and his family and now Lord Primly, she'd come to realize—she was not different than these people and they were not different than her. They were all broken people in some way, moving through life, carving out happiness when and where they could. The muscles of her throat worked. And she wanted to carve out that happiness with Gabriel. Jane squared her jaw. Whether he wished it or not. She was going to fight for him.

She located Gabriel with her gaze and found his stare trained across the room, upon an older, vaguely familiar stranger at the opposite end of the hall. The same man he'd been staring at earlier. "Who is that?"

Lord Primly followed her stare. "The unsmiling fellow?" That could be very nearly everyone present. "The Duke of Ravenscourt."

A loud humming filled her ears. She stomped on the earl's feet once more. "The Duke of Ravenscourt," she repeated back dumbly.

He nodded once.

The Duke of Ravenscourt. Her father. A man she'd caught but two glimpses of during her childhood. The blonde of his hair had been replaced by a steely gray and his form had more weight to it than she remembered. But it was him. She bit down hard on the inside of her cheek. How odd to attend the same social function as one's father but still have no idea that the man who'd sired you was just fifty feet away—until a chance look across the ballroom floor.

The music drew to a stop and Lord Primly made to escort her from the floor. "If you'll excuse me," Jane murmured. And of their own volition, her legs carried her those fifty feet to the figure she'd spent the course of her life hating. A man who'd never acknowledged her existence but who'd settled funds upon her regardless. Such a man must have cared—if even just a bit.

Alone, with a crowd of nobles likely too fearful to approach the austere lord, he sipped from a crystal champagne flute and eyed those in attendance with a kind of boredom from above the rim. Jane came to a stop before him. He flicked a cool gaze up and down her person.

She smoothed her palms along the front of her skirts. Of course, there was all manner of dictates on the rules of etiquette in terms of introductions. Yet this man was her father. Surely because of that, a different set of rules applied?

He broke the impasse. "May I help you?" Icy derision coated his question.

A shiver snaked down her spine and her impetuousness in coming here set off the first stirrings of uncertainty. Only, he was the one who'd wronged her through the years. She was, as Gabriel and Primly and Chloe had reminded her, worthy of being here. "I—" Jane angled her chin up. "My name is Jane Mun—Edgerton," she amended. "I am the Marchioness of Waverly."

He flicked an imaginary piece of lint from his sapphire coat sleeve. "I know who you are," he drawled in thick, bored tones.

She wrinkled her nose. The duke likely heard the scandalous tale of her hasty wedding. "No," she tried again. "I am…" She dropped her voice and spoke in hushed tones for his ears alone. "I am your daughter." The duke gave no outward reaction that he'd heard or cared about her admission. Coldness spread throughout her frame and she resisted the urge to fold her arms and rub warmth back into them.

"As I said, I know who you are."

Jane rocked back on her heels. This was the man her mother had loved? This unfeeling, remote being is who her mother had died of a broken heart for? She eyed him a moment and expected more of the burning vitriol she'd carried all these years. Where was the consuming hatred? The scathing words she'd wanted to level upon his head? It was gone. Instead, in its place was a freedom—a freedom from her past. She didn't need his recognition or his love. And there was something freeing in that revelation. A tremulous smile turned her lips. "I have hated you for so long." He stiffened at her words. "You are no father. Not in the ways that matter," she said more to herself. Jane squared her shoulders. "But you settled funds upon me that sustained me and gave me purpose. For that, I thank you."

He peered down the length of his hawkish nose at her. "Funds?"

The first stirrings of alarm set bells rang within her ears. "The three thousand pounds upon my birthday. This year."

His brow furrowed in deeper confusion and the bells chimed all the louder. "I didn't settle funds upon you. I told Waverly I'd not see a pound go to any bastard claiming to be my child."

The floor fell out from under Jane's feet and her world tilted.

With his words blaring in her ears, Jane spun on her heel and rushed from the hall.

She skirted the edge of the floor and weaved between couples and when she'd put the ballroom behind her, and with only her father's words for miserable company, she raced down the corridors. Her heart thundered in her breast and threatened to beat outside her chest. Lies. All of it. Lies. There had been no funds. She ran all the faster. Her breath came in harsh spurts that filled her ears.

Why would Gabriel do this? Why…? On a sob, she shoved open a door, stumbled into a dimly lit room, and then quickly closed the door behind her. Jane leaned against the wood panel and closed her eyes. A tear slid down her cheek, followed by another and another. There had never been any funds. No three thousand pounds with which to shape a life for herself. He had known as much and yet he'd come to her, with the promise of those funds, given up his freedom and the vow he'd taken to never wed—all for her.

"Wh-why would you d-do that, you silly man?" she rasped. Not of love. But of some misbegotten sense of guilt; a need to take care of others while never caring for himself—even her, a stranger who'd lied to him. And she'd taken the greatest something of all—his name. Then, it appeared they both had based their entire relationship on deception. Jane covered her face with her hands and tried to suck in breaths, but they caught as broken sobs until she had nothing left to cry.

She scrubbed her hands over her cheeks to drive back the remnants of useless tears and absently wandered about the empty library, replaying every moment since she'd tumbled from the alcove at the London Opera House. Gabriel's offer, their wedding, the terms of their marriage. All of it. Jane stared down into the cold, empty grate of the fireplace. She preferred a world in which she'd perceived him as the pompous and arrogant nobleman. Those sentiments fit neatly into the views and beliefs she'd developed all these years about noblemen. Those powerful nobles weren't supposed to care about anyone except themselves. But Gabriel did and that truth now shook the foundation she'd constructed all her beliefs, goals, and hopes upon.

With his sacrifice, he'd done something not her mother, nor her father, nor anyone else had ever done—he'd put her security and happiness first. She lowered her head to the cool mantel and pressed her eyes closed. All he would get from her was two months service as a companion until Chloe made a match.

How could she face him, a man she loved so deeply now knowing this? No wonder he wanted her gone. She stared absently down at her satin slippered feet.

A shimmery glint captured her notice and she welcomed the momentary diversion from her father, nay the duke's revelation. Jane dropped to her knees and hesitated. Then, casting a glance about, she picked up the necklace. There was nothing remarkable about the bauble. It did not gleam or shine like the diamonds and rubies donned by the ladies whose employ she'd once been in, and yet...She trailed her fingertips over the intricate heart pendant. There was something majestic in its simplicity. She made to set it on the mantel when a click sounded in the night. Jane started and spun about, her heart thundering hard.

A young woman stepped into the room. Her heart sank to her toes at the familiar plump form of the young lady who'd stood at that receiving line earlier that night. *The Duchess of Crawford.*

The woman froze at catching sight of her. With the thick veil of darkness, Jane could not make out a hint of the woman's thoughts. Whatever they were, they surely would not be kind ones for this interloper, her scandalous guest who'd snuck off and stolen a moment of privacy in her library.

Jane swallowed and was the first to break the silence. She cleared her throat. "Your Grace." She executed a curtsy Mrs. Belden would have had a difficult time finding fault with. "Forgive me. I—" She closed her mouth. What could she say? That the truth of her father's disdain coupled with her husband's great sacrifice had driven her here?

The duchess angled her head and moved deeper into the room. As she came closer, her brown eyes glinted with curiosity and an unexpected warmth from one of her esteemed status. "You?" she prodded. Her Grace's gaze lingered a moment upon Jane's cheeks and she gave thanks for the cover of darkness that, at the very least, hopefully obscured a hint of her tears.

Jane swallowed a sigh. Of course it would be too much to expect the woman would not want to know what had brought her to the duke's private libraries. With all the lies she'd already crafted, she at last offered this woman truth. "I desired a moment away from," *the misery of my circumstances,* "the festivities."

The twinkle in the duchess' eyes sparkled all the more. "You do not enjoy *ton* events?"

Perhaps the woman didn't remember who she was. After all, there was a sea of guests in the crowded ballroom. What was one more lady, even if Jane was one of the most gossiped about figures present? Folding her hands together, the cool metal of the pendant pressed hard into the palm of her hand. "It is a lovely ball." She prayed the other woman didn't hear that for the weak lie it was.

A sharp bark of laughter escaped the duchess. "Your tone and eyes are unconvincing, Lady Wa?" So, she did remember her.

"Jane," she hurriedly insisted as heat slapped her cheeks. Then didn't everyone now know of the scandalous by-blow wed to the marquess. "Forgive me." Mortification curled her toes in the soles of her slippers. "It was not my intention to offend."

The duchess gave a wave of a hand. "I assure you, Jane, I would be least offended by your opinion of Society events."

Those words suggested this woman, just a step below royalty, too, held an aversion to the frivolous pursuits of the *ton*, and gave Jane pause. A gentle smile lined the woman's lips. "They are rather lonely affairs at times, aren't they?" She turned her palms up. "I know that better than you might believe."

Life was a rather lonely affair at all times. With a slight nod, Jane looked down at the tips of her slippers. "Still, I should not be here. It was unpardonable of me to have taken leave to wander your home, Your Grace."

"Daisy," she insisted. "Please, Daisy. The whole duchess, Her Grace, business gets very tiring." The duchess took a step closer and then dropped her voice to a conspiratorial whisper. "And I assure you, I've wandered a good number of homes in search of my own moment of solitude during tedious Society affairs."

Jane shook her head frantically. "Oh, no. Your event is not tedious." Terrifying, yes. Tedious, no.

"And yet, you are here," the woman admonished contemplatively.

And yet, she was here. Her Grace's words provided Jane the necessary window with which to make her escape.

Except, the duchess glanced about the room, and her earlier amusement and gentle warmth slipped. Concern flooded her eyes as she skimmed her gaze about the room. What brought the hostess away from her own ball?

As though sensing her question, the Duchess of Crawford looked to Jane. "I lost something." She captured her lower lip between her teeth and worried the flesh. "It was a gift given me by my husband. It was…" The muscles of her throat worked. "*is* very precious, a treasure worn by others and I've gone and lost it." Ah, so this is what would take the woman away.

The thin chain in Jane's palms throbbed with warmth and she looked down at her tightly clasped fingers. She unfurled her hand and held the pendant up. "Is this perhaps it, Your Grace?"

The room rang with the woman's startled gasp. Relief washed over her face as she accepted the delicate necklace. "Thank you so very much," she said on a reverent whisper. Her gaze caressed the inanimate object with lovingness. "How very odd." she murmured more to herself. "I've heard told the clasp was broken and yet, this evening was the first time I've ever been parted with the piece."

Jane shifted. She'd not known people to look upon even other people with that gentle connectedness. In a rush to fill the awkward silence, she said, "I discovered it by the hearth, Your Grace." Clearing her throat, she dipped one more curtsy. "If you'll excuse me. I should return to the ballroom."

"Wait!" the woman's soft cry stayed her movements and she turned back, fisting her hands at her side. Of course it was too much to hope the powerful peer would forgive her presence in her library. "You are just married?"

Grief knifed through her. Yes. That was what she was. Married. An obligation. "I was, Your Grace."

The ghost of a smile danced on the woman's lips. "Daisy," the duchess absently corrected her again. She wandered closer to Jane and walked about her in a slow circle, as though taking her in.

Jane stiffened under the unrepentant scrutiny.

Then the woman froze and shifted her attention to the necklace in her hands. She turned it over in her palms, passing it back and forth, repeatedly. "Someone once told me the necklace finds its way to the person who is supposed to possess it."

Perhaps it was the tumult of her emotions, but she now struggled to follow the woman's words. She tipped her head. "Your Grace?"

The duchess blinked slowly. "It is meant to go to you."

Jane searched about in consternation. She wanted to understand the lovely woman. She did. The Duchess of Crawford could have, by all rights, been put out with Jane for her bold commandeering of her room. Yet, she'd not. She spoke with kindness and warmth. "I'm afraid I don't understand, Your Grace—Daisy," she corrected at the woman's pointed glance.

Daisy thrust the metal into her palms and the charge of the hot chain penetrated Jane's gloves. She gasped at the inexplicable warmth generated by the piece.

The duchess watched her closely. "There is a legend surrounding that necklace. It was given to several friends by an old gypsy woman. She promised the wearer of the pendant would earn the heart of a duke." There was a wistful quality to her words.

Jane bit the inside of her cheek to keep from saying that she'd long given up on dreams and fairytales. "I do not need the heart of a duke," she all but spat. "As you see, I am already wedded." *To a man who does not love me.* "There will be no I—" She let the words go unfinished. The woman gave her a probing stare. Jane held the long, gold chain out. "I thank you for your offer, but you've likely heard the details around my marriage to the marquess." She wagered she'd be hard-pressed to find a single servant, soldier, or member of polite Society who did not know of those circumstances.

Daisy held her palms up and shook her head. "You must." She pushed her hands forward, forcing the necklace closer to Jane.

Jane gently pushed back. "No, I cannot." Would not. "That is a…" She paused. "…kind," Peculiarly odd. "Gesture."

Then the woman's chocolate brown eyes went wide, giving her the look of a night owl startled from his perch. "You love your husband." She spoke with the same shock and awe of a person who'd just been told the world was, indeed, round.

Desperate to be free of this painfully awkward and too intimate discussion with this stranger, Jane cast a glance about. When she looked once more at the duchess, she found her patiently waiting, with a soft, almost sorrowful smile on her lips. Jane curled her fingers tightly about the necklace and welcomed the bite of the pendant into the fabric of her gloves. "I…do." Those words dragged from her, were a hopeful bid to quell the woman's probing questions.

She gave her a gentle smile. "I once believed my husband did not love me."

At that intimate revelation from her, a stranger, she stiffened. Then, a duchess was permitted that bold confidence and strength. Jane weighed the chain in her palm. "It is unusual to find a peer who believes in those sentiments." And yet the Duchess of Crawford did.

That glimmer lit her kindly eyes. "Nobles are to wed for marital connections and power and not much more, you think?"

She lifted her shoulders in a little shrug. "I do not know what a nobleman or lady should believe or do." As soon as those revealing words about her origins left her lips, she bit the inside of her cheek hard. "I'm merely a companion," she finished lamely. "I was not born to your world." She glanced over the duchess' small shoulders to the doorway. "I really should leave." She should never have come. To London. To Gabriel's home. Jane again held out the necklace.

Her Grace folded her hands behind her back, her meaning clear: she'd not take the piece.

"Surely, it matters to you more?" she asked, in a last bid to make the woman see reason.

"I searched for this necklace through the streets of Gipsy Hill. Do you know who found it?"

She shook her head.

"My husband."

Of course. The heart of a duke, located and gifted by the duke of her heart. How very fitting, and—"It is all the more reason that you cannot simply give it to me, a mere stranger."

Daisy looped her arm through Jane's and gently steered her over to the door. "I've kept this pendant longer than I had a right to. It represented the talisman I hung my hopes upon after..." A flash of sadness lit her eyes and the muscles of her throat worked. "After a very difficult time."

Curiosity struck, but Jane quickly tamped down the sentiment. As one who valued and protected her own past and privacy, this woman's world was her own, and she'd not infringe any more than she already had.

The duchess gently disentangled the necklace from Jane's fingers and then turned her about. "When you look at me, Jane, you likely see a duchess. Perhaps a noblewoman to be feared." Yes, those lofty nobles had never given her much reason to trust them or their intentions. She placed the cool chain about Jane's neck and fiddled with the clasp. "But I'm no different than you. I'm merely a woman who desired love."

A painful swell of emotion climbed Jane's throat and choked off words. A woman who desired love. She pressed her eyes closed. This woman, in one swift exchange no more than a handful of moments, should look into her soul and see the truths she kept from even herself. Since she'd been a girl in the nursery, she'd longed for the love and attention of someone—her mother, her nonexistent father, a servant, anyone. And now she was married to a man who, by his own admission, never would or could love her. The faint click of the clasp at last catching filled the room and brought her eyes open.

"There," the duchess murmured.

Jane touched the filigree heart. "I don't want the heart of a duke," she said, her voice whisper soft, wrenched from within her. *I only want Gabriel's heart.*

The young woman's smile widened. "Neither did I." Jane furrowed her brow. "I wanted only the heart of my duke. My husband. And you," she motioned to Jane, "shall have the heart of yours."

There was no man. Nor would there ever be. Not a gentleman and not with the aspirations Jane had for her finishing school. "There will be no man to possess my heart," she said, her tone flat, and she reached up to remove the gift.

Daisy took her by the hands once more and guided her through the remainder of the room to the doorway. "Ah, but you still don't realize it?"

"Realize what, Your Grace?"

"The necklace found you. You have no other choice but to find love." The duchess started for the door and just as the woman touched the handle, Jane called out.

"Your Grace?" The young lady turned back and looked at her. Jane folded her arms close to her chest. "Might I request a favor of you?"

The woman inclined her head. "Of course."

"Will you have my carriage readied? I find I cannot stay."

TWENTY-EIGHT

S he'd taken his damned carriage.

Seated in the confines of his brother's carriage, Gabriel stared with sightless eyes at the passing streets. She'd left. From across the ballroom floor he'd taken in her approaching the Duke of Ravenscourt and then her flight. It was as though she'd disappeared—a task not impossible in the lavish, opulent home of the Duke of Crawford.

And if it hadn't been for the Duchess of Crawford, he would still be wandering his host and hostess' blasted home.

She asked for her carriage.

He fisted his hands on his lap and willed the carriage faster. What in hell had that monster said to her? Given her the cut direct? Cast aspersions upon her character and credibility as he'd done when Gabriel had approached him days earlier? While his tortured mind ran through every horrifying possibility, the grating rumble of the wheels turning over the cobbled roads punctuated the quiet.

As the illegitimate daughter of a nobleman, Jane had gone through her life treated as though she were of lesser worth, a woman who'd been told by Society's dismissal that she did not matter. In his silence, in his blasted determination to protect himself from hurting or feeling, he'd committed the most egregious offense against her—he'd fed the very same belief the lady likely carried.

Jane had given him her love.

And he'd rejected her. Pain knifed away at his insides and he rubbed the dull place where his heart beat. He'd gone through the better part of his life believing he didn't care about anyone or anything

262

but the obligation he had to his siblings. But he'd been so very wrong. He cared and it was as his brother said—claiming he didn't care and believing himself incapable of love, or being loved, didn't make it true.

The carriage rumbled ahead and he damned the infernal ride. The traffic had clogged the streets and delayed his return home.

I should have told her. I should have let her know just how much she mattered to me. He should have given her the words she'd been denied the course of her life; not because it was an obligation owed, but because they were the words she deserved, the words in his heart. He was nothing without her. He'd been nothing, an empty, cold shell of a person before her. She'd made him smile and laugh, and teased him, and—

His townhouse pulled into focus. Gabriel rapped once on the ceiling and the conveyance rocked to an abrupt stop. He planted his feet upon the carriage floor to keep from pitching across the seat and then tossed the door open.

"My lord?" his driver called after him as he sprinted the remaining distance down the street. His pulse hammered wildly in his ears and his breath came in great, gasping pants that had nothing to do with his exertions. He skidded to a stop at the base of the stairs and then took them two at a time.

God love Joseph. The servant threw the door open in anticipation and Gabriel rushed inside. He shrugged out of his cloak and tossed it to a waiting servant. "My—"

"Her Ladyship is above stairs, my lord."

The words had no sooner left the older man's mouth than Gabriel took the marble stairs two at a time. He stumbled over his feet in his haste and righted himself. Then he reached the landing. With his heart hammering wildly, he raced to Jane's chamber door and tossed it open. He staggered inside and located her in the corner of the room.

She stood at the corner of the window, her mouth parted on a moue of surprise. "Gabe—"

"W-wait," he rasped, sticking out a finger. "Just w-wait." A slight frown played on her lips. "Please," he added. He dragged a hand through his hair, damp with perspiration from running through the London streets. "I've always been rubbish at talking to people, J-Jane."

Gabriel panted, damning his earlier exertions that made a muddle of his words. He rested his hands on his knees and drew in several, slow, steadying breaths. "My sisters, my brother, my mother. I have but one friend. And even him I'm a miserable bugger to."

She cocked her head as though trying to make sense of his words, except his thoughts tumbled around in his head, over each other, so that even he no longer knew what to say or how to say it.

He tried again. "I never wanted a wife. Or children." She folded her hands before her and he stared at those interlocked digits so tightly clasped her knuckles turned white. "Until you. And even that, not until tonight. At the duke's ball, and—"

"There was no three thousand pounds."

Her soft whispered words cut into his profession. Gabriel straightened and stared unblinking at his wife. He shook his head in an attempt to process. "How—?"

"My father," she said quietly. "He explained that he'd never settle any funds upon a bastard child." Gabriel curled his hands into tight fists, torn between wanting to take her in his arms and hunt her father down and hurt the beast as much as Jane now hurt. "Is that true?"

He unclenched his hands and gave a terse nod. "It is." With that utterance, the lie he'd never truly allowed himself to consider, wheedled around his brain, now damning and ugly for the deception he'd practiced. "I'd thought to—"

"Protect me," she supplied, taking a step toward him. "That is who you are, though, isn't it?" There was sadness to her tone that gutted him. "You would marry a woman you didn't even like—"

"I liked you quite well." Only, as those words left him, he grimaced at how inadequate they were. "Well, not quite at first." He pressed his fingers against his temples. He was mucking this up, quite badly. He'd venture no lady had ever been won with such unromantic sentiments. "You infuriated me and do you know why?" He let his hands fall to his side.

She shook her head back and forth in a slow motion.

Gabriel closed the distance between them and took her hands in his bringing them close to his chest. "Because you made me feel and

I'd spent my whole life trying to not feel anything. You terrified me with your bold challenges and your undaunted courage." Emotion balled in his throat. "I have not given of myself in thirty-two years. I have let no one in. Not my brother or my sisters. Not any woman." A dull flush stained his cheeks. "In any way."

Jane widened her eyes as an understanding flashed within their blue depths.

Except, there was no shame with that truth. "I have not given any piece of myself to any woman and for that, I am thankful."

Tears flooded her eyes. "Oh, Gabriel," she whispered, stroking his cheek.

"I was waiting for you." He captured her wrist in his hand and brought it to his lips. "I just didn't know it. Jane Edgerton, I love everything about you. I love you for having carved out a life and slipping into my home in order to survive. I love you for wanting to open a school, because it is admirable and good. I love you because…" He placed a kiss against her lips and the familiar spark that had always been between them ignited. "I love you because there is no other reason than that I do."

The muscles along the slim column of her neck moved. "Gabriel, you don't have to—"

He claimed her lips once more, silencing her. "My whole life I've done what I thought I was supposed to." It had been a futile attempt to right his sins. It had taken Jane to show him that those crimes belonged to his father. "This," he drew her hands to the place where his heart beat for her. "There is no logic or reason to this. This is me, a man in love with you and if you leave me to go to your school, it will devastate me. Don't leave me. I—"

Jane leaned up on tiptoes and kissed him. Gabriel closed his eyes a moment and, for the first time in his life, turned himself completely and fully over to another person.

Hesitantly, he clasped her at the waist and drew her closer. Then kissed her as he'd longed to since their first exchange in his library. Kissed her as he'd dreamed each night since then. Kissed her with who he was. He plundered her mouth with his over and over and their tongues danced in an age-old rhythm. Gabriel swept her into his arms and carried her over to the wide four-poster bed then gently laid her down. He shrugged out of his jacket and tossed it aside. He tugged his cravat off and then his waistcoat followed suit. All the while, his gaze remained trained on Jane in her mauve satin gown. As he joined her on the bed, she came up on her knees. He touched his lips to the rapidly beating pulse at her neck and she tipped her head back on a shuddery sigh. Gabriel nipped and tasted the flesh, while he worked his fingers over the bothersome row of buttons down the back of her gown. A hungry desire to at last know her in every way made his fingers clumsy and he cursed.

Jane smiled and stroked her fingers along his jaw. "Always so in control," she said softly.

Gabriel yanked at the row of buttons and tiny pearl pieces scattered about the bed and floor. "I have had no control since the moment you entered my life, Jane." With that, he pulled at the fabric of her gown tucked beneath her knees and pulled her dress overhead, baring her to his eyes. Desire slammed into him so hard, it sucked the air from his lungs. "I love you, Jane Edgerton."

In her life, she'd been Jane Munroe. Mrs. Jane Munroe. Miss Jane Munroe. But never before had she had a true name. Not until now. Now, she had one that bound her to a man in a way she'd sworn to never want, in ways that had posed a danger to her freedom and control.

Gabriel removed her chemise and revealed her naked frame to his gaze. Then, there was far greater danger in being the bitter, broken person she'd been all these years. A woman who could not forgive. A woman who could not forget. But this beautiful coming together with another person did not weaken her. It made her stronger. With that, a sense of peace filled her chest. It drove back the animosity that had consumed her all these years.

"You should hate me," he whispered and placed a kiss at the corner of her lips. "I lied to you about your funds."

Yes, but then life had taught her that sometimes in order to survive a person did what a person must. Gabriel placed a kiss at the opposite corner of her mouth. It did not make it right. It made it...life. "Do you want me to hate you?" she teased breathlessly as he moved his questing lips down her throat, to the swell of her breast.

He palmed the flesh and weighed them in his hands. A moan worked its way up her throat as he raised first her right breast to his mouth. "I have dreamed of doing this from the moment I kissed you." His breath fanned her nipple and the flesh pebbled with the gentle stirring of air.

Jane bit down hard on her lip and held her breath in anticipation as he closed his lips about the turgid bud. An agonized groan ripped from her throat and her hands automatically came up to clasp his head to her chest. He sucked at the flesh until a wild yearning pooled between her thighs. Then he shifted his attention to her other breast. "Y-you are c-certain you've never d-done this before," she cried out as he suckled her.

"Quite certain." He slid a hand between her legs and with his long fingers, stroked the thatch of golden curls that shielded her womanhood.

"You m-must think me a wanton," she rasped and splayed her legs wide, encouraging him to continue his quest.

"I think you perfect," he whispered and then slipped a finger inside her.

A keening moan echoed throughout the room as she tightened her legs reflexively about him. Then he slid another finger and she bucked in a desperate bid to be closer to him. He continued to work her, teasing the hot nub at her center until thought fled.

She cried out as he suddenly stopped. "Why—"

"I need to feel my skin upon yours," he whispered. Gabriel quickly removed his shirt. All the while, his wife's passion-glazed eyes took in his every movement. After he tugged free his boots and tossed them to the floor, he shucked off his breeches. Gabriel returned to Jane's arms. As he lowered himself from above her, he took her mouth under his once more. Heat spiraled in her belly and spread like a slow conflagration of desire for this man.

There had never been another but her. Tears popped behind her eyelashes and she blinked them away. But a lone drop slid down her cheek. He drew back and momentary horror stamped out the desire etched in the harshly angular planes of his face. "Have I hurt you?"

"No!" She wrapped her arms about him and drew him down to her. "I am just happy," she whispered and tilted her head to receive his kiss.

Gabriel groaned and shifted himself above her and then with his knee, parted her legs. He settled himself between her thighs. "You will drive me mad," he whispered and found her with his fingers. Then, he slowly slid himself into her. Jane brushed her fingertips through his hair. Agony ravaged his face as he moved within her tight, hot sheath. Her body closed around them, so perfectly suited to one another. "I love—" her words ended on a cry as he plunged deep inside her. *Bloody hell.*

He stiffened above her. "Forgive me," he said hoarsely, his tone harsh. "Did that hurt?"

Like the devil. "A bit," she squeezed out but then he moved a hand between their bodies and stroked her center. Again and again until the pain receded and all she felt was the shared connection between them. The hot blaze reignited by his movements spread through her and threatened to set her aflame.

He increased his rhythm moving in and out and she lifted her hips in time, taking him. The pressure built, pounding hard and fast inside her, and she stroked Gabriel's face with tremulous fingers. He clenched his eyes tightly closed. And the rightness of their joining sent her over the precipice and she shattered into a million shards with white light flashing behind her eyes. Gabriel joined her immediately on an agonized groan that went on forever as he pumped himself deeper and deeper, and then he collapsed atop her—spent and replete.

Jane sank into the satin coverlet with Gabriel's broad, powerful frame pressing down on her. Her heart pounded hard and fast. Or was that his? He rolled away from her and she mourned the loss, but he only flipped onto his side and drew her into the fold of his arms. She burrowed against the solid wall of her husband's chest. All these years she'd spent hating noblemen and the prospect of marriage, only to find she'd been saved—by the love of a lord.

EPILOGUE

1 month later

Jane's back ached. Then, a four-hour carriage ride along the rutted old Roman roads would do that to a person. She winced as the carriage hit another sizeable bump.

"Almost there, love," Gabriel confirmed.

She frowned. "You've said that eight times."

He winked. "Well, this time we really are almost there." The carriage hit another dip in the well-traveled road and pain radiated from her buttocks, up along her spine. She wrinkled her nose. Her husband had mysteriously ordered her valise and trunks packed and loaded that morning. He'd given no indication where they were going. Or when they would arrive. Or—

"Blast and damn," she mumbled as the carriage listed right and then it rocked to a blessed halt.

"We are here," he announced cheerfully and reached past her to shove the carriage door open. Leaving her sitting with her mouth open and closing, he stuck his head back inside the carriage. "Well, then. Aren't you going to step down?" He held his hand out and she accepted his fingers.

"I still do not see what has been so secretive," she complained. She'd enjoyed a splendid month, the truly wedded wife of the Marquess of Waverly and would have been content to forever stay in London, in the comfort of the only home she'd ever known. With his hands upon her shoulders, he guided her forward and then shifted her to the left.

"Just a bit further," he encouraged and then stopped.

270

Jane blinked several times at the stucco manor house with its shattered windows and crooked front door.

Gabriel tugged off his gloves and beat them together. "I..." He frowned. "I was assured by my man of business that it would suit." Then he returned his attention to the building and scowled. "Alas, it's a bloody mess. It can be fixed. We will fix it. You will fix it, as you see fit..."

She looked away from the old manor home and stared perplexedly at her husband. "Are we living here?" Though at this point, after hours within the confines of a carriage, she wasn't altogether certain where here was.

"Er." He yanked at his cravat. "I would rather wish you'd live with me. And it wouldn't be appropriate for me to live here. Not with you."

Jane scratched her brow. "I believe a man and his wife are permitted the luxury of sharing the same home, Gabriel."

"It is a school," he blurted, yanking his attention back to her.

Her heart started and she swung her gaze in the direction of the old manor home. A school. A school in which young women could attend and be free to exercise their minds and take part in real learning. A school where young ladies of uncertain circumstances might carve out a life for themselves. Love for Gabriel swelled in her heart and she touched trembling fingers to her lips.

"Or rather it is your school. To establish, run, and control as you see fit." He held his palms up. "I—" His gaze went to her fingers and then he took in her tear-filled eyes. He frowned. "If it does not suit, than you are free to—oomph."

Jane flung her arms about him and he staggered back. "It is perfect," she breathed against his lips and then pressed her mouth to his.

Gabriel took her lips in a gentle kiss. "You are perfect."

She drew back and cupped his face between her palms. "No, we are not perfect." They were two very imperfect people who'd found each other. She drew him down closer and then pressed her brow to his. "And yet, together, we somehow are."

He rubbed his thumb over her lower lip. "I love you, Jane Edgerton."

"And I love you, Gabriel Edgerton."

And after years of being forgotten, dismissed, and rejected, Jane had in Gabriel everything she'd never had and always wanted.

A family.

The End

AUTHOR'S NOTE

The dramatic opera written by Gioachino Rossini, La Cenerentola first premiered in January 1817 in Rome's Teatro Valle. When it first debuted it was met with a good deal of hostility. It shortly went on to become very popular. La Cenerentola then premiered in Lisbon in 1819, and eventually premiered in London in 1820, less than a year after Jane and Gabriel's first meeting in "To Love a Lord". As the libretto written by Jacopo Ferretti worked perfectly for Jane and Gabriel's relationship, I took the artistic liberty of moving up the London premier date.

BIOGRAPHY

Christi Caldwell is a USA Today Bestselling author of historical romance novels set in the Regency era. Christi blames Judith McNaught's "Whitney, My Love," for luring her into the world of historical romance. While sitting in her graduate school apartment at the University of Connecticut, Christi decided to set aside her notes and try her hand at writing romance. She believes the most perfect heroes and heroines have imperfections and rather enjoys tormenting them before crafting a well-deserved happily ever after!

When Christi isn't writing the stories of flawed heroes and heroines, she can be found in her Southern Connecticut home chasing around her feisty six-year-old son, and caring for twin princesses-in-training!

Visit www.christicaldwellauthor.com to learn more about what Christi is working on, or join her on Facebook at Christi Caldwell Author (for frequent updates, excerpts, and posts about her fun as a fulltime mom and writer) and Twitter @ChristiCaldwell (which she is still quite dreadful with).

OTHER BOOKS BY

CHRISTI CALDWELL

"Winning a Lady's Heart"
A Danby Novella

Author's Note: This is a novella that was originally available in A Summons From The Castle (The Regency Christmas Summons Collection). It is being published as an individual novella.

For Lady Alexandra, being the source of a cold, calculated wager is bad enough...but when it is waged by Nathaniel Michael Winters, 5th Earl of Pembroke, the man she's in love with, it results in a broken heart, the scandal of the season, and a summons from her grandfather – the Duke of Danby.

To escape Society's gossip, she hurries to her meeting with the duke, determined to put memories of the earl far behind. Except the duke has other plans for Alexandra...plans which include the 5th Earl of Pembroke!

"A Season of Hope"
A Danby Novella

Five years ago when her love, Marcus Wheatley, failed to return from fighting Napoleon's forces, Lady Olivia Foster buried her heart. Unable to betray Marcus's memory, Olivia has gone out of her way to run off prospective suitors. At three and twenty she considers herself firmly on the shelf. Her father, however, disagrees and accepts an offer for Olivia's hand in marriage. Yet it's Christmas, when anything can happen…

Olivia receives a well-timed summons from her grandfather, the Duke of Danby, and eagerly embraces the reprieve from her betrothal.

Only, when Olivia arrives at Danby Castle she realizes the Christmas season represents hope, second chances, and even miracles.

"Forever Betrothed, Never the Bride"
Book 1 in the Scandalous Seasons Series

Hopeless romantic Lady Emmaline Fitzhugh is tired of sitting with the wallflowers, waiting for her betrothed to come to his senses and marry her. When Emmaline reads one too many reports of his scandalous liaisons in the gossip rags, she takes matters into her own hands.

War-torn veteran Lord Drake devotes himself to forgetting his days on the Peninsula through an endless round of meaningless associations. He no longer wants to feel anything, but Lady Emmaline is making it hard to maintain a state of numbness. With her zest for life, she awakens his passion and desire for love.

The one woman Drake has spent the better part of his life avoiding is now the only woman he needs, but he is no longer a man worthy of his Emmaline. It is up to her to show him the healing power of love.

"Never Courted, Suddenly Wed"
Book 2 in the Scandalous Seasons Series

Christopher Ansley, Earl of Waxham, has constructed a perfect image for the *ton*–the ladies love him and his company is desired by all.

Only two people know the truth about Waxham's secret. Unfortunately, one of them is Miss Sophie Winters.

Sophie Winters has known Christopher since she was in leading strings. As children, they delighted in tormenting each other. Now at two and twenty, she still has a tendency to find herself in scrapes, and her marital prospects are slim.

When his father threatens to expose his shame to the *ton*, unless he weds Sophie for her dowry, Christopher concocts a plan to remain a bachelor. What he didn't plan on was falling in love with the lively, impetuous Sophie. As secrets are exposed, will Christopher's love be enough when she discovers his role in his father's scheme?

"*Always Proper, Suddenly Scandalous*"
Book 3 in the Scandalous Seasons Series

Geoffrey Winters, Viscount Redbrooke was not always the hard, unrelenting lord driven by propriety. After a tragic mistake, he resolved to honor his responsibility to the Redbrooke line and live a life, free of scandal. Knowing his duty is to wed a proper, respectable English miss, he selects Lady Beatrice Dennington, daughter of the Duke of Somerset, the perfect woman for him. Until he meets Miss Abigail Stone...

To distance herself from a personal scandal, Abigail Stone flees America to visit her uncle, the Duke of Somerset. Determined to never trust a man again, she is helplessly intrigued by the hard, too-proper Geoffrey. With his strict appreciation for decorum and order, he is nothing like the man' she's always dreamed of.

Abigail is everything Geoffrey does not need. She upends his carefully ordered world at every encounter. As they begin to care for one another, Abigail carefully guards the secret that resulted in her journey to England.

Only, if Geoffrey learns the truth about Abigail, he must decide which he holds most dear: his place in Society or Abigail's place in his heart.

"Always a Rogue, Forever Her Love"
Book 4 in the Scandalous Seasons Series

Miss Juliet Marshville is spitting mad. With one guardian missing, and the other singularly uninterested in her fate, she is at the mercy of her wastrel brother who loses her beloved childhood home to a man known as Sin. Determined to reclaim control of Rosecliff Cottage and her own fate, Juliet arranges a meeting with the notorious rogue and demands the return of her property.

Jonathan Tidemore, 5th Earl of Sinclair, known to the *ton* as Sin, is exceptionally lucky in life and at the gaming tables. He has just one problem. Well…four, really. His incorrigible sisters have driven off yet another governess. This time, however, his mother demands he find an appropriate replacement.

When Miss Juliet Marshville boldly demands the return of her precious cottage, he takes advantage of his sudden good fortune and puts an offer to her; turn his sisters into proper English ladies, and he'll return Rosecliff Cottage to Juliet's possession.

Jonathan comes to appreciate Juliet's spirit, courage, and clever wit, and decides to claim the fiery beauty as his mistress. Juliet, however, will be mistress for no man. Nor could she ever love a man who callously stole her home in a game of cards. As Jonathan begins to see Juliet as more than a spirited beauty to warm his bed, he realizes she could be a lady he could love the rest of his life, if only he can convince the proud Juliet that he's worthy of her hand and heart.

"A Marquess For Christmas"
Book 5 in the Scandalous Seasons Series

Lady Patrina Tidemore gave up on the ridiculous notion of true love after having her heart shattered and her trust destroyed by a black-hearted cad. Used as a pawn in a game of revenge against her brother, Patrina returns to London from a failed elopement with a tattered reputation and little hope for a respectable match. The only peace she finds is in her solitude on the cold winter days at Hyde Park. And even that is yanked from her by two little hellions who just happen to have a devastatingly handsome, but coldly aloof father, the Marquess of Beaufort. Something about the lord stirs the dreams she'd once carried for an honorable gentleman's love.

Weston Aldridge, the 4th Marquess of Beaufort was deceived and betrayed by his late wife. In her faithlessness, he's come to view women as self-serving, indulgent creatures. Except, after a series of chance encounters with Patrina, he comes to appreciate how uniquely different she is than all women he's ever known.

At the Christmastide season, a time of hope and new beginnings, Patrina and Weston, unexpectedly learn true love in one another. However, as Patrina's scandalous past threatens their future and the happiness of his children, they are both left to determine if love is enough.

"Once a Wallflower, At Last His Love"
Book 6 in the Scandalous Seasons Series

Responsible, practical Miss Hermione Rogers, has been crafting stories as the notorious Mr. Michael Michaelmas and selling them for a meager wage to support her siblings. The only real way to ensure her family's ruinous debts are paid, however, is to marry. Tall, thin, and plain, she has no expectation of success. In London for her first Season she seizes the chance to write the tale of a brooding duke. In her research, she finds Sebastian Fitzhugh, the 5th Duke of Mallen, who unfortunately is perfectly affable, charming, and so nicely…configured…he takes her breath away. He lacks all the character traits she needs for her story, but alas, any duke will have to do.

Sebastian Fitzhugh, the 5th Duke of Mallen has been deceived so many times during the high-stakes game of courtship, he's lost faith in Society women. Yet, after a chance encounter with Hermione, he finds himself intrigued. Not a woman he'd normally consider beautiful, the young lady's practical bent, her forthright nature and her tendency to turn up in the oddest places has his interests…roused. He'd like to trust her, he'd like to do a whole lot more with her too, but should he?

"In Need of a Duke"
A Prequel Novella to "The Heart of a Duke" Series by Christi Caldwell

In Need of a Duke: (Author's Note: This is a prequel novella to "The Heart of a Duke" series by Christi Caldwell. It was originally available in "The Heart of a Duke" Collection and is now being published as an individual novella.

It features a new prologue and epilogue.

Years earlier, a gypsy woman passed to Lady Aldora Adamson and her friends a heart pendant that promised them each the heart of a duke.

Now, a young lady, with her family facing ruin and scandal, Lady Aldora doesn't have time for mythical stories about cheap baubles. She needs to save her sisters and brother by marrying a titled gentleman with wealth and power to his name. She sets her bespectacled sights upon the Marquess of St. James.

Turned out by his father after a tragic scandal, Lord Michael Knightly has grown into a powerful, but self-made man. With the whispers and stares that still follow him, he would rather be anywhere but London…

Until he meets Lady Aldora, a young woman who mistakes him for his brother, the Marquess of St. James. The connection between Aldora and Michael is immediate and as they come to know one another, Aldora's feelings for Michael war with her sisterly responsibilities.

With her family's dire situation, a man of Michael's scandalous past will never do.

Ultimately, Aldora must choose between her responsibilities as a sister and her love for Michael.

"For Love of the Duke"
First Full-Length Book in the "Heart of a Duke" Series by Christi Caldwell

After the tragic death of his wife, Jasper, the 8th Duke of Bainbridge buried himself away in the dark cold walls of his home, Castle Blackwood. When he's coaxed out of his self-imposed exile to attend the amusements of the Frost Fair, his life is irrevocably changed by his fateful meeting with Lady Katherine Adamson.

With her tight brown ringlets and silly white-ruffled gowns, Lady Katherine Adamson has found her dance card empty for two Seasons. After her father's passing, Katherine learned the unreliability of men, and is determined to depend on no one, except herself. Until she meets Jasper…

In a desperate bid to avoid a match arranged by her family, Katherine makes the Duke of Bainbridge a shocking proposition—one that he accepts.

Only, as Katherine begins to love Jasper, she finds the arrangement agreed upon is not enough. And Jasper is left to decide if protecting his heart is more important than fighting for Katherine's love.

"More Than a Duke"
Book 2 in the "Heart of a Duke" Series by Christi Caldwell

Polite Society doesn't take Lady Anne Adamson seriously. However, Anne isn't just another pretty young miss. When she discovers her father betrayed her mother's love and her family descended into poverty, Anne comes up with a plan to marry a respectable, powerful, and honorable gentleman—a man nothing like her philandering father.

Armed with the heart of a duke pendant, fabled to land the wearer a duke's heart, she decides to enlist the aid of the notorious Harry, 6th Earl of Stanhope. A scoundrel with a scandalous past, he is the last gentleman she'd ever wed…however, his reputation marks him the perfect man to school her in the art of seduction so she might ensnare the illustrious Duke of Crawford.

Harry, the Earl of Stanhope is a jaded, cynical rogue who lives for his own pleasures. Having been thrown over by the only woman he ever loved so she could wed a duke, he's not at all surprised when Lady Anne approaches him with her scheme to capture another duke's affection. He's come to appreciate that all women are in fact greedy, title-grasping, self-indulgent creatures. And with Anne's history of grating on his every last nerve, she is the last woman he'd ever agree to school in the art of seduction. Only his friendship with the lady's sister compels him to help.

What begins as a pretend courtship, born of lessons on seduction, becomes something more leaving Anne to decide if she can give her heart to a reckless rogue, and Harry must decide if he's willing to again trust in a lady's love.

"The Love of a Rogue"
Book 3 in the "Heart of a Duke" Series by Christi Caldwell

Lady Imogen Moore hasn't had an easy time of it since she made her Come Out. With her betrothed, a powerful duke breaking it off to wed her sister, she's become the *tons* favorite piece of gossip. Never again wanting to experience the pain of a broken heart, she's resolved to make a match with a polite, respectable gentleman. The last thing she wants is another reckless rogue.

Lord Alex Edgerton has a problem. His brother, tired of Alex's carousing has charged him with chaperoning their remaining, unwed sister about *ton* events. Shopping? No, thank you. Attending the theatre? He'd rather be at Forbidden Pleasures with a scantily clad beauty upon his lap. The task of *chaperone* becomes even more of a bother when his sister drags along her dearest friend, Lady Imogen to social functions. The last thing he wants in his life is a young, innocent English miss.

Except, as Alex and Imogen are thrown together, passions flare and Alex comes to find he not only wants Imogen in his bed, but also in his heart. Yet now he must convince Imogen to risk all, on the heart of a rogue.

"Loved By a Duke"
Book 4 in the "Heart of a Duke" Series by Christi Caldwell

For ten years, Lady Daisy Meadows has been in love with Auric, the Duke of Crawford. Ever since his gallant rescue years earlier, Daisy knew she was destined to be his Duchess. Unfortunately, Auric sees her as his best friend's sister and nothing more. But perhaps, if she can manage to find the fabled heart of a duke pendant, she will win over the heart of her duke.

Auric, the Duke of Crawford enjoys Daisy's company. The last thing he is interested in however, is pursuing a romance with a woman he's known since she was in leading strings. This season, Daisy is turning up in the oddest places and he cannot help but notice that she is no longer a girl. But Auric wouldn't do something as foolhardy as to fall in love with Daisy. He couldn't. Not with the guilt he carries over his past sins...Not when he has no right to her heart...But perhaps, just perhaps, she can forgive the past and trust that he'd forever cherish her heart—but will she let him?

"Seduced By a Lady's Heart"
Book 1 in the "Lords of Honor" Series

You met Lieutenant Lucien Jones in "Forever Betrothed, Never the Bride" when he was a broken soldier returned from fighting Boney's forces. This is his story of triumph and happily-ever-after!

Lieutenant Lucien Jones, son of a viscount, returned from war, to find his wife and child dead. Blaming his father for the commission that sent him off to fight Boney's forces, he was content to languish at London Hospital...until offered employment on the Marquess of Drake's staff. Through his position, Lucien found purpose in life and is content to keep his past buried.

Lady Eloise Yardley has loved Lucien since they were children. Having long ago given up on the dream of him, she married another. Years later, she is a young, lonely widow who does not fit in with the ton. When Lucien's family enlists her aid to reunite father and son, she leaps at the opportunity to not only aid her former friend, but to also escape London.

Lucien doesn't know what scheme Eloise has concocted, but knowing her as he does, when she pays a visit to his employer, he knows she's up to something. The last thing he wants is the temptation that this new, older, mature Eloise presents; a tantalizing reminder of happier times and peace.

Yet Eloise is determined to win Lucien's love once and for all...if only Lucien can set aside the pain of his past and risk all on a lady's heart.

"My Lady of Deception"
Book 1 in the "Brethren of the Lords" Series

***This dark, sweeping Regency novel was previously only offered as part of the limited edition box sets: "From the Ballroom and Beyond", "Romancing

the Rogue", and *"Dark Deceptions"*. *Now, available for the first time on its own, exclusively through Amazon is "My Lady of Deception"*.

Everybody has a secret. Some are more dangerous than others.

For Georgina Wilcox, only child of the notorious traitor known as "The Fox", there are too many secrets to count. However, after her interference results in great tragedy, she resolves to never help another…until she meets Adam Markham.

Lord Adam Markham is captured by The Fox. Imprisoned, Adam loses everything he holds dear. As his days in captivity grow, he finds himself fascinated by the young maid, Georgina, who cares for him.

When the carefully crafted lies she's built between them begin to crumble, Georgina realizes she will do anything to prove her love and loyalty to Adam—even it means at the expense of her own life.

Non-Fiction Works by Christi Caldwell
Uninterrupted Joy: Memoir: My Journey through Infertility, Pregnancy, and Special Needs

The following journey was never intended for publication. It was written from a mother, to her unborn child. The words detailed her struggle through infertility and the joy of finally being pregnant. A stunning revelation at her son's birth opened a world of both fear and discovery. This is the story of one mother's love and hope and…her quest for uninterrupted joy.

COMING SEPTEMBER 2015

Book 2 in the Lords of Honor Series
"Saved By a Lady's Love"

A story of when Beauty met the Beast!

And coming October 2015

Book 6 in the Heart of a Duke series
"The Heart of a Scoundrel"

Featuring the Marquess of Rutland and Miss Phoebe Barrett!!

To receive the first look at covers, blurbs, and excerpts,
please sign up for my monthly newsletter!
http://eepurl.com/bj2twD